PATHS TO OTHERWHERE

By James P. Hogan

PATHS TO OTHERWHERE

JAMES P. HOGAN

A Baen Books Original

Baen Publishing Enterprises
P.O. Box 1403
Riverdale, NY 10471

ISBN: 0-671-87710-0

Cover art by Gary Ruddell

First printing, February 1996

Distributed by Simon & Schuster
1230 Avenue of the Americas
New York, NY 10020

Library of Congress Cataloging-in-Publication Data

Hogan, James P.
    Paths to otherwhere / James P. Hogan
        p. cm.
    ISBN 0-671-87710-0 (hc)
    I. Title.
PR6058. 0348P37 1996
823'.914—dc20

95-44433
CIP

Printed in the United States of America

TO

DAVID DEUTSCH

—an evening with whom was enough to inspire the b

And

SARAH LAWRENCE

—for introducing me to him.

The help of the following is gratefully appreciated:

- Dr. David Deutsch, Department of Physics, Oxford University, England, who finally explained quantum-mechan "paradoxes" in a way that made sense, and in doing so convinced me that the Many Worlds Interpretation is probal real.

- Don Peterson, of Los Alamos National Laboratory, for insights to life up "The Hill," both in and out of the labs, and some wonderful guided sightseeing.

- Russell Galen, of the Scovil, Chichak & Galen Literary Agency, for his encouragement at a time when it was neede relentless criticism, nevertheless, when that was needed, ai invaluable help in putting together the ideas that mattered.

- Karen Reedstrom, of the Objectivist Club of Michigan, fi great help with the research.

- Toren Smith, of San Francisco, for producing those odd bits of information that are never to hand when you need th

Prolog

The woman in the tan business suit sat in a p
recliner that looked like a dentist's chair. Her he
in a concave rest that kept it positioned exactly,
focal zone of the projection array a few inches ;
She was staring at one of the screens on a panel ir
of her. Leonard Sarvin, Deputy Director of the D
Research Administration, stood to one side, out
field being directed by the machine. His pri
assistant, John Fiske, was with him. The depar
had poured millions into this, and the Director was
harried by the President's office for a progress u
Jesse Willard, the National Laboratory's exec
director, watched from the other side of the chair,
the chief scientist of the project, who was handli
demonstration, checked other screens. Cabinet
equipment racks lined the partitioned space a
them. The hum of pumps and cooling fans came
other machinery beyond.

"It's quite straightforward." Kintner looked u
addressed the three visitors. "We're Black. The ma
plays Red. It's our move. But the bet has to be real
make it ten dollars, say. You've got three choices fc
the game will go: Win for Black, win for Red, or a
Winners divide the pot."

"What happens if we all lose?" Fiske asked.

1

Kintner smiled thinly. "Then I suppose thirty dollars goes to charity."

The two men from Washington looked at each other, as if checking for something they might have missed. They both shrugged together.

"Ten on Black," Sarvin said.

"Black," Fiske agreed. He looked at Kintner and Willard. "I mean . . . what else is there to say?"

The screen showed a position in a checkers game. Red was down to four men, one of them blocked, the others positioned hopelessly. Black still had five men, plus another two already crowned. No six-year-old could have lost from that position.

The woman in the chair continued staring with a puzzled expression, however. Her name was Jane. She had only recently been promoted to Fiske's personal secretary, and the role of being the guinea pig had fallen on her as the junior member of the party. Her eyes and common sense were telling her the same as the other two had said. And yet . . .

As she considered the three options in turn, DRAW seemed to shout insistently from somewhere deep in her mind. It made no sense; yet every instinct impelled her toward it. She bit her lip, uneasy at the thought of appearing foolish. But Kintner's instructions had been quite clear: "Forget everything you think you know. Just play your hunches."

"Ten on a draw," she said finally.

Beside her, Fiske laughed. "Okay. It's your money."

"Then let's see what happens," Willard said. "Would somebody care to decide the move?"

Sarvin and Fiske looked at each other again. Fiske pointed at the screen. "How about that guy to there? Move him up. Why take chances?"

"Looks good to me," Sarvin agreed.

"Very well," Willard said.

Kintner tapped at keys. The move appeared below the board, with a request to confirm. He hit the Y key.

And the board disappeared, to be replaced by the legend:

WHAT WE DIDN'T TELL YOU WAS THAT THE
SELF-DESTRUCTS AT THIS POINT.

NOBODY WINS

SORRY GUYS.

Willard's manner lost the flippancy that he ha
maintaining. "It doesn't predict the actual future
impossible on principle. But what the machine
is extract the probabilities of possible alternative
the weightings of the Multiverse branching str
ahead. And since it's driven by real future outcom
theoretical models or probabilities, it delivers a c
indication even if the truth is not as you've been
believe. Think what an impact this will have on st
policymaking. It could enable us to restore the
world balance."

Just at that moment, it was having an impact on
things too. Jane, still coupled into the machine, was
vivid premonitions of where more in life was headin
just a checkers game. For months now she had been
Jack's line about doors he could open for her
department, a marriage that was just a pretense. . .
could she have been so naive? Fancy dinners on his e:
account, a few nights in hotels when they went o
like this—and she'd thought she was heading for th
time social circuit and a career? *WRONG! WR*
WRONG! the machine was telling her. Everything
that future felt bad. There was nothing specific th
could pinpoint; just overwhelming forebodings of
hurt, shame, ridicule. But it felt as certain as the
of the checkers game had a few minutes earlier.

She sat up sharply, her eyes blazing at him. Fisl
the change in her and shook his head, mystified.
what is it?"

There was no way that she could control the indig
boiling up inside. At the same time, in an officia
and with others present, the moment was not appro
for confrontation.

She got up. "We have to talk—later," she said t

Then, to the others, "I'm sorry. Will you excuse me, please?" And with that, she walked quickly from the scene.

Sarvin frowned. Fiske looked appealingly at the scientists. "I'm sorry. . . . I really don't know what that was all about." He made a helpless gesture, as if trusting them to understand.

"It's nobody's fault," Kintner said. "The process does have deeper side-effects. We're still learning about them ourselves."

They were getting reports of strange happenings from a number of places where research was being conducted. The world didn't need this loose in it as well, on top of everything else, he told himself.

"It's too potent to be left out there for any foreign power to harness and exploit," Kintner told Willard later, when they were alone in Willard's office. "The whole thing has to be brought under official direction. All other projects should be terminated. Get the best people in the field here and put everything under one centralized authority, where it can be controlled."

"I already talked to Sarvin about it," Willard said. "He's making the same recommendation. We're trying to schedule a meeting in Washington with the Security Council about it for next week."

Chapter O

Sometimes Hugh Brenner thought he'd been b
the wrong planet. It seemed as obvious as anything
be that people achieved more when they learned
along than they did when they fought over things.
put as much time and energy into fixing problems i
of blaming each other for being the problem, there w
be any problems left. So far they'd had two ful
rehearsals for wiping out what passed as civilizatio
time it looked as if things might be leading up to tl
performance.

He looked from the car along a rubble-strewn side
while they waited for the lights to change on th
mile-long slum of University Avenue leading to the ca
An orator in a forage-style cap and gray-shirted u1
was pounding the air and shouting into a microphon
a raised stand. Below, a line of linebacker-size Gra'
stood facing a crowd of a couple of hundred, mainly st
and local derelicts. A banner above the stand
NATIONALIST ACTION COALITION. Youths in parkas and l
jackets were gathered farther along the block. Arou1
corner, police in riot gear stood behind armored van
mesh-covered windows.

"Looks like more trouble today," Chris said fro
passenger seat. Hugh's route into Berkeley brough
past the pile of one-room rental conversions that

shared with nine other students. Not many sophomores drove these days. As part of the measures to prevent Detroit from closing down altogether, regulations and taxes were designed to clear older cars off the roads. The light turned green below the cluster surveillance cameras covering the intersection. Hugh sighed and shook his head as he eased the car forward. It was a GM Ocelot that he'd bought used and well worn, built south of the border.

Behind them, Alice turned to peer through the rear window. She had started appearing with Chris two or three mornings a week, almost a month ago now. Hugh didn't know much more about her than that she could have looked better if she had a good meal more often; she came from San Antonio; and she was majoring in political sociology, whatever that was. Hugh didn't have much time for politics. A physicist of twenty-eight, unattached, with no dependents, no dependencies, no payments, he was one of those oddities who still thought life could be simple and honest.

"At least they've got plans for *doing* something," Alice said, turning back.

"It's all a mess and too far gone," Hugh answered. "What's anyone going to do now?"

"Well, somebody has to. How else are we going to get things back on track?"

Hugh knew the line: *Security is Strength. Pride through Duty. Honor and Sacrifice.* Liberals and speculators were the cause of all the problems. Chris had been sounding more radical lately. Hugh had wondered where he'd been getting it from. He wasn't in a mood to be indoctrinated just now. "Chris says you want to come over to the lab and see our machine, Alice," he said to change the subject.

"The QUIC," Chris said, turning his head to look back.

"You mean so you can show me how smart scientists are?" Alice replied.

Chris shrugged indifferently. "You don't have to. I just thought you might want to see something different. If you'd rather stick to another day of same-as-usual, that's okay by me."

Most people at college would know enough to be familiar with the gist.

"Something to do with things being waves and particles at the same time, isn't it?" she said.

Hugh nodded. "Things like photons and electrons, that people usually think of as particles, can also interfere with each other like waves." He made throwing motions in the air with both hands. "You know when you toss a couple of stones into a pond—each one makes circles of waves that spread out. Where the circles start to overlap, you get a criss-cross effect of flat spots and rough spots. That's called an interference pattern."

"Okay. . . . And quantum whatevers do the same thing?"

"Right. Except there's a difference: They can do it with themselves—apparently. It's as if you only threw one stone, but you still get the pattern."

Alice thought about it, made a face, and shook her head. "That doesn't make sense."

"Which is why they used to be called paradoxes. But the answer turns out to be that what the particle—or whatever—is interacting with isn't itself, inexplicably, in *the* universe, but counterparts of itself, or 'ghosts,' if you like, in these other universes that you read about. In fact, that was what persuaded most physicists to accept them as real: the way they explain the paradoxes."

Chris reappeared in the doorway from the office. "Just routine stuff, mainly," he told Hugh. "You've got a note to meet Theo in Strahan's office at eleven sharp." Theo Jantowitz was the professor that Hugh worked with—Chris was one of their technical assistants. Stan Strahan ran the department.

"Probably to do with these government people who are supposed to be coming today," Hugh said.

"What do they want?" Chris asked.

"You tell me. Nosing around the project, I guess."

Alice looked puzzled. "I thought that you guys were working on something to do with evolution. What does the government care about giraffes' necks or where chickens and eggs come from?"

"Tell me something that the government doesn't care about," Chris snorted.

"It started out as something to do with evolution, but it's kind of taken on a life of its own," Hugh said. "We'll find out soon enough what they want. Anyway . . ." He indicated one of the regular, five-foot-high cabinets. Its side panels had been left off for easy access, revealing several racks of electronics filling the lower part. The top section consisted of a metal frame holding three tiers of aluminum boxes, each about the size of a paperback book, arranged in rows. Another cubicle stood behind, and a confusion of pipes, metal coils, and valves connected to a cooling system stacked by the wall. "That's it. Meet the QUantum Interference Correlator. QUIC, this is Alice."

He waited while her eyes darted uncertainly, seeking a hint for a hopefully sensible question to ask. She didn't make a joke by talking to it. Too intense. The ones who were into politics were always too intense.

"Okay, so these other universes are real," she said at last. "This machine here—you're saying that it connects to them somehow?"

"Kind of. Interference between universes at the quantum level means that information transfer takes place between them." Hugh patted the top bank of silver boxes. "The guts of it all is in these. They contain a special kind of circuit chip with precisely configured helical structures integrated into the electronics. Think of them as molecular-scale antennas. They tune to the quantum-level information leakage and couple to their other-universe counterparts, just like the 'ghost' particles."

"Oka—ay . . ."

Hugh tapped one of the boxes again. "So this machine is actually a lot bigger than what you see. It operates in combination with thousands of copies of itself, that exist in other universes."

Chris stood by them, watching the befuddled look spread across Alice's face and enjoying it. She shook her head. "This is getting weird. I mean . . . So what does it do?"

Hugh rolled a chair up to the console. "Well, let's have a look and see. You can be driver." Alice sat down and waited while he tapped in a line of text. When he had finished, the words on the screen in front of her read:

This is a test sentence to show what the QUIC can do.

He indicated it with a nod. "Now you just copy what I've typed there again, underneath. But I want you to make an error in it somewhere." As she was about to begin, Hugh said, "Remember, there are thousands of other Alices at thousands of other machines in thousands of other universes, all doing the same thing."

She hesitated, eying him suspiciously. "You're sure this isn't some kind of joke?"

"Just go ahead and do it," Chris said behind her.

"Make a mistake somewhere, right? Anywhere I like."

Hugh nodded. Alice started copying the line. The timing of the characters did not synchronize with her keystrokes— they appeared after varying delays of fractions of a second. She either failed to notice or didn't mention it. When she got to the word *sentence* she typed, *s-e-n-t-e-m-c-e. . . .* But on the screen, the word appeared correctly. She blinked and glanced up at the other two. They said nothing. She finished typing.

"It's a con," she accused. "The copy is automatic. What I do doesn't make any difference."

"That's what you'd think," Hugh agreed. "But in fact what's going on is a lot more interesting. See, the machine doesn't only respond to what *you* type. It combines it with what all the other Alices are typing too. They all put in an error somewhere as well, but they didn't all pick the same place. Statistically, the odds of any given place being picked are low. So, the letter that you picked got typed right far more often than it got typed wrong, and the machine went by the majority vote. And the same was true for every other choice too. So all the Alices got a correct sentence, and they're probably all staring pretty much the way that you're staring at me right now."

"A self-correcting keyboard," Chris said. "Like it?"

The tech who had been working on the cabinet was watching. "Neat, eh?" he said to Alice.

She slumped back in the chair. Finally her defenses were down. "This isn't real," she muttered.

"Oh, it's real," Hugh assured her.

She found that she could make the cursor trace an almost perfect circle on the screen—because the random wobbles made among the Alices in the many universes tended to cancel each other out.

Or, instead of combining the results from all universes together, the machine could simply deliver the first response from any of them. In simple problems like matching shapes and finding names on a street map, in all but one try out of twenty, the machine had the solution before she did. It meant that another Alice somewhere had found it faster.

Chris had moved away to talk to the tech working on the cabinet. Alice looked up at Hugh. He had smooth, tanned features with high cheeks and deep, distant brown eyes, the legacy of a dash of Cherokee somewhere back in the gene line. His hair was black and wavy, collar length; his face was fringed by a wisp of beard and another across his upper lip, forming a humorous excuse for a mustache. Her calculating eyes regarded him curiously. The line of the mouth softened a fraction. He saw that expression two or three times a week. The offer was there: frank, unashamedly opportunistic—ready to trade in the sophomore for a lean, laid-back, not-bad-looking postdoc. Mobile too.

No, he liked life simple, he told himself. And it was already complicated enough. Don't even think about it. Besides, cutting Chris out like that wouldn't have been his style.

"Alice," he said, lowering his voice, "there are problems that I don't need." He gave her an easy smile and shook his head. "Even with thousands of me out there to think about them."

It could be tempting, though. For a moment the thought

came into his head of asking her if she had a friend who wasn't attached right now. Then, after a second or two, he dismissed it. He wondered as he did so how many of the other Hughs in the other universes had made the same decision.

Chapter Two

Allegedly the two visitors were scientists, not bureaucrats—although Jantowitz maintained that once Government got into science it made little difference. Stan Strahan, the head of Biophysics, brought them down to the lab after lunching with the faculty dean. He didn't say where they were from or what the reason was for their interest in the work at Berkeley.

The first, Strahan introduced as Dr. Kintner. He was a biggish man in his mid-to-late fifties. Although his belt had probably inched out a notch or two in the last fifteen years, he was trim enough for his age and still hefty around the shoulders. He had a smooth, expressive face with a high forehead accentuated by receding hair, and wore gold-framed bifocals, a charcoal-stripe suit, and subdued maroon necktie. Hugh thought he smiled too much, with a geniality that became condescending. He distrusted smiling people from the government. There was always the possibility that they might be here to help him.

Kintner's companion's name was Ducaine, again a doctor. He was in his mid thirties, with a heavy, rounded jaw, protruding eyes that stared intently, and a florid complexion, which with a halo of crinkly, overgrown, yellow hair, gave him a wild look. He was wearing a tweed jacket with knitted tie. From the moment that Strahan showed them into the lab, Ducaine's gaze darted ceaselessly this way and that over the equipment. Hugh was unable to tell whether it signified complete cluelessness or an expert's sure and silent assessment.

Strahan pointed out the component parts of the QUIC, which they had evidently talked about over lunch. Ducaine stooped to peer at the antenna-boxes in the top frame of the main cabinet, then transferred his attention to an uncased module that Strahan offered as a sample. "What discrimination method do you use on the coupling from the antenna chips?" Ducaine inquired. Strahan nodded at Hugh to take it.

"You mean for directionality resolution?" Hugh said.

Ducaine's yellow halo bobbed vigorously. "Yes. Multiphase arrays? Masked sequential? Group extraction filtering?"

"Multiple phased arrays," Hugh said.

"Your own design?"

"Mainly—although the basic idea was published a few years ago. We added a filter stage that performs partial extractions as a second stage."

"Snell's Algorithm?"

"A variation of it, yes."

"Hm. Interesting." Ducaine turned the assembly over to inspect the other side. Definitely not bureaucrats, Hugh told himself—and not amateurs when it came to the science, either.

"And yet the project originated from work concerning evolution," Kintner said, directing himself at Jantowitz to bring the professor more into the conversation. "It must have taken a remarkable insight to connect Multiverse cross-communication with evolutionary dynamics. What prompted it?"

Strahan had explained over lunch that it had been generally conceded for some time that the theory was in trouble. While few seriously doubted that evolution happened, it had become increasingly clear that the mechanism traditionally upheld as the driving force— natural selection, or the progressive accumulation of random mutations—did not possess the innovative power to explain what was observed.

Jantowitz had developed a hypothesis that the geometric configuration of DNA could cause it to function as an antenna. He was a theoretician. Circuits and chips were not his line, which was why he had teamed up with somebody like Hugh. Hugh's thesis had been to test the idea by attempting to build an artificial device to do the same thing.

Jantowitz regarded the visitors balefully through heavy, horn-rimmed glasses. He never allowed himself to be enticed into returning smiles. "The evidence that Darwin predicted would be everywhere found for the gradual changes that he proposed—found, it has not been. The intermediate forms do not exist." He didn't like officialdom in any form. But he evaded rather than confronted. His way of putting off people who irritated him was to provide answers that had no connection with the questions asked.

Jantowitz was in his early sixties, getting somewhat corpulent now, with a snub nose and thick lips that thrust forward to give him an appearance of gazing disapprovingly on everything that he scrutinized—which was often the case. He had a head of white but full, wavy hair, and a matching droopy mustache. But for his clothes, he might have looked quite distinguished. They gave the impression of having been thrown at him and somehow stuck, rather than put on, and clashed colors and styles with a determined consistency that Hugh thought was surely genetic in origin. Today he was wearing a tan lab coat unbuttoned to reveal a red-and-blue check hunting shirt and the collar of a hand-knitted gray cardigan that he had owned for as long as Hugh had worked with him, and which Hugh sometimes suspected he'd been born in.

Ducaine tried to pick up the gist of what Jantowitz was saying. "You couldn't have bursts of rapid evolutionary change instead, separated by long periods of stability? Wouldn't that explain the absence of intermediate forms?"

"Waves and weather, the superficial aspects of geography,

they might shape," Jantowitz said. "But to build mountains and move continents, you must have deeper forces." The visitors looked at Strahan for enlightenment.

"Explanations along those lines were tried, but they didn't really work," he said. "Every cell is a miniature factory containing millions of specialized parts, all interdependent. On every level up to a complete organism, too many unlikely changes would have to take place at the same time to transform one viable form into another. It would be like mixing parts from an auto engine and a washing machine. The in-between forms wouldn't be functional."

"It sounds as if you're saying that evolution can't happen at all," Kintner remarked.

"Not in the time that the evidence points to," Strahan agreed. "Even with the most generous allowances that you can plausibly make, all the calculations said that what had happened couldn't have."

"So how are we here?"

"If the Earth were a few million times older, then, maybe, something like the orthodox mechanism might have been adequate," Strahan said. He waved a hand. "But not as things are. Something more had to be going on."

"And your suggestion was quantum-level communication arising from the DNA structure tuning to leakage frequencies," Ducaine said, looking at Jantowitz.

They went on to talk in a little more detail about the origins of the QUIC. The basic idea had been that the same interference that made particles appear to interact with themselves, and which had linked the machines being operated by the juxtaposition of Alices, also enabled certain biological molecules in different universes—specifically, the nucleic acids and their evolutionary predecessors—to communicate naturally. The information accumulated in the genomes of the species making up the Earth's biosphere was not a product of the evolution taking place on just one Earth, but from a huge ensemble of Earths exchanging results. Hence, there was no need for the computer to have been running for millions of times longer to have produced the super-computation that had resulted. It consisted of countless "regular" computers cooperating in parallel.

Whether or not the model was correct had never been established. The work had been completely sidetracked into developing the hardware, and the QUIC was the outcome of it.

When the talk reached this point, it became clear that it was not curiosity about evolution that had brought Kintner and Ducaine to Berkeley. Their questions had been for form's sake. What they really wanted to hear about was the QUIC hardware and its underlying multiple-universe physics. It turned out that they were fully conversant with Hugh and Jantowitz's published papers. They showed great interest in the theoretical basics that Hugh had employed in his designs and asked for copies of his calculations and schematics. And then they departed, still without giving any hint of where they had come from or why, leaving the campus after a final session alone with Strahan in his office upstairs.

"Okay, Stan, would you mind telling us what all that was about?" Hugh invited when he and Jantowitz made their way up to Strahan's office a quarter of an hour after Kintner and Ducaine had gone. "Those two were not dummies from some PR office putting together a career guide for the schools. They're right out on the edge of this business. What does the government want with QUIC?"

Strahan had been expecting it and had prepared a line to stall things until he heard definite word from the Board. But after putting up with two hours of what had amounted to cross-examination, Hugh was in no mood for stalling. Beside him, Jantowitz simply stood with his lower lip thrust out in a way that dared Strahan to try it. Strahan capitulated with a sigh. He sank back in his chair and showed his palms in a conciliatory gesture.

"Okay, I'll be straight. It isn't the QUIC per se that they're worried about. It's the whole field of MV physics.

Apparently it has defense implications. The federal government have got their own thing going, and they want to classify all allied work."

"*Classify it?*" Hugh exploded. "Evolution? What the hell kind of defense implication is there in that?"

"Oh, come on, Hugh," Strahan said tiredly. "You know it isn't that. It's the physics. They're concerned with how the QUIC works. And in any case, don't try that one on me. You know as well as I do that the QUIC hasn't had much to do with evolution for a long time now."

"Why do they want to put it under wraps? What kind of work are they doing?"

"I really didn't ask."

Jantowitz brought them both back from a line that was leading nowhere. "What is it, then, you are telling us?" he said. "Are they wishing to take control over our project, these governments peoples?"

Strahan massaged his temples for a moment, then looked up. "Oh hell, I really didn't want this to be so soon. . . . It's worse than that. They're closing it down."

Hugh stared disbelievingly. "You're not serious."

"I wish I weren't. They're serious all right."

"But . . . it's *ours!* We created it. It's opening up a whole new world. . . ."

"I think that may be the problem," Strahan said. "It's opening up more of a new world than you think."

"What are you talking about?"

"Let's just say I get the feeling that they're a bit farther ahead than they're letting on. This work leads into areas that they don't want everybody in the world picking up on."

"Like what?"

"Would you believe they didn't tell me?"

Hugh shook his head protestingly. He didn't expect answers, but now it was he who needed to stall while he pulled his thoughts back together. "You can't let them," was all he could muster finally.

"Hugh, it's out of our hands."

Hugh's color deepened, and his breathing became short. Jantowitz knew that for most of the time he tended to be fairly easygoing. His ability to escape totally into his work kept him detached from the worst of life's stresses and tribulations. But on the occasions when he did lose his cool, it could be spectacular. Now everything that he had worked for in years was about to be snatched away, and Jantowitz saw one of those occasions about to happen. He caught Hugh's sleeve and tugged lightly.

"Come, Hugh," he urged. "Time it is now for us to get some coffee, I think. Cooler heads make the better sense, yes? Maybe we come back tomorrow and talk with Stan some more, when we have together our questions thought out."

Hugh drew back, exhaling a long breath. He nodded. "I guess you're right."

"I'm really sorry about it, guys. Believe me," Strahan said.

They left the building and went to the snack restaurant situated on-campus. By the time they sat down, Hugh had lapsed into brooding restlessness. Jantowitz did little to lift him out of it.

"The protesting will do you no good. It just makes ulcers faster," he said. "These situations, I have seen before. Everybody fights for the same moneys from the government's pig-trough. And on top of this, you have all the administrators and faculty heads who think they make good politicians, caring more about being somebody at Washington cocktail parties more than they care about science. No one will be on your side."

"What are you saying, then?" Hugh asked him. "We just let them wrap it up and walk away, without even trying to fight them?"

"I'm simply saying that perhaps the time has come to be a little philosophical. We have nothing to fight them with," Jantowitz replied.

But then events took an unforeseen turn. People from an undisclosed department in Washington appeared at

Berkeley a week later and quizzed Hugh and Jantowitz separately on their backgrounds and experience. Soon after that, Kintner came to California again with another colleague, called Mulgrave, to talk to them some more, this time in the federal offices across the Bay in downtown San Francisco. It turned out that Hugh and Jantowitz's work didn't have to be wasted after all. All work on the new physics, they were told, was being concentrated under government direction. Subject to satisfactory background checks for the necessary security clearances, they were offered positions on the official program.

All they knew about it at that stage was that it was run by the Defense Research Administration and would involve moving from California. But really, there was little choice. As Jantowitz had prophesied, no serious internal opposition materialized to terminating the Berkeley project. Hugh's work was his passion, while Jantowitz, at his age, had no other future.

The offers were subsequently confirmed.

And accepted.

Chapter Three

The trouble with the machine was that it gave anyone who coupled into it, and who allowed their mind to dwell upon the matter, a pretty good idea of what, generally, could be believed about the official pronouncements that they were supposed to live with. Since the environment was a political one, with misinformation and doubletalk having been the accepted management style for years, this meant that nobody trusted anyone or believed anything that the machine associated with negative feelings. Least of all did the powers in charge have any trust in the loyalty of their employees. But the world situation was critical and getting worse, and this research could provide the means for reversing it. The work had to go on. Consequently, security assumed a more crucial importance than was usual even for a classified program. The project's Security Officer, who reported directly to Willard, the Laboratory's overall director, figured prominently in all decision making. His name was Bruce Calom.

"I still have reservations about this Dr. Brenner from Berkeley," he said, bringing a photo and evaluation summary up on the conference room screen. "Several of the staff members at Berkeley considered him irresponsible because he talks too freely with students about inter-departmental affairs that are not generally considered to be undergraduates' business. His reply is that enabling young people to practice making competent judgments is what universities are supposed to be for. To me that spells risky."

The meeting was to review the new names recently confirmed as recruited to the project. With Calom were Jesse Willard, executive director, and Edward Kintner, Chief Scientist of the Octagon Project.

"I see you've added a personal endorsement, Ed," Willard commented, looking at the requisition file.

"We need his expertise," Kintner replied simply. "The work that he's done there is brilliant. Neville Ducaine went over those designs of his and says they're as advanced conceptually as anything we're using here."

"I still want it on record that I don't like it," Calom said.

"Do you have something specific?" Kintner asked.

"Just a gut-feel that comes after years of experience. I don't need any machine to tell me." Calom had said the same thing before the offer was made, but the scientists' arguments had prevailed. He knew that Kintner used the machine to guide his decisions, which no doubt meant that Kintner didn't trust half the things that Calom said. He himself had an antipathy toward intellectuals, and scientists in particular—which didn't help matters.

Kintner regarded him equably through his gold-rimmed bifocals. "If everybody at this establishment could be guaranteed to come risk-free, you wouldn't have a job, Bruce," he said. "I'm sure we can control the problematical aspects. In fact, if he possesses precisely the kind of specialized knowledge that we don't want being spread around, this might be the best place to keep an eye on him. We can put him under special surveillance."

Willard nodded at Calom. "Do it, effective from his date of arrival. Get an extended background check on him too."

Kintner had known Calom's attitude, of course. But Kintner's enhanced premonitions had been different. Evidently, what had sounded warning bells for Calom wasn't necessarily bad news for everyone else. When Kintner had coupled into the machine and contemplated future prospects, he had been gripped by a sense of breathtaking possibilities that had excited the scientist part of him. The certainty impressed itself that there could be new discoveries far beyond anything glimpsed so far. But only in association with the option of hiring Brenner. It vanished for every alternative. The machine could not be specific beyond that. So Kintner had lodged his vote, and the others could reconcile themselves in whatever way they chose.

Willard looked down at his file again. "Very well, then, we need his expertise. And this Polish mathematician who's coming with him—nothing further to report there?"

Calom shook his head. "Nobody's got much on him either way. He and Brenner have worked together at Berkeley for four years now. His professional and academic record is solid. Apart from that, he seems to have discovered how to stay invisible to most of the system. We'll put him under observation with Brenner."

The offer to Jantowitz had been on Kintner's recommendation too. The man's theoretical knowledge was impressive. And why not somebody with experience in biophysics? They already had people from just about every other discipline on board. The project was a long way past being just research into the strange side of basic physics, as it had begun. Now there didn't seem to be an area of human thought, action, or humanity's very existence that didn't stand to be affected.

Chapter Four

Hugh and Jantowitz received letters confirming that they would be joining an as-yet undesignated project located in New Mexico. Enclosed were plane tickets to Albuquerque/Santa Fe. For a mailing address, they were given a Post Office box number in Los Alamos. Their instructions were to report to the Assistant Chief Personnel Officer in the Administration Building at the TA-3 site of the Los Alamos National Laboratory. Temporary accommodation had been arranged for them in the town.

A young, tight-jawed Army captain called Hemel met them at the airport. There were also three other arrivals for the National Laboratory—two men and a woman, all traveling singly. They said little as Hemel and a guard in fatigue dress, carrying an automatic rifle, escorted them from the arrivals concourse.

The airport had a wartime feel about it, with the National Guard patrolling the terminal building and armored cars on standby outside. Northern New Mexico was not a safe area these days. Urban terrorists driven out of the ghettos by police countermeasures and gang rivalries competed with back-to-the-wild survivalists for territories and spoils. Isolated residences were being abandoned, and some outlying communities lived virtually under siege.

Outside, a green minibus was waiting, with DEFENSE

RESEARCH ADMINISTRATION painted on its sides. In addition
to the driver, there was a second guard, occupying a rear-
facing seat at the back. Before the bus moved out, Hemel
called somewhere by radio and received confirmation that
the road was clear. They left the urban area on Highway
25 toward Santa Fe, following the wide, flat valley of the
Rio Grande. The crumbling red peaks of the Sandia Range
stood jagged through the heat haze to the right. Hugh's
main impressions, fresh from the crush and commotion
of the Bay Area, were of the vastness, the emptiness, and
the dryness.

Jantowitz, sitting opposite, had maintained his usual
taciturnity through most of the trip. He always seemed
to dress for winter in Illinois, and had on a mangled black
homburg and tan raincoat that he wore with the belt tied
behind to avoid the bother of fastening it. A helicopter
that had appeared several times passed overhead again.
The noise stirred Jantowitz out of whatever thoughts had
been preoccupying him. He turned from the window and
gestured. "Not much city life here. I told you you should
see more there when you could. Young peoples need the
chance to make the mistakes to learn from."

"Oh, I saw all the life I needed," Hugh answered.
"Anyway, it'll be healthier here. High-desert climate. Good
air. People probably get out a lot."

"Do you still do the jogging and that kind of thing?"
Jantowitz asked the question warily, as if he were inviting
a confession.

"Sure. It's supposed to make you live longer."

Jantowitz wrinkled his nose. "To me, it has always seemed
that the things people do to live longer would give them
the least reason for wanting to. Too much health is bad
for you, I suspect. Is like money. Too much, then you
start the worry that now you lose it, and the worry makes
you sick."

"That's a new one, Theo. I'm not sure what a doctor
would say about it, though."

"Pah! Doctors. What do they know? Just body-mechanics."

Jantowitz looked back at the window and told the desert, "Four doctors who tell me to live healthier, I have buried."

Hugh looked around the bus casually. The two men were talking earnestly in lowered voices near the front. The woman was sitting in a closer seat, reading a typewritten document on a briefcase resting on her knee. Thirtyish, Hugh judged; could be quite attractive if she dressed a little more femininely and didn't look so intense. She sensed him watching her and looked across.

"Hi," he volunteered. She regarded him blankly, as if he had said something in an obscure dialect of Swahili. The moment dragged like a joke fallen flat at a royal table. "Er, I guess we're both working at the same place. We just got in from California. I'm Hugh."

Her eyes remained expressionless. "To save us both a lot of time, if you're wondering if I screw, the answer's no," she informed him. "And in any case, I don't like being picked up on busses." With that, she returned to her reading.

"Well, excuse me. . . ." Hugh looked back out at the distant side of the valley. Scratch one off the list, he told himself.

At Santa Fe they exited the highway and turned north amid dun-colored, adobe-style houses spread out among sandy hills spattered with juniper, piñon, and desert pine. On the climb up to Los Alamos, the landscape became bleaker and rockier. Deep canyons gouged their way between long fingers of flat-topped mesa. Ahead to the west, the hills rose toward the greater summits of the Jemez Mountains, purple and hazy in the distance.

Los Alamos, extending ribbonlike along the top of a mesa, appeared suddenly as the bus came over a rise after a winding, uphill section of road. It was young as towns go, most of it dating from within the last half century. There were still some buildings going back to the "secret city" of the Manhattan Project in the early 1940s, but most had been replaced in the growth by a regular, open community that had accompanied the founding and expansion of the National Laboratory in the postwar years. Then, in more recent times, the civilian programs had been gradually axed or hived off to other departments, and the remainder consolidated under the DRA to concentrate on defense-related work. Much of the openness was lost; fences and guard posts appeared around places that had been accessible; in many ways the area had reacquired something of its former character.

The bus passed the airstrip on the approach into the town, and then traversed the central area, where the World War Two research had been concentrated. Then they followed the extension eastward into more residential surroundings and turned off to the right. Captain Hemel looked back from his seat by the driver. "This is 43rd Street now. That's where you two will be staying until you get something more permanent. It's a private boardinghouse, run by a Mrs. Ryecroft. We know her well. She puts up a lot of people from the Lab."

They stopped outside an older two-story house, probably going back to the fifties, sheltering from the world and time behind a barricade of laurel and a wicket fence choked with roses. It had been repainted fairly recently, pale yellow with white sills and trim, in a brave attempt to relieve the dusty torpor of the street. The drapes in the windows looked clean but old. A fading Old Glory, discolored by the sun, was painted on the mailbox.

"Try a little sugar with the acid and razor blades for breakfast next time," Hugh said to the woman with the briefcase as they climbed out.

While Hemel led the way up the porch steps and rang the doorbell, the driver unloaded the bags. Somewhere inside the house, a dog began yapping. It started off another dog with a deeper bark somewhere across the street. Jantowitz's mouth tightened. Hugh shrugged resignedly. All his life, it seemed, he'd been plagued by yappy dogs.

There was bustling behind the door, and a female baritone voice yelled, "Shut up, Selby! It's okay." Then the door opened, and Mrs. Ryecroft appeared. "Ahah! You have to be the professor and the doctor. I get professors and doctors all the time. Sometimes I think I could start my own university here." She didn't lower the volume. Her accent was from New England, maybe near Boston.

She was heavy around the middle, with a large nose, wide mouth, and features that had once been firm now rounding out above the beginnings of a second chin. A white top retained large, sagging breasts, while her lower half was squeezed into pink stretch-slacks that, with her weight, the indecency laws should have had something to say about. In addition, she wore a purple head scarf knotted at the front.

Hemel introduced everybody and produced a document for her to sign. It made Hugh feel like a package being delivered. Hemel reminded Hugh and Jantowitz that they would be collected at 9:00 the next morning, and then returned to the bus. The driver deposited the last of the bags in the front hallway and followed. Mrs. Ryecroft closed the door. A terrier with hair that looked impenetrable falling over its eyes had singled out Jantowitz for a confrontation and was emitting curious, whirringlike noises, presumably supposed to be snarls.

"Don't worry about her," Mrs. Ryecroft foghorned. "She'll quieten down when she gets used to you. She's a Yorkshire, so I call her Selby. Selby's a town in Yorkshire, England. I spent a vacation near there with my husband when he was alive. They eat blood pudding for breakfast. Would you believe that?" Jantowitz blinked at her through his heavy-rimmed lenses. Outside, the sound came of the bus starting and pulling away.

"Did you, er, bring the custom back here?" Hugh asked.

"You're kidding. I wouldn't give that stuff to Selby." She handed each of them a ring with two keys. "One's for the room. One's for the front door. I lock it at ten. Come on up. I'll show you the rooms now."

The decor was traditional, striving to preserve its memories: floral carpets; heavy drapes with tasseled ties;

vases and brass; pictures of a mountain lake and forest, house by a bridge, dark-skinned girl with flowers. But the inferior staining of the hall table and chairs failed to hide the scratches and patchy repairs. The good furniture had gone. Her world was coming apart—like everything else, everywhere.

She wheezed up the stairs ahead of them, the expanse of pink stretch-slacks convulsing obscenely. "It's all guests up here. I have my own suite downstairs, past the kitchen. Breakfast is at seven-thirty, dinner at six. Call before five if you want something kept late—they work all hours at the Lab. Visitors are okay, but no drunks, drugs, or smoking in the rooms. The local watch officer will want to know you. He stops by once a week. And remember you've got fourteen days to register your address with the Sheriff's department."

Jantowitz took the first room, which was across the landing from the top of the stairs. Hugh's was along a short passageway. It was plain but clean, with a double-size bed, wall closet, two upright chairs at a table by the window, and a small writing desk in one corner.

"This'll be fine," Hugh said.

"Is there anything you don't eat, any special diets?" Mrs. Ryecroft asked.

He shook his head. "Pretty much anything's okay with me. I'm an omnivore."

"I've got Mexican on for tonight, tacos and enchiladas. That okay?"

"Sounds great."

She indicated the door across the passage with a wave of her hand. "You've got an English guy called David Wallis in there. Been here a few weeks. He's okay—about your age, I'd say. You'll meet him later when he gets back. He's a university guy too—from a place called Cambridge. Ever been there?"

"I know of it," Hugh said.

"The only other person right now is across on the other side of the stairs. Ingram—some kind of engineer. But you don't see much of him."

"Mrs. Ryecroft." Jantowitz's voice came from his room at the head of the stairs.

"What?" Her response would have been fitting had he been on the far side of the street.

Hugh looked out. Jantowitz appeared in his doorway, steering Selby not ungently but firmly around the doorpost with a foot. "Mrs. Ryecroft, I am sorry, but the room is now my space and paid for, and the animals I cannot have. Will you talk to her or whatever it is that you do, please?"

"Is he gonna be a problem?" Mrs. Ryecroft muttered at Hugh.

"I think he has an allergy," Hugh whispered, naming the first thing that came to mind. "He's okay."

"Oh, okay." She bustled away back along the passageway.

It was defensiveness, Hugh decided. Her noise and bluster tried to present a defiant face, and overcompensated. Underneath it, she was scared and insecure. Everybody was.

He moved to the window and lifted aside the net to peer out. The room was at the rear of the house. The yard was paved for a short distance, with weeds sprouting through cracks. Farther back was a forgotten lawn with seats and a garden table. Wooden slat fences separated it from adjoining yards to the sides and rear. In one of them, children were playing on a creaky swing set. A small, yapping dog pranced around them. Hugh sighed and let the net fall back again.

Chapter Five

David Wallis came in shortly before six. He was breezy and direct in the way that old movies liked to depict as characteristically British. No garish dress, cosmetics, or hair coloring; instead, naturally sandy hair cut short and conventionally, a fresh complexion, and a patterned woolen sweater with plain twill pants. No mirror glasses to be inscrutable behind, nor display of the calculated offensiveness that many seemed to mistake for being assertive. He greeted the arrivals with a solid handshake and a grin that came easily. "So you're the new faces that we've been expecting. Not that I've been here that long myself. As Mrs. R.'s probably told you, I'm not used to these wide open spaces."

Ingram, the engineer, did not put in an appearance that evening. Over dinner, Hugh and Jantowitz learned that Dave was an optical electronics specialist, single, and liked cars and anything mechanical. He also confided, since they'd find out for themselves tomorrow, anyway, that he was with the project that they would be joining. He didn't respond when Hugh probed for a hint of what the project was about.

After taking care of the guests, Mrs. Ryecroft left them to have her own meal in the kitchen. Jantowitz excused himself too, saying that he was tired after the day's traveling and would read a little, then retire early. Hugh and Dave were left to finish their coffee alone.

"What is there to do in the evenings?" Hugh asked.

"What kind of thing are you looking for?"

Hugh shrugged. "Nothing special. Just to look around, see where the people go. Get a drink, maybe."

"There's a Community Center here in town that most Lab people use. Also, a couple of other places that are a notch or two above your average redneck stomping shops and watering holes."

"Are you busy?"

"I am tonight. We're working a late session."

"Does that happen often?"

"There's a lot going on."

"How far from here is it?"

"Oh, we're only at TA-3—across the bridge on the South Mesa. It's walkable, but there's a bus I can catch in half an hour. Why do things the hard way?"

"You don't have any wheels, then?" Hugh said.

Dave shook his head. "Too much hassle getting the permits. Anyway, the Lab runs its own shuttle busses around the area. They'll take you to most of the places you'll want to go. There's a pickup point on Trinity Drive, just at the end of the street."

"Is it safe around here?" Hugh asked.

"Not too bad. Why?"

"Driving from the airport this afternoon felt like we were going through a war zone."

Dave sighed. "It's getting crazy out there," he agreed. "And places like this can become special targets—along with the people who work in them. You know how it is: eco-terrorists, anarchist guerrillas—the ones who think that science is the cause of all the world's problems. A month or two ago, they got one of the beam-weapons designers with a car bomb. Nasty. But he had this place out in the middle of nowhere that he'd built himself and wouldn't leave. You'll be all right up here in town. This location's like a fortress."

Hugh digested the information, then changed the subject. "You didn't have any trouble getting in here? I mean, being from another country—a high-security place like this."

"I worked on military stuff before, which probably helped," Dave answered. "The Mother Country and the States are closer than most people realize when it comes to skullduggery and intrigue. But it was all up in the air for a while. At one point I almost told them to forget it. I'd already got an offer from Eurospace Engineering in Germany—straight satellite optronics."

"Without all the security hassle?" Hugh said.

"A lot less hassle, anyway."

"So why didn't you take it?"

Dave shrugged. "I was too hooked on MV physics. The work at Cambridge had run out of funding, and it wasn't going to be renewed—due to pressure from the U.S., I suspect. Coming over here was the only way to stay in the field. I'm sure you know yourself how it is."

Hugh knew exactly how it was. Working in the new physics of quantum-connected universes generated a curiosity that was compulsive.

"MV physics" was a professional's term. The "parallel universes" that Hugh had talked about to Alice accorded with the popular conception of the subject, but was a simplification. The other realities existed not as discrete, separate entities stacked like the pages of a book, but as a smoothly varying continuum. Hence, the Alices that he had described were not "other" Alices, existing detached and apart from each other, but different components of the same "super-Alice," all acting in different ways in their variously differing circumstances.

This peculiar conclusion followed from one of the earliest questions that quantum mechanics had addressed. The question had to do with the fact that many processes in physics have several possible outcomes—such as which particular level, of the various permissible levels that exist, an excited atom will return to after absorbing energy. In a given case, there was no way of knowing in advance which of the alternatives would actually occur, although the probabilities could be calculated very accurately. How, then, did Nature "choose" which of the possible outcomes would become real? Various explanations had been considered in almost a century of argument, none of them satisfactory. All they seemed to agree on was that reality was a lot stranger than unaided imagination was probably capable of conceiving.

The currently accepted answer was known as the Many Worlds Interpretation. According to this view, *all* of the possibilities did, in fact happen and were equally real! Each alternative led to a different region of reality, which in turn included all the possible consequences. The "true" universe, or "Multiverse"—hence MV—thus forms an enormous branching structure, extending in virtually an infinite number of dimensions, in which everything that could happen, future and past as well as present, exists somewhere. Nearby parts of the Multiverse tend to be similar. More distant regions become progressively more different. Different in what way depends on the direction.

The sequence of events making up an individual's experience represents merely one possible path through the totality, determined by chance, choice, or more generally a combination of both. This picture accommodated and resolved the classical conflict of determinism and free will: In the Multiverse, everything is determinate; which parts of it a particular consciousness will come to know, however, are not.

Dave declined to answer when Hugh asked how MV physics was being applied at Los Alamos. "You don't talk about what you don't have to," he said. "They'll tell you what they want, when they want to."

That was fair enough, Hugh thought. He wasn't in Berkeley now. "What kind of thing were you doing at Cambridge, then?" he asked instead.

Dave hesitated for a second. "I was in an experimental psychology lab." Hugh frowned. He hadn't heard of any related work in that field. "Part of a group studying intuition and the roots of human genius," Dave said.

"What does MV work have to do with things like that?"

"Sorry, Hugh. That's all you get." Dave looked at his watch. He stood up and moved to the door. "Well, I probably won't see you again tonight. What's your schedule for tomorrow?"

"We're being collected first thing," Hugh answered.

"Okay. I'll probably bump into you sometime later in the lab. Have fun." He disappeared, and Hugh heard him putting on his coat in the hall. Hugh sipped his coffee, staring distantly at the empty doorway. His own MV expertise spanned the physics in general, and he could see how it would be relevant to any likely application here. But why Theo? What could be going on that would have room for a mathematical biophysicist? It was the first time that he'd really stopped to ask himself the question. Dave certainly wasn't giving anything away.

"Okay, Dave, I guess I can see your point," he called out absently. "I mean, for all you know, I could be undercover security, trying to catch you out, couldn't I?"

Dave stuck his head back around the door. "Oh, I don't think so," he said lightly. "I didn't, even before you arrived."

Hugh sent him a puzzled look. "How could you? We've only just met. How could you have formed any opinions about me before?"

Dave smiled at him mysteriously. "You'll find out," he said.

Calom's office was plain and utilitarian considering his exalted-sounding rank—certainly more so than would have been typical for a university department head. The desk was regular service style: gray-painted metal with a vinyl top, side extension for dual-screen com unit and hardcopier; a table with several leather-backed steel chairs occupying one corner; and a unit of bookshelves and three metal filing cabinets to complete the furnishings. The walls carried maps of the world, the U.S.A., New Mexico, and the Los Alamos area; an organization chart of personnel and departments; framed citations, photographs of groups in uniform, and military insignia.

The secretary who had brought Hugh from Personnel left, closing the door. Calom indicated the visitor's chair, and Hugh sat down. Calom sat back and contemplated him in silence for several seconds over steepled fingers. He had an open face that stared squarely, almost impertinently, with raised eyebrows and questioning mouth. The lines were lean and firm in the way that goes with a body kept in good shape. His hair was cropped close, almost to the skull; his eyes were clear, gray, unsmiling. He was wearing a loose gray jacket over a black, polo-neck sweater.

Hugh returned his stare evenly, not allowing himself to be cowed. He didn't like military or security mentalities, the business of violence that they dealt in, or the way they seemed to consider it their privilege to violate with impunity what were supposed to be everyone's rights. In his view, their kind of professional paranoia had brought the world to its present condition. But it wasn't his place to say so here. He just let it show.

Calom brought his hands down to the arms of his chair but remained resting easily. "Yes, Dr. Brenner, I know what you're thinking. Science should be honest and open. We have all the knowledge we need to build a better world. The politics of greed and power that I represent are what keep it divided. I do know the line." His voice had a dispassionate quality, with a hint of an almost extinguished accent—English or Australian, Hugh wasn't sure which.

The flattened vowels accentuated the cynicism of someone who was long past expecting good from either the world or anybody in it.

The pause hung in the air. It was a test. Hugh could either affirm himself now, or concede the status game permanently. "I guess that doesn't leave a lot for me to add," he said, drawling the words, keeping a relaxed exterior.

Calom acknowledged with a brief upturn of his mouth. "Very well. Then let me make my position plain too. That way we'll both know where we stand from the start. I don't have much use for long speeches. Intellectuals are not my favorite people, Dr. Brenner. Especially overprotected academics who think that an aptitude for playing computer games gives them something to say about how things should be run in the real world. Force runs the world, and always has. Force created the country that makes your work possible, and made the laws that protect your paycheck. So we both depend on the same system for our survival, just as the system depends on us to do our part. The difference is that I understand and accept. You do not, which means that your discretion and reliability are suspect. My job is to make sure that the privileges that your work here will necessitate being extended to you are not abused."

Hugh pursed his lips and drew a long breath. There was no point in being drawn into a clash of opinions. Probably that was what Calom wanted. He said, "Well, that just about spells it out. I don't really have too many questions."

Calom continued looking at him for a moment longer. "Good." He sat forward to separate out some of the papers on his desk. "Your clearance is S3/2. That covers Octagon, which is the official designation of the project you'll be working with, Central Resources, and certain facilities outside the advanced weapons programs. These declarations and waivers need to be signed, as you were advised."

Hugh turned the papers around and scanned them briefly. They bound him against disclosure in any form, without countersigned permission, of any information acquired as a result of his work, not only for the duration but indefinitely thereafter. All rights to the contrary implied or expressed, were hereby waived—demonstrating them to be, indeed, quite alienable. So were rights against search of person, and property, workplace, or residence, which could now be violated on demand by DRA representatives or their authorized agents. There was no point in objecting now. As Calom had said, he'd been advised what the job would entail. Hugh dashed signatures and initials in the spaces indicated and returned the papers wordlessly.

Calom reformed the sheets into a stack. "Surprising as it may sound, life here can be quite agreeable, Dr. Brenner," he said. "Forget about the world's imperfections. You're not going to change anything. It only takes a small effort to fit in. I recommend strongly for your own peace of mind that you try it."

The same secretary came to take Hugh back to Personnel, where Jantowitz had at last completed the preliminaries. They had lunch in the TA-3 cafeteria. Then, a serious-looking young man who looked like a technician appeared and announced that he was to take them over to "Polk." Presumably this was where Octagon was housed. It turned out to be on the far side of the main complex, TA-3, that they were in. The technician took them across in one of the electric, golf-car-like buggies that staff used for shuttling about the compound. On the way over, he answered that his name was Roger, and said very little else. Hugh wondered if all of life here was the same festival of mirth and hilarity as his impressions so far.

The Polk Annex extension consisted of several new buildings added to the west side of TA-3 in recent years. The one that Roger brought them to bore the uninformative inscription P2 on a plate by the front doors. It was not especially imposing from the outside—a two-story frontage of black, one-way glass, and sides of gray, fluted walls, featureless except for a row of widely spaced windows

high up, running all the way to the rear. It put Hugh more
in mind of a concrete battleship with rectangular portholes
than a building. A perimeter road ran behind, separating
the rear from the gravel strip running beside the inner of
the two chain-link boundary fences.

Roger took them up to a row of offices in the front
section and knocked on a door bearing Kintner's name.
Kintner's voice called "Come." Roger pushed open the
door, motioned the new arrivals through, and departed.

Kintner was behind a desk facing the room diagonally
from one corner. He treated them to a welcoming smile
and indicated chairs standing by a wall. Hugh and Jantowitz
drew out one each. Kintner tapped at a com unit beside
him and addressed the blank screen. "Rose, our new men
are here. Would you ask Neville and Sam to join us, please?"

The surroundings felt almost cheerful after the metallic
starkness that Calom surrounded himself with. Wooden
desk, chairs, and credenza. A commendable attempt by
the carpet to inject color. Even a few family pictures
among the degrees and diplomas on the ego wall. In
one of them, a younger Kintner in mountaineering garb
posed triumphantly on a snowy summit.

"I take it you're done at Personnel?" Kintner said. "All
sorted out? No hitches?" Jantowitz said there were a couple
of details that needed checking—nothing serious. Some
time-filling chatter followed about the area in general and
the desert climate. As he watched the mouth talking, the
ever-mobile eyes assessing, Hugh had the same feeling
that he'd experienced on the previous occasions that he'd
met Kintner—of interacting with a charade. The words
were reassuring, the expressions amiable. But somehow
the conviction persisted that the real person who existed
somewhere remote behind the camouflage was made of
very different material.

The door opened again, and the two people that Kintner
had sent for arrived. The first was Neville Ducaine, whom
they knew from his original visit with Kintner to Berkeley.
With Ducaine was an Oriental whom Kintner introduced

as Sam Phniangsak. ". . . known universally here as just 'Sam.'" He was of middling height, a little on the chubby side, and wearing a green, open-neck shirt with khaki fatigue pants. His face had a jovial set to it, and he regarded the new arrivals with dark and intelligent, yet playful eyes.

"Most of the scientists here are longstanding establishment people like Neville," Kintner said. "But we do have a few, like yourselves, who've been brought into the project from outside because of their MV experience. Sam is from Thailand originally. He's here as what I suppose you could think of as a consultant."

"So you are a physicist also?" Jantowitz said, looking at Sam.

Sam shook his head. "Actually my qualification for being here is Buddhist philosophy." He grinned at the look on Jantowitz's face. Hugh got the feeling that he was used to surprising people in this way.

The eyes behind the bifocals were amused too. "Our work here goes beyond the things that most people in the MV field are aware of," Kintner said. "You'll see for yourselves shortly. Octagon is organized broadly into an Engineering Group, a Theoretical Group, and supporting services. Because of your specialties, I'm assigning you to different teams. Professor Jantowitz will be joining Peter Mulgrave's Theoretical Group." Mulgrave was another whom they had met in the course of the interviews. "Peter is away today, unfortunately. But Sam can show you around and should be able to answer most of your questions."

Most men would have felt an impulse to make their mark in some way at that point. Jantowitz just nodded.

Kintner turned to Hugh. "Dr. Brenner. You will be going to the Engineering Group, which is headed by Neville. You can talk specifics when he shows you the lab. But first, while we're all together, I want to say a few words about the background to what we're doing here and what it all means. Neville and Sam have heard this before, but it's important enough that you can't hear it too many times. Bluntly, the business that we're in is survival. Survival of our kind, of our culture." He placed his palms flat on the desk, letting the mood of the room shift to a more somber note. Then he went on:

"I don't have to tell you that things are in a bad way. You see it every time you look at a news screen. I'm not talking about our domestic stresses. China, with client states in Africa, faces Japan and its alliances in the Moslem world. The big clash is going to come in Asia, over the immensely resource-rich parts of what used to be the Soviet empire. When it does, Europe will be drawn in, and then everybody else too. That much is the public's general perception, and it pretty much spells things out the way they are—as far as it goes. However, the real picture is more ugly and goes back a lot farther. Now I'll tell you the other part that you won't read in the headlines.

"The reason why the West will have no choice but to get involved is that, ultimately, we are the target. History is filled with accounts of how the wealth of our civilization was built on the exploitation of other peoples. Much of that is true. Some would argue that such were the ways of the times. The point that matters, however, is that the larger part of the world accepts it uncritically, or has been encouraged to do so because it's the kind of motivator that arouses masses and turns them into followers. In other words, most of the world out there that's differently colored from us and outnumbers us five to one is itching to settle a long list of grievances, real and imagined, that have been building up for centuries. In the past, they've never had the political power or the weaponry to do much about it. Now all that's changed."

Kintner paused to invite comment. Hugh glanced around. Jantowitz remained inscrutable. Ducaine and Sam looked at the floor. Nobody said anything. Kintner continued:

"The present standoff in the East is just the preliminary. Whichever power prevails will control two thirds of the world's population. Then they'll come for us, for the throat. It will be genocidal—a war of extermination. Nothing will be barred. Already we have muon-catalyzed fusion bombs the size of gallon cans, orbiting beam weapons, nerve toxins that can incapacitate whole cities, gene-specific viruses that can be made race-selective. More is being developed every day.

"We can wait passively and be resigned. Or we can seek a solution. But any solution will require a ruthlessly candid approach, with no agonizing over religious, moral, or other values. We must cultivate the ability to look at human society with cold objectivity, and to analyze and discuss our conclusions without loss of discretion or undue humility. The best interests of all of us demand recognition of such virtues. Do not deviate from them."

Kintner's voice, though quiet, had taken on a sharper edge. From where Hugh was sitting, light from the window gleamed from the lenses, blotting out the eyes behind. The faceless head, its brow high and rounded, jaw moving hollowly, looked for a moment like a skull.

Finally, Hugh thought.

He was hearing the remote operator at last.

Chapter Seven

Hugh was not sure what he expected to find in the austere, blockhouselike, rear section of P2 Building. Some kind of super-weapon, maybe? Or an elaborate control center serving some arcane purpose. But the warren of labs, work areas, and cubbyholes full of machinery that Ducaine took him through after they left Kintner's office and went back to the ground floor typified research environments everywhere. Without the TV-monitored security booths to get into the building, and coded finger-box locks on the doors inside, it could have been back in Berkeley.

There were more names and faces to try to remember. Hugh saw Roger again, working intently on the circuitry inside a rack slid out from a cabinet, and as uncommunicative as ever. The cabinet was one of several positioned around a partitioned space containing a recliner that resembled a dentist's chair, with a framework above containing electronics and other hardware. Hugh had noticed several similar chairs tucked away here and there, and more of them in open parts of the floor. In one that they passed, a girl was sitting with her eyes closed, while a woman and a man watched over the shoulder of a technician operating a console nearby. Ducaine didn't elect to explain what was going on.

As was typical of MV work, there was a lot of regular, production-style photographic, etching, and crystal-growing

51

equipment. The field was too new to have attracted specialized manufacturers to cater to it yet; hence, antenna chips and associated close-coupled optronics were usually made by the researchers themselves. The information that the special hardware acquired could then be processed by more conventional means. In the central part of the building, Ducaine took Hugh through several large rooms full of power distribution and conditioning equipment, and then on to workshops and stores at the back. From there, they ascended a staircase to the upper level.

The windows that Hugh had seen from the outside belonged to a periphery of rooms and offices running around the outside, separated by corridors from a central core. For the most part, these housed Peter Mulgrave's Theoretical Group, which Jantowitz would be joining. Presumably theoreticians needed airier and lighter surroundings for inspiration. There were also a secretarial section, conference facilities, and a library.

They moved on into the core area. And there were the computers that Hugh had been expecting. The concentration of raw, brute-strength, number-guzzling power was colossal. There were tiers of Cray, TMC, Hitachi, and other supers, front-ended by cabinets of specialized optical-frequency processors buffering the antenna-chip arrays. Almost all of it was configured around massive parallel architectures and stacked pipelines fed by recirculating "racetrack" molecular mass-memory arrays— numerical earth-movers optimized for plowing through gigantic fields of data. Hugh knew the kind of techniques that this work required. He had never seen them amassed in such density.

There were offices, graphics rooms, and simulator setups used for software development. A few of the machines were reserved for the programmers. The rest of the hardware, however, belonged to the system at the heart of the Octagon project, which Hugh now learned was known as the QUAntum Detection & Amplification of Radiation device, or "QUADAR."

"Impressed?" Ducaine asked, unable to contain a smile.

Hugh raised his eyebrows. "Whatever this thing does, I've got a feeling that it's going to make the QUIC look pretty puny," he replied.

"A lot of the work going on at the moment is upgrading to more powerful phase discrimination amplifiers," Ducaine said. "Next week it will be even more impressive."

The QUADAR was not a discrete machine, or even any discernible focal point of activity, but a collective term for the whole system, extending through the building as a score of different experiments. In the midst of it all they came across Dave Wallis. He was standing at a console with a girl in a white lab smock, keying in numbers as she read them from a list. Behind them were racks of circuitry draped in cables, and another of the padded recliners.

"You've met Sam," Ducaine said to Hugh. "Here are two more people who were brought in from outside: David Wallis and Sarah Pacey. . . . This is Dr. Hugh Brenner, from U.C. Berkeley—one of the new hands that you've heard about."

Dave nodded at Hugh. "We already met."

"Last night. We're both staying at the same place across the bridge," Hugh explained.

"Well, that helps," Ducaine said. "Then you probably know that Dave came here from England." Hugh nodded. "Sarah's from Texas, originally."

"Austin," Sarah said.

She was slim to the verge of being skinny, with a long face hollowed at the cheeks, and wide, dark eyes with heavy lids. A straight, thin nose, pert mouth, and tapering chin gave a lean firmness that was attractive, though not in any way that would be called glamorous. Her hair was between fair and auburn, falling in loose waves to the nape of her neck. She regarded Hugh with a distancing look, not committing herself one way or the other.

"But she came to us from Japan," Ducaine informed him. "From an exchange program with Osaka University. Sarah's the artistic one among us."

Artists got involved in MV work too? Hugh looked from one to another of them questioningly. It seemed a strange kind of qualification.

"Basically, it was to do with the physics of inspiration and creativity," Sarah told Hugh. "I don't know what kind of MV work you were involved in. It connects with just about everything."

Hugh was already beginning to realize that. His background was pure physics; Jantowitz's, evolutionary dynamics. Dave had said that he had been involved with the psychology of intuition and genius. Sam was a philosopher. Now an artist. Hugh frowned, searching for a common thread to it all.

Ducaine watched his face. "Let's tie it all together for you," he said. Then, to Dave, "Can we break in here and give Hugh a demo?"

"If we can just get this finished first." Dave resumed tapping at the console.

"Has Jeff clued you in on capturing an initialization profile yet?" Ducaine asked him.

Dave shook his head. "Not really. We're still working on it."

Ducaine produced a pocket communicator and held it close to the side of his face. "Jeff Berres." There was a pause. "Hello, Jeff?" The communicator squawked something unintelligible from where Hugh was. "Jeff, this is Neville. I'm at E13 right now. We've got a new man here, and I want to run a demo. Can you get over here and fix the profile for us?"

The communicator squawked something that sounded like "Gimmeaminutewillya."

Dave finished what he had been doing and said, "All set."

Ducaine waved in the direction of the chair. Hugh looked at it uncertainly. "Yes." Ducaine's halo of yellow hair bobbed. "Take a seat."

Hugh lowered himself into the chair. It was comfortable enough, with soft arms and a concave rest at the back, seemingly to keep the occupier's head still. At the console,

Dave flipped switches and checked responses on a screen. Ducaine turned toward Hugh and pressed his palms together for a second.

"I like to tell this as a kind of fable," he said. "With somebody from your background it's especially appropriate. Imagine that long ago, life had progressed to something like amoebas, floating aimlessly in their ponds and tidal pools. The individuals that happened to encounter nutrients thrived; the ones that drifted into toxic areas didn't. Those that got carried up to where the sunshine was did better than those that stayed down in the dark." He paused. Hugh watched him from the chair, unable to guess where this might be leading.

"Then, rudimentary light-sensitivity appeared, and the ability to sense chemical gradients. Think what a survival advantage those things were! They made possible the emergence of purposefully directed behavior. What began as vague instincts to follow what 'felt right' about which way to move in the pond—'hunches' about what lay ahead, if you will—led eventually to the sophisticated mechanisms that we find associated with eyeballs and noses today."

Then a bearded man in a light gray overjacket appeared and took over from Dave at the console. Presumably this was Jeff.

"How do you want the modal distribution?" he asked Ducaine.

"Standard for now. We'll tune it for specifics when he's imprinted. This is Dr. Hugh Brenner, by the way, Jeff. He's just joined us. Jeff Berres, Signal Processing."

Berres sent Hugh a nod as he worked. Hugh returned it. An exchange of technical jargon between Berres and Ducaine followed, which meant nothing to Hugh. Then Ducaine resumed.

"Something very different from any of the other primates happened in the ancestral hominid line. Life became purposeful—capable of more than just animal-like reaction to immediate circumstances. Faculties emerged of intuition, creativity, abstract reasoning, that set man in a class apart from everything else in the animal world." Ducaine's eyes seemed to enlarge in their intensity, making Hugh feel as if he were being peered at through a microscope. "What do you think it was, Dr. Brenner? The growth of the human brain has never been satisfactorily explained by simple survival needs or any mechanism of basic selection. What happened that made it unique?"

Intuition and the roots of genius? Wisdom? Creativity? The words went through Hugh's mind again. But how did any of it relate to MV physics? . . .

Unless Ducaine was saying that the brain was somehow able to use information propagating at the quantum level. Hugh stared up at him in astonishment. "Are you saying that it responds to Multiverse communication?"

"Exactly!" The halo of yellow hair danced in a frenzy. "And is that really so strange, when you think about it? If things as crude as arrangements of lenses, metal slits, and photographic film can make quantum events observable macroscopically, why couldn't a billion years of evolution produce a molecular quantum-event detector—that's what a retina or any other nerve-ending is, after all—and neural amplifying mechanism capable of delivering survival-oriented information to the brain?"

There was no need for Ducaine to spell out the rest of the analogy. What he had described was the human basis for knowing, because it "felt right," which path to steer behaviorally through the Multiverse "pond." The amoeba selected a direction that felt desirable to move in by responding to information coming from a place where life would be better. In the Multiverse, some choices of action led to consequences that were preferable to others. Since everything in the Multiverse was equally real, such differences could signal themselves backward in what was normally perceived as "time." Some individuals were better than others at sensing them. They tended to make good teachers and leaders. People thought of them as being unusually gifted with "intuition" and "anticipation." It all fitted.

Hugh was only beginning to grasp the enormity of what this portended, when Berres spoke from the console again.

"Okay, I think we're close. Let's try and zero in now." He took a pen from his shirt pocket and pulled across a piece of paper that was lying on the console. "Hugh, I've just written a letter on this sheet here. It's either an *A*, a *B*, or a *C*. Say which you think." Hugh looked perplexedly at Ducaine. Guessing games? What did this have to do with MV physics—or any other kind?

"None of them stands out for any reason?" Ducaine said.

"No."

"Then just guess."

Hugh shrugged. "*B*."

"Uh-huh." Berres checked something on a screen and entered codes. To one side, Sarah and Dave were watching. Dave winked at Hugh mysteriously. Berres wrote on the paper again. "*X*, *Y*, or *Z*?" he said.

"*Z*."

Another adjustment. "*R*, *S*, or *T*?"

This time, Hugh was conscious of something having changed subtly. He didn't feel the same casual indifference that he had before, in the way he might have played a children's game. As he visualized the letters in his mind, the *R* seemed to take on a special significance somehow. It was a vague feeling only, but definitely there. "*R*," he replied.

"Ri-ght. Now we've gotcha." Berres made some final additions, then scribbled once more. "*U*, *V*, *W*," he shot at Hugh.

Now there was no doubt. The answer was shouting inside Hugh's head—far more strongly than just a hunch. "*W*." And even as he said it, he *knew* he was right. Ducaine was looking satisfied, not even bothering to check with Berres.

What in hell was going on?

Ducaine stepped forward into Hugh's field of vision again. "So now we know the physical basis for how such faculties work. The equipment that evolution has provided us with is fine for planning a birthday party or a vacation trip. But, as countless wars, political catastrophes, and other disasters have shown, it has proved inadequate for dealing with the complexities that our uniqueness makes it possible for us to create." He paused to let Hugh absorb that much. "Better understanding of how the senses worked enabled devices to be built to enhance them, such as telescopes and sound amplifiers." Ducaine turned and waved a hand to indicate their surroundings generally. "So why not an intuition amplifier?"

Hugh moved his eyes to take in the arrays of focusing optronics inches above his head. What this had to mean was that the QUADAR was able to sort out quantum-level data percolating back from the forward direction in time, and assemble it into usable information that a brain could work with. The incredulity must have registered on his face. Ducaine nodded and smiled.

"Yes, I think you've got it, Dr. Brenner. That example we just showed you with the letters reflected a situation involving certainty. By the time Jeff asked you the question, he'd already written down the letter. Now let's bring probability into it." He produced a six-sided die and held it up for Hugh to see. Then he clasped it in a fist as if to roll it on the console top. "Any bets?" he said to Hugh.

This didn't make sense. *Five* was impressing itself in Hugh's mind—not as insistently as the *W* had before; but it was clear. And yet, that shouldn't have been so. In the dimension of the Multiverse that represented the possible outcomes, the timeline ahead split six ways with equal probability, none of which ought to be favored. So why was he conscious of any preference at all? But there was nothing but to go with it. "Five," he told Ducaine.

Ducaine rolled the die—and five it was. He repeated the process twice more. On each occasion Hugh called five, and five came up. Something very strange was going on. On the next try, Hugh felt five yet again, and said so. But this time the die showed a 2. Then Ducaine held the die in front of Hugh's face and let him see all of it. It was a fake. Four of its sides carried 5, the other two, 3 and 2.

"The machine can't predict the future that will actually happen—that's impossible, of course. What it can do is tell you which way to bet. And it will do so even when your ideas on what the rules are turn out to be mistaken because you were deliberately deceived. But isn't that what we mean by 'intuition,' after all—getting the odds right when it flies in the face of what everyone else thinks is common sense?

"And that, Dr. Brenner, is what the QUADAR is all about. It doesn't add to mental faculties, but enhances to an extraordinary degree that peculiar human ability which is present to a greater or lesser degree in everyone. It amplifies foresight in the way that a telescope amplifies eyesight.

"The purpose of the Octagon project is to provide a decision-making aid for government in the hope that it will reveal a path for avoiding the calamity that our experts say is inevitable. I don't have to tell you how invaluable such a measure would be in times such as we are living in."

Hugh could see that. But also, still coupled into the machine, he could see more. He could see his options in life beckoning with greater or lesser appeal. The main path standing out was the project that he was now committed to and had resolved to make the best of. But only premonitions of disappointment, frustration, and eventual conflict came back to him from that direction. There was no detailed image, nothing specific. He *felt*, rather than saw, eventual betrayal, then himself being discarded. Those who demanded loyalty had none to offer in return.

His first reaction was an impulse to protest out loud. Berres and Ducaine were watching him, as if expecting some such violent reaction. But Hugh suppressed it. Because, besides the treachery and pretense, he had glimpsed something else too.

Coming to Los Alamos had felt like the last phase of a nightmare that had been closing around him for years. But suddenly he felt, as surely as he had ever felt anything, that Octagon also contained the key to the way out. Here, on this one path before him, lay not only the possibility of escaping from all of it, but to do so permanently.

The machine had looked into the maze ahead and extracted that much. What it hadn't told him was how.

Chapter Eight

Hugh had gotten the impression that Dave and Sarah were closer than being just colleagues in the same lab. In the days that followed, they made no particular attempt to hide the fact. They lunched together in the TA-3 cafeteria, and Dave usually had something planned with Sarah for the few evenings on which they were both free. There was nothing especially surprising about two young people being drawn to each other, of course; even more so if it relieved the oppressiveness of the unfamiliar world that they had all been brought into. On the Sunday following Hugh and Jantowitz's arrival, Dave told Mrs. Ryecroft not to set a place for him that evening, since Sarah had invited him to dinner at her place. Sarah had been at Los Alamos a little longer, and had moved into apartments that the Laboratory owned north of the central district. However, the afternoon was black with thunderstorms, and shortly before five o'clock Dave called Mrs. Ryecroft and asked if there were any electrical problems at the house.

"No, everything's fine here," she trumpeted back into the phone. "Why? What's up?"

"We've got a power-out here at Sarah's. I think it's affecting this whole part of town," Dave told her.

"What about your dinner date?"

"I think it's a case of taking a rain check—literally. Could you fit a couple of late additions in over there?"

"When have I ever turned anyone away? Sure, bring her over. There's plenty. I'm sure Hugh could use the company."

Sarah was not a stranger to the house. In fact, she had lodged there herself when she first came to Los Alamos.

"I swear you're getting skinnier," Mrs. Ryecroft said as she watched Sarah shred lettuce for the salad. "They should have let you stay here for a few more weeks. I'd have put some meat on those bones. What are you feeding yourself on over at that place they put you in? Music might be food enough for love but it doesn't have enough calories."

"I do okay. I'm probably still adapting to the altitude," Sarah answered without looking up.

At a worktop to one side, Hugh finished filling two glasses from a bottle of Paisano. "You should do this more often," he told Sarah. "Be more like one of the family."

"Boy, couldn't we use more of that these days," Mrs. Ryecroft muttered.

"I think I had enough of family life growing up in one," Sarah said. There was little warmth in her voice or expression. Hugh looked at her for a few seconds, inviting more, but the distant attitude that she had displayed since their first meeting hadn't changed.

He picked up the glasses. "Well, I'll take these on through."

"We'll be about fifteen minutes," Mrs. Ryecroft called after him.

"Okay."

"Are you sure the professor won't be showing up?"

"No. He'll be tied up until late."

"I'll leave his in the refrigerator, then."

"That'll be fine."

So far, Jantowitz hadn't had as much access to the machine as he had hoped, due to the upgrade work that had been going on. That work had been completed late on Saturday, however, and he had gone in on Sunday with Sam to catch up.

Hugh carried the glasses through into the hallway just as the street door opened and Ingram, the engineer who was also the only other resident presently, entered. He was remarkably unremarkable in dress and appearance, qualifying for "average" on just about every characteristic that could be named. He rarely spoke, never took dinner, and nobody in the house had any idea which part of the Lab he worked in. Dave said he could have vanished in a crowd of three.

"Hi," Hugh greeted automatically. Ingram nodded an acknowledgement and disappeared upstairs. Hugh shrugged and carried on into the living room where Dave was sitting on the couch, staring absently at the TV with its sound turned down. It showed scuffles breaking out at a Grayshirts rally in Albuquerque.

"Is it me, Dave?" Hugh asked, passing one of the glasses. "Sarah's still giving me the treatment. Ingram talks to me like I'm a piece of the furniture. What's your secret for getting along with them? If it's that accent, I'll take lessons."

"Cheers." Dave took the glass and tried a sip. "I don't know about Ingram, but with everyone who works in P2 it's the machine. It creates paranoia. Nobody trusts anybody because they're never sure what little secrets they might have glimpsed into. And we've all got them, haven't we?" He tasted the wine again and smiled. "You could call it a guilt amplifier, I suppose. It's the reason why the whole place is so obsessed with security."

Hugh remained standing and contemplated the window moodily. The "side effect" that he had experienced from the QUADAR was an unavoidable consequence of being connected to it. Every contemplated course of action or proposal from somebody else carried connotations of good, bad, indifferent, or otherwise, derived from the probable outcomes. What came through as feeling good to one person didn't necessarily affect everyone else the same way. Thus, negative premonitions didn't always imply insincerity. A whole new set of rules for social interaction in the workplace was having to be worked out. It was common knowledge that Kintner used the machine as an aid to administrative decisions. The object at the end of it all, he pointed out, was to guide national policymaking. Learning how to use the technology was as important as getting it to work right.

It made Hugh feel more like a subject in a social-engineering experiment than a free, working scientist. Nobody doubted that whatever insights the project revealed would be monopolized for the political and military advantage of the West. There would be no sharing with the world generally. It was ironic to find himself thinking such thoughts at Los Alamos of all places.

"The Caloms of the world should appreciate it," Dave said.

"There's somebody else that I seem to affect the wrong way."

"Oh, he's like that with everyone, even Kintner." Dave glanced at the screen and added distantly, "Sometimes I think I should have taken that Eurospace job in Germany."

"Ask the machine the next time you're hooked up."

"It's too late. That option lies in the past now. Hence, the machine no longer has access to that region of the branching structure."

Hugh thought for a moment. "Of course. It would have to work that way, wouldn't it."

"So maybe there's still need for something like Sam's mystical insights yet," Dave said.

Hugh turned and looked down at him over the rim of the glass while he tasted his own drink. "Do you really think there's something to it—direct experience of reality and all that stuff?" he asked.

"I'd say there has to be," Dave answered. "It's difficult to imagine that they could all have been wrong for thousands of years. What they say is too similar. They must be on to something. . . . Anyhow, the powers that be, here, seem to think so. They brought him in as an advisor on the project."

"True." Hugh hadn't grasped the full implication of that

before. It added yet another perspective to what they were doing. "Well, he's someone that Sarah ought to take to better, anyhow," he said absently. "She was in Japan before she came here, right? Does she have a thing about the East?"

"I think she's got more of a thing about affairs that don't work out," Dave said. "She went there to forget about one. I've never asked about the details."

"Better not get too attached, then, by the sound of it," Hugh commented.

Dave shrugged. "Artists," he replied, as if that explained everything.

Sarah came through from the kitchen, holding a glass. The way the conversation hung suddenly was impossible to miss. "Hello, my radar says you two are talking about me," she said.

"Yes." Dave agreed without hesitation. "Hugh thinks he must be using the wrong soap or something. Apparently, you're not being very nice to him. I tried telling him it's probably just the P2 crabs, but it really ought to come from you." Hugh had to remind himself that this kind of candidness was simply Dave's way. It saved a lot of complications—but it took some getting used to.

Sarah looked at Hugh, sighed heavily, and then actually managed a thin smile. "I'm sorry. It wasn't personal. As Dave says, it's that place. It gets to everybody."

That was all it needed. "It's okay. I think I'm beginning to understand," Hugh told her. "Don't worry about it."

She nodded in the direction of the screen, which was showing riot police forming up and attracting missiles from all factions of the crowd. "What's happening here?"

"The voting majority expressing its rational preference," Dave answered laconically.

Sarah lowered herself onto the arm of the couch next to him. "Why is it the story of so much of history? So much violence and destructiveness. People spend most of their time squandering the talents and resources that could have solved the problems that they fight about.

There's enough to be depressed about, even without the machine."

"Ah. But the machine will give the world the means of overcoming all that," Dave intoned grandiosely. "Technologically augmented wisdom, whereby humanity will finally rise above such failings." He raised his glass and drank to the prospect.

Sarah snorted derisively. "You mean like all the other magic solutions we've been hearing for two thousand years that were going to do the same thing? Gee, who do I write my check to?"

"If I didn't know you better, I'd think you were losing faith in the cause," Dave said.

"Cause? It was never my cause." She looked at Hugh. "In Osaka we were beginning to interpret creative human vision in MV terms—you know, the sudden flash of insight that seems to come from nowhere. That was the cause I was dedicated to. Then the Japanese government got involved, and all foreigners were let go."

"The same as here," Hugh said.

"It's happening everywhere," Dave agreed.

Sarah nodded. "And when I got back here, this was all there was." She waved her free hand vaguely. "This is how it's being run. The world's being sold out again. I think Oppenheimer was right. Maybe, if I had the chance, I'd keep up the tradition."

In his room upstairs, Ingram raised his eyebrows as he listened in, making a routine check on the voice quality being picked up by the microphone concealed in the living room's ceiling light. Calom would like this, he thought to himself. In the multichannel recorder disguised as a video cassette player, he adjusted the levels on the wire from the living room to reduce background noise from the TV. Satisfied, he closed the unit, took off the headset, and returned it to his briefcase along with the tapes covering the previous twenty-four hours. Minutes later, he left the house as unceremoniously as he had entered it.

✧   ✧   ✧

Meanwhile, in a part of the P2 building, Jantowitz settled himself in the QUADAR coupler while Sam, standing at the control console, loaded his initialization profile from the system's files. Jantowitz was taking his introduction to the machine's capabilities slow and easily. The others in the building were mostly technicians testing the newly installed amplifiers. The researchers wouldn't be in until the next morning.

"So why is it you are here with this project?" Jantowitz asked as Sam tapped in commands and checked the screen.

"You already know why," Sam said. "They wanted to know if the effects that the QUADAR produces are similar to the insights attributed to traditional Eastern mystical philosophies. That's my department." He smiled, knowing full well that that wasn't what Jantowitz had meant at all.

"Yes, their reasons, I know," Jantowitz said. "It is *your* reason I wish to hear."

Sam answered after a pause, without looking up. "Pursuing the rational kind of knowledge that this side of the world has produced doesn't seem to have done much to increase humanity's wisdom. The intuitive path that my discipline follows is supposed to see beyond the delusions that cause all the problems." He shrugged. "Maybe I can bring such insights into what is going on here, before it is turned into a political weapon. I don't know."

"So it is to the Buddha you would steer us, and back from the Bomb," Jantowitz said.

"You could put it that way."

"A tall order, to me it would seem."

"I can only try, if the opportunity presents itself. Otherwise, I shall hope to learn."

Jantowitz studied the Oriental curiously from the chair. "Tell me, how similar is it?" he said. "When your intuition is enhanced by the QUADAR, is the experience anything like that of directly heightened consciousness? All this—" Jantowitz waved a hand to indicate the surroundings. "Is it just an expensive way of repeating what you have been doing for two thousand years that we have discovered?"

"Similar in some ways, not so in others," Sam replied. "From my own experiments, I am confident that the things that have been described for centuries as mystical insight are results of abnormal Multiverse sensitivity—either acquired accidentally or developed through training. There is that much in common. The difference is in the direction that consciousness looks in—the part of the Multiverse from which information enters awareness. In the traditional meditative state, the mind expands into the present. Its experience is of *knowing*—direct perception of a timeless reality that transcends the limited world of the senses. The QUADAR, by contrast, tunes to the future. It delivers an experience of feelings and premonitions. One reveals what is; the other, what could be. Actuality versus potential."

Jantowitz recognized the feeling of the field coming into focus when he suddenly knew, a fraction of a second before it happened, that Sam was going to take one of the pens from his shirt pocket. "We are tuned in now, yes?" he said.

Sam nodded and wrote something on a scrap of paper. "Getting the knack, eh? A quick routine check, then. Which number, 1 to 5?"

"Three," Jantowitz said.

"Again."

"Three again, it is."

"And again."

"Five."

"Good. Okay, we were going to look at some of the ways of untangling probabilities, weren't we. . . ."

Jantowitz was already letting his mind wander through a miscellany of thoughts, examining them in the light of the machine's illumination. To his surprise, he immediately picked up a feeling of something puzzling virtually about to happen. He focused on Sam as a possible cause of it, but all he got from that direction was the corroboration of total integrity that Sam's image always evoked. Of this one person, at least, Jantowitz had no doubts. He never became this friendly with people so soon after meeting them. For that matter, it was rare for him to get especially friendly with anybody.

A strange, detached feeling came over Jantowitz, unlike anything that he had experienced previously on the machine. But he'd had only brief, introductory sessions. There was a lot more for him to learn yet. He didn't pay much heed.

Then Hugh sauntered in, dripping wet in a parka with the hood thrown back, and carrying a black nylon briefcase. "Wow, it's bucketing down out there," he said. "I thought the storm had eased off, but it started up again and caught me halfway. . . . Oh, you're busy. Didn't mean to interrupt."

"It's all right. We were just starting," Jantowitz said. "So what is this new dedication that all of a sudden we are favored with? Sunday night, you are working?"

"Oh, it's pretty dead at the house. Dave's gone over to Sarah's place for dinner. I thought I'd spend the evening catching up on some background reading." Hugh looked to the side. "Sam, could I borrow that manual on vector filtering that you showed us a couple of days ago? I can let you have it back tomorrow."

"Sure. It's over in the desk."

Jantowitz turned his head and blinked, puzzled. Sam seemed to have shifted position somehow, although Jantowitz had no recollection of seeing him move. He had been standing at the console, talking to Jantowitz. Now, suddenly, he was over at the far wall, by one of the equipment cubicles. He walked over to a desk nearby and opened a drawer. Hugh joined him, leaving a trail of water drops across the floor.

"Yes, here it is," Sam said, producing a blue binder. "Keep it as long as you like. I'll let you know if I need it."

"Thanks." Hugh took the binder and slipped it into his briefcase.

"I was just about to couple Theo in," Sam said. "Stick around and watch if you like."

Now Jantowitz was even more bemused. He was already coupled in. What in hell was Sam talking about?

Hugh moved back to the door. "No, I'll be getting back.

It wouldn't be much fun staying around in these clothes, anyway. I'll see you tomorrow. I told Mrs. R. you'd be late, Theo. She'll leave something in the refrige—"

"Theo? *Theo, are you all right?*" Sam's voice interrupted, sounding alarmed. Jantowitz looked back toward the desk. Sam wasn't there. Jantowitz located him a moment later, now at the console again, holding the pen.

Suddenly, Jantowitz wasn't so sure that he was all right. "Why shouldn't I be?" he demanded obstinately, all the same.

"You didn't seem to be registering anything I was saying."

"Were you saying something? Sorry. I was listening to Hugh."

Now it was Sam's turn to look perplexed. "Hugh? What do you mean? I don't understand."

"Hugh." Jantowitz snapped the word challengingly, certain now that something was very wrong. Sam turned his hands palms-upward and returned a bewildered expression. Jantowitz jerked his head back toward the doorway. There was no sign of Hugh. "He was here just a moment ago. He came in to borrow . . ." Jantowitz's voice trailed away. The floor between the doorway and the desk was quite dry.

"Nobody has been here, Theo," Sam said, speaking with the exaggerated calm of somebody worried and trying not to sound it.

Jantowitz swallowed. After a few seconds, he said, "Sam, would you do something for me, please? Look in the lower right-hand drawer of that desk over there and tell me if there's a blue manual on vector filtering there."

"I know there is. I put it there on Friday." Sam looked puzzled. "But how could you know that?"

"Just look and see if it's still there," Jantowitz said.

Sam stared at him oddly for a moment, then shrugged and walked over to the desk. "Here it is. Satisfied?" He held up the blue binder that Jantowitz had seen Hugh take just a few minutes before. "Now would you tell me what this is all about?"

"Sam, could we please terminate this experiment?" Jantowitz replied shakily. "The explanations, I would prefer to leave for the moment, if you don't mind. For now, there is much thinking that alone, I must do. Suddenly, very mysterious it becomes, this whole business that we have going on here."

Chapter Nine

The next morning, Hugh was sitting back in one of the couplers in the Vector Dynamics section, which was the group that Ducaine had assigned him to. He waited while Ducaine and an engineer named Phil Moody discussed the results of the last test. They were running a long series of guessing games with numbers, first with the new amplifiers switched in, then with them out, in order to measure how much performance was improved. The routine was already tedious, repetitive, and boring. Such was much of the real work of science.

Periodically, he heard stories about neighbors who didn't talk to each other for years until there was a power outage, and suddenly there was no TV. There ought to be power outages more often, Hugh thought—perhaps an obligatory one every week, like the old-time sabbath. Sarah had opened up at last over dinner, talking about her work in Japan, and Dave had revealed an inexhaustible supply of anecdotes which his dry delivery rendered hilarious. Mrs. Ryecroft had been drawn into joining them at the table, then opened a bottle of brandy afterward. "This is the way life used to be," she had told everybody. "Would you believe people actually knew how to get along once? They used to get together like this, have parties. Now they're only interested in what they can cheat each other out of." After another glass she started reminiscing about her dead husband and became tearful over what she was going to do if she had to sell the house.

Then Jantowitz had returned earlier than expected, mumbling just a few semicomprehensible words in response to their greetings and going straight up to his room. He had been equally withdrawn over breakfast, said little to Hugh on the way to the lab, and promptly disappeared on arriving there to go and find Sam. Hugh hadn't seen him since.

Afterward, Sarah had reverted to somber mode over the aggressiveness that seemed to dominate human nature. She had an interest in history as well as the visual arts. War horrified her. She saw nothing noble or heroic in it; only the raw reality of people being deliberately brutalized and incited to hate and kill one another. Her revulsion made her shake visibly when she talked about it. Yet she had come to Los Alamos. Her time in Japan had left her with a fascination to understand more of the human mind. Now, this place alone, ironically, held the promise of an insight into the source of its highest faculties.

Ducaine looked up and toward Hugh. Unquestioning intellect committed to the service of everything that Sarah abhorred, Hugh reflected. No wonder her situation got her down at times. "Okay, Hugh, we're going to run another five sets with the same weightings as the last, but at higher power. The range is still ten. All right?"

"Ready when you are," Hugh returned. Moody tapped at the console. Hugh experienced the by-now-familiar feeling of the world suddenly taking on a changed aspect of significance and associations. Dave described it as the feelings-equivalent of false-color graphics with the contrast enhanced. Hugh didn't find the metaphor compelling. He saw geometry with the perspective distorted.

"Go," Ducaine instructed.

"Eight," Hugh responded.

"Next."

"Mm . . . two."

"Next."

An impression of emotional shallowness formed when Hugh concentrated on Ducaine and allowed his mind to probe. He sensed the imperviousness to feeling that Sarah said made her shudder. Contrast Sam, who radiated simple love for everything that lived, and made everyone feel precious. . . .

And suddenly the lab had vanished, and Hugh was sitting facing a gray metal desk in a room with filing cabinets to one side and maps on the walls. Calom was talking to him from behind the desk. He realized with a jolt that he was in Calom's office.

"You might think of it as no more than a flouting of college rules, Dr. Brenner, but you're out of that environment now. Do you realize that this makes you liable to criminal prosecution?"

Hugh looked around in bewilderment. They were alone. Then he looked down and saw that he was wearing the blue-patterned shirt that he'd worn yesterday. But he'd spilt gravy on it last night, when he helped clear the dishes after dinner, and a moment ago, in the lab, he'd been in the buff-colored one that he had put on clean that morning. What in God's name was this?

"Well?" Calom demanded.

Hugh looked at his watch. The time was about what it had been when he was calling numbers to Ducaine; the date hadn't changed. There had been no time for him to have had some kind of blackout.

"I asked you a simple question," Calom said. "Since you are new here, and I'm satisfied that your action was not malicious, I had intended to let the incident pass this once. But if your only answer is to persist in this stubborn silence, I might be forced to revise that judgment. So what have you to say?"

"I—I . . ." Hugh could only shake his head. "I don't know how to explain this. Something's happened. . . . I honestly don't know what you're talking about."

"Oh, Dr. Brenner, *please*," Calom groaned impatiently.

"No, look . . . I don't know what I'm doing here, what this is about . . . Anything."

"You're being ridiculous."

"Really, I'm being serious. I'm having some kind of mental aberration. I don't understand it."

"You sound quite coherent. You knew what this was all about a moment ago."

Hugh shook his head helplessly again. "A moment ago I was in the lab, coupled into the QUADAR—running tests with Ducaine. Now I'm here all of a sudden. That's all I know."

Calom gave him a long, dubious look, then pushed across a thick blue binder that was lying on the desk. "You know what that is?" he said.

Hugh turned it to read the cover, then nodded. "A manual on vector filtering techniques. Sam Phniangsak showed it to Theo and me last week."

"Anything else about it?" Calom asked.

Hugh shrugged. "No. Like what?"

"You were stopped taking it out of the main gate in a briefcase last night. Restricted information, Dr. Brenner. It doesn't leave the building."

Hugh stared at him incredulously. "That's insane. I wasn't here anytime yesterday."

"The gate log says you were. So does the P2 access record."

"It wasn't me," Hugh insisted.

"Oh, come on. You were identified by two guards and the duty officer. What kind of game is this? I'd have credited somebody of your intelligence with something better."

"But *I wasn't here* last night, I tell you! I was at dinner with friends."

"Five minutes ago you admitted that you were here."

"I told you, five minutes ago I was in the lab."

"I think this has become preposterous enough," Calom said, sounding short.

Hugh sighed. "Look, I know you think of us as rather naive, childish people. But I'd hardly be this stupid.

Something strange has happened to me. Maybe somebody sitting here five minutes ago knew what you were talking about and agreed, but it wasn't *me*. This isn't some silly excuse. I can't tell you any more."

Calom studied him for several seconds. Finally he said soberly, "Stay where you are. Let's get a professional opinion on this." He turned to the com terminal on one side, touched a key, and addressed somebody on the screen. "Get me the Medical Department, Emergency Room."

Hugh sank back in the chair and closed his eyes. His mind was still too much in shock to attempt making sense of it. Calom's voice came again. "Calom here. We've got a case of some kind of sudden amnesia or something here. Can you get somebody over to my office right away? . . ."

Hugh let his head hang back. It thudded unexpectedly against a headrest. The acoustics of the surroundings had changed suddenly.

"Hugh!" Somebody was shaking him. He opened his eyes to find Ducaine peering down at him. "Are you okay?"

Hugh blinked and looked around. Phil Moody was behind Ducaine, and a couple of technicians were coming across the lab floor. "What happened?" he mumbled.

"You blacked out for a few minutes. Do you feel all right?"

"I guess so. . . . I'm a bit confused."

"Let's get you off the system. I think we'd better get a medic over and check you out. Okay, people, that's it for now. Everybody take a break, go get some coffee or something, okay?"

Shortly afterward, in the middle of an impromptu meeting in one of the Engineering Group offices, Jeff Berres suddenly started talking in a way that made no sense. He claimed that he was not there but hooked into a coupler in the Signals Processing section. A few minutes later he returned to normal just as suddenly, with no recollection of the incident.

✧   ✧   ✧

Kintner had been in conference with Jantowitz and Sam since first thing that morning. Reports were sent in to them of the events concerning Hugh and Berres. Half an hour later, Kintner issued a directive for all on-line coupling to the QUADAR to be suspended until further notice.

Chapter Ten

Were the experiences that Hugh and Jantowitz had reported—and also, it turned out, an Engineering Group technician called Joyce Theale, but hers wasn't known about until later—simply a case of artificially induced hallucinations? Brain surgeons had known since the 1940s that electrical stimulation of specific points on the cortex could evoke vividly detailed sensory impressions. At first these had been thought to be stored memories reactivated, but further investigation revealed that much of the content was being manufactured internally by the brain, as in dreams. Was the QUADAR somehow doing the same thing?

"No, I'm pretty sure we can rule that out," Peter Mulgrave told the meeting that Kintner called in the upper-level conference room, behind the executive offices, later that afternoon. Mulgrave was lean, pallid, and gaunt-faced, and seemed to carry a shadow around his chin at any time of day. "Cadaverous" was the word that came to Hugh's mind. "Theo's and Hugh's accounts corroborate each other too well—unless anybody here accepts the idea of shared dreams."

"I think we're agreed on that," Kintner said from the end of the table, across the corner from Willard, who had joined them and was presiding. Kintner looked around. Nobody dissented. Besides Hugh, Jantowitz, and Sam, one of Mulgrave's theoreticians, Helen Almer was present; also, Ducaine, Berres, and Joyce Theale from Ducaine's group. The various section heads would be updated later. The purpose of this get-together was simply to try to find out what had happened from the people directly involved.

"Then we're only left with one other explanation," Helen Almer said. It was the one that Sam and Jantowitz had been deliberating with Kintner since first thing that morning. "The QUADAR is adding a transverse component to the normal flow of subjective experience through the MV. It's inducing a sideways wobble into adjacent regions."

"Do we have any idea how?" Willard asked.

Ducaine shook his head. Mulgrave shrugged. "We still don't understand the phenomenon of consciousness," Kintner said. "Without a model, the precise mechanism of how the system interacts with it must remain an unknown." Which was as much as Ducaine and Mulgrave had expressed.

The Multiverse formed a continuum that became progressively more different from familiar reality in a practically infinite number of ways as it extended away in practically an infinite number of dimensions. Each of these realities—"cross sections" of the Multiverse, as it were—would include its own variant, or "copy," of the inhabitants of the familiar world too—like the Alices operating different versions of the QUIC back at Berkeley.

Normally, the sequence of impressions perceived by a particular consciousness took place strictly in the "forward" direction where consequences followed causes, creating the experience of causally connected time. Each such consciousness kept to its own parallel track like a runner in a race, believing it to be all that existed. With no information reaching it of anything outside its own lane, its awareness did not extend into even the regions immediately next door.

Helen Almer was saying that the QUADAR could change this. Under certain conditions—nobody knew exactly what, yet, but the higher operating power of the new amplifiers apparently played a part—it could cause the flow of awareness to veer sideways. Instead of progressing to its own future, the consciousness of a person subject to the effect "changed lanes" to occupy a copy of that person inhabiting a nearby part of the Multiverse. What had been demonstrated, in other words, was the staggering fact that it was possible to experience directly the alternate realities whose existence, up until now, had only been inferred from abstract theory or the operation of devices like the QUIC. The diverted personality evidently carried its own memories with it; hence, the reality in which it found itself did not, in general, accord with its remembered past.

As with the Alices and the QUICs, it followed that countless other Octagon teams in other universes had upgraded their systems too, and personas taking part in those tests were just as likely to take over their other selves in this reality. That, of course, was what must have happened to Jeff Berres, who was nowhere near a coupler at the time when he was briefly "possessed." Joyce Theale seemed to be another case of the same, having experienced several minutes of total blankness while operating a terminal in the library—although she hadn't spoken to anyone at the time.

A disturbing thought was that just because this Kintner in this reality had called a halt to further testing, it didn't follow that all the other Kintners would necessarily do the same. That meant that "visitors" from other Octagon projects could still show up, whether tests were being continued in this particular one or not. It all depended on how the connections were made between one reality and another, and in an effective infinity of possibilities, that was something that nobody knew anything about.

In fact, two incidents had occurred since the tests were halted that sounded like just the kind of thing that would be expected. At lunchtime, a physicist with Mulgrave's group tail-ended a car on Central Avenue, claiming afterward that she had blacked out and had no recollection of the event. Then, barely an hour before the present meeting, a programmer had found himself abruptly transported to another part of the building with no idea how he came to be there. Mere coincidence? Both on the day that the upgrades to the machine became operational? Nobody around the table thought so.

The next question, naturally, was what to do. "Obviously we have to involve Washington," Willard said. "The implications are too serious for anyone here to decide. That's why I'm sitting in."

Kintner could hardly disagree. All the same, he pinched his nose dubiously and seemed unwilling to leave things at that. Finally, he said, "True, of course. But Washington is going to need more facts than we are in a position to supply as things stand. They'll need more than this to go on."

"What are you proposing?" Willard asked.

"In view of the world situation, we should make it our business to give Washington minimum cause for delay," Kintner replied. "I suggest that we resume limited tests aimed at answering some of the more obvious questions that are going to be asked. For example, is this thing controllable? Is it possible to somehow select which 'direction' you move in?"

"What other side effects might there be?" Mulgrave threw in.

"Nothing adverse, it appears," Kintner returned evenly.

"You don't *know* that, Edward," Helen Almer cautioned.

"We are going into people's heads," Mulgrave said.

Ducaine frowned down at his hands. "I'd hardly call blacking out at the wheel of a car nothing adverse," he said. "It might have been just a tail-end bump this time. Next time could be a lot worse."

"The cause of that was in a different universe," Kintner pointed out. "If other versions of this meeting decide to resume testing, the effects may show in our universe, and there's nothing we can do about it." He had a point. Ducaine grunted and fell silent. Kintner went on, "All we stand to achieve by not acting likewise is that developments in *our* universe—which affect our future and over which we have some control—will be needlessly delayed."

"And I guess all the other Kintners will have thought the same thing," Berres concluded.

"My point exactly," Kintner said.

Mulgrave brought a hand up to his brow and shook his head. This was getting too bizarre. The others exchanged baffled looks. "The psychology of what's going on here is fascinating," Sam murmured.

Hugh looked around. All very well, but nobody was doing much volunteering. The machine was beginning to have weird effects, and none of them wanted to be the first to find out what else it might do. Of course they didn't. The emotional associations that the machine returned when they contemplated the future of the project were mixed. But with Hugh it was different. His first experience with the QUADAR had imbued him with the certainty that the project held the key to a very different and vastly better future. That hadn't changed, although he still had no idea how to interpret the oracle. But passively surrendering the initiative to Washington couldn't be the way to go.

"I have a suggestion," he said after the silence had persisted for what was beginning to feel like a long time.

Kintner raised his eyebrows. "Well?"

"I'll be one of the test pilots. I'm new here—I don't represent a lot of specialized investment. That way, if anything unexpected does happen, it won't affect the experienced people."

Several surprised looks came from around the table. Kintner frowned for a moment. Not that he was about to pass such an offer up. It was just a case of finding the right words. "Very magnanimous," he commented.

Not really. It was just that if there really were any serious risks involved, Hugh was fairly sure that the QUADAR would have given him some hint of the fact. But there was no need for everyone to know that.

"If it could be as important as you say, then we should

keep moving," he said. "Hell, it's no more than we expect thousands of other guys to risk all the time."

Kintner nodded. That said it for him as well as anything could have. He looked at Ducaine. "Neville?"

"It makes a lot of sense. Good man, Hugh," Ducaine replied.

"Peter?" Kintner invited.

Mulgrave looked from him to Ducaine, to Hugh, and then back. "Well, if it's okay by Neville . . . It's his department. What else can I say? Sure, let's go with it."

Kintner gave Willard an inquiring look. Willard nodded. "Agreed, then," Kintner pronounced.

"Hmph." Jantowitz wrinkled his nose and snorted. "Well, he is not the only one here who is new. What does an old man have to lose? Never in the years we work together have I let him make the fool on his own. Me too, also, you can count in."

Hugh was impatient to get back to the machine already. He would have made the same offer anyway, he suspected, regardless of good or bad premonitions.

Chapter Eleven

The mountains west of Los Alamos are part of an immense, circular rim, fifty-five miles around, known as the Valle Grande. Rising from a bowl at 8,000 feet to peaks as high as 12,000 feet, it forms one of the world's largest calderas, or collapsed volcanoes. Rocks ejected from a titanic explosion around a million years ago have been identified as far away as Kansas and Louisiana. Subsequent minor eruptions have left their mark as clusters of cones and exposed plugs standing inside the principal basin.

With activity slowed while management talked to Washington, Sarah decided that she needed to get out, away from the restrictions and the paranoia if only for a day. Dave didn't need much persuading; Hugh managed to work in a break to join them. The regulations required lab personnel to keep recreational activities within ten miles of the town unless specifically cleared with the local police department. But everyone knew what regulations were for. None of them had a vehicle. Sam, however, drove a comfortably depreciated Jeep that would be ideal for an expedition to see some of the surroundings, and they talked him into joining them. "Contrition afterward is always easier than permission beforehand," he declared solemnly.

"Is that a piece of old Thai wisdom, Sam?" Sarah asked him out of curiosity.

"Not as far as I know. I heard it from somebody who was Irish," Sam replied.

Following the traffic incident on Central Avenue involving the physicist, there had been a proposal that those like Hugh and Jantowitz—plus a number of others by now—who would be carrying on as experimental subjects should discontinue driving. But then it was realized that *anyone* who normally used the machine—in other words not just those individuals—might still be doing so in other universes, and so was just as likely to appear suddenly in their parallel self in this universe. There simply weren't enough drivers available to chauffeur everyone on the project around. Kintner therefore settled for the next best thing he could think of, which was to stress to his own "test pilots" the importance of being prepared for sudden situations that might call for some quick action—and hope that his various counterparts in other realities would have the reciprocal decency to do likewise.

They left the Jeep off the road at a place where a rocky spur jutted out to overlook a canyon, and a trail began a meandering descent down the side. Here and there, they caught glints of a creek far away at the bottom. None of them expected to be breaking any hiking records that day. They would find a spot for a mid-afternoon lunch, perhaps explore around the cliff bases for a while, and get back to town in time to clean up and eat out somewhere for a change. That sounded like the kind of day they were all in the mood for.

The trail plunged and rose across a series of descending humps of broken rock sparsely covered with juniper and clumps of cactus. The air lower down in the canyon was heavy and still. Dave and Sarah led; Sam followed a few yards behind them; Hugh brought up the rear. At one point Sam hissed a warning. A few yards ahead of Dave, a brown, mottle-patterned snake that he hadn't noticed was curled on a rock about six feet to one side of the trail.

They filed past very cautiously. The snake slid off into a crack, evidently unimpressed.

"It's so quiet and peaceful," Sarah said a short distance farther down. "We could be a million miles away from that place, and you wouldn't know the difference."

"It sounds terrible, but why does it feel so great to get away from people?" Dave tossed over his shoulder from the front.

"Give 'em time, they'll get here," Hugh said. "I guess that's one thing to be said for economic slumps. Without it, there'd probably have been a theme park down here already."

Sam shaded his eyes to study a rock terrace a little above them, paralleling the trail with a line of low cliffs rising on the far side of it. The others stopped and waited. "They probably wouldn't be the first," he said. "I think there might have been Indian dwellings along there once. See those lines of holes? They don't look natural. That's where they would have fixed the ends of the roof poles. They used to build lean-to houses out from the rocks." He pointed. "That cave could have been a back room to one of them."

"How long ago?" Sarah asked.

"Oh, anywhere from about five to eight hundred years."

"Hm. I can't see much to make poles out of here," Dave said, looking around.

"The climate was different then," Sam said. "This valley was probably quite green. They cultivated all kinds of crops, kept animals."

"So is that why they're not around anymore?" Hugh said.

Sam nodded. "There are some well-documented ruins down near the Lab, along the road out toward White Rock. There was water there when they were lived in, but not these days. As the climate got drier, the women had to go farther and farther to fetch water. Before the settlement was abandoned, apparently they were having to go two to three miles, practically down to the Rio Grande, and then all the way back up. Imagine doing that twice a day with a stone jar on your head." He thought for a moment and chuckled. "Maybe that's where the saying 'Not tonight, I've got a headache' started. That would have got the guys' attention all right, wouldn't it?"

They began moving again. "I wonder what kind of a world view they had, whether they saw reality the same way as we do," Sarah mused. "That was one of the things that struck me in Japan. The East might have picked up a few Western ways superficially, but the more you get to know them, the more you realize that there's still a different outlook underneath." She turned her head to glance back. "That's why you're here, isn't it, Sam? To see if traditional Eastern methods can be applied to interpreting what the QUADAR is uncovering."

"Everything leads to its opposite. Poles are joined by the same axis," Sam replied enigmatically. He smiled as he looked from side to side, thumbs hooked in the straps of his pack, admiring the surroundings. A hawk drifted down from its station to investigate the intruders, circled at a distance to check them out from all angles, then spread sail to be carried lazily back upward aboard its thermal.

"Science and insight," Hugh said from the rear. "Opposite poles of knowledge: one rational; the other, intuitive."

"You've got it," Sam said.

Hugh had been getting curious about this. The notion that the Western and Eastern approaches might have arrived at the same fundamental truths from different directions was hardly a new one. Commentators from both schools had been making the suggestion since the mid twentieth century. Schrödinger's cat conundrum could have been a Zen paradox about being and not being at the same time; Bell's theorem and Hindu sages taught the interconnectedness of all things; modern physics in its culmination had joined Buddhist wisdom in reducing space, time, and the breaking down of the world into objects and events to illusory constructs of the intellect.

"So what are you finding, Sam? Do they come together somehow?" he asked.

"It's interesting," Sam replied. "I think maybe they do— in the Multiverse. Things do exist and not exist, happen and not happen, at the same time. In this universe and countless more like it we're hiking down a trail, while in others we're doing something different. It's all real. One connected whole. Your actions determine what part of the potential you actualize. You see—people thought East and West were opposites. But they lead you to each other, like north and south."

Dave had stopped again, and Sarah likewise. Sam was still talking when he and Hugh drew up with them. "What's up?" Hugh inquired, seeing nothing to attract undue attention. Then he noticed that Dave was frowning and looking around as if everything about him was suddenly strange.

"Dave?" Sarah peered at him. "Dave, what is it?"

Dave registered each of them in turn. An odd smile played on his face. Hugh realized what had happened a split second before Dave spoke. "Oh, sorry. . . . I imagine that you're all probably familiar with this kind of thing by now. But I'm not actually 'yours,' if you know what I mean. I've just arrived."

They were all intelligent, rational people. They knew the situation, and after a few moments of initial befuddlement nobody had to ask what was going on. Even so, the whole business was so outlandish that for several seconds they could do no more than stand staring and mouthing incoherencies. A reflex made Sarah withdraw her hand from resting lightly on Dave's arm.

Dave went on, "I take it we're off on a hike somewhere. Good idea. Do some clear thinking away from it all. I wish somebody in my universe had suggested it. I've spent practically all day hooked into that bloody machine. Our Kintner runs a tough ship. It seems as if you might have been blessed with a milder variant of him. I was in a universe a little while ago where he'd put a military cordon around the whole P2 area and wasn't letting anyone out. Luckily I didn't stay there too long."

Sam recovered from his surprise first. "You, ah, seem to have become quite a traveler already," he remarked.

"Reality surfing," Dave agreed. "It could catch on." There was an awkward silence while he waited for them to adjust fully.

"Couldn't that be a bit hard on the copies?" Sarah said at last. She eyed him dubiously. "Not to mention whoever else happens to be around." And she had a point, of course.

"Oh, it's early days yet," Dave said cheerfully. "These things will get sorted out in time." He made a face and moistened his lips. "I don't know what my alter ego here has been doing with this body, but it's got one hell of a thirst. Do we have anything to drink?"

Hugh was carrying a pack frame with a small ice chest; Sam had the food. "I could use one too. Let's take a break for a few minutes," he said.

"Fine," Sam agreed.

Hugh unslung the pack, squatted down on a rock, and began unfastening the chest. The others found places around. "So your team is hard at it today—back where you're from," he said to Dave. It was like talking to somebody they'd met coming the other way along the trail. The whole situation was crazy, but what else was there to do? Dave accepted a can of soda and popped the tab. "What kind of things are you finding out?" Hugh asked. "How about directional controllability? Are you making any progress there? We're not getting anywhere with it."

He presumed that Dave would know what he meant. So far, the machine would "flip" a subject's awareness into a nearby copy of his or her self (or more accurately, into an extension of the "superself") suddenly and unpredictably. Nobody had found a way of initiating the process voluntarily or of steering it in any particular "direction"; neither could they control when to "return." The machine just did its own whimsical thing when it chose to, and nobody knew why.

Dave lifted the can and drank gratefully. "From what I heard, I thought you were trying the same approach we are," he answered.

"What are you talking about?" Hugh said.

Dave gestured with the can and looked at Sam. "When I showed up here—weren't you talking about traditional Eastern mind-training? We think Sam might be the pointer to the answer. He—our Sam, that is—seems to be making some progress. I've been trying to duplicate what he says he does, but with me it's all still pretty chaotic. Hopefully, it just needs practice."

"I was hoping to experiment with just that, but Peter and Neville wanted to try a software approach," Sam said. "So I left them to it."

Hugh was about to open a can for himself, when Dave gave a start and looked at the can in his own hand as if it had suddenly materialized there. He blinked, shook his head, and peered down at the rock that he was sitting on. This time it was Hugh's turn to be a second ahead. "Oh, so you're back," he said.

Dave's features knitted uncomprehendingly for an instant, then relaxed into a grin. "It happened to me, didn't it?" he said.

"Uh-huh," Hugh confirmed.

"But we learned something from your counterpart," Sam told him. "This is starting to get interesting."

"It's getting goddamn weird," Sarah said, shaking her head.

"I want to try out what the other Dave suggested," Sam said. "Can we call Peter now? I'd like to see if we can schedule some machine time as soon as we get back."

"I thought we were all having dinner somewhere tonight," Hugh said.

"I'll take a rain check," Sam said. "This has got me intrigued. Do you have the phone, Dave?"

Dave produced a mobile and passed it across. Sam entered Peter Mulgrave's personal code and waited. Several seconds went by, but a connection confirmation failed to appear. Then the unit displayed: CONNECT FAIL ERROR.

"Hm. Looks like a glitch in the system," Sam said and tried again. The result was the same.

"Let me see," Dave said, holding out a hand. He looked worried all of a sudden. Sam passed the unit back to him. Dave entered a command, checked the display, entered something more. A shrill, fragmented whine interspersed with static came from the audio.

"This could be trouble," Dave muttered, rising to his feet. "Get the stuff picked up, guys. We need to get out of here."

Chapter Twelve

"Bush gangs, ghetto fighters from the cities," Dave said as they hurriedly collected things together. "They're all over these parts. We shouldn't have come out this far."

"But what does it have to do with the phone?" Hugh asked.

"They use jammers—obviously they're not going to mess with anyone who could have police choppers here in minutes. So it means there are some in this area. And from the sound of that signal, I'd say they're pretty close."

There was little talk as the party hastened back up the trail, conserving their breath for the ascent.

They saw the truck as they came over the rocky spur at the top of the trail—an old camper, modified with crash bumpers, window mesh, dirt wheels, and heavy suspension, and painted black with gaudy ornamentation in gold and red. It was parked at an angle across the front of Sam's Jeep, blocking it from the road. A rusting maroon pickup, loaded with boxes, bundles, and assorted junk, stood behind, preventing the Jeep from backing up. Several figures were lounging round, apparently waiting. Some of them were holding guns. They straightened up when the returning party came into view. More appeared from the open door of the camper. Sam, who had assumed the lead, stopped to survey the situation. The others drew up apprehensively on either side of him.

A cold, shaky feeling took hold of Hugh as he realized that this was serious. Action heroics had never been his line. Like most men he fantasized from time to time about dealing with tricky situations. When the reality occurred, his brain invariably seized up, finally managing to figure out what he should have done, usually days later. "What do we do now?" he whispered.

"Better leave this to me," Sam murmured, keeping his gaze fixed ahead.

"What do you know about situations like this?" Dave muttered on Sam's other side.

"Nothing. I'm just hoping I'm a faster learner."

Great, Hugh thought, and felt sick.

A low growl came from behind them. "Why don't you jus' keep on movin'?" a voice said, smooth but menacing. "Y' can't be fixin' on standin' there all day." Hugh looked back. Two more men had stepped out from the rocks flanking the path. The one who had spoken was fortyish, lean but muscular, with a ragged black mustache, stubbly chin, and dark, beady eyes. He was wearing a padded work vest over a heavy plaid shirt, and a wide-brimmed leather hat. He was also toting a shotgun, trained skyward but with the breech closed. The other, taller but younger, was holding a large, savage-looking dog, black with brown flashes on the muzzle and chest, on a chain. His mouth was drawn back and twitched in a suppressed, imbecilic snigger. He gave the impression of being just itching to set the dog free. Sam motioned resignedly to the others with his head. They moved on down the rest of the way to where the vehicles were standing. Stubble-chin and the Sniggerer followed.

An older man, broad and deep-chested, gray hair held back by a red and white bandana, wearing faded denim, was in the center of the group standing waiting. He was carrying a pistol in a holster attached to a studded belt. There were two more men, one maybe nineteen, the other in his thirties, and a woman aged somewhere in between. All were dressed garishly but shabbily. The woman and the kid had hunting rifles and mean expressions; the other, holding an automatic military model, greeted the arrivals with a crooked, toothy grin. An older woman had come to the door of the camper, one hand restraining a boy of about eight. There was a face that also looked like a child's at one of the camper's windows. Another woman was in the driver's seat of the maroon pickup—a blonde, her hair straggly and dirty.

The man with the automatic and the toothy grin looked Sam up and down. "Well, well, looks like we got us a fat Chink here. Been hiking with the kids, huh? Now ain't that nice? We thought we'd better stop and make sure you was all okay. You know, you can run into some mean people out here if you don't watch out." A guffaw came from the imbecile holding the dog.

Hugh could sense Sarah shaking even with Sam between them. Dave, on the far side of her, stood rigidly immobile. Hugh stole a glance at Sam, expecting to find something of the same, but Sam's expression was calm and devoid of fear. Somehow it even managed to hint that, despite the odds and the guns, he, ultimately, was in control. The older man with the bandana, who looked as if he was in charge, seemed to pick up on it too and eyed Sam with less certainty than the situation would appear to have warranted.

"Do strangers make you that afraid?" Sam said.

The stubble-chinned man behind spat into the dust. "You're crazy, Slope. Ain't us that's got much reason to be."

"But you're the ones who are acting like it."

"Let's just say we're good when it comes to stayin' alive."

"Perhaps you've been picking the wrong neighbors."

The Kid lowered his gun threateningly. "You got a smart mouth there, fat man. I'm not sure I like it." This wasn't following the script. It made him nervous. He needed to *see* some effect.

"Go ahead, shoot me. It won't make you feel better," Sam said. "What's troubling you is inside. I didn't put it there." The Kid cocked the hammer and aimed. Sam met his gaze. The leader in the bandana raised a restraining hand.

"That's a fancy rig you got there," Toothy Grin said, inclining his head at the Jeep. "I could use me a set o' wheels like that."

Sam offered the keys. "Take it if you insist. But what good would it do you in the end? A new kick for a month, six months? It won't solve anything. It carries a homing beacon that can be remote activated, anyway."

The Red Bandana spoke finally. "Getting by from day to day's good enough for us. What else you got? Got money? Electronics? Any guns?" He turned his head a fraction. "Quit bein' a damn fool, Jabe, and check out the wagon. You know what to look for. Hit the phone if it don't pull out." The Kid uncocked the rifle sullenly, moved a step forward, and snatched the keys from Sam's hand. The Bandana motioned to the girl. "Get them pack bags."

"Is this how you teach them?" Sam indicated the camper door, where a girl, watching wide-eyed, had appeared behind the boy. "This is the way they will live? Have you any idea what you are wasting, what every one of them could become?"

"They'll know how to stay alive. That's a pretty good start," Toothy told him.

Sam shook his head. "If they last. That boy is sick. He needs help."

The Bandana looked back—just a glance, but it showed worry. The woman wrapped an arm around the boy and drew him closer protectively. Their two reactions were enough. They knew.

Sam moved forward. Toothy Grin snapped down his automatic in warning, but Sam ignored him and squatted down in front of the doorway to peer at the boy's face. It was pallid and clammy, the eyes showing white below the irises. Sam smiled and spoke encouragingly, as if the others weren't there. "Hi. How are you today? Could do with feeling a little better, maybe, eh?" He raised an eyelid gently, then laid his fingers on the boy's forehead.

"We tried our best. What is it?" the woman asked in a fearful voice. "I think Marcy's coming down with it too."

Hugh saw then what Sam must have recognized from the start. Desert banditry was not these people's way. They were not natural predators, incorrigibles; just once-ordinary people, pushed beyond the limit.

Sam felt the glands in the boy's throat, evoking a wince. "Oh, a little sore there, eh? Can I see your tongue, little fella?" The boy stared back defiantly without moving.

"Open your mouth, Charlie," the Red Bandana ordered. He had moved up behind Sam and was watching. Charlie poked out his tongue impudently, then let his mouth open wider when Sam pushed his chin with a finger.

"You could use a good meal," Sam said. "I've got some things in my lunch that you'd like—nice and cool, easy to swallow." He looked up over his shoulder at the Bandana. "There are some drugs in the Jeep that would probably help too—if that assistant of yours hasn't wrecked the medical kit already."

"Jabe, come out of there," the Bandana called to the Jeep.

The Kid looked back from where he was leaning in on the driver's side. "Hell, not just yet. I got a whole—"

"Dammit, I said get yourself out o' there!"

Back with Hugh, Dave and Sarah were beginning to breathe more easily. While Stubble Chin covered them and the girl was taking the packs, the Imbecile had gone forward with Sam and was standing a few feet back with the dog straining on its chain. Still squatting, Sam studied the animal for a few seconds, then looked up. "Let it go," he said. The Imbecile looked at the Bandana for guidance and got none. His face creased with the agony of having to make a decision. He unsnapped the collar link.

The dog sprung forward like a greyhound coming out of its trap, but Sam didn't move. Maybe the unexpected confused it. Or perhaps it was the sight of Sam befriending

Charlie, or the absence of any trigger scent of exuded fear. Then again, maybe Sam was simply a good judge of animals. But the dog halted just feet from him and stood growling suspiciously. Sam grinned—taking care not to bare his teeth—and, slowly enough not to alarm, not far enough to intrude into the dog's space, held out a hand. The dog's ears pricked, its tail swished. Sam waited, letting it take its own time. It edged nearer and sniffed. Sam opened his palm. The dog sniffed again, nuzzled, then licked. Sam waited a few seconds, then ran a finger lightly up its muzzle and scratched between its ears.

"Well, I'll be darned," the Bandana breathed.

"I think we could find a treat for you too, guy," Sam said to the dog. It lolled its tongue out at him and seemed to understand.

The Bandana squatted down by Sam and indicated Charlie with a nod. He spoke in a low, gruff voice. "What do you reckon? Could it be something real bad?"

Now Hugh understood what Sam had done. It went deeper than just demonstrating absence of fear. Fear and insecurity were these people's whole problem. Sam had shown that he had what, deep down, they desperately craved. Even if it didn't register consciously, they would reach out, as the dog had.

"I am not a doctor," Sam answered. "We're with the Lab. There are people there who could put you onto the right facilities in town."

"It's a trick," the girl said. "Don't believe 'em. When did them down there ever care about any of us?"

"We don't have money to pay. We don't have shit anymore," Toothy Grin said. He sounded bitter. Hugh guessed he was Charlie's father.

"There are ways," Sarah said, unable to stay out of it now. "They haven't cut everything back. You can still get help for a new start."

"If you can show 'em how you're gonna earn it," the Bandana said. "What in hell are we supposed to do?"

"That can get sorted out later," Hugh said.

"Ain't the way I was told," the Bandana replied.

"Maybe you were told wrong," Sam suggested.

"At least talk to the right people," Sarah implored. "We could even bring them out to meet you somewhere, if that would make it easier."

The Bandana looked doubtfully at Sam. Sam nodded affirmation. "You'd do that, for us?" the Bandana said. "Why? . . ."

"To save their chicken asses, why else?" the girl said. "Can't you see, the minute they're outta here they're gonna go straight—"

There was a faint *whoosh* of parted air and then a dull *splat*, followed instantly by two more. The dog collapsed, blood gushing into the sand. At the same instant, lights brighter than the sun erupted, blinding everyone. Hugh found himself on his face in the dirt, covering his ears against a thunder of detonations paralyzing his brain.

The chopper came up from below the rim of the canyon, where the cliffs had muffled its approach. While captors and captives alike were still reeling and staggering in shock, helmeted figures in the mottled combat garb of the New Mexico Anti Terrorism Force leaped from the side doors and secured the vehicles. At the same time, the two squads that had been landed on the far side of the ridge behind, and moved down on foot to launch the initial flash-grenade assault, broke cover and moved in along the road from both sides.

By the time Hugh began recovering his senses, Stubble Chin and Toothy were groaning on the ground with troopers standing over them. Others had the Kid spread against the Jeep, and the Bandana against the camper, while three more tried to restrain the girl, who was spitting and clawing. The Imbecile was on his knees, gibbering over the body of the dog. A short distance away, the blonde was being hauled out of the pickup, which had run off the road and hit some rocks. She must have tried to get away with her vision still ruined.

Sam was on his knees, looking around in bewilderment.

Hugh shook his head in protest. This was all wrong. It didn't need to be this way. Charlie was screaming in terror as a trooper pulled him away from his mother's grasp. The mother was wailing. Inside the camper, the young girl was screaming.

"Fuck you!" the older girl shrieked as she bit and struggled. *"I knew it was a fuckin' setup. Fuck all of you!"* A trooper felled her with a closed fist.

An officer from the chopper stood hands on hips, his lip curled distastefully. Sarah grabbed his arm. Somebody behind pulled her back.

"You don't understand!" she shouted. "They're not what you think. This isn't necessary. You don't have to do this. . . ."

He regarded her coldly. "These trash are all the same. We know how to deal with 'em. Save all the crap, lady. I think you're pretty lucky to be in one piece."

A mile away, parked on a high bend in the road from where he had followed the action, Ingram lowered the binoculars. Not bad, he thought to himself. NMATF's response time was getting better. The extra training they'd been putting in lately must be paying off.

He radioed a message back to Calom's office saying that the subjects were now safely in the charge of the State authorities and he was signing off for the day. It was fortunate that his mobile phone used military circuits unaffected by amateur jamming, he told himself as he pulled away.

Chapter Thirteen

As was to be expected, the authorities took a serious view of the affair. As far as they were concerned, newcomers whose value to the project was still to be proved had gotten themselves within a hair's breadth of being killed by violating clearly spelled-out rules, and endangered others involved in extricating them. The timely arrival of the NMATF unit was attributed vaguely to "an anonymous call." The incident seemed to vindicate Calom's earlier misgivings. Sam's case was less clear. Although it was generally held that he should have known better, he had never given any actual undertaking to behave himself or be bound by the prevailing regulations. Introduced to the project at the instigation of some high-ups in Washington, he had been confronted with demands to sign the usual papers, cheerfully declined—and been brought in anyway.

The internal "tribunal" took place in a meeting room in the TA-3 Administration Building the following day—there would be criminal proceedings later to deal with the itinerants. Willard presided. A chagrined Kintner, who didn't need reminding of who it was that had opposed Calom's doubts, read the list of condemnations and censures. For the most part, Calom let Kintner do the talking, enjoying his discomfort. Ducaine sat in as a token representative of the three from his group. It seemed implicit that Sam could speak for himself.

Regardless of how much she and the others might have been at fault, Sarah was still incensed. "They had ceased being threatening," she insisted as soon as she got an opportunity. "Sam had turned them right around. They would have been willing to—"

"Had they demanded money and other valuables, and was one of them in the process of searching your vehicle, which was obstructed from leaving?" Calom interrupted in a bored voice. He had a full account from the officer commanding the NMATF unit, a Major Schalger, whom he'd known personally for a long time.

"Well, yes, to begin with. But—"

"Were some of them holding guns, or were they not?"

"Not actually aimed at anyone. There wasn't any need to make a war out of—"

"And had they interfered with public communications in the vicinity?"

"Blame me, not these three," Sam said, intervening. "I have been here longer. I drove the Jeep."

Calom took no notice and turned to the others on the panel. "Those are the facts, and the court will draw the obvious conclusions. I don't have time to listen to talk about unfortunates being misunderstood. They knew what they were asking for. If they weren't the worst of the scum that's out there, then it makes the point that these people were lucky. The ATUs are trained to go in fast and hit hard. They don't conduct opinion polls first."

Sarah still wouldn't let things rest. "But can't you see? It's *we* who are making the rules that say it has to be that way. Sam showed us a whole different approach." She looked appealingly at Kintner. "And maybe the world's the way it is for the same reason. We make our own reality. Giving Washington this machine isn't going to change anything. It'll just become another weapon. Get them to listen to people like Sam."

But Kintner either didn't hear, or had heard it all too often. Hugh, Dave, Sarah, and Sam were told to wait in an adjoining room.

"They don't have the backgrounds to be trusted with regular responsibilities in this kind of environment," Calom said when the room was cleared. "Either dispense with them or restrict their movements to the town, using ILBs if necessary. I can't be responsible for security otherwise." An Individual Locator Beacon was an electronic device, usually a bracelet, worn by offenders on parole and in other cases that required movement to be monitored. It kept track of its ground coordinates from satellite transmissions and emitted a signal if moved outside a prescribed boundary.

Willard studied the backs of his hands, evidently less than enthused. "That could be difficult in Sam's case," he said without looking up. "We all know he's not going anywhere. And making him an example would just be inviting political fights with the wrong people. And for what?" In other words, Sam had friends. Calom knew this, of course, and had expressed an opinion for the record. He would leave the political shoe shuffling to those whose business it was.

Ducaine looked from one to another. "Well, it shouldn't be difficult to find grounds for making an exception in his case, should it . . . ?"

Kintner thought he had it. "We have to treat him as a special resource. This unanticipated ability of the QUADAR to divert consciousness into adjacent parts of the Multiverse could open up a new realm of potential if only we knew how to control and direct it. And it seems from what they gleaned via Dave that Sam could be the key. In view of the unconventional approach that he brings to bear on the problem, I would recommend against imposing any psychological pressures likely to impair his sensitivity or judgment."

So there it was. They could let Sam off the hook and keep the peace with the Olympians beyond Willard, at the same time justifying the decision with a reason that all could pretend was the real one. Nobody dissented. Sam was called back in on his own and offered the deal.

"Yes, your point is perfectly clear," he said when he had heard them out. "But aren't you missing the far more significant one?"

Kintner looked puzzled and glanced at Ducaine, who returned an equally uncomprehending shake of his head. "What do you mean?" Kintner asked Sam.

"What happened yesterday. I don't mean the encounter with those misguided people. But before that—when Dave was briefly taken over by a different version of himself."

Calom remained inscrutable. The other three looked confused. "That's what we've just been talking about," Ducaine said. "He indicated that your techniques of mental training might be the answer to controlling these flips that the QUADAR makes."

Sam smiled and shook his head. "Yes, what you say is true. But the truly significant thing was not what he said, but *the fact that he was saying it!*" He waited a few seconds, then went on, "This is no longer just a question of perceiving other realities directly. What these 'flips' demonstrate is the possibility of *meaningful communication between them!* Think what that means."

Sam and the others had talked about it the previous evening. The possibilities were stupefying. The knowledge existing in all the universes could—in principle—be pooled. Scientific discoveries, engineering designs and inventions, technologies, philosophies, artistic creations—anything produced by any one universe could be made available to all the rest. The multiplication of human productivity that it implied staggered the imagination. The "information trade" (physical objects, of course, didn't move between universes) that could follow out of it would make the effects of knowledge transmission by language, and a whole history of global commerce, seem paltry by comparison.

The room went very quiet. But what Sam's listeners were seeing suddenly was the prospect of presenting Washington with a bonanza beyond anyone's expectations— one that would allay thoughts of blame for what had happened the previous day and quickly put them to rest.

"*If* we can learn how to direct the process," Kintner said.

Which made Sam indispensable. The others presumed that he had thus purchased his own extrication—it was what they would have done in his position in the circumstances. But when Calom began talking along lines of removing Hugh and his companions with as little fuss and complication as possible, Sam interrupted by shaking his head again. He had been expecting this.

"You still haven't thought the whole thing through," he said. "Other versions of them will still be using the machine in other universes—universes, for example, in which yesterday's events never happened at all. Those other versions are liable to appear in their copies here at any time—just as one of Dave's did. Do you want to let them go back to the wide world out there, knowing that this could happen to any of them at any time? Or would you rather have them here, where you can keep an eye on them?"

Nobody could dispute the point.

After a brief discussion, Hugh and the others were brought back in and advised that since their work was valuable to the project, further proceedings would be waived and action limited to confining their movements to the city limits until further notice. This could be by their agreement, else they would be required to carry ILBs.

"What happens if we fail to comply, with or without them?" Dave asked.

"Is that a refusal?" Calom asked.

"No. Just curious."

"Then the offer of a waiver is withdrawn, making you all liable to criminal prosecution for violation of the security acts," Kintner replied. It was a bluff, but it enabled the powers to exit and keep face. Sam signaled with a barely perceptible nod for them to accept. Willard warned that they would probably be called as witnesses at some later date in the proceedings against the itinerants. And with that the matter was closed.

❖   ❖   ❖

That evening, Dave and Sarah disappeared to commiserate, celebrate, or share whatever other feelings the day had evoked in them, privately somewhere. Mrs. Ryecroft went out after dinner to play cards with friends, and Ingram hadn't been seen since breakfast. Hugh and Jantowitz were left with the house to themselves. The professor had little to say about the incident or the official handling of it. He had always confined his advice and criticisms to subjects concerning their work, and kept any opinions on what Hugh chose to do outside the lab to himself. Neither did it seem there were going to be any speeches now. Instead, Jantowitz produced a couple of handwritten sheets torn from a pad and passed them across from his armchair in the living room, where Hugh was using a laptop on the coffee table. The writing was in Polish—blue ballpoint, closely spaced, text interspersed with mathematical notation.

"Somebody from back home?" Hugh said, then saw that it wasn't a letter. "Wait a minute, this is your writing, right?"

"Yes," Jantowitz agreed.

Hugh shrugged. "I don't read Polish, Theo. What is it?"

"I'm not absolutely sure."

Hugh sat back from the keyboard. Obviously he was supposed to ask the question. "Oka-ay?"

Jantowitz explained, "Yesterday, while you are out enjoying the countryside and being mugged, this in my office, I find. But the recollection of writing it, there is none. So I conclude that some time in the day a blankout I must have had there without realizing it, and my other self who visits, he leaves this." He interrogated Hugh with his eyes to make sure this was registering. "At least one Jantowitz, it seems, has decided that he could do better if he can get many Jantowitzes working together. It's an interesting thought he has, yes?"

Hugh nodded slowly. "The others and I were talking about something like that—after what happened to Dave."

"So you understand what this might mean?"

"I think so, yes." One of the reasons why Hugh and Jantowitz worked well together was that they thought the same way and could communicate effectively without having to spell everything out. "So what does it say?" Hugh asked, inclining his head in the direction of the papers.

"The main problem that they are having there is to find a way to direct the machine such that what kind of universe the awareness is diverted to, they can choose."

"Hm. That sounds familiar," Hugh said.

"Yes, but the approach that they are considering, it is not. You see, what is it that happens, they ask, when the machine makes this decision to send you sideways as well as forward? Something, somewhere in the machine must cause it, they argue. Maybe some unusual state of the software, or a complexity in the field dynamics . . . But something happens in there that causes these flips to take place. And if we knew what they were, then maybe we can find directional correlations."

Hugh stared at him thoughtfully. It made sense. Events had causes. Something changing inside the machine made the flips happen. Possibly those changes could be identified and related in some systematic way to the direction across the Multiverse in which a flip took place. If so, the implication was that maybe direction could be selected by inducing the required changes deliberately. That would give them an alternative approach to complement Sam's. Whereas Sam hoped to be guided to a target universe by its qualities, Jantowitz was proposing "aiming" from this universe by setting the machine up appropriately. Sam's method would be that of a homing missile; Jantowitz would use artillery.

"It's a thought," Hugh agreed finally. "But what if it's triggered chaotically, or by some amplification of quantum events? You'd never be able to establish a control algorithm then." In other words, what if the cause-effect correlation that Jantowitz was talking about turned out to be random?

Jantowitz shrugged. "He who doesn't look never finds out. To win the prize, you must first buy the ticket."

Hugh rubbed his chin. "It might take a lot of time to get any kind of pattern out of it," he observed doubtfully.

Jantowitz took back the sheets of paper and waved them in the air. "Maybe I need less time if I use a lot of Jantowitzes," he suggested.

Of course. Another Jantowitz somewhere had thought of it first and was recruiting others to take on different parts of the investigation and pool results.

Hugh nodded. "It's the same principle we used with the QUIC."

"Yes, which is probably why the scientists here don't think to apply it," Jantowitz said. "Today I talk to Peter Mulgrave, and he agrees we try. Probably you all will hear more about it tomorrow."

It was an example of trans-Multiverse communication happening already. Hugh recalled the intimation that the machine had given on his first day, of unimagined consequences emerging from the project. Already they were glimpsing possibilities that went way beyond anything that had been dreamed of then. For the first time, Hugh got the feeling that this was only a beginning. It could end up leading . . . just about anywhere.

The proto-cells in Ducaine's pond had a vague perception of light reaching them from somewhere. They knew there were places around them to explore out there. But they were still a long way from becoming fish.

Chapter Fourteen

After some practice, Sam discovered that when coupled into the machine he could induce a "flip" on demand by conscious volition. He was unable to choose or influence in advance any aspect of the reality that he flipped himself into. As with the spontaneous flips induced by the machine—for the time being, at least—that was a matter of pure caprice. But it was a beginning. Possibly the art of control would come later. The next thing to find out was whether his years of training were necessary for mastering the knack, or if, with guidance, it was accessible to the uninitiated.

"The problem has always been that the experience can only be known directly." Sam was standing in front of Hugh, who was in one of the recliners in the Vector Dynamics section. They were running full-blown tests, with Hugh hooked up to a battery of ECG and EEG recorders, pulse and blood-pressure monitors, and various other physiological sensors. Ducaine and a scattering of technical staff attended to the banks of associated equipment all around. "It produces an awareness unlike that revealed by the senses. Since language refers to the world of everyday perceptions, it is inadequate to describe it. Modern physics has to resort to mathematics for the same reason."

"I've got all that. But I'm still not sure what I'm supposed to concentrate *on*," Hugh said.

"That's the whole point. Forget all the stories you've heard about mustering powers of concentration, or whatever. That isn't what we're doing." Sam sought an analogy. "Think of a neurotic workaholic who has never relaxed for a moment in his life. Hyperactivity and tension is the only existence he's ever known. That's your mind. For the first time ever, it must learn how not to *do* anything. Let it discover how to just *be*."

This had been going on for half the morning. Hugh relaxed and tried to get comfortable. A knee at an awkward angle or a piece of clothing pulled too tight could become excruciatingly distracting at just the wrong time. Once more, he began the process that he had been through a dozen times of trying to empty his mind of thoughts. . . . But the act of trying was, itself, a thought. Thinking about not thinking was thinking. Don't think about anything, Sam had said. Focus upon a point, and then let the point dissolve into nothing . . . whatever that meant. It was all very well for him to talk. His people took years over this. Hugh had had since yesterday. Dave hadn't managed any better. Neither had Phil Moody or any of the others who had tried. . . .

Wait a minute. He was wandering away, letting thoughts connect together into a train again—just what he wasn't supposed to do. Back up and try again, he told himself.

Nothing, right? Okay, nothing. . . .

But they were always there, thoughts. Dave had said it was like shining a flashlamp around a dark attic, picking out one item at a time, jumping from one thing to another and realizing what a disorderly, jumbled mess it all was. It seemed a wonder that anything coherent or worthwhile ever came out of it. Conflicts and tangled feelings everywhere, any of which could get the upper hand with just a little push and take control. No wonder people sometimes felt they weren't the same person from one day to the next. . . .

No, stop all this. Nothing, right? Let it all become still, like ripples dying away on a pond. When the water is still, then you can see through it. . . .

Like the amoebas in Neville Ducaine's pond. Did the mind's activity somehow muddy the waters locally in the Multiverse pond? Is clearing them what this is really all about? An interesting point to take up with Theo. . . . Theo's group . . . Wonder if they're finding anything that looks like directional correlations. How would you map it? What kind of attributes would define the coordinate axes? . . .

Nothing, right?

Calm . . . Still . . . Not a thought. That's better.

Maybe it'll work this time. . . . No, don't think about it.

Just learn to *be*. Be one with everything around—right?

What in hell does that mean? I'm in here, and everything else is out there. How can you be one with it? Well, try.

Okay. Become aware of the environment of sound. Fans, motors, equipment operating. A hammer tapping some distance away, scraping of something being moved across the floor. A hollow, lower-pitched, background of ventilation and power plant. Surprising how much was there that you'd never noticed before. Sam's voice murmuring to somebody.

"No, don't get any wrong ideas. I'm not into this popular stuff about truths that are closed to Western science. I think Neville's right in saying that what happened differently with the human brain was that it evolved an ability to read MV signals. We enhance that ability through training; you do it by building instruments. It's the same reality, but interpreted in different ways. You can break down and analyze the signals with precision; we put together the message that they carry."

Had anyone been talking about anything like this when they began this test run? Hugh felt as if there could have been a discontinuity—except that for all he knew he might simply have dozed off for a moment. Staying awake was supposed to be a problem with Eastern mystics too.

Then, somewhere in the background, a female voice said, "How are those field sampling routines working out?" It sounded like Joyce Theale.

"Not bad," someone answered. "We're getting pretty good resolution."

Joyce Theale hadn't been anywhere around when Hugh began the test. He opened his eyes. "I think we have it," he announced. Everyone in the vicinity focused on him in interest.

"Joyce wasn't here when I coupled in," Hugh said.

"I just arrived from the coffee lounge a moment ago." She held up a cup. "Sorry."

"What's your check number?" Phil Moody asked him.

"Fifty-three," Hugh answered. At the beginning of the test he had memorized a random number generated from the time intervals between radioactive decays of a sample of thorium.

Moody looked at what the operator had written in the log. "Yup, fifty-three. That's what we've got here too."

Hugh nodded resignedly. They didn't have it yet. The number was a product of fundamental quantum uncertainty. Even in another version of this same test being carried out in an immediately adjacent part of the Multiverse, a different quantum state would, in general, have occurred, yielding a different number. He was still in the same universe.

Sam found that he could reverse the flip and bring himself back again—although still with no control over the reality that his detour took him into. Apart from that, nothing much new happened for a week. Hugh and the others tried to emulate him but with increasing frustration. Kintner put in more frequent appearances, impatient for results.

Then Mulgrave and Jantowitz produced the results of a study that the Theoretical Group had made of how various physical quantities measured inside the machine had altered when Sam made his successful transitions. On each occasion, the event had been accompanied by a characteristic resonance in the spectrum of energy fluxes associated with antenna array—a hyper-dimensional wave complex referred to as the "A-field." And, more interesting: mathematical analysis showed the A-field in this condition to be inherently unstable, liable to go into self-induced resonance spontaneously. The situation was something like the complex exchange of energy between beans shaken in a bowl, where one bean can suddenly and unpredictably acquire a disproportionate amount of momentum and be ejected. Radioactive nuclei randomly eject particles and break down in the same kind of way. It suggested that what Sam had learned to do was nudge the system into doing what it was highly prone to anyway—like triggering a mass of delicately balanced snow into an avalanche.

"What we have to begin with, it is random resonances that cause the process with Sam, just as with anyone else," Jantowitz told the weekly informal progress meeting. "But then Sam learns how to trigger the resonance. That is the difference."

This suggested an intriguing possibility. Kintner voiced it. "So if we can find a way of inducing these resonances in some other way, then perhaps we can trigger the process ourselves, with anyone—without their having to learn how to do what, at present, it seems only Sam can do."

"Yes, that's the point," Mulgrave confirmed.

The next day, Kintner talked with Ducaine and the principal engineering physicists about possible ways of adding feedback circuits into parts of the antenna array to generate controllable resonances. Hugh was included also, because of his experience with the QUIC design. A further week of experimenting on lab benches showed that the effect could be achieved surprisingly easily. Accordingly, modifications aimed at enabling "forced flips" were incorporated into one of the on-line couplers, and the control software updated to handle them. Hugh's name was drawn for the first trial run.

Two days of system checkout and calibration followed. Then, finally, Hugh lowered himself back once more into the seat before Sam, Jantowitz, Ducaine, Kintner, and a mixed technical audience, and technicians began attaching the various body sensors.

As always, there were last-minute fussings with detail, and hurriedly convened mini-conferences. Ducaine and a couple of engineers poked around in an opened cabinet, while Kintner stood to one side with Sam and Mulgrave, exchanging nods and head waggings. Hugh waited in the coupler, acutely conscious of the fact that in this context "trial" was a euphemism for "finding out what happens." None of the lab bench tests or computer simulations could predict what effect a deliberately induced resonance would have on a human consciousness. This was the only way. But then again, what reason was there to feel apprehensive? He'd been through the process before. The only difference this time would be that it would take place at a chosen moment, instead of when the right conditions happened to come about spontaneously in the machine's A-field.

Wouldn't it?

The only honest answer was that nobody knew. That was why they had drawn names for the first trial.

The other act of faith—which everyone must have appreciated, although it had hardly been mentioned openly—was that mimicking the field configuration that had been measured when Sam made his reverse transitions would be enough to bring Hugh back also. In short, if the first part of the test worked but the second part didn't, Hugh would be in a jam.

Ducaine closed the cabinet and turned away. Kintner moved to the middle of the floor and called for attention. "Okay, everyone, let's get it on the road. We're going as the revised spec, but with scan resolution increased by ten for a hundred points every millisecond to catch the peaks. Okay on that, Jeff?"

Jeff Berres entered commands to one of the monitor consoles and confirmed, "Got it."

"Amplifiers, Neville?"

"Looking okay," Ducaine said.

"Okay there, Hugh?"

"I've been okay here for the last half hour."

"This is the easy ride," Sam called across. "Think about anything you want. No more need to worry about just 'being.' "

Hugh thought about being a human cannonball with a charge of unknown power about to be detonated, and no parachute.

"Have we got a check number?" Kintner asked.

"Check number is seventy-six," an operator returned.

"Seventy-six," Hugh repeated.

"Timing down at ten seconds from . . . *now*," Ducaine informed everyone. ". . . Two . . . One. We have regular connect."

Hugh felt the sensation that was now familiar, of his mind slumping like a suddenly heavy and tired body, and fingers of awareness stealing into it from a peculiar elsewhere that seemed to lie within. The premonitions of complex but eventually positive outcomes associated with the project had grown stronger in the past couple of weeks, meaning that such a future was more probable. Presumably, then, recent events had turned more in that direction.

Kintner scanned quickly over screens and displays. "Continue," he instructed. This was the part that was new.

"Initiating forcing function," Ducaine announced. "We're on a ten-second count from . . . *now*. . . . Seven . . ."

Suddenly, Hugh caught a flood of confusion with strong negative emotional overtones coming from right ahead.

"Four . . . Three . . . Two . . ."

And Hugh was lying in a bed. He sat up in alarm. He had never seen the room before. There were clothes and female makeup articles scattered on a vanity, more clothes draped over a chair, books piled on top of a scratched chest of drawers, and posters hung in a vain attempt to brighten shabby walls. Then footsteps sounded outside. The door opened, and a girl came in. She was fairly tall, dressed in a black sweater, and had her hair tied in a ponytail. With her was a blonde with sharp, pallid features, wearing a pink T-shirt and jeans. They looked alarmed. The blonde's face was familiar. It took Hugh a second or two to place her.

It was Alice. Alice, Chris's girlfriend who studied political sociology back at Berkeley.

Chapter Fifteen

"Hugh, there's trouble. We have to move," the girl with the ponytail muttered. Voices were yelling elsewhere in the house, with the sounds of doors banging and footsteps pounding on stairs. She picked up a leather shoulder-bag that was propped by the wall and handed it to Alice. "They're in there." Alice nodded and hurried back out.

Hugh looked about him dazedly. "Where are my clothes?"

The girl gave him an odd look, picked up a sweater and pants from the chair and thrust them at him. "What's happened to your memory? You got paint all over them last night. Chris gave you those."

Hugh began struggling into them. "You mean Chris from the lab?"

"Well, of course. . . ."

A man in a black leather jacket came in through the open door, thickset and swarthy, with a black beret. "Maggie, we have to get the man away." He looked at Hugh. "Do you have a car?" Hugh could only look toward Maggie.

She frowned at him, then looked back at the man in the black beret and nodded. "Sure, we've got one. What's going on, Don?"

"There's a van full of guys pulled up along the street,

that we don't like. Val thinks it could be a raid. We need both of you downstairs." He disappeared back out again.

Hugh felt in the pants pocket and pulled out keys. They were his, all right. He recognized his own shoes by the bed. Maggie held them ready to hand to him while he pulled on his socks. "You don't mind helping us out, do you, Hugh?" she said. "That guy you met last night, he's kind of important. It's probably him that they're after."

They came out onto a landing of an older house. There were boxes stacked beside an open closet, with piles of paper on shelves inside. A crash sounded from below, followed by breaking glass, a scream, and confused shouting. A man in his twenties, wearing a padded work vest, came out of a room opposite. "They're coming across the street. This could get nasty." He kept his hand inside the vest. Hugh thought he had a gun.

"Who are they?" Maggie asked him.

"I'm not sure."

"Come on," she said to Hugh, and he followed her down a level. The noise intensified. Several figures in hard helmets ran by brandishing what looked like pick handles. Don came out of a doorway to one side, accompanied by Alice, still holding the leather bag that Maggie had given her upstairs, and a bearded man carrying a bulky black travel carryall.

"You'll have to take him out through the shop," Don told Maggie. He nodded curtly at the youth in the work vest, who had come down with them. "Ernie, go with them. Call Fay later. We'll make contact through her." He handed Maggie a document folder. She took it, saying nothing, and began descending the stairs. Hugh hesitated, still hopelessly bewildered. Don shoved him urgently. "Go! Get outta here!" Hugh followed after Maggie, with Ernie and the bearded man close behind.

In the hallway below, figures were tussling and swinging blows inside the front door, which had been smashed in. One was lying motionless. More were fighting in a room to one side, where Hugh caught a glimpse of a man in a ski mask swinging a sledgehammer at what looked like a photocopying machine. Something crashed through the pane beside the door. More men in ski masks appeared. A shot sounded from above, and one of them staggered. Maggie ran to a passage leading to the rear of the house, the bearded man keeping close behind. Hugh followed with Ernie.

They went down a back staircase to a large room containing computers and printing machinery. There were piles of boxes, and shelves with stacks of printed sheets carrying the heading SDA. A figure straightened up from behind one of the machines. It was Chris. "I should never have gotten you into this," he shouted at Hugh. "Get out. I'll catch you later." Hugh could only gape, too dumbfounded to respond. Maggie pulled him away and took them out through a side door and hurried across a yard connecting to a narrow street at the back. More figures in masks were already approaching from the corner, some of them brandishing baseball bats.

Ernie produced the gun that he had been nursing.

"Which way?" Maggie asked Hugh desperately. Hugh could only look first one way, then the other. He turned up his hands, clueless.

"Who is this asshole?" the bearded man demanded, glancing from Maggie to Ernie and now visibly alarmed.

Maggie grabbed the front of Hugh's shirt and shook him. "Hugh, for Christ's sake, *where did you park the goddamn car?*"

". . . cardiac rate is shooting up, with rapid eye agitation. Skin resistance has dropped. God, he's practically in shock." Different voices, changed acoustics.

"I think the inverse function works, Neville." Kintner's. "Are you with us again, Hugh? . . . Ah, yes, you're back."

Hugh sat up, blinking. It took him a few seconds to get his bearings. "Get Calom over here," he said. "We have to talk right away."

✧   ✧   ✧

Calom joined Hugh and Kintner upstairs in Kintner's office less than ten minutes later. Still shaky, Hugh described his experience. He concluded: "It might not have happened yet in this reality. If not, maybe there's a chance of stopping it."

Calom regarded Hugh searchingly while he went over the salient points in his mind. "Who is this Chris Gelling again, that you're so concerned about?" he asked finally.

"He was an undergrad who worked with us at Berkeley—computing science."

"Had you known him to be politically active?"

"Not before he took up with Alice, no."

"It doesn't sound as if he was the only one with a proclivity for politically active female students," Calom remarked pointedly.

Hugh spread his hands. "Give me a break. I'm not responsible for what some other version of myself gets into in another universe."

True, but it suggested that there had been a time when the Hugh in this universe came close. Calom didn't choose to make an issue of it at this point, however. "Very well. I'll pass this on to the appropriate authorities. We'll see what happens," he said.

Hugh was summoned back to Kintner's office an hour later. Calom was with him again. They wasted no time on preliminaries.

"I've talked to some people," Calom said. "They're going to need more information to be able to do anything. They would have preferred talking to you directly, but owing to the unusual nature of the source we had to plead security." Hugh nodded that he understood and sat down in a chair that Kintner indicated.

"This girl Alice at Berkeley, do you know her full name?" Calom asked.

"No, I never asked."

"She was a student?"

"Right."

"In what department?"

"Political science, I guess. She was taking political sociology."

"The house you described—is that where she's living currently?"

"I'm not sure. I presume so."

"When you were at Berkeley, did you know where she lived?"

"I used to pick Chris up near San Pablo and Burnette, so it was probably around there."

"Did it look like that area?"

"I wasn't paying much attention to the scenery. But from the little I saw out back of the house, it could have been."

Normally, Hugh wouldn't have been as forthcoming. But if he wanted help, he had to cooperate. The more he delayed things, the less chance there would be of doing any good. He assumed that everything was being recorded. Kintner listened without interrupting. This was Calom's department.

Calom went on, "This man Don, who seemed to have some authority. How would you describe him?"

"Oh . . . short, broad—solid looking. Dark skin with black hair about down to here." Hugh touched his collar. "Maybe Hispanic. Wide eyes, dark, kind of intense. Black leather jacket and a beret."

"Clean shaven?"

"Well, a bit stubbly—but I guess so. No beard or mustache or anything."

"But this person they seemed so intent on getting away, he did have a beard."

"Right."

"What else can you remember about him?"

Hugh racked his memory but had to give up. "This sounds dumb, but so much was going on. All I remember is the beard."

"Could you recognize him again from a photograph?"

"Yes, probably."

"And the other names you heard were? . . ."

"The guy who came out with us was Ernie. And let me

see . . . there was a Tim and a Val. And Maggie—I never saw her before."

"Didn't you say Ernie was to make contact again by calling somebody called Fay?"

"Oh yes, Fay, that's right."

Calom gave him a long, final, penetrating stare. "And the material that you saw in the print shop, it had the letters SDA?"

"SDA. Yes."

"Anything else you can think of that might be significant?"

Hugh went back over it all, then shook his head. "No, I don't think so. That's it."

Calom glanced at Kintner, but Kintner had nothing to add. "Thank you, Dr. Brenner. You've been most helpful," Calom said.

Immediately after the interview, Calom and Kintner went to see Willard on the executive floor of the Administration Building.

"Don sounds like Don Sengro, a political militant that the National Action Coalition uses for dirty work that they don't want to be associated with openly," Calom told them. "Federal intelligence agencies have suspected a link between NAC and the Student Democratic Alliance for a long time. The Beard was almost certainly Martin Selucci, a big NAC wheel that a lot of people would like to silence. The raid could have been by any one of a number of ultra-right-backed outfits, probably with that intention. He's been holed up out of sight for weeks somewhere in northern California, and nobody knew where."

He turned to Willard. It was the first time that either of them had seen Calom visibly excited. "Can you see what this *means!* We can acquire possibly invaluable information that might not be accessible in this universe. And we can do it without compromising operations in this universe at all. If you thought you had something extra for Washington before, then what about this? It could be the intelligence profession's dream machine!"

Willard was nodding thoughtfully. "Ye-es. . . . Yes, fascinating."

Kintner listened and understood. But it seemed that the philosophical side could wait a little longer. He cleared his throat. "Fascinating," he agreed. "But shouldn't we be concerned about the more practical side, just at the moment—doing something to avert the business in Berkeley?"

Calom turned his head and seemed to take a moment to register what he meant. "Oh, I should have told you," he said. "You don't have to worry. I'm afraid I was taking advantage of the situation and drawing Brenner out a little. That business all happened yesterday—or at least, something very like it did. Dr. Brenner's friend is fine. He wasn't even at the house. It appears that he moved into Brenner's old apartment with Alice soon after Brenner left to move to Los Alamos. The two of them spent most of yesterday there—probably screwing."

Chapter Sixteen

Dave had never been able to master Sam's method, either. But, like Hugh, he transferred successfully when the machine initiated the process, and found himself temporarily in Germany, having taken the position with Eurospace Engineering that he'd told Hugh he almost decided on before accepting the offer for Los Alamos. And similarly with Sarah, who had a confused experience among people who were unfamiliar, in a city she didn't recognize, with no idea what was going on.

It appeared that actively driving the resonances, instead of just allowing them to arise from random fluctuations within the machine, increased the amount of sideslip into other realities, and hence the possible diversity of experience. The branching structure was highly chaotic: seemingly trivial differences in past happenings could lead to wildly altered outcomes. In Hugh's case, for example, a presumably different reaction to Alice when she visited the QUIC lab had resulted in his not moving to Los Alamos at all! And this was understandable, given the effect that associating with political activists would very likely have on his chances of being hired. He was tempted to call Chris in Berkeley, but Calom put a ban on all contact. In view of recent transgressions, Hugh felt it wisest to comply.

Now everybody in Octagon wanted to get in on the act, and access to the system became limited while more couplers were being modified. But the excursions out into the Multiverse were still completely random affairs. To make them directable in any meaningful sense, or even to go back to the same region of the Multiverse a second time, would require some system of repeatable "coordinates." Devising such a system implied having a notion of something corresponding to direction. And being able to define directions implied figuring out a systematic way of organizing the accumulating information into some kind of map. This became the main preoccupation of the Theoretical Group, keeping Jantowitz away out of sight for much of the time. As a result, Hugh spent more of his out-of-work hours getting to know Dave and Sarah.

The TV in the living room of Sarah's apartment on Canyon Road was showing an old newsreel of Stalin, Roosevelt, and Churchill, the three principal Allied leaders in World War Two, at the conference held at Yalta in the Crimea in February, 1945, where they drew up plans for the final phase of the German war and the shaping of the post-war world. Sarah came out of the bedroom muttering something that began with "China rat man . . ." and began putting towels that she was carrying back in a closet.

Hugh looked across from the table in the living room, where he was browsing in one of her books that he had taken from a shelf. Dave clattered about in the kitchen area behind, fixing coffee. "What's that all about?" Hugh asked idly.

"When is your birthday?" Sarah asked in reply.

"What is this? Are we into birth signs all of a sudden?"

"Just tell me."

"August 8. Why?"

Sarah thought for a moment. "This year, that will be on a Tuesday," she informed him.

"Really? Well, if you say so, I guess. I don't know. How do you know?"

"For any particular year, a twelve-digit number will give you the date that the first Monday of every month falls on. The number for this year begins with 624, which tells you that the first Monday in January falls on the sixth, the first Monday in February, on the second, and so on. Get it?"

Hugh frowned, but nodded. "Okay. So what's all the business with China and rats?"

"That's how you remember the twelve-digit number. It's based on a phonetic alphabet. 6 is 'j,' 'sh,' or 'ch'; 2 is 'n'; 4 is 'r,' and it goes on. Just consonants. You fill in vowels to make up something you can remember. The eighth digit is a 7, which says August 7 will be Monday, and so August 8 must be Tuesday. See?"

Hugh stared at her for a second or two. "Sure, it's great. I'm impressed." He gestured invitingly. "So . . . is this a new hobby that you're into, or something?"

"Nothing moves physically between universes," Sarah replied. "You can't bring back notes or pictures of what you find. So if a trade in information is ever going to happen, it will have to be done by memory training."

"It's an old art that this gives a whole new field of application for," Dave threw in. "Rhyme and rhythm. Homer's epics were preserved orally for six hundred years before they got written down. Religious processions around cathedrals and monasteries were designed to have set parts of the litany recited at specific places. It helped fix recall by association."

Hugh sat back, put down the book, and stared across at Sarah. It was obvious, really. He had been too wrapped up in the physics to think about it.

"Just think," she said. "If you learned how to do it, you might bring back a new Shakespeare play that he never wrote in this universe. What do you reckon the rights might be worth?"

Hugh smiled. "Getting a bit carried away now, aren't we? You're talking about realities that are way, way different, now. All we're doing is wobbling off track a little bit into close variations of the one we've got."

"And look at the discontinuities that all three of us have

experienced already," Sarah said. "And it's still early days. The machine's range will be extended more somehow."

"Somehow," Dave repeated vaguely. How was not obvious. It was something that was already being talked about in the labs. Ducaine feared that they might be approaching the system's design limits.

The conversation trailed off as their attention shifted to the TV. It was showing more figures in old-fashioned suits and uniforms, shaking hands, smiling and posing for the camera. The commentator's voiceover continued:

"In July there was a further conference at Potsdam, although by that time President Roosevelt was dead and had been succeeded by a new face, Harry Truman. Attlee had become the new British Prime Minister. . . ." The gist of the documentary was that the breakup of the European colonial empires and eventual arming and backlash of the non-white races had been foreseen back then. The Cold War with Russia had been engineered as an elaborate pretext to develop the weapons which alone could preserve the West. Russia and America had always been comrades at heart, just as in the great joint crusade against Nazism. Their revolutions had been fought for the same ideals against similar monarchal tyrannies. Earlier, the news had reported that Congress had approved more military aid to Russia, and that U.S. ground forces would be moving to positions in the Urals.

"Oh, I get so tired of all this," Sarah sighed. "Just think, if we could find the right direction, there must be a part of the Multiverse where Sam's kind of world exists. Imagine finding out what it was like, even if just for an hour."

Hugh smiled. "What's Sam's kind of world?" he asked.

"Oh . . ." Sarah waved toward the TV. "One that isn't run by people strutting around full of self-importance and with power over the lives of millions. Where people are honest and simple and decent, and value each other for what they are instead of what they own. . . . I'm not saying that reason and rationality aren't important. But maybe what we need more of is Sam's kind of knowledge—some way of bringing the two together into a better balance somehow."

"So do we take it that the rational pursuit of self-interest isn't the way?" Hugh said. It was a gentle dig, his way of saying that they'd heard this before, and he agreed with her.

"Not sufficient, anyway," she replied. "It was the European nations rationally pursuing what they perceived as their rational self-interests, at the culmination of an Age of Reason, that gave us World War One. And we've been dealing with the consequences ever since." She looked for support to the only European present. "Right, Dave?"

Dave nodded. "That must have been a significant Multiverse branch point right there. It generated a whole region evolved from a common ancestral universe where the Western world tore itself apart."

"And we're stuck in the middle of it," Sarah said.

Hugh picked up his mug. "Common ancestral universe," he repeated. "I like that. It's a good way to put it."

Sarah stirred milk into her coffee. Dave leaned forward and sipped his black. After a short silence Dave said to Hugh, "What led Theo into looking for an MV connection to evolution? I always thought evolution was on pretty solid ground."

"Oh, it is," Hugh answered. "In the sense that nobody's saying it didn't happen. But the traditional mechanism for explaining it doesn't work."

"You mean natural selection?"

"Right. It can account for small adaptations within limits, and maybe a few species; but for the big picture, something a lot deeper has to be going on. Theo came up with this idea that DNA might be an MV antenna, so what you've really got is lots of evolutionary processes exchanging information in parallel."

"Communication between universes—just what we've been talking about," Sarah said after a few seconds. "Except that the information we're talking about is cultural, not genetic. It's history repeating itself at a higher level." That hadn't occurred to Hugh before.

"So is that how evolution happens?" Dave asked. "Parallel processing via the MV—that's what drives it?"

"I'd say the jury's still out," Hugh replied. "The work is still to be done. We got sidetracked with the QUIC and never really came to anything conclusive."

"Oh, so *that's* where the QUIC idea came from," Sarah said.

"We were trying to prove the feasibility of Theo's idea by mimicking it artificially," Hugh told them. "The QUIC operated by coupling to its MV counterparts—the way Theo thought DNA does. Apparently the approach is unique. I don't think anyone else is doing anything like it. That was why Kintner and Ducaine got all excited when they came to Berkeley to see it. The technique effectively boosted the power of the basic system by . . ."

"What's happened to it?" Dave asked. "Is it suspended, will we be taking it over here at Los Alamos, or what?"

"It sounds spooky—but interesting," Sarah said. "I hope they do start it up again here."

Then they both realized that Hugh wasn't listening. His voice had trailed away in mid sentence, and he was sitting back in his chair with a faraway, unblinking expression on his face.

"Hugh, are you all right?" Dave asked.

"I think it might be a transfer," Sarah whispered. They waited, wondering what variant of reality this Hugh would turn out to be from.

But it wasn't a transfer. After a few more seconds Hugh—still "their" Hugh—focused back inside the room and looked at each of them strangely in turn. "It boosted the power," he said. "We could apply the same method here. It wouldn't take much to do it, either."

Dave blinked. "Here? You mean to the QUADAR?"

"Exactly."

Dave and Sarah looked at each other, searching for the implication. Sarah got to it first. "Are you saying we might

be able to boost the QUADAR's range farther after all?"
she said.

Hugh gave her a strange, crooked-mouthed look, as if
he were still having difficulty with the possibilities unfolding
in his mind.

"Boost the QUADAR's range?" he repeated. "Look . . .
Willard and the others are all worked up about a spooks'
machine that might let them peek into the house next
door." He shook his head. "That's just a bicycle wobbling
out of its lane." Hugh paused to look from one to the
other again. "Guys . . . we can give them something that
will *fly!*"

Hugh put the idea to Jantowitz as soon as he got back
to Mrs. Ryecroft's. They discussed it late into the night.
First thing the next morning, they went to see Kintner.

Chapter Seventeen

Howard Turner was a neurophysiologist in Peter Mulgrave's group. After decoupling from a session on the machine, he acted strangely, saying little and directing hostile, suspicious looks at everything and everybody about him, then disappeared into his office, refusing to take calls. He emerged several hours later and announced that science was wasted in a world ruled by fools and tutored by liars. He then walked out of LANL, leaving the contents of his desk and office untouched. On being subsequently contacted by DRA Security, he informed them that he intended leaving the country to join a children's orphanage in Paraguay. He wasn't interested in the proper termination procedures. Sure, he'd sign anything they wanted him to.

Sam explained it as QUADAR-enhanced insight: amplified MV receptivity of the kind that he believed accounted for much of human nature unexplained through the ages. Ducaine used his amoeba-in-the-pond analogy to illustrate that feedback from future branchings of the Multiverse caused certain courses of action to "feel right." Some individuals were better than others at discerning them. Sam believed that the "moral sense" that made humans unique was a result of the same kind of process operating to evaluate behavior in general rather than specific actions—consciousness learning to steer itself toward better futures through the confusion of choices that life offers. Simply put, exercising some restraint and adhering to certain standards tended to result in societies that were better for all in the long run and thus took on the attribute of being "right" as opposed to "wrong." Various religions and philosophic schools had interpreted essentially the same message in different ways, usually with concepts of "gods" that conveyed in some way or other which was which. For the best part of a thousand years, philosophers had been trying to derive a moral code rationally from logical foundations, and had failed. How could it have been otherwise before the underlying physics was discovered? The reality was neither supernatural nor deducible logically from premises that failed to comprehend the Multiverse.

Through to the Middle Ages, the physical world had presented a baffling variety of moving objects, winds, tides, stresses, and forces that kept a pantheon of deities and spirits occupied full-time to manage. Then Newton reduced everything to three laws and put them all out of work permanently.

"I think we might be on the verge of taking it beyond the realm of just physics," Sam told the weekly progress review group.

"Er, what do you mean—extending it into the humanities or something?" Jeff Berres said. He was a pure nuts and bolts man, not really interested in philosophical ramifications.

"They won't love you if you steal it from them, Sam," Helen Almer commented. "They've been trying to imitate physics for years."

Sam shook his head. "That wasn't what I meant. I meant everything—every kind of knowledge. If the Multiverse works the way I'm beginning to think it does, then 'physics' expands to cover just about everything contained within the human experience."

While Sam talked about reducing even mystical insights to comprehensible terms, the official response to Hugh's vision of reaching far-off, undreamed-of worlds was being decided over a teleconference hookup to Washington.

Leonard Sarvin, Deputy Director of the Defense Research Administration, spoke out of a screen in Willard's office. "Oh, don't get me wrong. It's making a *big* impact here. The President wants to be kept informed personally on a continual basis. But it's the intelligence potential that we want to see developed. If this new angle is going to be of any practical use, we need to concentrate on getting into worlds that are close—real close. Nobody's interested in boosting the range to something that would lose all connection with what we know. See what I'm getting at? Okay, so suppose we find out all kinds of stuff about some wacko world where the Chinese got to the Moon first and a communist revolution happened in America. Who *cares?* Nothing about it would be relevant to *our* situation. For what's been put into this, we want something out of it that we can use."

Calom and Willard were in their respective offices in Administration, while Kintner was connected in from the Octagon building. The scientist part of Kintner was reluctant to let things just go at that. "The individual who conceived the idea—Dr. Brenner—based it on a parallel amplification process that he and Jantowitz devised while they were at Berkeley," he said. "Their method is unique. We have rare talent here. The consequences of demotivating it could be unfortunate, to say the least."

The other participant from Washington was a General Ventz, from some undisclosed part of the Defense Department underworld, who was being brought in to take care of security at the more general level of significance that the project was taking on. Internal affairs at Los Alamos were still Calom's department. Ventz confined himself purely to carrying out his task, with no desire to get embroiled in the scientific issues and the complications surrounding them.

"That's a specification matter," he said. His voice was a gravelly baritone, sounding each syllable deliberately. He was lean and tanned with hollow cheeks, a sharp nose, and white, crinkly hair. His hands, which appeared on-screen from time to time to pat his hair or adjust his tie, were large and sinewy. "It's just a question of defining what the goals are and making it clear who's in charge."

Willard gnawed his lip. He took orders relayed from Sarvin's boss by Sarvin, not from Ventz. But this wasn't the time to make a confrontation out of it. "It may not be that straightforward," he said. "The people we listened to a few minutes ago are already working under protest . . . to some degree." Calom had presented a surveillance update, which included material from the bugs and taps in Sarah's apartment. "It wouldn't take much to push them into open defiance after the last incident. I wouldn't want to risk that."

Ventz snorted. "Are you saying you ask their cooperation as a *favor*? What kind of place are you operating there? You tell them what you want, and you expect it to get done. That's their job. That's all there is to it. Period."

"This is not a military objective," Calom put in, sounding curt. "It's not quite the same thing as ordering people where to point their guns and shoot."

"Hell, it's still a—"

"Gentlemen . . ." Sarvin intervened at last. "Why don't we play it diplomatically and leave them some leeway as a fallback option?" he suggested. "As an opener we pitch the hard line—and who knows, they might buy it. If they do, we've got no problem. But if it looks as if they're about to choke on it, we can back off and say okay to some range-boosting work as a concession."

"I could go along with that," Kintner agreed.

Ventz grimaced. "Concession" didn't seem to be a word that sat too easily. "Provided the mainline project stays on track," Sarvin threw in to make his point. Ventz emitted a sigh, compressed his mouth, nodded tightly, and let it go at that.

"I'll issue a policy directive stating that greater range is not our aim at the present time," Willard said. "Effort is to be focused on achieving directability."

So there it was. Long-range voyaging out across the

Multiverse was dead. The only question was how best to couch it without alienating the workers.

"Any other points?" Sarvin invited. Nobody had any. He checked his agenda. "I think that covers local Octagon matters. We just need Jesse to stay on line for a couple of general points," he told Calom and Kintner. "You are excused, gentlemen. Thanks for joining us."

"Shall I talk to Professor Jantowitz and Dr. Brenner to let them know the decision in advance?" Kintner asked.

"Yes, I think that would be best, Ed," Willard replied.

Kintner nodded. "Very well. In that case, good day." He vanished from the others' screens. Calom did the same a few seconds later.

Sarvin waited for a moment, and then resumed in a lowered tone. "What about this loose cannon that we've got? How exposed are we?" Nobody needed to be told that he meant Turner.

"I don't understand how it could happen," Ventz declared, showing his hands. "I mean, you're supposed to have an internal security operation out there, right? What were they doing? Don't they keep profiles? They should be able to tell when these screws are about to come loose."

"I suggest that you acquaint yourself more with the pertinent facts before making such insinuations," Willard returned.

"The facts are simply that—"

"*Gentlemen* . . . let's concern ourselves with the present," Sarvin pleaded. The other two fell silent. "Jesse," Sarvin said. "What can we say about the subject's condition and the likely risk factor?"

"He has a full working knowledge of all aspects of Octagon, including the recent functional extensions," Willard answered. He looked down at his hands, hesitating, and then back up. "Calom profiles him as unstable and unpredictable. His attitude is not cooperative. He has indicated intent that has to be categorized as hostile."

"And the exposure risk? . . ." Ventz prompted. Willard did not respond.

"In Colonel Calom's estimation," Sarvin said.

Willard licked his lips. "Significant," he told them.

A somber silence persisted. Then Sarvin said, "We take it that you will refer the matter to the appropriate agency, General."

Ventz nodded.

Hugh was boiling when he and Jantowitz came out of Kintner's office on the upper floor of the Octagon building and turned along the corridor. "Theo, they can't do this! We're talking about something that could be the biggest thing since the invention of speech, and all they can see is another toy for the NSA? What kind of people are we working for? No wonder the world's in a mess. I quit. I'm out. I don't care what bullshit I've signed. I'll find somebody else who'll push this thing to its potential. I'll even go over to the Chinese if that's what it takes."

Two secretaries going the other way with armfuls of folders raised their eyebrows. Jantowitz steered him firmly in the direction of the Theoretical Group's offices. "Is what it will take to get yourself shot, that kind of talking. You know there is nowhere else that you will find such opportunities. Nowhere."

"Opportunities for what, Theo? For making a personal contribution to creating the Global Police State? We could forget the need for any of all that—permanently. They know it, too. They'd all be out of work. That's what this is really all about."

Jantowitz poured coffee into two mugs from the communal pot in the secretarial area and led Hugh into his office.

"Well, they can't force us, Theo," Hugh resumed. "This isn't some slave labor—"

"Take this and shut up. You are young enough to know everything, except that one should listen twice as much as one speaks. That is why, the God, two ears and one mouth he gives us, yes?" Hugh took a sip, started to say something more, checked himself, and acquiesced with a sigh. "I want you to see this," Jantowitz said, moving across to one of the display units by his desk.

He activated the screen and juggled with codes and mnemonics while Hugh leaned against a chair and watched. Finally, Jantowitz produced an image consisting of a vaguely outlined banded structure for most of the lower half, and above, a streaky, branching pattern going into hazy whorls about several blobs. Hugh recognized it as representing a section of a crudely defined mathematical phase space with complex structure showing chaotic properties. The fuzziness and lack of detail indicated that the plot was not a theoretical construct, but had been generated from very approximate experimental data.

Jantowitz tapped keys to show a series of sections in turn, giving the feel of movement and the structures extending in multiple directions. He looked at Hugh questioningly.

Hugh's belligerence with politics had already subsided. Mentally he was back in the Multiverse again. "Is this what I think it is?" he breathed.

Jantowitz nodded. "Just a rough sketch, we have yet. But the beginnings of a map of the territory are here. You see there"—he indicated the lower area of the screen—"the blue areas in this whole zone show us, I am almost sure, a region of universes in which you and I, we did not come to Los Alamos at all. But you see also from those stripes—the condition also depends on some alternating higher-level factor that as yet I have not identified." He pointed again. "Then we have this island function here—it seems to be the worlds that contain your escapade with the itinerants. It is a restricted domain, as you see. Very likely, many factors had to be just right, and so in most universes it never happens. You were in one of the unlucky ones, it seems."

Hugh stared wonderingly. He felt as if he were one of Ducaine's amoebas seeing a sonar scan of its pond—or the immediately surrounding part of it, anyway—for the first time. "What parameters are correlating with the attributes?" he asked finally. In other words, when the machine caused a flip to happen, what measurable aspects of its operating state related to identifiable characteristics of the universe that the flip took place into? Or in short, what was Jantowitz varying to generate the maps?

"I have found that extracting complex components from the resonance field equations gives progressions that seem to have some physical meaning," Jantowitz replied. He brought a new image onto another screen and went on, "Now take a look at these. They are field plots mapped into projections of MV space. I assume the forms here are familiar, yes?"

Hugh recognized the spiraling pattern of trajectories starting from diverse points around a phase space, gravitating inward to the curious regions of stability known as mathematical "attractors"—unexpected zones of equilibrium that some physical processes with an otherwise inherent tendency to chaotic instability would settle into and thereafter resist further departures from. Attractor theory had done much to explain the long-term stability exhibited by biological species and genetic combinations, in contrast to the perpetual change that traditional selection theory predicted. Application of the mathematics of attractors had involved Jantowitz in evolution in the first place.

"The whole structure revolves around strong attractors," Jantowitz said. "So you see what this means. In theory, yes, an infinity of universes is possible, just as an effectively infinite number of different animals is possible. But in reality they converge around a limited number of stable solutions. So the scale of the problem reduces vastly."

They had been hoping for something like this. It meant that specifying an infinite number of coordinates to achieve directability wouldn't be called for—which was just as well, for it would have been impossible.

"So this could be the breakthrough," Hugh murmured, still awed.

Jantowitz nodded. "Exactly so, yes. And that is my point.

Is not a time to talk like you do, about quitting the business. Better it is to know when to cooperate a little. What sense is it to go making trouble now, when all the things we need, we have here?" His voice fell to a lower, conspiratorial note. "And more, when we are in the ahead-of-the-game situation that will buy us the time also, yes?"

Hugh looked at him uncertainly. "What are you getting at, Theo?" he asked.

Jantowitz gestured toward the screen. "Already, here, we are close to giving them the directability that they want. When Peter Mulgrave and Ed Kintner see this, then very happy peoples they will become. So, when we work in their time and the other scientists here are involved also, we work hard and make good progress." He licked his lips below his walrus mustache. "But also we work in our own time. And that is when we make for ourselves the machine that will fly across the Multiverse."

Hugh shook his head, as if doubting that he could have heard correctly. "Do it ourselves? You mean unofficially—with no authorization? Theo, you're crazy."

"Crazy, maybe. Insane? No." The eyes behind the Coke-bottle lenses glinted deviously. Jantowitz went on, keeping his voice low, "You say yourself, it wouldn't take much for anybody who understands the QUIC. For software, we have access here already to everything we need. As well, we will need modified antenna arrays and replacement amplifier modules for the couplers. Dave is the hardware expert, yes? So he takes care of that. Then you have to duplicate our special chips we have at Berkeley." Jantowitz pointed a finger downward at the floor. "All the equipment is there downstairs." He paused and studied Hugh's face. But Hugh was still having too much of a problem absorbing it to be capable of a response just yet. Jantowitz went on:

"Yes, I know what it is you are thinking. How we do our own project like this up here when all these peoples, they come and they go all the time like is railroad station. Well, answer is, we don't try to do it up here." Hugh frowned, now not following at all. Jantowitz pointed at the floor again. "You know area downstairs between power conditioning and crystal shop, yes?"

Hugh nodded. There was a warren of rooms and spaces on the lower floor behind the bays of power conditioning equipment for the computers upstairs, and the shops and instrument stores to the rear. "What about it?"

"Is place down there designated N2 that two of Jeff Berres's people use temporarily before they move upstairs," Jantowitz said. "Computer terminals and desk space it has, and recess at back with two couplers. Enclosed and secluded. And right now, is not used." Jantowitz turned a hand to indicate himself. "You see, the eccentric Polish professor, this is, who cannot work with the interruptions all the time and the distractions. So, to Peter Mulgrave and Kintner I go, and I tell them that if for the machine, directability Washington wants, then the peace and the privacy to work in, I must have."

"You figure that's all you have to do? They'll give it to you just like that?" Hugh sounded doubtful.

"I don't know. I tell you before, you must first buy a ticket if you want to win the prize."

Hugh refused to believe it could be that easy. "Okay, suppose they did. Our design specs for the QUIC were impounded and classified, remember?"

"Mmm . . . But not before I post encrypted backups to an address that I happen to have on a confidential network," Jantowitz murmured.

Hugh sank down in a chair, shaking his head at the audacity of it. Jantowitz waited for a few seconds, then shrugged. "Of course if you young peoples are all just the talk and the wind, then it doesn't happen, I guess. So the wooden heads in Washington run science and make the rules, and you've asked for what you get. It's your world."

"What made you think of it?" Hugh asked after another pause to digest the enormity of what Jantowitz was proposing.

"Your idea it was, not mine," Jantowitz said.

"What are you talking about? Theo, you *are* crazy."

"Bits and pieces I get as notes left by different Jantowitzes. But it seems the idea originates with some other version of you who is in another universe somewhere. So maybe you are trailing behind the Hughs who don't waste their time getting mad over politics."

The whole situation was crazy. Hugh shook his head and sighed in a way that said okay, he was in. "Let's just hope that Calom and the management here don't hit on the idea of pooling their marbles between universes too."

"A likely possibility, it is not," Jantowitz said. "Sharing information is the way of scientists. These others, always they want to restrict information. So they don't think to work together. That way, we always stay ahead."

Jantowitz showed no sign of doubt or reservation. Hugh slumped back, nodding. It felt like a new twist in the path that had been beckoning him onward from the beginning. Of course he would go with it. What other choice did he have now?

Chapter Eighteen

Throughout her life, Sarah had gone through periods of experiencing unusually lucid dreams. Typically this would go on for a few weeks, perhaps caused by a passing emotional state or events taking place in her life at the time. Unlike ordinary dreams, which were vague, incoherent, and evaporated soon after she awoke, these were vividly real, and persisted. The minuteness of detail that they could capture astonished her. A street scene might contain every line of the doors and windows of a building, even the individual bricks forming the walls; people that she encountered were complete to every hair on their head and the wrinkles in their clothes. She found that she could consciously make a point of observing such things closely to check. At times the illusion could be so compelling that it would take several minutes for her to be sure that she was finally awake. And even then, sometimes she wasn't—sure; or, on occasions, as it turned out, awake either.

Somehow, the textbook explanations that she was creating it all from stored experiences didn't ring true. If minds were able to hold and organize such vast amounts of detail, why couldn't they be accessed consciously—as would seem a more useful mechanism to have evolved? And why, if they were little more than aimless assemblings of elements swirling around in her head in the way the experts said, did the same images and places recur repeatedly? It was coming from "outside" in some way or other, Sarah was convinced.

The other thing she was convinced of was that in some mysterious way many of the situations that she found herself in were connected. She dreamed on occasions of a broad, crescent-shaped thoroughfare busy with traffic, amid soaring, brightly lit, unusually styled buildings; of being in a fast-moving mass-transit vehicle with colorfully dressed people; of a street system with multiple levels connected by ramps; of a place that she lived in, with views from high up and bridges to other nearby towers. None of the scenes had anything in common, and yet she *knew* that they were parts of the same city; that the fragmented glimpses were from an existence that some version of herself was leading . . . "somewhere." But it never amounted to more than that obstinate certainty of feeling that people can take it into their heads to harbor toward anything, that no amount of reasoning or contrary evidence will budge.

At college she became interested in a theory that she came across of a possible connection between MV sensitivity and artistic inspiration, and after completing an introductory study, joined a research program being set up in Japan at the University of Osaka. The researchers at Osaka were also investigating certain kinds of dreams in the context of MV communication, and were looking for subjects with a high proclivity for dreaming lucidly. Sarah became closely involved for two years, and though the technology used in Osaka was nowhere near what existed at Los Alamos, her experience and the unique perspective that she had acquired to MV phenomena were sufficient to admit her to the project when she returned to the U.S. With her disposition toward the intuitive and insightful, as opposed to the rationalist-materialist world view of the hard sciences, and her penchant for things oriental, it was natural that she came to rely a lot for guidance on the views and advice of Sam Phniangsak.

They were in a corner of the Theoretical Group's

statistical lab. Sam was at a desk console, reviewing some files. Sarah had joined him after taking part in a series of machine runs. Hugh and Dave had disappeared, probably downstairs with Jantowitz. Jantowitz had prevailed upon Peter Mulgrave for a retreat where he could work undisturbed, and Mulgrave had obtained Kintner's agreement to let him use the N2 area that had been vacated recently. Already, it was referred to generally as Jantowitz's "Bolthole." Hugh and Dave seemed to have gotten deeply involved with him in his work on directability. They had all stayed into the early hours both last night and the night before. When Sarah expressed curiosity about what they were doing, Dave had been strangely uncommunicative.

"I used to dream about being in a very different world— modern in some ways, and yet quaintly old-fashioned at the same time," she told Sam. "There were different scenes, but somehow I knew they were all parts of the same picture. I kept finding myself back in the same settings, over and over." She looked across at where he was tapping keys intermittently, listening as he scanned the screen. "The system they had at Osaka consolidated the effect. I'm certain it was a connection to another part of the MV."

"Could be," Sam agreed. "Perhaps it's there all the time, but the deluge of sensory data coming through in the normal waking state swamps it out."

Sarah thought for a moment, staring at him. "That's what it's all about, isn't it—the mental training. You suppress external distractions willfully, which lets you focus on MV information consciously. You shift your awareness from outside to what's coming through inside."

Sam beamed. "You see how easy it is to understand if you're allowed to put it in your own terms," he said.

"You think I really was seeing pieces of a world that actually exists somewhere?" Sarah asked him.

"Look what the machine can already let you do. So why not without it? At our present state of knowledge, I wouldn't rule out anything."

Sarah looked distantly toward the window. "It had such

an exciting feel about it. Everyone was content, free to live how they wanted. So unlike this one. Do you think anything perfectible could ever come out of this mess that we've gotten ourselves into?"

"What makes you think that any world is perfectible?" Sam queried.

She shrugged. "It's what philosophers ask, isn't it?"

"Yes. And when, after a lifetime of arguing about it, they finally arrive at the conclusion which should have been obvious in the first place—that it isn't—it depresses them, sometimes to the point of suicide. But that's their own fault for asking the wrong question."

"What question should they ask, then?"

"If the world is improvable—which, of course, it is. And if the net achievement of a lifetime is to contribute anything at all to that end, no matter how small, then that life was well spent. Be content to have done a modest amount of good. Untold misery has been caused by zealots trying to cure all of the world's evils."

Sarah propped her chin on her hand and watched him while he carried on editing. "Why aren't people like you running the world?" she asked.

"I suppose people who don't especially desire power over others aren't very likely to attain it," Sam replied. "Although I believe there are some islands in the Indian Ocean where being the chief is considered a lousy job, and nobody wants it. It's probably the most enlightened political system that this planet has produced so far."

"Why do some people want power over others?"

"Why do people crave after anything? Probably because they believe that acquiring it will make them secure and happy."

"But they always seem to be the most insecure and least happy," Sarah said.

"Because their beliefs are based on delusion. If you have the power, then others do not. Whatever you demand exclusively, others cannot have. So your imagined happiness depends on possessing what you deny others the right to possess. So how can your happiness last when it's obvious that everyone else will try to take it away?"

"What's the answer, then?" Sarah asked. "What will make everyone happy? Is there an answer?"

Sam closed the file he had been working on and sat back in his chair. "What the Buddhists teach is to free yourself from the three great evils in life: greed—which means all kinds of craving—hatred, and delusion. But delusion is really the cause of the other two. We crave that which we delude ourselves into thinking will bring happiness; we hate those whom we delude ourselves into thinking stand to stop us from getting it." He stood up and moved over to the window to look out at the starkness of concrete buildings and chain link fences.

"But when you cease to hate, you see yourself in others. How, then, can you inflict cruelty on them? For thousands of years people have tried fear, force, reason, and persuasion to restrain humanity's excesses—all failures. But the effective way requires no elaborate policing or large institutions. Just simple compassion. When you yourself *feel* the pain and humiliation of others, how can you hurt them?"

"You know, sometimes Dave and Hugh and I talk about 'Sam's world,'" Sarah said. "I think you've just summed it up. People helping each other, instead of thinking that any gain has to be someone else's loss. It really isn't a zero sum game, is it?"

Sam turned from the window and smiled. "There's an old Chinese fable about the difference between Heaven and Hell. Both are great palaces set out with tables for a luxurious banquet. The only thing is, the chopsticks are all four feet long. In Hell, everyone tries to feed themselves, and they get nowhere. But in Heaven each person feeds the one opposite, and they all have a good time. I think that just about sums it—"

Suddenly Sam was gone, and Sarah found herself in another room entirely. It seemed to be a records office, with a row of file cabinets, a microfiche reader and storage trays, printer terminal and copier. She was standing in front of one of the file cabinets, a drawer pulled halfway out, with a folder open in her hand. The tag on it read: TURNER, HOWARD L. It was all so sudden. She was too befuddled even to recognize the name. She looked around, trying to make sense of the situation.

Then a door opened behind her. She whirled around, still clutching the file folder. A balding, bespectacled man in white shirtsleeves was standing in the doorway. His expression was grim. "I thought I saw you sneaking in here. What do you think you're doing? No, don't move. You just stay right there, young lady, while I call security."

The office that Sarah had found herself in was at the back of the Administration Building and belonged to a section of the personnel department that handled social and recreational matters. The file was an unrestricted one maintained by the Lab's Sports & Social Club. She would never have gotten near Turner's official personnel record— or anyone else's, for that matter.

Calom arrived from upstairs in the same building a quarter of an hour later. In answer to his questions, Sarah could only state simply that she had no recollection of going there and knew of no reason why she should want to. Calom was sufficiently familiar by this time with the strange effects of the QUADAR not to reject her story out of hand. He called Sam in P2 building, who confirmed that Sarah's manner had changed suddenly in the middle of their conversation, and she had left on what sounded like a pretext. From the time between her leaving the statistics lab and being accosted in the Administration Building, it was clear that she must have gone there directly.

"Obviously, it was another transfer," she told Calom wearily as they went through it all yet again. Why did security mentalities insist on looking for ulterior motives in everything? "Some version of myself in another reality had a reason for wanting to contact him." The file related to the Howard Turner who had walked out and announced his intention of quitting the whole business. "Maybe the information was lost there, or maybe she couldn't get to it—I've no way of knowing."

"What dealings have you had with Howard Turner as yourself—in this reality?" Calom persisted.

"None. I knew him by sight, that's about all. I exchanged maybe a dozen words with him since I came to Los Alamos."

"What kind of things did you talk about?"

"Talk? We didn't talk about anything. It was probably just things like, 'Good morning,' or 'Have you seen Ducaine anywhere?' I don't remember every word I say to everybody."

"You had no dealings with him outside the lab? Political interests in common, maybe? . . . Or a more personal relationship?"

Sarah stared in disbelief. "Are you asking me if we were *fucking?*"

"People do. You wouldn't be the first. It happens all the time," Calom said expressionlessly.

"I'm not hearing this. It isn't real." Sarah shook her head and held her composure with an effort. "No. We were not lovers. I don't know anything about him." She looked across the office and saw to her astonishment that Calom was still skeptical. "You can't assume that whatever's true in some other universe has to be reflected here," she said. "There can be abrupt transitions to something totally different. . . . The Calom in that universe could be a spy for the Chinese. You see what I'm getting at. Whatever he's involved in has nothing to do with you. It's the same with me. Maybe in whatever reality this other version of me came from, it might have been . . . as you say—or whatever. But *she* is not me. I can't speak for her or answer for her."

Calom continued staring at her for several seconds more, then rose to his feet with a nod. "Don't discuss this conversation with anyone else," he said. "I might want to talk to you again."

As Calom moved to the door Sarah said on impulse,

"What happens to somebody like Turner in a situation like this?"

He stopped with his hand on the doorknob and looked back. "Since he's in violation of the security acts he could be detained or prevented from leaving the country. It really isn't your concern, Ms. Pacey. I suggest that you confine your attention to the work that you were brought here to do, and leave others to theirs. That way all of us will get along fine."

On returning to his own office, Calom called Kintner to advise his findings. "I'm satisfied that it's the way she describes," Calom said. "She's telling as much as she knows."

"It's just part of the situation that surrounds this whole project, I'm afraid," Kintner told him. "Anyone connected with it can cease being 'themselves' at any time. It's something we're going to have to learn to live with."

Calom didn't look very comforted. "Not if they're going to use it as an opportunity to try and get information in ways that they would never risk in their own world," he objected. "That's completely unacceptable."

"Why?" Kintner asked. "Whatever information they take back to their own reality can hardly have any effect in this one, can it? You'd only be protecting some other administration in a different universe, not our administration in this one."

This whole business was unsettling enough without getting into logical debates with somebody like Kintner. Calom pointed out what merely seemed to him to be common sense. "But suppose that the Sarah Pacey who was here temporarily did gain access to something sensitive, and later came back again. She could communicate it to others in this world. So we *are* compromised. That's not a situation that I can tolerate."

Kintner could see the reason for the misunderstanding now. Calom had no concept of the dimensionality of the Multiverse. Kintner searched for a way of getting the point across without being demeaning. "I don't think the risk is as bad as you may think," he said finally. "There are as good as an infinite number of other realities. That means that the chances of hitting the same one twice in random transfers are virtually nonexistent."

"Random transfers for the present," Calom agreed. "But what if you people succeed in achieving repeatability— or some other versions of you in all these other realities out there do? Isn't your objective exactly what I'm talking about?"

Kintner blinked. Calom had him. He had thought it through from the perspective of his own priorities and hit on a valid point that had escaped Kintner. Indeed, if a solution to repeatability existed—and it didn't need the scientists in this reality to find it—it *could* be a problem.

He looked out at the security chief with a sudden new respect. "What are you proposing—short of keeping everyone confined or under permanent observation?" he asked. He had intended the remark to be flippant, but the look on Calom's face gave him the feeling that Calom might indeed have been considering just that.

"Introduce a system of randomized ID codes that all Octagon personnel will be required to memorize," Calom replied. "To be used for gaining admission into the facility or access to restricted records."

Kintner considered it. This would certainly be the time to start experimenting with solutions. "Very well," he agreed. "Prepare a proposal along those lines for Jesse, and I'll endorse it." Calom nodded and was about to clear down. Kintner stopped him with a gesture. "There was one other thing, while you're on the line. This business with Jantowitz and the others going it alone for longer ranges . . ." It was no longer just Jantowitz, Hugh, and Dave. Dave and Hugh had brought Sarah in. Jantowitz had decided that he needed additional help, and had included Sam also.

"Yes?" Calom said.

The scheme was no secret, of course, due to Calom's surveillance. Calom had given a full account to Willard, who had acquainted Kintner with the situation and invited his opinion. General Ventz, of course, would never have condoned it. But since Ventz's area of responsibility lay specifically *outside* the National Laboratory, Willard didn't see any particular reason why it should be made his business.

"Jesse's right," Kintner said. "Dammit, *we* run this project, not Ventz. They're our people, and I don't think we should risk alienating them. Also, it would be a mistake to reveal your surveillance over something like this. We're making good progress, and their contribution is invaluable. So I think our response should be to act as if we don't know, let them carry on, and keep an eye on them. To be honest, I'm curious to see what they come up with."

"That's fine by me." Calom had no quarrel with anything that kept Ventz in his place.

"So, I can tell Jesse that we are in agreement?" Kintner checked.

"Yes," Calom said.

Chapter Nineteen

Sarah grew more disturbed when she got a chance to think things over. She didn't believe that any version of herself would have gotten involved with Turner in a personal way. He was married, introverted, not at all her type. The suggestion simply wasn't credible. The more likely explanation was that a Sarah in a different reality had needed to find out something that she hadn't wanted to risk being caught looking for in her own world. So she had made the attempt using the version of herself who existed in this one. Whoever was in charge of the operation back home hadn't allowed enough time for her to complete the task, and she had been brought back too soon, leaving her suddenly reinstated alternate self to handle the explanations. The question that remained, of course, was: What had the other Sarah been looking for? If it wasn't anything personal, it could only have had to do with something that had come to her attention concerning Turner's situation generally.

"It had to be something pretty ordinary to be in an office like that," she said to Dave, back at her apartment on the day the extra restrictions were announced. "Yet she went to all that trouble to avoid being discovered. So the information itself wasn't particularly sensitive. What she was hiding was the fact that she was looking for it. In other words, it was what she already knew that was making

her nervous, not anything that she expected to find in
the file." She was sitting in the armchair by the window,
restless and tense, a half-drunk cup of coffee beside her.
She hadn't touched the tacos that they had picked up on
the way back from the lab.

Dave looked at her from the table. "What would she
find in a social–club file?" he said. "It could only have
been something domestic—home address, relatives,
something like that."

"Exactly. And that says she couldn't have known him
very well, just the same as I don't."

Dave thought about it as he chewed. "You think she
wanted to contact him for some reason?"

"Perhaps. Or just to check up on him, maybe."

"What for?"

Sarah clutched her shoulders with crossed arms, as if
she were feeling cold. "Look, I don't know if this place is
making me as paranoid as the rest or something. . . . But
do you think they'd really just let him just walk away like
that—knowing what he knew, acting the way he did? They'd
see it as a security disaster waiting to happen."

A similar thought had crossed Dave's mind, but he'd
kept it to himself. "You think the other Sarah had reason
to suspect that something might have happened to him?"
he said. "That's what she was trying to check—to see if
he was okay?"

"How can I know? But why else wouldn't she have risked
following it up in her own universe if it wasn't to do with
something like that?"

"Actually, something like that did occur to me," Dave
admitted.

"Then why didn't you say so?"

He shrugged. "Maybe I was wondering if I was getting
a bit paranoid too."

They looked across the room at each other long and
silently, both searching for confirmation that they weren't
reading more into this than was there. Finally, Sarah said,
"We can still check it out, Dave."

Dave frowned. "How do you mean?"

"I didn't get a chance to register much because Hollings showed up almost immediately. But I remember seeing the name Turner and a New York address on a form at the front of the file. The area code of the number was 212, so it must have been Manhattan. If we go through the Turners in the directory, we might find one who's connected with him and might know something."

Dave made a face. "It's a pretty common name. How many do you figure there could be in a place like Manhattan?"

"Less than infinity, Dave. In fact, it's less than four columns of a standard page. I checked before we left today." Sarah stared at him. "An hour at the most."

She was insisting, not suggesting. Dave downed some coffee and nodded. "They're two hours ahead of us there. We'll make a start as soon as I finish this. You get another cup of that down you and tie your nerves back together. With the tension you're putting out, it's a wonder the air isn't crackling."

Sarah didn't smile. "Dave, if something has . . . happened to him, then it's proof as far as I'm concerned. Coincidences like that just don't happen." Dave nodded and said nothing.

Some calls didn't produce answers; others just got recordings. But Turner number eleven had a cousin working for the government in New Mexico, sure enough—coating fence posts in one of the state penitentiaries. Turner number twenty-one was a woman who kept insisting shrilly to Dave that he had it wrong—the Turner that he wanted was in Mexico, not New Mexico. Turner number thirty had relatives in the Santa Fe area all right, but the last of them had died in 1975. Turner number forty-two tried to interest Sarah in life insurance. Then it was Dave's turn again.

"Hello?" A man's voice—quiet, sounding around middle-aged.

"Oh, hi. My name is David Wallis. I'm trying to locate

somebody called Turner and I'm hoping you might be able to help. I believe he has family in Manhattan somewhere."

"Who is it you're looking for?"

"His name is Howard Turner, Howard L. He's a neuroscientist. The last I heard he was with a government project in New Mexico."

There was a pause. "Who is this again, please?" the voice asked.

"David Wallis. I'm a friend of his from way back."

"You're English, aren't you?"

"That's right. I work in a similar line."

"Howard was never in England, far as I know."

Dave nodded rapidly at Sarah and stuck up a thumb. She moved closer, gripping his arm. "I met him at a conference. But it sounds as if you know him, right?"

"My brother, yes."

Dave couldn't suppress a grin. "That's great. Look . . . it is Mr. Turner, I take it?"

"Yes."

"I heard from a friend that Howard is planning on moving to South America. I just wanted to get in touch before he leaves. As far as I know he's left his job already. Do you happen to know his whereabouts?" There was a silence. "Or maybe someone else who might know how he can be reached?"

Finally the voice replied hollowly, "I'm afraid that won't be possible, Mr. Wallis. Howard isn't going anywhere. His car was forced off the road somewhere near El Paso late last night. The police say it was a marauding gang from across the border. He and his wife were both killed."

Mrs. Ryecroft came out of the kitchen to clear the last of the dishes from the dinner table. Hugh poured coffee for himself and Jantowitz. The professor was perusing an article in a folded physics journal propped in one hand, and acknowledged with a grunt.

"Did you like the pie?" she asked at her usual megaphone level.

"It was great," Hugh said.

"Well, if you start acting funny, we'll know it wasn't my cooking," Mrs. Ryecroft said as she went back out. The official story put out in the town was that a chemical had got into the water supply at TA-3, and some of the personnel working there were liable to temporary bouts of confusion and possible memory loss. Anyone witnessing such an occurrence was to contact the authorities on an emergency number.

Emma, one of Mrs. Ryecroft's card-playing friends, who was visiting, resumed talking as Mrs. Ryecroft came back into the kitchen. Confused fighting was going on in the border region between Iran and Pakistan, and aircraft from a U.S. carrier force to the south had shot down four planes that it was claimed had attempted an attack. Emma had a son in one of the air bases in Arabia, which had gone to high-alert status.

"I heard there was more trouble down at that Iranian store at the other end of town last night. Seems there was some people arrested."

"There's always somebody who's not happy unless they're making some kind of trouble," Mrs. Ryecroft said.

"Well I don't think it's right, them coming here and living off us while our boys have to be over there, risking to get killed, and trying to sort out their problems. They should be made to go back and take care of their own problems."

"Well, it wouldn't surprise me if they get closed down. . . . Selby, will you get out from under my feet."

"Seems to me they should be closed down, too. I think everybody should have to—"

The phone rang. Mrs. Ryecroft answered it.

"Here, a paper from Russia we have, analyzing genome stabilities as mathematical attractors," Jantowitz said, motioning at Hugh with his magazine.

"Let me see."

"Hugh-ugh. It's for you-ou." Mrs. Ryecroft reappeared in the kitchen doorway and brought the phone over. Hugh took it.

"Hello? Hugh Brenner here."

"It's Dave. Look, something's come up. I can't go into it now, but Sarah and I have to talk to you right away. Can you meet us at Rustlers in, say, fifteen minutes?" Rustlers was a coffee lounge that they used, near the center of town.

"Well . . . sure, I guess."

"See you there." Dave hung up.

Hugh took a long drink of his coffee and stood up. "Change of plan. I have to leave," he announced. Jantowitz was absorbed in his article again and just grunted.

Mrs. Ryecroft peered from the kitchen. "Are you okay? This isn't the sudden kind of acting funny that we're supposed to watch out for?"

Hugh grinned. "No, I'm normal. It's just something urgent that's come up. I'll see you later." He emptied his cup and left the room.

In a monitoring room used by Security in the basement of the TA-3 Administration Building across town, the duty operator who had been listening tapped a key. The recorder reset, ready for the next call.

Hugh found Dave and Sarah at a booth by the window, looking pink in the glow reflected off the sidewalk from the neon sign above the door. Dave had on a parka over a dark sweater. Sarah was in a light raincoat and a woolen hat. She looked drawn and tense. The other occupants were clustered at the far end. Hugh ordered a sweet tea at the counter, brought it back, and sat down.

"We know why the other Sarah was interested in Howard Turner," Dave said. Hugh simply returned a questioning look, and Dave went on to relate the story. Sarah stared at Hugh, watching his reaction, giving no indication of her own thoughts. Dave concluded, "I've worked among these kinds of people before, but I've never seen anything like this. This isn't just another classified program. It's obviously considered crucial to national interests, and when you've got that, nothing else matters. Sarah's pretty shaken up. I am too. This is scary, Hugh."

"So what are you saying?" Hugh muttered, propping his face against a hand. "We can't very well walk away. You've just told me what can happen." Hardly constructive, but those were the first words that came to mind.

Dave shook his head. "Nobody's talking about quitting. I just don't want any of us to be under any illusions about the way things are, that's all."

Hugh turned his face toward Sarah. "And that's how you feel too? We're still in business the way we planned?"

She looked at him as if he ought to have known better. "What made you think it might be any different?"

"I thought for a moment that maybe you were about to tell me that you were having second thoughts—that you were through helping them produce their machine," Hugh said. "We can't risk antagonizing anyone any more right now. They'd come up with more restrictions that would make life impossible."

Dave had apparently been thinking the same. "We can still go through motions that will keep everyone happy," he said to Sarah. "It doesn't mean that we can't still press ahead with *our* machine."

Sarah looked at each of them in turn for a second and shook her head. "You don't understand," she said. "I can take nasty things happening in life without freaking out. And sure, I want to see if this idea of Theo's will work, just as much as you do. But that isn't what this is all about. For me, there's more to this whole situation. It goes a lot deeper." She paused to compose her words.

"This whole place—the project, the people who run it. It's everything that I hate about the world. But walking out wouldn't be the answer. It wouldn't be the way to change anything."

This was a new turn on things. Hugh glanced uncertainly at Dave. "What do you imagine you can change?" he said to Sarah.

She sighed and looked down. "I don't know. Probably

not much. But little things can add up. That's the real reason why Sam is here too. Had you figured that out?"

"Ah, I thought we'd get to Sam," Dave said. "It sounded a bit like his ants moving mountains."

Sarah went on, "He says that all evil is rooted in delusion. One of the biggest delusions is believing that enemies can be destroyed by violence. It simply creates bigger enemies. The only way to destroy an enemy totally and permanently is to make him a friend."

"So is that what you're going to do with the people here?" Dave asked, smiling—not unkindly.

Sarah's face remained serious. "This is something that's important to me, Dave. I want to know if I can see people the way he sees them—to care, unconditionally. Of course it's easy to get along with people that you agree with. It's when you don't that it means something. That's when you learn how not to hate." She looked from one to the other again. "Okay, maybe I won't change the world. But I might learn to change something in myself. Maybe that's as much as one person can do. . . . And what better opportunity could there be to find out than this?"

Chapter Twenty

Bruce Calom was English originally, the son of a police sergeant who said that no country could survive that fined people for working honestly and awarded cash prizes to punks and "yobs"; he died when Calom was ten, shot in a drugs raid in London's East End. Calom had joined the regular British military when he was eighteen, flown on helicopter assaults in the Gulf War, and then graduated with a specialist counter-terrorism unit, taking part in irregular actions in southeast Europe, the Middle East, and Africa as political abominations created by the diplomacy of plunder and two futile world wars fell apart. He had transferred to the U.S. for two years as an advisor to Special Forces and Rangers, accepted an offer to stay permanently, and moved into intelligence with the DoD. The position at Los Alamos had followed.

Order and stability, he believed, were the essential foundation for any society that hoped to preserve a worthwhile quality of life, and endure. He had seen what happened in places where the rule of law broke down, and armed mobs and criminals took over. That no government was perfect, he would have been the first to agree; but any form of it was better than none at all. And firmness was necessary to maintain it. He had no patience for intellectuals and academics prattling about their precious rights and freedoms, secure in protected havens that soldiers had fought to create. So on the scale of survivorship that was his way of measuring worth, his kind ranked higher. They would always exist, with or without those who depended on their protection; the converse was not true. The knowledge was a source of inner satisfaction. That it was not currently fashionable to acknowledge the fact made no difference.

Thus, Calom had always been sure in his attitudes, confident that the images he held of the world reflected what was really out there. It came as something of a shock, therefore, to learn that two of just such people—and, furthermore, among the youngest, recently recruited to the project—had been uneasy about Howard Turner when no question had crossed Calom's mind. It wasn't that he had any reason to reject the official story, even now—he had received a copy of the police report the same morning that he listened to the tapes of Sarah Pacey and David Wallis from the tap on her phone. Whether it was true was not the point. The fact remained that they had been suspicious enough to check and find out, while he, the professional who prided himself on taking nothing at face value, hadn't thought to ask.

Calom went over to the P2 facility late that same afternoon, ostensibly to verify the implementation of the new measures that he had agreed with Kintner. He questioned the guards at the security checkpoints covering the entrances to the building, and then went inside to observe the procedures being followed by the technical staff. On the upper level, his tour brought him eventually to the Engineering Group's labs and offices behind the computing area.

He found Sarah working alone at a terminal in a graphics lab of the Signal Processing section. Her gaze lingered on him a shade longer than casually when he appeared, but she said nothing and carried on with what she was doing. Calom came in and looked at the screen in front of her. It was filled with programming symbols that meant nothing to him.

"I mentioned that I might want to talk to you again about Howard Turner," he said. "I received a report from the Sheriff's Department this morning. It seems that he was the victim of a gang attack."

"Oh, no!" Sarah groaned and sat back in her chair, doing a good job of looking as if she hadn't known.

"I'm afraid so. In Texas—down near the border, the night before last."

Sarah shook her head and sighed. "That's awful. Why do these things have to happen?"

"A sign of the times we live in," Calom said. "I had no idea when we talked yesterday. I'm sorry if some of my questions were a bit . . . pointed."

Sarah went through the motions of digesting the information, then looked at him questioningly. "Why are you telling me? You still think I might have had some connection with him in this world, don't you?"

"Not especially. You'd probably have heard sooner or later. I suppose I felt that if it came from us first, you'd be less likely to jump to any rash conclusions." And in a way that was true. Calom realized as he spoke that the real reason why he had come here was an irrational feeling that his bringing the news himself would somehow convey that *he* had not been involved in what had happened. For some reason it mattered to him. What she might think of others was not something he could influence.

This time it was her turn to interrogate him. She did so silently, with her eyes. He could read in them that she didn't believe him. Yet at the same time the accusation that he would have expected to accompany her conviction wasn't there. More, if anything, he was aware of a searching curiosity to know how *he* felt. It was one of the rare moments in his life when he felt confused.

"Wouldn't some people think that it happened at an amazingly convenient time?" Sarah said at last.

"Roofing contractors find hailstorms convenient. It doesn't follow that they cause them," Calom pointed out.

"So you think coincidences like that happen?" she asked.

"I think you watch too many movies," he replied.

He waited for some reaction of scorn or derision. Instead, she continued regarding him with the same mixture of doubt and curiosity. "It's important to you, isn't it—this whole system that you work for," she said finally. "I mean, it isn't just a job. You do it because you believe in it."

The remark was so unlike anything that Calom was accustomed to that none of his standard defenses was appropriate; he responded candidly. "Yes, if you must know. Evil people exist. You either defend yourself, or you go under. That's the way the world is."

"Do *they* think you're just defending yourself?" Sarah asked. "Or do they see a threat that's evil too?"

"That's just the way it is," Calom said again. "Wishing otherwise won't change anything." He hoped this wasn't about to turn into a debate. He'd heard the line before from the same kind of people, and he knew that neither of them was going to change the views of the other. Changing people's views wasn't his business, and he considered that those who tried to make it their business were wasting their time. And he had no reason to alter his own views. If they didn't follow from the obvious, he wouldn't have held them.

But Sarah sensed the impasse and steered them away. Again Calom was surprised. Intellectuals usually reveled in confrontation. He suspected they did it as a demonstration, compensating verbally for what they lacked the nerve to risk physically. "I've been trying to place your accent," she said. "What is it, Australian or something? I met a few of them when I was in Japan."

"English—a long time ago. I started out in London."

"You'd think I'd have known. Dave's English. But you don't sound like him."

"Londoners sound different—plus, being over here for years changes it. Most Americans guess Australian. Don't worry about it." This was a novelty. Calom wasn't used to people being at ease in his presence.

"What brought you here?" Sarah asked.

"The Service. I used to be with the British military—airborne and later counter-insurgency. A few of us came over on an advisor exchange scheme when urban guerrillas started becoming a problem here." Calom shrugged. "I guess I just liked the climate and stayed."

"Do you go back there often?"

He shook his head. "There's nothing to go back for. They've given the store away. All of Europe's the same. The Asians are just waiting to move in—China or Japan, whichever comes out on top in Siberia. It's going to happen."

A strained look came over Sarah's face. She looked away. "How is it that other people don't seem to feel the revulsion that I do for war and everything connected with it? . . . Kids who've never harmed anyone being taken away from their homes and brutalized into killing each other. Sometimes the thought makes me physically sick. How can anyone release weapons over cities full of defenseless people? I can't comprehend how anyone can even design them."

"It's not so strange," Calom said. "I think you'll find that most people feel the same way. But they do what they have to."

Sarah shook her head insistently. "It's what they're conditioned to do. Normal, sane people don't incinerate others alive, blow off their limbs, shred them with fragmentation bombs. . . . It's as if they have some kind of switch inside them that can be pulled to let them go away and do unspeakable things. Then they can come back and be switched off again, and play with their grandchildren as if none of it ever happened."

"Is that how you think it works?" Calom said.

"I don't know. That's how it seems. All I know is that I couldn't do it," she told him.

"Not even if everything you cared for was threatened?"

"There has to be a better way."

"People have been saying that for thousands of years. They've never found one."

"And look what the cost has been."

Both of them could see that they were not going to get anywhere—but even that was communication of a kind. "Oh, of course it's a nice thought," Calom agreed. "But you're up against human nature. And you won't change that."

"Maybe human nature doesn't need changing. Maybe it just needs to be left alone, to be what it wants to be," Sarah suggested.

Calom shook his head. "Not in the real world. I know. I've seen too much of it." He moved to the doorway, then stopped and looked back as a new thought occurred to him. His mouth took on the semblance of a smile. "But if you find another one that's different, let me know."

In the Bolthole on the lower level of the Octagon building, Sam Phniangsak sat back in one of the two couplers in the screened-off area at the rear, waiting to be thrown farther out into the Multiverse—assuming that the QUIC modifications worked—than anyone had ventured before. Jantowitz completed checks on the special modules that they had substituted in the antenna array. They were crude prototypes that Dave and Hugh had scraped together quickly, and Jantowitz's modified software was at the bare-bones stage. The goal for now was simply to prove the principle. Improvements could come later. The others were upstairs at their regular work—having them all down here together would have been too conspicuous.

"Very well, we seem to be okay," Jantowitz said, scanning his displays. "The parallel coupling, we have established." The hardware was communicating with copies of itself in surrounding realities. "We are active. You should be feeling MV connectivity now."

"Check," Sam confirmed.

"And now I have a forcing function specified." Jantowitz peered over his spectacles from the console. "Where this will send you, my friend, I don't know. Return initiation is programmed for three minutes. With all the unknowns, that should be long enough, I think."

Sam tried returning one of his jovial grins, couldn't quite manage it, and made do instead with a nod.

"Target acquired. Low-level attack bearing one thirty-six, range eleven five: five of them, coming in fast!"

"Switch to red. Lock on automatic."

"Bear Two, register on TAC six and confirm."

Sam looked around in bewilderment. He was standing with head and shoulders protruding from a hatch in an armored vehicle the size of a house, a huge gun protruding from a turret above him, a boxlike rack containing missiles swiveling around on one side. The voices were coming through headphones attached to a helmet. He was wearing a heavy, padded uniform with belt and sidearm, binoculars, accessories, and pouches. They were stationary on a road stretching across open terrain, bleak and wintry, with low hills in the distance, the sky in one direction black with smoke. The road was crowded with bedraggled soldiers who looked Asiatic, mingled in disorder with trudging refugees. There were old people, children; others sat or lay among their bundles, too exhausted to move. Some never would. More fighting vehicles and military trucks were strung out among them.

"BEAR TWO ACKNOWLEDGE!"

"Phniangsak, are you reading?"

Did it mean him? The air cracked with sudden concussions hitting his ears. A wall of flame engulfed the column on one side. People were running, screaming, some of them alight. More noise added to the din as missiles streaked up into the sky from close by, followed by gunfire.

Somebody below grabbed him and hauled him down roughly into a claustrophobic compartment of machinery, electronics, and sweating bodies. An officer in a leather skullcap and flak jacket yanked off Sam's helmet and phones, at the same time yelling into the stem mike of his own headset.

"Bear Two reading. Tracking on TAC. Scope, back up on manual." He looked more Arabic than Oriental, with large brown eyes and a heavy mustache. The confined space rang with a hammering noise as a weapon somewhere on the vehicle commenced firing.

Another of the crew shouted from his console. "Two air-launched cruise acquired from sat fix. Computers analyze attack profile veering west, upwind. Gas! It's gonna be gas!"

The mustached officer looked at Sam. "The hatch! Seal for gas!" Sam gaped back helplessly. The officer shoved him aside, causing Sam to strike his head painfully on a valve, and hauled himself up onto the step where Sam had been standing. The face of a woman appeared above, contorted in terror. She had an arm clawing frantically inside the hatch and was trying to pull something up after her. It was a child. Sam watched in horror as the officer seized a rifle from a rack and clubbed her away from the opening with the butt, then slammed the hatch and secured it.

Sam felt blood running down his face. The mustached officer peered at him. "Why the refugees?" Sam asked weakly. "Why are they killing those people?"

"I think he's freaked. We've lost this guy," the officer called over his shoulder. He shook his head and spoke to Sam. "Take it easy. It's the Whites. They're behind everything. They always have been. They want us to wipe each other out. I saw it in the Gulf. Then they think they'll take over again. But it won't be that way. We remember. You'll see."

Sam closed his eyes. "No, no, no," he groaned.

"Yes, I'm afraid. Time, it is to disturb you. A pity, since you look so peaceful," Jantowitz said.

Chapter Twenty-one

Kintner instructed all scientific and engineering grades to be present at the next weekly progress meeting, which was normally attended only by section heads and above. This meant everyone except technicians, secretarial staff, and maintenance and service personnel. He moved the meeting to the conference facility on the upper level to accommodate the larger-than-usual numbers.

The room filled well ahead of time, buzzing with curiosity and speculation. Sarah guessed it would be an official version and cover-up of what had happened to Turner. Jantowitz said it would be to urge more effort on cracking the directability problem. Phil Moody thought that as a new security measure the town would be closed, and all who used the QUADAR restricted to moving within its confines. One of the theoreticians predicted a major Asian war imminent. Sam adopted his usual wait-and-see attitude, and Hugh followed his example.

Kintner arrived and took his place between Mulgrave and Ducaine at the table facing the room, and for a while business had to do with routine matters: testing of the modified software had hit a few snags but was proceeding; somebody had an idea for stabilizing certain modes of A-field resonance that prompted some discussion; the soap in the men's rooms was gritty and made everyone smell like disinfectant, and could they find a different supplier?

That kind worked better for getting grease off. Then could they have a regular kind as well for people who hadn't been working on anything greasy? It was all standard government issue. Well, was there anything that said you couldn't supplement it from outside? Why not bring your own? Why should you have to? You didn't have to bring your own light bulbs. The subject was discussed for as long as some of the technical debates. Finally Kintner delegated it to Ducaine to delegate to somebody else after the meeting. He then cleared his throat and looked around. The room fell quiet as the mood adjusted to a more appropriate note.

"The reason why I wanted all of you here today is to inform you of some important changes that will be taking place in the organization of this project, commencing virtually immediately. Since everyone here will be affected, it's important that you all understand something of the background." Kintner paused and looked around. Attentive expressions had settled on all sides.

"I don't have to remind you of the importance of this project to the vital interests not only of this nation, but of our entire Western heritage. We expect major hostilities to break out in Asia before very much longer—according to the consensus of our analysts, a year at most. Europe will be drawn in, and ourselves then or later, either aligned with one of the rival power blocs or as eventual antagonists of whichever side emerges from the initial conflict." As Kintner had said, nobody in the room needed reminding. They had all heard it from him innumerable times. It was the standard wisdom of the day. He continued:

"We are now learning that this is not some accidental whim of fate unfolding, but the culmination of deliberate policies that were set in motion by alien interests envious of our success, over half a century ago. When World War Two ended, the leaders of the historical and cultural tradition that we refer to broadly as the Western world—ourselves, Europe, and the former Greater Russian sphere—foresaw that those interests would one day acquire the technologies that *we* had created, and move against us with their superior numbers. Because of the general war weariness and misguided idealism of the times, they were unable to acknowledge such realities openly. Therefore, they created an elaborate deception which made it possible for us to develop the weapons which alone were capable of redressing such a numerical imbalance. Our possession of those weapons kept the real threat in check for fifty years." That was the standard line, dispensed universally. Hugh had no particular reason to disbelieve it, although Sarah said it was a distortion of what had really happened.

Kintner went on, "That ended when the Soviet corner of the alliance was undermined and fell apart. Their former territories are now being contested. Unless we take measures to protect them, ours will be next." Kintner paused and swept his eyes round the room again. On either side of him, Mulgrave and Ducaine sat facing the room impassively like attending acolytes at an address by a bishop. He made an empty-handed gesture. "Protect them with what? Since the turn of the century our opponents have been arming openly and matching us. Their numerical preponderance has increased. Their zealousness to right past wrongs—for the most part fabricated by unscrupulous opportunists—leaves them unamenable to reason."

He raised an arm in a sweeping gesture to indicate not just the room but the whole facility around them. "Ingenuity, not force, is the answer. We believe that the understanding of MV phenomena that has been achieved here at the LANL is unique in the world at the present time. That is why all work has been concentrated and placed under military security. Initially, the aim was to provide our political leadership with a means of finding an optimum path through the difficult choices ahead. Then, more recently, we stumbled—there's no other word for it—upon the remarkable possibility of being able to actually experience nearby areas of the Multiverse directly. Applied intelligently, such a capability offers the prospect of deducing facts about our own world that could never be ascertained purely from the information accessible within it." Thus far, Kintner had given a potted version of his routine pep talk and summarized what everyone already knew. The audience waited, sensing that he had come to whatever he had called them together to announce.

"Washington considers rapid development of such a capability crucially important—which is why we've all been under pressure. But more is involved than just providing capability. For its potential to be realized, that capability has to be made available to the appropriate intelligence-gathering agencies. For them to use it effectively, they need to begin gaining experience at the earliest opportunity that it's possible to arrange. And we for our part need their inputs to guide us in producing what's wanted." The gold-framed bifocals swept around the room one last time.

"It has therefore been decided to implement close working relationships between us without further delay. To that end, an advance team of intelligence operatives selected for their technical backgrounds will be arriving early next week to commence familiarization training. A part of the facility will be set aside for their use while an extension of the QUADAR is being installed in additional space to be provided alongside this building. This ancillary project will operate under direct orders from Washington, but with a local coordinator who will liaise via the Laboratory's General Director. Its code designation will be 'Polygon.' "

"What they're telling people about the Russians isn't true," Sarah said to Hugh and Sam over lunch in the TA-3 cafeteria later. Dave was with Jantowitz in the Bolthole. They had completed another of the special hardware modules the previous evening and were using the lunch hour to test it. "There was never any secret understanding after World War Two. You've only got to read what was written at the time. It was real. Communism was real. We were all set to annihilate each other. The

Soviet empire bankrupted itself trying to keep up. They weren't undermined by the Chinese."

"That isn't the way people are hearing it," Hugh remarked. It wasn't his subject. He had never really understood what the European wars of the last century had been about, or why America had to get involved. He took another bite from his burger. He'd been inclined to go for the fish, but changed his mind on overhearing someone remark that it didn't taste right.

"It's just brainwashing and propaganda, setting them up for next time," Sarah said. She shook her head in short, rapid movements and looked at Sam as if for support. "I don't believe anything that comes from governments. They lie habitually and compulsively. It's their way of life. Why can't people like you run the world, Sam?"

Sam considered the question while he finished chewing a mouthful of salad. He had been quieter than usual for the past several days. "Perhaps if I tried to run the world, I would no longer be a person like me," he replied finally.

It wasn't quite the kind of answer that Sarah had expected. "You think that just having power can change anyone?" she said. "It doesn't simply attract people who are corrupt already?"

"I think it's an extremely complex question that I don't have the answer to," Sam said.

"Is that really so, though, Sam?" Hugh queried. "I mean, if circumstances had been different, could you ever have ended up as a completely different person— say, doing the kind of work that, oh . . . Calom does, for instance?"

"Oh, very easily," Sam answered in a curiously quiet voice. "I *know*."

The communicator in Hugh's shirt pocket buzzed. He fished it out and held it by his face. "Hugh Brenner."

Ducaine's voice squawked at him. "Hugh, Neville here. We're ready to try driving the forcing function this afternoon. Jeff's people are practically done on the hardware. It's your turn in one of the hot seats, so we'll want you back here first thing after lunch."

"I'll be there," Hugh replied.

It was a first attempt at using information from Jantowitz's map. So far, the system could be forced into a resonance that would induce a transfer, but the mode of resonance was random: there was no way of knowing what kind of reality the transfer would be to. Now, some of Peter Mulgrave's people had used Jantowitz's results to generate a set of constraints that they believed could be imposed to confer something corresponding crudely to direction. The hope was to be able to launch a transfer on specific bearings, rather than simply letting it jump where it would. Achieving that much would at least enable "shots" to be clustered, hence opening up the possibility of repeat visits to the same reality—which was what Washington was particularly interested in. Figuring out how the bearings tied in with particular targets could come later.

Since this was official work, the tests were all short-range excursions into the MV neighborhood, showing near-variations of the familiar world for the most part, but with occasional abrupt changes in the way that was becoming familiar.

In the course of the tests, Hugh found himself suddenly in the middle of a meeting with Ducaine and others, not knowing what was being discussed—they all knew the routine too, of course, so there was no cause for surprise; next he was sitting in the lab, doing nothing of special interest; then on a phone, with no idea whom he was talking to; he found himself sitting in the same coupler, not realizing he had transferred at all until the random number checks were compared; then he was in the medical office, feeling extremely queasy after a fish lunch that had upset a number of people; and finally he was jogging on a trail along the edge of South Mesa, with no clue as to why he wasn't working.

It was all fairly routine, ending with a half-hour general

discussion in the machine area to review the day's findings. The only unusual thing had been a couple of instances where the correct resonance had occurred, but no transfer had followed. This had not happened before, when no attempt was being made to direct the transfer. It wasn't an intermittent fault, which was the first guess, for the same thing turned out to have happened with several other subjects too that afternoon, using different couplers. Mulgrave assigned it for further investigation in the morning.

Afterward, Hugh went with Jantowitz to the cafeteria for a snack dinner. Then, bringing back sandwiches in a bag to keep them going later, they returned to P2 Building and went through to the Bolthole. Jantowitz was curious to try out the new technique with one of their longer-range, "QUICkened" couplers.

"Remember you are no longer the tourist," Jantowitz said from the console. "Now it is time to start the working visits, yes? We need for the maps all information on where it takes you: who is the President; what things are in the news; what are the movies they watch; what is their politics, their economics, their sciences, their history. Everything you can bring back, we need."

"You're sure that's a complete enough list?" Hugh said dryly from the coupler. "I mean, I am going to have all of fifteen minutes there. I'd hate to waste half of it by running out of things to do."

"Probably enough it is for now," Jantowitz said in all seriousness, watching the screens. "Now, attention please. Hardware check is okay. The parallel coupling, is active, yes. MV connectivity should be established."

Hugh felt the Multiverse opening out in his mind. "Check."

"Forcing function is primed, and . . . initiated." Jantowitz looked at Hugh expectantly. When Hugh continued staring back at him, his expression changed to a frown. "You are still here?" he said after a few seconds.

Hugh spread his hands and shrugged. "Zilch. Nothing's happening. It's doing it again."

Jantowitz inspected another screen of data. "You are right. We have resonance; but transfer connection we do not have."

"Unlucky," Hugh said. "In all the tests we ran this afternoon, this happened twice. Now we get it first time."

"Let me be sure that I have these settings correct." Jantowitz lapsed into semi-intelligible mutterings as he reverified codes and numbers. Hugh waited, wondering if the mapmaking task was really practicable. Every minor variation of any situation or event represented a potentially different dimension in MV space. How could they hope to put together a map of something like that? Even somebody as stubborn as Jantowitz had to be aware that this could be insurmountable.

"It looks okay. So we try a different set," Jantowitz said finally, rekeying a string. "Again, please." But the result was the same as before. So were the next five combinations that he tried.

"Theo, this isn't the way it was this afternoon," Hugh said. "There has to be something radically wrong. Maybe it isn't the same thing at all. It could be Dave's hardware."

"The hardware, we tested at lunchtime. It tested okay," Jantowitz insisted.

"Then it has to be in your driving code somewhere. The only thing we can do is abandon this run and go through the whole thing line by line."

Jantowitz shook his head obstinately. "The codes and the forcing function, I have checked. It is activating, but we do not achieve a connection to anything out there. The machine is trying to send you somewhere, but the Multiverse is saying you can't go. Something is happening that we have not seen before."

The next two tries were the same. And the next. At Hugh's insistence they repeated all the tests on the special hardware module that Dave and Jantowitz had conducted earlier. Then they verified that Jantowitz was following the same procedure as had been used earlier. They reinstalled the software and retested it. By 2:00 A.M. Hugh was back in the coupler for another try. The same thing happened again.

"Theo, give it up," Hugh said wearily. "It's time to go away and do some more head-scratching."

"Perhaps if the gain factors on those loops, I reduce to give more bandwidth. . . ."

"You've done all you can do here, and I need some coffee."

"And suppose we avoid that region completely and set all theta values negative. . . ."

"Are people like you born obstinate, or did you have to work at it?" Hugh said testily.

"I *beg* your pardon!" the distinguished-looking man with the white mustache and the dark suit, sitting in the seat alongside him exclaimed in an outraged voice.

The back of the van ahead, framed in the windshield, was getting bigger at an alarming rate. *"Watch it, man!"* somebody else shouted from behind.

Hugh tensed, waiting an agonizing split second for the driver to react; then a pit opened in his stomach as he realized that *he* was the driver—on the wrong side of the car. He wrenched the wheel desperately, hitting the brakes. *Wrong way!*—traffic coming straight at him; but no—it was on the wrong side of the road. No time to think, just get out of the way. They hit the grass verge on the far side amid cars swerving and honking, brakes screeching.

"Jesus bloody Christ!" a different voice from behind yelled as the car bumped to a halt.

Hugh stared at the unfamiliar dash panel layout, found the key, and turned it to kill the motor. He threw a helpless look over his shoulder. Two more men in suits, one pink with anger, the other looking terrified, were straightening themselves up after being shaken all over the rear seat.

"You said knew your way about over here," the one in the passenger seat blared irascibly. The vehicles that had halted around them were not models that Hugh recognized. The houses were different.

"Decided yer've 'ad enough of life, 'ave yer?" a truck driver called, glowering down from his cab. English accents. Cars had stopped. A couple of drivers were getting out.

"Extraordinary! Never seen anything like it in all me life," one of the two behind muttered.

"Get him out of there. Let John drive, for God's sake."

Even though he himself was the intruder, Hugh hated the Hugh who was supposed to have been here—where he belonged—who it seemed, somehow, had gotten him into this. There was a peal of rising and falling siren notes, and a white police car appeared from the opposite direction, lights flashing, and drew up in front of them. Two officers in peaked caps got out and strode over. Hugh wound down the window resignedly. He pictured Theo back in the lab, probably scanning through a magazine and munching on a sandwich while he waited for the transfer to time out— and he hated him too. Get all the information you can. It was preposterous.

"Everybody all right here? . . . Good. Could I see your driving license and proof of insurance, please, sir?"

Hugh looked up ferociously. He'd had it with this whole stupid business. What was there to say?

"Can you tell me who the President of the United States is, what's in the news today, and the top five movies?" he asked. "And while you're at it, how would you summarize the current political system, economic situation, and the state of scientific progress?"

He felt a malevolent inner satisfaction at the startled look on the policeman's face. *He* would only have to wait this out for another ten-or-so minutes. His unknown, hated other self could do the explaining when he took over again.

Chapter Twenty-two

The officer who would take charge of Polygon locally and coordinate with Willard was introduced as a Colonel Elson, reporting directly to General Ventz in Washington. Elson was a squat, solidly built man with pink, fiery features, crinkly yellow hair, and a pugnacious disposition that made him treat everyone as if they were subordinates in the Army. But he got things done. He appeared one day amid a group of engineers surveying the proposed site adjacent to P2; in the course of the next few days he organized a whirlwind series of technical meetings between Octagon people and DoD-assigned specialists flown in from various places; and in less than two weeks results were apparent.

Two portable, windowless, single-story office buildings arrived on enormous trailers and were set in place next to P2. Construction teams erected a fence on three sides, which with one wall of P2 formed a compound within the TA-3 site. Over the following days, a procession of trucks began delivering crates, furnishings, machines, and supplies. Army Engineering Corps crews connected utilities; antenna arrays and communications dishes sprouted on the roofs; NSA technicians moved in to install the specialized equipment. Armored cables laid in a concrete-lined trench connected to the P2 building. A security checkpoint was established to control access from the side door of P2, while a guard post commanded a gate through the fence to the general TA-3 area.

Meanwhile, the first of the intelligence personnel who would be operating Polygon arrived to commence their familiarization training. Pending completion of their new facility, several rooms on the upper level of Octagon were reserved for their use. They were intense, unsmiling people, who did not mix with the project personnel, ate and spent their off-duty time separately, and when they talked outside their own group at all, did so only in reference to the work at hand. Their unvarying attire—male and female alike—consisted of loose-fitting black pants, soft shoes, and a lightweight gray polo-neck sweater. They quickly became known throughout the project as "the spooks."

While the spooks were settling in and becoming part of the P2 background scenery, the scientists turned more of their attention to the growing mystery of understanding what linked the bewildering varieties of other selves that their experiments were beginning to reveal. It seemed that everyone existed as just one instance of countless alternate personalities scattered across the Multiverse yet all somehow connected together. What, exactly, was it, the scientists asked themselves, that ended up thus connected?

"What do we mean by a 'personality'?" Peter Mulgrave asked the people sitting and sprawled around his office. It was one of the informal gatherings that could happen at any time, especially when problem areas were being encountered that could produce thoughts at odd moments. A lot of them had decided to take a break from the experimental work in any case. Activity with the couplers was continually being interrupted by computer down-outs resulting from the work in progress on the link to Polygon. Jantowitz was there, along with Ducaine from the Engineering Group, Helen Almer from Mulgrave's group, and Dennis Ursell, one of the mathematicians.

"What I mean is, all these things we've been calling

'copies' of ourselves are obviously connected together somehow. But into what? What is this . . . 'entity' that they form? What property of identity do they all share that defines it?"

It wasn't the first time that such a question had come up. Ducaine voiced one of the common speculations more or less automatically. "Genetic signature?" he suggested. "Individuals in other realities who possess the same genotype." Somebody had proposed it after hearing about Jantowitz's earlier work involving DNA and MV communication.

Mulgrave shook his head. "It sounds too contrived. Do you mean that if you changed one gene in me, then I wouldn't be me anymore? I can't really buy it, Neville. Besides, we had a case the other day where somebody— you, in fact, wasn't it, Helen?—saw themselves in a mirror during a transfer and had different color eyes."

"Right," Helen Almer confirmed.

"So there. Altered genotype, but still connected," Mulgrave concluded.

"Your other self, she couldn't the tinted contacts have been wearing in the eyes, I suppose?" Jantowitz said, after a pause.

"No, I checked," Almer replied. It was surprising how good they were all getting at thinking of things like that. Nobody bothered bringing up any of the other possibilities that had been talked about before.

Mulgrave made a brief gesture toward Ursell and went on, "Dennis has been having a look at Theo's model of stable regions of MV space forming attractors. We think that these things we call copy personalities might possess the same kind of structure: connected systems of attractors extending across the Multiverse. Exactly what defines them, we don't know. But a big part of the project that I can see ahead of us is finding out."

Jantowitz sat forward in his seat, interested. Now that Mulgrave had said it, it seemed an obvious possibility to have considered earlier. And it had an immediate bearing on the problems that he and Hugh had been running into.

Basically, Mulgrave was suggesting that the various "personas" that a subject could find him or herself transferred to were not distributed all over the Multiverse, but clustered in certain preferred regions of it. The nearest comparable thing that came into Jantowitz's mind was the strange mathematical object known as the Mandelbrot Set, from the branch of mathematics that deals with complex numbers.

The infinity of ordinary numbers can be represented by the infinity of points on a line. In an analogous way, complex numbers correspond to the points of a plane. The Mandelbrot Set is the collection of all the complex numbers that exhibit a particular property when processed in a special way, and it can be illustrated graphically by showing the regions that those numbers occupy on such a plane. The pattern that results is astoundingly complex and defies all intuition. At first sight it appears to consist of odd-shaped islands fringed by wartlike buds, but increasing the magnification reveals more of them, no two ever exactly alike, down to any level of magnitude without limit. Furthermore, none of them is isolated; although the filaments might be invisible below a given scale, all parts of the Set retain a peculiar connectedness. Mulgrave was saying that the continuity of individual identity across Multiverse space arose from a similar kind of connectedness in an entity not yet understood. The others in the room got the gist without its needing to be spelled out.

There was a short silence while they entertained their various thoughts about it. Then Helen Almer said, "These . . ." She looked around. "What are we calling the persons who make up this . . . what is it, this kind of 'total self'? We need a different word than 'copies.' I don't think it really applies."

"It might not even be accurate," Mulgrave said. "If the Multiverse gets more different as you move farther away, why shouldn't the people in it?" He paused inquiringly.

No one disagreed. "I thought, maybe, 'connected analogs' captures the concept better," he suggested.

"Very well, these connected analogs . . ." Almer said.

"We could call them Conans," Ursell threw in, smirking.

". . . if they exist as restricted island regions, it would explain why we couldn't always get a transfer when we tried directing the flip. Maybe we were trying to project somebody to a part of the MV where there wasn't any analog of them to project into." Which was a technical way of saying that there were worlds in which no version of a particular individual existed, either because they had died from some cause, or because they had never been born.

Mulgrave nodded that this was the point he had wanted to make. "Exactly. And it would explain why we always got a transfer before: When the system was unconstrained and free to do its own thing, it followed the continuity and always made a connection."

Jantowitz leaned back and stared at the far wall. It also explained why the problem had been worse when he and Hugh tried directing transfers over greater ranges. Nearby worlds—the kind being explored in the official tests— would generally be similar to the home world, and the chances of having an analog in them would be high. More distant regions, on the other hand, would contain relatively few connected analogs, making the chances of hitting one correspondingly less.

What this suggested was that he and Hugh had been going about things in the wrong way. Blindly giving the system a set of "bearings" and hoping that it would find an analog there to connect to was absurdly inefficient. That Hugh had made any transfer at all over longer ranges was probably pure luck. The better way would be to let the machine find islands of connectivity by free-flipping; then use the drive parameters to force repeat visits back to the same place. Jantowitz nodded vigorously, causing Mulgrave to stop in mid sentence. The others stared at him curiously. Yes, yes, he told himself: *That* was the way the system should be used.

✧   ✧   ✧

Not far away, in a part of the Theoretical Group's lab area outside Sam Phniangsak's office, Sam summarized his background and its relevance to MV theory. Four spooks, all in their late twenties to early thirties, three men and a woman, listened expressionlessly. He explained his belief that from time to time through history, individuals had appeared with exceptional sensitivity to information diffusing from other parts of the total reality that was only now being recognized. Such individuals tended to be viewed as "inspired," and their visions attributed to various traditional supernatural sources. Usually they were unable to interpret them in any other way themselves.

"Are there any questions?" the spook who seemed to be the most senior asked his squad before they moved on to the next item on their itinerary.

"I have a question," one of the men said. He was taut and athletically muscular, with sandy hair, tanned features, and wide, china-blue eyes. His name was Kerney.

"Yes?" Sam acknowledged.

"Is this tantamount to scientific proof that God exists? Is the Bible now validated by physics?"

Sam studied him for several seconds, searching for terms that would be acceptable to both of them. In the end he replied, "The world that we see is governed by processes beyond the ability of any human mind to comprehend, which can only make us conscious of our limitations. And in subtle and complex ways, what we come to experience is determined by our decisions and actions. So it should be possible to find the better paths, if only we can learn to read the signs. This is all that true religion has ever tried to say. The concept of 'God' seems as valid a way to describe such workings as any other."

"Thank you."

Sam was unable to tell if he had made any impression. Then he noticed Dave by some cubicles in the background, motioning to catch his attention. He seemed to be trying to signal without making it obvious to everyone that something was urgent. Sam indicated with a nod to the leader of the group that he was through.

"Your talk was appreciated, sir. We are grateful for your time." The other three murmured their concurrence, and they all left.

Sam went over to join Dave. "What is it?" Sam asked in a low voice.

"It's Sarah. Since the schedule's all messed up today, we decided to slip in an extra run with one of the special couplers down in the hole. But they downed the main computers half an hour earlier than they were supposed to. It cut the connection dead, without executing the return sequence. She's still out there. There's no way to get her back."

They left the work area and hurried down to the Bolthole. Sarah was in one of the couplers at the rear, comatose and looking restful. Sam ran quickly through the status indicators on the screens. The system was dead. It might as well not have been there.

"You don't automatically return on deactivation," Dave said needlessly. They had talked about the possibility, but it wasn't something that any of them had cared to play with. He was clearly worried, speaking for the sake of something to say.

Sam patted Sarah's cheeks, lifted an eyelid, tested her pulse at the temple. She seemed normal enough physically, anyway. He moved to the console and tapped in the call code for Operations Control. A few seconds later a man's face appeared on one of the screens.

"Ops, this is Alan. Oh, hello, Sam."

"Hi. Who's supervising there?" Sam asked.

"Lester, but he's up to his ears right now. Can I help?"

"This down-out that we've got. It came on early, and we were just about to go live. How long is it going to be this time? Does anyone know?"

Alan looked surprised. "That shouldn't have happened. We weren't showing any time slots for couplers. That was why Colonel Elson across the way told us to go ahead."

"Er, yes . . . Maybe someone forgot to log it. But it's messed us up. Can you tell us when we're due up again?"

Alan didn't look very reassuring. "There's some major reprogramming going on for the link to the new building," he said. "It isn't going to be today, I can tell you that much for sure."

Chapter Twenty-three

Sarah was in an airy, sunny room, with large picture windows on two sides forming the corner opposite the door, and a central skylight above. It seemed to be some kind of workroom or studio, with framed and unframed pictures covering the walls, more standing in a rack on one side, and shelves loaded with books, jars and cans, brushes and paints, and other items that she recognized as artist's materials. There was an easel with a canvas mounted; a table below one of the windows, with matting and framing tools in a rack above; a scarred wooden desk in a corner; and a chest of wide, flat drawers—the kind used for storing prints and drawings—nearer the door. An armchair stood by a low side table, and plants in hanging pots over the window ledges added some color and freshness. The abruptness of the transition from the machine environment of Los Alamos emphasized the calm and serenity. She was getting more used to finding herself in unfamiliar situations by now. Her immediate reaction to this instance was regret that it would be for only twenty minutes at most.

She herself was sitting before a large, flat screen, more than two feet across, supported on a jointed brace that enabled it to pivot to any angle like a draftsman's table. It seemed to be a kind of electronic painting system, and had a keyboard of unfamiliar pattern below, and a horizontal surface to one side, covered in sketches and notes. A strip across the top of the screen presented a palette of colors, and there was a rack containing styluses with various-shaped tips—apparently free moving, with no wire connections. The whole thing had a more stylish look about it than the equipment she was used to; less stark and utilitarian.

The partly finished picture was a street scene set against a background of splendid buildings. The people in it were flamboyantly dressed, all, it seemed, striking dramatic poses and showing purposeful faces. The unfinished side of the scene showed blocked outlines and skeleton forms with details yet to be worked in, all rendered remarkably like a canvas development using the techniques that artists were familiar with and preferred. She had seen nothing like this in her own world.

She got up and wandered around the room, inspecting the pictures on the walls. Although the themes were varied, from landscapes to portraits, lone figures to city scenes, abstracts and studies, there was an eerie feeling of recognizing in works she had never seen before a common element that she knew was "her." The whole room was an expression of "her." She moved to the windows and looked out over a small grassy court with ornamental pond, bordered by a white stone balustrade entwined in greenery and roses. Beyond and below was water bounded on the far side by a shore of tree-covered hills dotted with villas. She went out through a glass door. The air was warm, scented by blossoms. The stretch of water below was an inlet, opening to islands and ocean away to the left. The sky was blue and sunny, with gossamer streamers of cloud high up. A gray and white cat curled on top of the balustrade turned its head to regard her lazily for a moment, then resumed contemplating the scene. She rather envied the Sarah who inhabited this world, she decided.

She walked slowly around the pond and looked back at the house, presumably hers. It was comfortably roomy, with outside steps leading up to a balcony framed between high bay windows, and the main roof sloping to a higher level. The studio formed an extension at one end, balanced by a glass-enclosed patio and greenhouse at the other. It all looked well kept and maintained.

Something beeped once at her waist. She realized that she was wearing a white, shirtlike top with loose rust-colored slacks. There was a gadget with buttons, vaguely resembling a TV remote, in a pouch attached to her belt. She took it out and studied it, but could make nothing of it. It didn't beep again. She put it back in the pouch and turned to look out over the balustrade.

Below were terraced shrubs and flower beds above a lawn. A dark-skinned woman in a floppy hat was hoeing weeds from one of the beds. A girl of perhaps four, wearing a plain cotton dress, was watching. She looked up when she caught the movement above. Sarah made a small wave with her fingers. The child seemed confused and clutched at a leg of the woman's baggy pants. Sarah shrugged and went back into the house.

The studio door on the far side opened into a short hallway that led to a sitting room with casual, comfortable decor and furnishings. Shelves of books lined one end, and a corner was fitted out as an entertainment center, with a large screen angled at 45 degrees to the room, and equipment around it that she didn't understand. There was a brick fireplace halfway along, and above it a large, framed picture that she knew again instinctively as "hers." It was a striking composition that seemed dedicated to lauding the strength and grandeur of three eagles.

From the sitting room, an archway with folding partition doors led to a more formal room, with armchairs and a couch richly upholstered in a striped, silky material. It had a regency style table and upright chairs, bureau, and cabinets, all in polished walnut, and a baby grand piano in the bay of one of the windows that she had seen from the outside. Past that was a dining room, equally sumptuous, with lots of chinaware and glass.

As curious as any woman in a new house, and sure by this time that she was alone, she abandoned caution and

went on through to where the kitchen had to be. The girl
who was in there began speaking just as Sarah came through
the door, then stopped abruptly.

She was maybe eighteen, thin, with long, braided hair
and a flat-nosed oriental face, dressed in a white blouse
and navy skirt. The man with her was a few years older,
also swarthy. They looked at Sarah uncertainly. She smiled
in a way that she hoped would be natural, intending to
walk through to another door that she could see at the
far end. But the effect on the girl seemed to be to make
her nervous. The young man stiffened, and for a moment
met Sarah's gaze with what seemed to be defiance; then
he lowered his eyes. Ungracious houseguests? Surly
relatives? Sarah didn't need to find out. She walked past
them to the other doorway and came out into a passage
that brought her to the front hall. A living room opened
on one side, and stairs with thick carpeting and carved
bannisters led upward toward the higher end of the house.

More to just get away and be on her own again, she
began climbing the stairs. When she reached the landing
that formed a corner halfway up, a chime sounded from
the front door below. She stopped and hesitated. . . . But
she could hardly leave whoever it was standing there. In
any case, she would only be around for a few more minutes,
she told herself. And she was curious. She went back down.
Just as she got to the bottom of the stairs, the girl who
had been in the kitchen came running into the hall.

"I'm sorry, ma'am. I was drying my hands." She hovered
anxiously, as if expecting Sarah to move aside.

"It's okay," Sarah said, puzzled, and opened the door.

The eyebrows of the woman standing on the other side
of it shot upward in surprise. She was tall, somewhat older
than Sarah (at least, older than Sarah presumed herself
to be; the long-jump experiments hadn't established yet
if age correlated across transfers), and overdressed for what
appeared to be the climate—gaudily in Sarah's opinion—
with tucks and folds, lace and trim, festoons of jewelry,
and a wide-brimmed sun hat decked in flowers. With her

was a shorter, plumper woman with dark hair, as much ornamentation, and an even more ridiculous hat. A large car, white, gleaming, and looking very luxurious, stood in the gravel driveway behind them. A brown-skinned man was sitting in the driver's seat.

They marched in, depositing hats, shoulder wraps, and purses on the girl's outstretched arm as if she were a hall stand and not giving her a second glance. "Michelle!" the tall woman exulted. (That was another thing—as analogs became more remote, their names tended to change along with everything else.) "I know this is terrible of us, but you're such a darling that you can't possibly mind. Mae and I were over at Julia's and got away early, and it was so close that we couldn't resist stopping by. If you're good and promise not to talk any of that nonsense about artists needing privacy, we might even treat you to lunch. Artists need to be sociable, just like the rest of us. We mustn't let you lose the knack."

Sarah waited, still holding the door. The tall woman looked at her oddly, then glanced in the direction of the girl, who was hanging the hats and other things. "Is your friend coming in too?" Sarah inquired, indicating the car with a nod.

"*What?*" the tall woman gasped. Behind her, the girl dropped one of the purses and stooped hastily to pick it up.

"*Really!*" the plump woman exclaimed. She had turned pink and sounded outraged. "Gwen, perhaps we ought to go," she said to the taller one.

Suddenly Sarah thought that maybe she didn't like this world so much after all. And especially, she was beginning to suspect, she wouldn't like at all the version of herself who came with it.

Gwen drew herself upright, her expression disdainful. "If it's *really* so inconvenient, Michelle, you've only to say so. But that's hardly a justification for personal insults. I'm quite shocked. In fact, more than shocked. This isn't like you at all."

"I'm not sure I want to stay now, anyway," Mae said

primly as Sarah closed the door. She turned and snapped her fingers at the girl. "My things."

"Suit yourself," Sarah said disinterestedly, opening the door again.

"*Michelle!*" Gwen screeched. From the frantic movements of her eyes toward the girl and back, Sarah gathered that she had broken a taboo. Dazed by what was happening, the girl held out one of the wraps toward Mae.

"No, you stupid creature. That's the wrong one!" Mae told her vexedly. Flustered, the girl offered it to Gwen.

Gwen pushed it away and turned her back on her. "No, Mae, I won't hear of it. We will *not* be pushed out into the street like common hussies. Michelle, something's the matter with you. Let's go inside. We need to talk . . ." she gave a long, pointed look in the direction of the girl, "privately."

Only minutes to go, Sarah thought to herself. What the hell? She took the wrap from the girl and thrust it into Gwen's hands. The girl, completely bewildered, turned and retrieved Mae's wrap and hat from where she had hung them.

"We're not leaving! Are you deaf?" Mae shoved them back at the girl savagely, knocking the hat out of her hands and causing her to lose her balance so that she stepped on it. "*You little cretin! Look what you've done!*" Mae shouted.

The girl spread her hands helplessly. "The mistress says one thing, you tell me another. How do I know what I am supposed to do . . . ?" She subsided abruptly, evidently realizing that her outburst transcended the bounds.

Gwen stared at her speechlessly for several seconds. Then she turned her head slowly toward Sarah. "Well?" It was as if she expected Sarah to do something.

"I am sorry. Everything is happening so strange all of a sudden. I get confused," the girl was saying frantically.

"She talked back at me," Gwen said in a disbelieving voice.

"Frankly I'm not surprised, considering the hard time we're giving her," Sarah said.

"Oh God. I think I need to sit down," Mae faltered weakly.

Gwen had turned a shade paler. "You can't *condone* it. She must be corrected." She looked at Sarah demandingly. Sarah could only stare back mutely. Gwen gave a haughty snort, produced a device similar to the one at Sarah's belt, and pointed it at the girl. The girl cringed, then emitted a cry as her arm convulsed in a spasm that lasted for several seconds. Then Sarah realized with horror what the metal bracelet around the girl's wrist was. She had noticed it in the kitchen and taken it to be a piece of plain jewelry. The young man in the kitchen had been wearing one too. And the woman gardener at the back of the house . . . And then she remembered, sickeningly. So had the child who was with her.

"Get out! Get out, both of you!" she screamed, seizing an arm of each of them and propelling them violently back through the doorway. *"Bitches! Monsters!"* A torrent of wraps, hats, and purses spilling contents down the steps followed. Sarah slammed the door and turned her back to it, breathing furiously. The girl watched, awed, and then retreated back toward the kitchen.

Sarah stood with her eyes closed, debating with herself whether to follow after her and try to explain. Explain what? What did she have to say that could mean anything here? Then, as she collected her thoughts together again, she remembered something that she had noticed on her way through the dining room. She found a way back there, avoiding the kitchen.

It was one of the ornamental plates mounted along the ledge running high up on the walls all around the room. Three flags behind three faces, and below, inscribed on a golden scroll among foliations, the words "GRAND ALLIANCE," and the dates 1939-1946. The flags had caught her eye, though the significance had failed to register at the time. They were Old Glory of the USA, the British Union Jack . . . and the black swastika in a white circle on a red ground of the Third Reich. The faces, she could see now, closer up, were Roosevelt, Hitler, and one that Sarah didn't recognize.

"The grandeur that was Rome." . . . Three eagles.

She made her way shakily back to the sitting room where the bookshelves were and began scanning the titles. Would her alter ego also share her interest in history? *Heritage in Jeopardy*. A quick perusal of the flap copy showed it to be an account of how America had come to the aid of Britain and Germany in their fight to save Europe from Asiatic barbarism in the form of Soviet Russia, later allied with Japan. *Stalin, the Perverted Genius*: personifying hatred going back to the Mongols. *Red Terror*: socialist atrocities—persecutions, exterminations, death camps— that the war was fought to ensure could never happen again. Also, there was a set of *Encyclopaedia Britannica*. Although there couldn't be much time left, Sarah collected an armful of volumes and carried them over to the large table. She sat down and began flipping pages, absorbing headings, dates, figures as fast as she could, using all the techniques she had been practicing.

World War Two had started in late 1939, yes . . . but with *Stalin's* attack on Poland! Sarah was aware that both Germany and Russia had invaded Poland from opposite sides, but in the history taught in her world, the Russians' involvement was played down because they had later became allies. Here it was the other way around. Germany had allied with Poland against the communists, and Britain and France had joined them in 1940 when Poland was overrun. There had been no hostilities in the west; no Dunkirk; no Fall of France; no Battle of Britain. Instead of Churchill, Britain had been led by Halifax, who gave up his peerage to become Prime Minister.

Sarah became too engrossed to notice that it was way past the time when she should have been brought back.

When the Russians reached the Rhine, took Persia, and threatened Egypt from Palestine, and Japan moved against European possessions in Asia, America launched a Pacific campaign. The tide gradually turned in both eastern and western theaters. Japan fell first, then realigned against the Soviets, and a massive strategic air bombardment developed as the ring closed, culminating in the nuclear destruction of Moscow, Leningrad, Stalingrad, and Vladivostok.

Sarah had just begun reading about the establishment of a rigid postwar colonial world order under the hegemony of unchallenged U.S.-British-German military supremacy, when the front door chime sounded again. She heard the serving girl's footsteps clatter across the hall, and then voices. Then the sounds of a number of people approaching. Only then did she register with sudden alarm that it was long past the time when she should have been recalled.

The man who entered was wearing a light gray suit and spectacles, and smiled reassuringly. The woman with him, in a dark jacket and skirt with a white blouse, was unsmiling and matronish. Two men in white smocks, broad shouldered and hefty, followed behind them. A man and woman in uniforms that looked like police waited just inside the doorway.

"Now, Michelle, there's no need to be alarmed," the man in the gray suit said. "We're here to help you. You've been having a tough time lately, isn't that right?" She stood up, but there was nowhere to go. The orderlies were moving around to get behind her. There was no point in resisting.

They took her to some kind of a clinic in a town not far away, and from there to a hospital. They talked unctuously and smiled, but there was something behind it all that Sarah found chilling. She sensed fear. Beneath the harshness and the arrogance they were insecure. She didn't seem to understand that violating their code was a threat to everybody. The little that she said made no sense to them. Obviously she was very sick. They gave her a tranquilizer to help her sleep. Tomorrow, they told her, she would go to a place where she could rest. The last thing she knew before she passed out was terror at the thought of being trapped in this nightmare.

But she woke up to Sam shaking her. "She's back," she

heard him say. The relief in his voice was like a huge weight lifting. "Okay, Sarah, you're fine. . . ." His voice sounded less direct as he turned to address someone else. "I think she's okay."

Sarah put her arms out and hugged him.

Chapter Twenty-four

"Fascinating!" Kintner pronounced after listening to the surveillance tape of Sarah describing her experience to Sam and Jantowitz. "We allied with the other side, so the received wisdom became that Hitler helped save the West from Asiatic hordes. Afterward, we joined in a comfortable carving-up of the world with his successors. That's why there has never been an immoral war: the winners always write the histories. Does that sound cynical? Oh, but who am I talking to? I hardly have to tell *you* about such things, do I?"

Sarah had "returned" early the following morning, when the system was restored after an all-night session by the engineers installing the Polygon equipment. She seemed fine as far as Sam could tell, but he told her to go and get a proper medical check nevertheless, on some pretext. Dave and Hugh had taken her back to her apartment to shower and change, and then for breakfast, in the course of which she had presumably told them her story. She repeated it for Sam and Jantowitz after returning to the lab around mid morning. Throughout her extended time in the coupler, the rest of the group had kept at least one of their number in the Bolthole at all times to intercept anyone wandering in. By morning they were getting very concerned. However, Jantowitz persuaded them to at least wait to give something a chance of happening when the system came up again. When it did, she recovered promptly, none the worse except for some stiffness, a pronounced weariness, and the emotional effects of her experience.

Calom inserted a different cartridge into the com unit by Kintner's desk. "This is Sam talking to all of them later this afternoon, after he and Jantowitz had discussed things in Sam's office," he said.

"All of them together in the Bolthole at the same time?" Kintner remarked. "Starting to get a little careless, aren't they?"

"They had been very anxious," Calom said. "A sudden relief from stress makes people drop their guard."

The screen showed the view looking down over the Bolthole floor area, with Sam half turned away, Jantowitz partly visible, and the back of a head that looked like Dave's. It had been recorded by a miniature camera installed behind a ventilator grille by one of Calom's people the night that Peter Mulgrave gave Jantowitz use of the space.

Sam's voice came over the audio. "Well, we've discovered something else that's new. When the connection is broken suddenly, without the shutdown sequence being executed, awareness consolidates somehow in the analog. You don't simply come back in the way we assumed."

"It was scary," Sarah said from somewhere off–screen. "I was really beginning to think I was trapped there."

"So long as you're over it now," Dave said.

Sam went on, "About these long jumps. There's a moral question we have to face, that Theo and I have talked about. I'm sure we're not the only ones that it has occurred to. Hugh almost got four people killed not long ago. Now Sarah has landed another version of herself into what kind of trouble, we can't imagine. She might be a very different Sarah from the one we know, but that's not the issue." He gestured briefly. "You can see the problem. Short-range transfers are almost invariably to worlds similar to this one—with analogs doing the same things as ourselves, here at Los Alamos, among people who understand what's going on. But over the longer ranges that we're getting into down here, that doesn't apply. The analogs exist in situations that are totally different, where people know nothing about transfers or what to expect—probably in worlds where no machine like this was ever built at all. And in cases like that, these sudden intrusions could be disastrous."

Dave's voice came through again, and the head in the foreground turned. "What are you saying, Sam? That we should call off the whole thing and stick to the short-range official program—now, just when we're getting somewhere?"

"Maybe just that—for now, anyway," Sam answered.

"Oh, I hope not," Kintner murmured in an aside to Calom.

"Hell, no." Hugh's voice this time. "The risk works both ways. I'll take mine."

Sarah spoke. "But you don't have a right to force it on an analog who doesn't have any choice. Sam's got a point, Hugh."

A short silence fell, broken eventually by Dave. "I hate to say this, but it sounds to me as if we're telling ourselves that the powers in charge are right."

"Hardly for the same motive, though," Hugh said.

"Maybe. But it doesn't change the facts," Dave replied.

"Well, thank you for crediting us with something," Kintner muttered.

Some inconsequential discussion followed on whether it might be possible to control the return process from the other end somehow. Sam had made attempts to signal back by altering the field configuration in the same kind of way that he had been able to force a flip, but with negative results. The chances of achieving anything in that direction appeared slim. Then Jantowitz, who had not figured in the exchange so far, moved into view.

"Maybe there is a way," he said. "If I can provide the coordinate numbers that will send you back again to the same places, what we do is this. First, we let the machine find us the connection to where an analog exists. We send

you through for just the quick look to see the situation—
a few seconds is all, maybe. And then we bring you back.
You say then 'yes it is okay there,' and you go back; or
you tell us, 'no, abort,' in which case you don't, and we
leave it alone. In that way, the risks, they are minimized."

"It's a thought," Dave agreed.

Sam considered the proposition. "*If* we can get a
workable system of coordinates. We must have
repeatability."

The suggestion put a new light on things. The upshot,
after more debating, was that the group would press ahead
cautiously along the lines that Jantowitz had proposed.

"This arrangement of leaving them alone is working out
extremely well," Kintner said to Calom. "They have given
themselves the strongest motivation to make the process
repeatable. And repeatability is what Washington wants
us to achieve."

Calom said nothing. At first, the decision to allow the
Bolthole group to proceed without interference had been
a purely internal matter within LANL and the DRA. Now
there was Polygon, with its connections to Washington.
Polygon was supposed to be kept up to date on all
developments taking place in Octagon. Covering something
like this up could create a dangerous situation for Sarvin
in the political rivalry that Calom's instincts told him would
emerge sooner or later.

Hugh came out of a store in town after finally making
a trip that he'd been putting off for weeks to get himself
some more socks, underwear, a couple of shirts, and another
pair of tan casual pants to work in. Why was it, he wondered,
that women seemed to love to shop, while men hated it?
Maybe another of Nature's ways of tricking them into being
compatible.

Older people said that the stores were not like they
used to be in years gone by. There was less variety these
days—fewer choices and styles; just piles of the same
identical products everywhere, getting shoddier all the

time. And from the old movies and pictures that Hugh saw, the towns and streets used to be brighter, somehow, and more cheerful in appearance too. Things seemed to have been better kept and maintained—less of the peeling paint, faded signs, cracking pavement, and decaying timbers that made everywhere look so tired and exhausted these days. It was as if people back then believed in a future that it was worth making some effort for.

A girl that he recognized came out of a pharmacy door just ahead of him. She was almost his height, with shoulder-length blond hair and fresh, open features—not at all bad. Today she was wearing a brown suedette jacket with light blue jeans. She was from the Lab, though not with the project. They had caught each other's eye and exchanged smiles occasionally in the TA-3 cafeteria. She paused for him to catch up when she saw him.

"Oh, don't worry, you're not being followed," Hugh called ahead. "I had to come into town to do some chores."

"You don't exactly look the type to be worried about."

"Going that way?" Hugh asked needlessly, indicating with a nod of his head.

"Yes—catching the one-forty shuttle at the Post Office."

"Me too. Mind if I tag along?"

"Sure."

"We could even practice the dying art of talking to each other," Hugh said. "I heard somewhere that people used to do things like that." She gave him one of her smiles. They began walking again, past the shopping center.

"You're with Octagon, right?" she said. "Over at the back in P2? They just put up a couple of new buildings there."

"Right." He didn't volunteer anything further, and presumed she'd know better than to ask.

"I'm with the FEL laser people in R3—a number hacker. My name's Irene, by the way."

"Hi. I'm Hugh."

"What kind of background are you from?—I mean workwise."

"I started out in physics. These days, you name it."

She glanced at him, as if deciding finally that he could be interesting. "I heard you're from California."

"Hey, what's this? People talking about me already? Hear my side before you listen to any of it."

"I didn't hear anything bad."

"Who told you?"

"Oh, a friend of Sarah who goes with that English guy you work with mentioned it—what's his name?"

"Dave Wallis."

"That's him. . . . You're in the same lodgings, right?"

Hugh nodded. "On Forty-third Street."

"So what part of California are you from?"

"I moved here from Berkeley—I was at the University there. But I'm originally from farther north—Chico. How about you?"

"East Coast. I used to be with what's left of NASA, but there's no money in science for science's sake anymore. Anything that doesn't *have* to be right because it's military is being run by lawyers and bureaucrats. They tell you what results they want your research to produce, to fit with their policy. It's crazy."

She talked easily and pleasantly. Hugh decided that he liked this person. Maybe the Brenner penchant for unerringly drawing the wrong kinds of female had changed. Surely he was due an evening off for a change. Where could he invite her out? A dance at the Lab social center? A drink somewhere? But not right now. Save it till they were just getting off the shuttle bus. Don't rush things, he told himself.

They came to the open square in front of the public library. A small crowd was listening to a man talking about Jesus, while another man and a woman who were obviously with him stood a short way back, holding bibles. Two young children were handing out pamphlets with a religious picture on the front. One of them came up to Hugh—a brown-skinned girl of perhaps ten, with long hair and big, round, intensely deep eyes. She offered him one of her pamphlets. Hugh grinned and took one. The girl returned a wisp of a smile and moved away.

"Why encourage them like that?" Irene asked as they moved on.

"Oh, why spoil a kid's day?" Hugh answered, realizing only as he spoke that her voice had changed. She sounded sharp and irritable.

"But that's not the point. Isn't there enough superstition and unreason in the world as it is? It's because too many people tolerate it. That's why the world is coming apart the way it is, and you're helping it along. I mean . . . don't you *care*?"

Hugh felt as if he'd pressed a button and started off some kind of taped reflex. He answered perfectly honestly. "What, you mean if other people want to live their lives in their own way and raise their own kids according to what they believe in? No, I don't care."

"Well, you should."

Hugh sighed. "Why does everyone have to have ideas about how I should live and what I ought to think? I don't go around telling everyone to be like me. But first those people are wrong for being the way they are, and now I am. Couldn't that have something to do with what's wrong with the world, too?"

There was a prickliness between them now, and it wasn't going to go away. They went back to TA-3 together, but the talk between them was perfunctory and remained distant. He didn't bother asking her out when they got off the bus. Instead, he spent the evening debugging software.

Everyone had an answer to everything, that they wanted to impose on everyone else. Nobody could just let others be. Except for a rare few like Theo and Sam, maybe. But how many took any notice?

Chapter Twenty-five

Jantowitz and Ursell came up with a solution to the repeatability problem less than a week later. Subjects could be sent back to the same reality time after time. The results were duly reported to Washington, and Willard received a personal message of congratulations from the President. The way was now clear for Polygon to become operational as planned. Willard judged this to be the opportune time to level with Sarvin. Willard's nature was not to play at intrigues, and he had been uncomfortable for some time about the unauthorized work that he had been allowing to continue.

They met in the first-class passengers' courtesy lounge at Los Angeles International Airport. Sarvin was en route for Washington, returning after a three-day getaway in Hawaii, and in good spirits; Willard had come out to the West Coast to meet with some of the contractors involved with projects at Los Alamos.

"Leonard, today we have a happy President because of the news from the Lab," Willard said over his bourbon. "And that's good news for both of us, right?"

"It's given me the first break that I've managed to enjoy for a long time, and that's not something that happens every day," Sarvin agreed.

Willard nodded in a way that said it confirmed what he had been hoping to hear. He lowered his voice. "Then there's something that you ought to know about."

"Don't tell me you're going to spoil it now?"

Willard shook his head. "It's just that you should know the full story of how it came about. . . ." He looked around and leaned closer over the arm of his chair. Sarvin waited, puzzled now. Willard sipped his drink and paused to choose his words. "You remember that proposition that those two people we brought in from Berkeley came up with— Brenner and the Polish professor?"

"They wanted to try for longer hops." Sarvin said. "The word from on-high was no-go. Our problems are closer to home."

"Right." Willard nodded. "Well, after they were turned down, they came up with a scheme to do it themselves on the side, in their own time. We were aware of it, naturally—from our surveillance. Anyway, Ed Kintner figured that letting them go ahead would be the best way to get them motivated into producing what Washington wanted—and avoid internal hassles at the same time. It sounded good to me. So I said what the hell and agreed."

Sarvin was frowning. "You mean you overrode policy? You let them do it?"

"Well, we didn't actually override anything. The official work went ahead as directed. It was more a case of exercising discretion where judgment of internal affairs was concerned." Willard saw that Sarvin might come around, and pressed his point. "Scientists can be notoriously temperamental to handle. I didn't want to go creating complications that would go bouncing up and down the line. . . . And it paid off, Leonard. We wouldn't be celebrating right now if we'd gone the official route."

Sarvin considered the situation. Starting a fight now would only risk appearing petty. He had always thought of himself as a practical kind of man. Wasn't it the results that were supposed to matter? "Who else out there knows?" he asked.

"Just Ed Kintner and Calom. Five people are involved: Jantowitz and Brenner; Wallis, the optronics man from England; his girlfriend, Sarah Pacey; and Sam Phniangsak."

"Him again?" Sarvin breathed.

"We've got everything on tape, and access into their files. They keep it to an out-of-the-way place downstairs that Ed arranged for them to use. As the proposal said before it was turned down, all it needed was a few hardware changes and some special software."

Sarvin worried at one of his front teeth with a knuckle. "This whole MV thing is going to get political now that the military are involved. We don't need something like this in the closet, Jesse."

"I know. That's why I wanted to bring it up. It's gained us the immediate objective. Now we can think about regularizing the longer-term situation."

Sarvin sat back and reflected for a while. Willard attended to his drink and remained silent. At length Sarvin asked, "What kind of results are these people getting?"

"Actually, quite remarkable," Willard replied. "To be frank, I think it would be a tragedy to terminate what they're doing, just arbitrarily. It might not be wise from the point of view of further productivity, either."

"I want to see all the surveillance material that you've collected, plus an evaluation," Sarvin said. "And from now on I'm to be kept posted on new developments as they happen, via encrypted transmissions direct to Washington. I'll give you a decision on it when I've got a better idea what we're talking about."

"I'll get Calom onto it first thing," Willard promised.

He felt relieved. It could have gone a lot worse.

Calom appeared in one of the data analysis labs, where Sarah was sorting field profiles on a screen according to the system of categories that Mulgrave and Jantowitz had devised. It was the quiet period around early evening, when the day workers had left and those who would be staying late disappeared for a meal break. No one else was in the vicinity.

"Good evening, Ms. Pacey," he said.

"Oh . . . hello."

"Working late again. I'm glad that you are able to muster such dedication in spite of your reservations."

Sarah shrugged. "Where else is there to go if you want to work on MV science? Your people have seen to that." She appended a note to an index and filed it. "Anyway, there isn't a lot else to do in this town."

"Where's David Wallis?" Calom inquired, looking around.

"Is our private life part of the official program to be checked up on too, now?"

"Nothing official. I was just curious."

"Is there anything you're not curious about?"

"It comes with the job." Calom smiled faintly. "But you ought to approve. Isn't curiosity supposed to be a quality of good scientists too?" He came into the room and moved across the floor to stand behind her.

"Dave will be helping Jantowitz downstairs later," Sarah said, keeping her eyes ahead. "They're probably over in the cafeteria, getting something to eat." She didn't know if Calom was staring at her, or contemplating the screen over her shoulder with the routine inquisitiveness that he directed toward everything. When the silence had persisted for a while, she asked, "What happened in the end with those itinerants?"

It was a question that Calom had been expecting for some time. "I really can't say," he replied. "It's a matter for the state authorities, so not something I've made it my business to follow up."

"But I thought we were supposed to be called as witnesses. I haven't heard anything. It isn't right. We could have cleared them—or at least helped put things in perspective. Those people weren't criminals—not the hard-core kind that was assumed."

Calom sighed. "Still convinced of the inherent goodness of human nature, eh?"

"Not with everyone. Just mostly."

"Yet at the same time you abhor war, which has always been humanity's prime preoccupation. A contradiction. You can't be unaware of it."

"A preoccupation of leaders, you mean," Sarah retorted. "They lie. They betray the people who trust them. And they survive because people like you are loyal to them." She gave him a withering look. "You still don't believe they could have murdered Howard Turner, do you? Or if you do, you won't admit it. Why is it so hard to accept? They're the same people who brought you Stalingrad and the Somme, Hamburg and Hiroshima."

"I told you before, I think you watch too many movies." Calom moved around to read the manufacturer's label on the equipment that she was operating. Before she could pick up on the theme, he went on, "They simply accept the world as they find it. If you want the real source of what puts them where they are, look to your precious masses. You can't have leaders without followers. Get rid of one bad one, and by tomorrow they'll have found themselves another."

"Not if they were left alone."

"But they don't want to leave everyone else alone. They'll swarm after anyone who tells them that their petty hatreds and bigotries are justified, and delight in killing each other rather than question them."

Sarah sat back from the console and looked at him. "So why not try telling them the truth instead?"

"They don't want truth. It's not often obvious what the truth is. It can be complicated, and then not turn out to be what they want to hear. They want simplicity and certainty. People are never more ferocious than when their prejudices are being threatened. Then truth becomes the enemy, and they'll die fighting it."

He moved away a few feet and paused to trace a finger along a bundle of cables running into one of the cabinets serving the coupler area. Sarah regarded him: lean and wiry, in a navy blazer and black polo-neck; taut features, close-cropped hair; his eyes, old for his years. They had seen a lot. His remark about certainty had hit home. She wondered how far it applied to her. Had he said it as a hint for her to examine her own premises?

She had been working at the mental exercises that Sam described, to see if they altered her or her attitudes in any way. Now she found that, either for that reason or because something about Calom was different, although her feelings about the things he symbolized hadn't changed, she was no longer able to personify them in him. For the first time she was aware of him as just a lonely, disillusioned human being. In a way he was like Sam—doing what he was able to, armed with the principles that he believed in. Neither had delusions about the world. Calom saw it as it was; Sam saw what could be.

"They were going to call it Oracle at one time. Did you know that?" Calom stepped back and ran his eye over the equipment panels. "It was more appropriate to the original goal of helping with policy decisions. But somebody thought it might tip the opposition off, so they made it Octagon instead."

"No, I didn't know that. I guess everything's changed beyond recognition."

"It does still perform the original function, though—right?" Calom checked. "What it did before you discovered this business about wobbling off into other worlds. It does still do that?"

"Oh yes. Some groups are still working on it. It just isn't the only priority anymore."

Calom looked along the cabinets. "It looks like the inside of a smart laundromat," he commented. "What do they do?"

Sarah got up from the graphics screen and crossed the floor to where he was standing. "Really, they're all just front-end encoders for the big machines next door. They transform raw Multiverse field samplings into data streams that can be processed."

"None of these is the oracle that sees into the future, then?" he said.

"It can't tell the future." Sarah started answering before she realized that he was being facetious. She carried on anyway, "What it does do is weight the probabilities of the possible outcomes of a course of action. Any value judgment is purely subjective."

"You mean, what's likely to happen is woven into what's out there," Calom said. "Whether it actually does happen, and whether I like it or not, depends on me."

"Exactly . . . Well, pretty close." Sarah had the feeling that he knew more than he was letting on. She had noticed before his Socratic way of drawing people out to reveal themselves.

He moved to the control console and tapped experimentally at a few of the keys on the supervisory panel—at present inactive. Then he turned to look at the coupler itself, stooping to inspect the antenna array frame over the recliner from all angles. "But this is where it all comes together. Even after all the computers in this building have done their thing, the result of it all still can't be printed out or put on a screen in a way that means anything. It still has to be funneled into a brain. The only processing system capable of making sense of it is the one that needed three billion years of evolution to learn how."

"It's not really that different from a telescope having to deliver ultimately to an eye," Sarah said. She added dryly, "You seem to have done your homework."

Calom prodded the recliner's padding here and there, then turned and sat down in it. "Ah, well, knowing what's going on is my job, isn't it?" Sarah didn't respond. He spread his elbows loosely on the rests and tried them for comfort, like a prospective buyer in a furniture store. "Better than the dentist's. This would pass in first class. You mean they pay you for lying in these all day?"

"Does your dentist?"

Calom smiled and eased himself back. "So," he said, letting his head fall back into the support and gazing at the equipment above him, "if I wanted to ask your oracle something, how would I talk to it?"

"You focus your thoughts on the option that you're considering, and . . . just open your mind up to what comes back."

"How do I read it when it does?"

"You'll know."

Silence fell for a couple of seconds. "Do you know, I've never tried this myself," Calom said. "Now I'm curious. I saw the confusion that it created among the others when they all rushed into it at the beginning of the program, and decided to have nothing to do with it. But it would be a shame to have to leave this place one day and not know what it was like. Don't you think so? How long would it take to set up?"

Sarah was taken by surprise. "Now, you mean? You want to try it right now?"

"Why not? It seems like a quiet time. Is there much involved?"

There was no reason to refuse, and in any case Sarah was hardly in a position to. "We'd have to go through a one-time personal calibration procedure that takes about five minutes. The file gets stored, so you're set for future runs afterward." She moved to the console and indicated it with a gesture. "I can do it if you want."

"Okay," Calom told her. It was really what he had come here for. "Let's go for the ride."

Sarah initiated the system and took him through the routine of tuning the system to his personal response pattern. By the time he was able to call numbers that she jotted on a pad, he was visibly impressed. She ran some tests involving randomizing to verify that the effect vanished when there was no bias in the future outcome, and ended by saving the file. "That's it. You're in touch with the universe," she told him.

Calom wasn't sure what he was supposed to feel. He hadn't gone into some kind of trance in the way he had half expected. He still had all his faculties and was fully aware of everything about him. In a way, it seemed anticlimactic. "What do I do?" he asked. "Am I supposed to reach out somehow?"

"Let it come to you. It's better if you close your eyes."

Calom did. "It's still . . ." he began, and then his voice

trailed away. There was a sensation of his mind opening up into a limitless void, as if he had existed all through his life in a cave, and the walls of the cave and the mountain that contained it had suddenly fallen away. He was suspended in a web of frozen time—not simply a single, linear time, but a superposition of alternate futures enmeshing him from every direction. And as he moved his vantage point mentally, the whole constellation altered to become a dance of changing patterns that defied comprehension.

At first his mind reeled. Then, gradually, he remembered what Sarah had said and made himself focus on images. There were whores in Santa Fe. He had thought of going there that evening. Warmth and company, just for a short while; the odor of a feminine room. He contemplated the prospect: of changing, leaving his apartment, driving down into the valley; a couple of drinks, a solitary dinner; then Madeline's place on the edge of town, maybe? . . . Impressions filled his mind of embitterment, futility, weary disillusionment. Probably accurate, he conceded; but it could as easily have been dredged up from any of a thousand memories as be a revelation of anything in the future.

Intrigued now, he gathered his thoughts and focused on the real problem that had brought him here. Should he go over Willard's head and have the illicit work down in the Bolthole discontinued? When he looked in that direction in the new light shed by the machine, all that came back were premonitions of ongoing antagonisms and a numbing, all-enveloping sense of entrapment. There was no future that way with any incentive. The alternative, then, was to let things continue as they were—at least, for the time being—against what felt like his better judgment. He considered that.

And there, like a light in a fog, Calom sensed the one way through the maze that led ultimately to peace in his troubled life. He had no specifics; it would be risky. But it was the only path that beckoned. And then something else came tumbling out of the confusion of tangled impressions and feelings. Amidst it all, the issue of Howard Turner was immensely significant. That was as much as the oracle could tell him.

He brooded for a long time after returning to his office in the Administration Building. Then he picked up the phone and placed a call to Major Mike Schlager of the New Mexico Anti-Terrorist Force.

They met late that evening in a bar on the outskirts of Santa Fe. "I need some information that I don't want to get through the system," Calom said. Schlager nodded. "It concerns somebody from the Lab who got canceled not long ago. His name was Howard Turner. The line is that he got in the way of lowlife from over the border, down near El Paso. I want to know if there was any internal involvement by the firm."

Schlager considered the request. It sounded straightforward enough. "What did this guy do?" he asked curiously.

"He wanted to go and work in an orphanage with kids," Calom replied.

Schlager raised his eyebrows. Calom's need to know could have been for any of a number of reasons, none of which made any difference. That was how the network functioned. "I'll see what I can dig up," he promised.

Chapter Twenty-six

The Bolthole group established that repeatability also worked with the long-range jumps that they were experimenting with. A further, surprising discovery in the course of their explorations was that connected analogs were not necessarily the same age. In fact, over far enough ranges, they didn't even need to be similar in physical appearance. This made a kind of sense, for as Mulgrave had observed a long time before, if, in general, worlds grew progressively more different the farther apart they were across the Multiverse, why shouldn't the same apply to the individuals within them? But it made the question of exactly what it was that remained "connected" all the more mysterious.

Jantowitz gazed approvingly at the handsome young man staring out of the mirror above the bathroom washbasin. He judged himself to be somewhere in his mid twenties, and had dark, curly hair and attractively rugged features with deep brown eyes shaded by pronounced, curving lashes. When he experimented, he found that he had a smile that came naturally, revealing white, even teeth. And the broad shoulders, solid chest, and slim hips that came with it all was something that the younger Jantowitz had never been blessed with at any stage. Not bad at all, he thought—even if he did say so himself.

He was wearing a dark red shirt with casual gray pants something like jeans, but not the same pattern. The bathroom looked like that of a private house. It was clean, cheerfully colorful, and cluttered with bottles and toilet articles all over the place, travel posters on the walls, and a rack stuffed with magazines between the pedestal sink and the tub. Jantowitz examined a few of them curiously. They were printed in Polish and covered computers, political humor and satire, theater, cartoons, and popular science. Loud music and the noise of many voices came from beyond the door. Students, Jantowitz told himself. A party. He hadn't been to a good party for years.

He moved to the door and was exhilarated to feel himself light on his feet, his body lithe and muscular. Curious, he opened the door and stepped out into a downstairs hallway, pausing to adjust his nonexistent spectacles. The house was filled with young people sitting and standing, holding drinks, chattering and laughing. There was dancing in a room opening off on the far side from the front door. A youth who had been waiting nearby went into the bathroom and closed the door.

Then a girl in a short red coat detached herself from a group talking loudly at the bottom of the stairs and came over, smiling. She was slim and good looking, with long, fair hair hanging loose, and white purse slung over a shoulder. "What kept you so long? I thought you'd fallen asleep in there."

"Oh, sorry," Jantowitz said, not catching on. "Were you waiting?"

She slid an arm around his neck and rubbed suggestively against him. "Yes, but not for that. . . . And just so that you know, I asked Anna and she said it wasn't and never had been. So there."

"Oh," Jantowitz said.

The girl turned away toward the front door, at the same time reaching for his hand. When he continued standing where he was, she looked back, seemingly surprised. "Well?" she said.

"Well what?"

She leaned closer and murmured in a more intimate tone, "Are we going?"

Jantowitz was about to ask where, when he suddenly understood. For a second or two he just stood frozen in disbelief. Then, slowly, a gleam came into his eyes. "Why, yes," he said. "Of course."

She looked at him oddly. "Well, I'm glad about that. . . . You're sure you haven't changed your mind?"

"No, not at all," he said hastily, and began following after her.

"Don't you want your coat?"

Jantowitz looked cluelessly at the coats hanging thick on pegs by the door, piled on the hall table, and draped over the bannister. Hell, what did it matter? He rummaged through the pegs and pulled out a blue zippered jacket that looked about his size.

"You're leaving, then, Alma?" a girl's voice called out above the din behind them as he pulled it on.

"Parties are for when there's nothing better to do," the girl in the red coat's voice answered laughingly. So, her name was Alma?

"Have fun."

"That's the whole idea."

A young man in a sweater moved close to Jantowitz and grinned knowingly. "You won't enjoy her, you know, Gustav," he murmured. "Take my word."

"Why not?" Jantowitz asked him. (He was Gustav?)

"I didn't." He nudged Jantowitz playfully in the ribs. "Just joking. No, really we're all jealous. She's gorgeous. Oh, by the way, how is it looking for Monday?"

"Er, fine," Jantowitz told him.

"They'll be there?"

"Yes."

A frown. "But I thought you said it looked fine."

"Oh, my misunderstanding. I meant no."

"Good. . . . Well, take care."

Alma was waiting, holding the door. Jantowitz went out.

She slipped an arm through his as they began walking. The street was narrow with houses on both sides, and led to a wider thoroughfare where he could see lights and traffic. He hesitated for a few paces, then put an arm around Alma's waist and drew her closer. "That's better," she said, and turned her face to kiss him on the cheek. "I thought you'd gone cold all of a sudden."

Her hip felt firm and round, and rocked seductively as she walked. He licked his lips in the darkness. "Do you think I'm crazy?" he answered.

Then he felt the car keys in the jacket pocket, and his pace slowed involuntarily. Not his jacket. The keys wouldn't fit his car, even if he knew where his car was. He thought frantically. "What's up?" Alma asked him.

"Erm . . . do you have a car that we can use?" he said.

She looked puzzled. "But of course I do. That's where we're going. Yours is being fixed. Isn't that why you came with Zep?"

"Oh, yes."

They came out onto the wider street among shops, restaurants, and a couple of bars, and started walking past parked cars. The first two were Russian, well made and expensive, and the next, German. Beyond that, Alma opened the door of a low, sporty looking model, silver gray in the streetlights, and then went around to the driver's side. Jantowitz got in and closed his door. He sneaked a look across the car as Alma climbed in beside him. Her legs were long and shapely beneath a short, tight skirt. She had a perfume that was captivating. Jantowitz decided that he had just become a lapsed atheist.

"You said it was about ten minutes from here to your place?" she said as she closed her door. She looked at him expectantly. He stared back, helpless. She smiled. "But that's a long time. Just to get us there . . ." Soft hands pulled his face closer. She turned her face toward him, her lips pouting.

❖   ❖   ❖

"Just checking," a voice said. Jantowitz opened his eyes and blinked. "How is it? Do we send you back or abort?" Dave was standing in front of him. Hugh was behind, at the console.

"No, no, we don't abort," Jantowitz said hurriedly. "Very interesting, it is."

"Okay." Hugh reached toward the keyboard.

"No, wait!" Jantowitz thought frantically. There was no point in going back now. He had no idea where Gustav's place was. But Alma had said about ten minutes. Give them fifteen to be sure. "Not right away," Jantowitz said. "I would like to verify your parameters for the z-matrix first."

"Sure." Hugh voided the entry and shrugged. Dave looked surprised. They had succeeded twice already in making a transfer back to a previously located analog, once with Hugh as the subject, once with Dave. Jantowitz got up, went over to the console, and began running through test screens. The other two thought he was being overly fastidious but said nothing. The professor was notorious for being finicky and plodding, but events had proved him right more than once. A full quarter of an hour went by before he pronounced himself satisfied and went back to the coupler.

"A brandy," Alma's voice said. "Peach if you've got it."

They were in the living room of a house or apartment, with the lighting low and music playing. Again the surroundings looked studentish—but comfortable. He was sitting on the edge of an armchair, staring at a cabinet with several doors as if about to open one. He could smell perfume on his face and taste lipstick. His shirt was unbuttoned, and he became conscious of having a strong erection. Peach brandy? He stared perplexedly at the doors and opened one at random. It contained stationery and cardboard boxes.

"Don't you know where your drinks are now?" Alma said behind him. He turned his head. She was perched against the arm of a couch, her shoes kicked off in the middle of the floor, skirt high on her thighs, blouse open, revealing a lacy red bra.

"You see what you do to me," he said. His voice sounded firm and jovial. That's better, he told himself. Get into the swing of this. He tried the door next and found bits of electrical gadgetry, more boxes, and some tools.

"You're *sure* you're all right?" Alma said, sounding worried.

"Why shouldn't I be all right?"

"Gustav, you just told me back in the car that you'd had a total blackout, were wearing somebody else's jacket, and couldn't remember how you got there. . . . I mean, there isn't any need to make up weird excuses. We don't *have* to do this."

"No, no! It's okay." He threw open another door. Bottles and glasses. "See," he said, pointing triumphantly. "Now, peach brandy? . . . Oh dear, I think I'm out of it. How about regular?"

"Okay, that'll be fine."

He poured her a brandy, and then as an afterthought added a stiff scotch for himself. Alma was back on her feet when he rose and turned, holding the glasses.

"Do we want coffee?" Alma asked, at the same time answering her own question with a shake of her head. "Let's take these with us." She moved toward the doorway that they had presumably entered by. Jantowitz followed, hypnotized by the sight of her swaying beneath the skirt. "Which way?" she called over her shoulder as she came out into a hall. "Here?"

"Yes." It wasn't. "No, I mean there." This time he was lucky.

The bedroom was plain and masculine, but warm and inviting.

"Oh, I like it. It's kind of cozy . . . and so 'you.' " Alma set her drink down on the bedside table and turned back the cover and sheet. Then, with Jantowitz watching, fascinated, she unsnapped her skirt and stepped out of it, peeled off her blouse, and stretched herself out. Her breasts were firm and full, and the rest of her body perfect. The miniature excuse for panties matched her bra. "Are you coming to bed, or standing there all night?" she said.

For a moment Jantowitz felt himself starting to balk. Then he pulled himself together and sent her what he hoped was a confident, reassuring grin. "Just admiring the view. Can you blame me?"

Alma smiled, but had to work at holding it against rising bemusement as she watched him tear a shoe off after getting the lace into a knot that wouldn't untie, fumble his shirt into an inside-out tangle, and then almost fall over with a foot caught in his pants. "Take it easy, Gustav. We do have all night."

Her skin was soft, her kisses delicious, the nipples under the bra, hard and eager. "I didn't know I could get so wet," she whispered.

"Time check, Theo. Is everything okay?"

Jantowitz's eyes shot open. "Yes, is okay."

"Just thought we'd better make sure—you know, since you were out for a while before we sent you back again. Can't be too careful, and all that, eh?" Dave grinned at him inanely.

"I said is okay. Hit the return," Jantowitz snapped. At the console, Hugh looked over the screens and frowned. "Well, what the matter is the hell with you?" Jantowitz demanded after several seconds had gone by.

"We may have a problem here. The coupling gain has zeroed," Hugh said.

"What! Is not possible."

Dave went back and looked over Hugh's shoulder. "He's right, Theo. I think we've lost it. You'd better come and take a look."

Jantowitz jumped up from the coupler and marched across. The matrix defining the director parameters was corrupted, with no hope of recovery.

"*Pah! Idiots!*" Jantowitz fumed. "A simple job it is here

that I give you, and what is this? Two stupids, I get! Scientists, you think you will be one day? How will this work ever get done?" He threw up his hands in hopelessness and, muttering Polish profanities, stamped away out of the lab.

Hugh and Dave looked at each other in astonishment. Both together, they shook their heads, nonplussed. "I guess that's it for today," Hugh said. He turned back to the console and began shutting down the system.

Chapter Twenty-seven

"Damn!" Peter Mulgrave said. "Okay, never mind. We'll brief somebody else to fill in, and then see you later. I hope it isn't anything serious. . . . Yes, okay. Bye for now." He took the communicator from his face and returned it to his shirt pocket. "That was Helen Almer now," he informed the people in his office. "Her car won't start. She's stuck over at TA-15 and won't be able to make it. But never mind, we can improvise without her. Let's go along to the lab, then." He rose from behind the desk and ushered the others toward the door.

Dennis Ursell got up to lead the way. Colonel Elson followed with the two technical officers who had accompanied him from the Polygon compound. They walked a short distance to one of the coupler areas used by the Theoretical Group. With repeatability finally cracked, the next objective was to achieve what Ursell had dubbed an "intersection," from the mathematical definition of the term. The several tries made so far had all encountered hitches of one kind or another. Rather than just explain it, Mulgrave had invited Elson over to see the next attempt live for himself.

Several technicians were at nearby consoles, with two couplers initiated and ready to go on-line. "Helen won't be here," Mulgrave told everybody. "She's stuck over at Pat's place with a sulking car." He turned to Elson, his mouth twitching and a light the bright side of funereal hovering discernibly in his eyes. It was the closest that any of them had seen his features come to manic laughter. "Perhaps one of the gentlemen with you could assist instead, Colonel? There isn't very much to it. It just involves a session in a coupler and following a simple procedure after transferring. The experiment requires two subjects, you see. Dennis here will be the other, since it's all his idea."

"Lieutenant Stachel, would you care to volunteer?" Elson said to one of the officers.

"I'd be happy to, sir."

Mulgrave knew Stachel's face from the earlier familiarization training. He indicated one of the two couplers with a wave. "If you'd just take that one." The lieutenant moved past the console and sat down. "The name's Stachel," Mulgrave repeated to the technician at the console. "I assume we have him profiled."

The technician tapped keys and consulted a screen. "Right, got it. Loading now."

Dennis Ursell had begun moving toward the other coupler. When he was a pace or two away from it, however, he stopped and looked around strangely. Mulgrave's eyes were on the lieutenant, and he didn't notice. The technician operating the coupler that Ursell had been about to occupy watched him suspiciously. She had seen enough incoming transfers by now to know the signs.

Ursell took in the situation calmly for several seconds, and then his expression changed to a smile. "Are we doing what I think we're doing, here?" he inquired, speaking to no one in particular. "About to attempt an intersection transfer, right? But where's Helen Almer? Did she get called away?"

Elson, Stachel in the coupler, and the other officer from Polygon were still relatively new to all this and didn't catch on immediately. Mulgrave, however, turned toward Ursell, looked him up and down, and nodded knowingly. "Just joined us, eh? I presume you're from somewhere pretty close."

Ursell nodded. "It's got to be from a universe practically next door."

Mulgrave explained to Elson and the two officers, "There are nearby parts of the MV in which they've already started the test. An analog of Dennis in one of them is coupled into the machine there and has taken over this Dennis here."

"That's correct," Ursell confirmed. "This whole scene looks identical to the one I was in a moment ago—except that I'm standing here and not in a coupler. And with us the other subject was Helen, not the lieutenant."

"It was supposed to be Helen here too, but she's stranded over at TA-15 with a dud car," Mulgrave said.

Ursell thought for a second. "In that case—" The wall phone on one side of the lab area interrupted him. One of the technicians picked it up. "It's okay, Rich. I've got a feeling it might be for me," Ursell called out. The technician held the phone out as Ursell came over. Ursell took it. "Hello?" Then, without waiting for a response, "Is this who I think it is?" He listened for a moment, then his face split into a grin. "Yes, it is. . . . Two-seven-five-zero, check? . . . So where are you? No, don't tell me. Let me guess. You're over at TA-15, yes? . . . Great! . . . Because Peter just told me that your analog was stranded there. This is absolutely terrific. I guess we open some champagne with the team when we get back, eh? . . . Well, see if you can get a ride over here before we're pulled back. It would be quite a historic encounter. . . . I hope so. 'Bye." He hung up the phone and looked across at Mulgrave. "Sorry, Peter, but I guess our world beat yours on this one. That was Helen—*our* Helen. She's over at TA-15 right now, transferred into your Helen. It went okay. The intersection function works."

Essentially, Ursell had derived a mathematical function describing the set of an individual's connected analogs extending across MV space. Regions where the sets corresponding to two different individuals "intersected," or overlapped, ought, therefore, to define worlds containing analogs of both of them. The way to test Ursell's theory was by using it to successfully transfer two subjects into the same alternate reality simultaneously. How would the researchers know for sure that both subjects had indeed arrived in the same world? Simply by arranging for them to make contact when they got there.

Hugh and Dave proceeded to modify the second coupler that they had available in the Bolthole in order to try intersections of their own at longer ranges. With the analogs scattered wider and found in more unlikely circumstances in worlds that diverged farther, making contact at the other end tended to present more formidable problems.

"It looks okay," Dave said. "Nothing threatening, no hazard. Check again in about ten minutes." Jantowitz looked back at the console and keyed in a command. By moving his eyes Dave was just able to glimpse Hugh for a moment, insensible in the other coupler. . . .

Then he was back once more in what he presumed from his brief, several-second assessment was a schoolroom. He checked his watch. It showed 3:20.

A lot of children, aged about eleven or twelve, were facing him from rows of desks with books opened on top. They seemed very orderly and regimented. The boys all had blue shirts and navy ties, and sat on one side; the girls were in light gray blouses and sat on the other. The room was stark and utilitarian. A serious atmosphere seemed to permeate the place. The children waited. Dave smiled. They looked uncomfortable, as if inured, perhaps, to the idea that teachers only smiled sarcastically.

From the corner of his eye he saw a desk with papers on top, facing the class. He turned to move closer to it, and in doing so saw the portrait in a gilt frame above the chalkboard. It was of a man with white hair and a white mustache, wearing a dark suit, painted imposingly in the manner of national leaders and famous figures. Dave had no idea who the man was. But he did recognize the faces of Stalin and Lenin flanking it in smaller frames. And there was a flag: red, bearing a former-Soviet hammer-and-sickle emblem in gold, with a British Union Jack inset in the upper left corner. Where the hell was he now?

A sheet of paper, taped to the top of the desk, showed names corresponding to the places in the room. *John Aston . . . Bryan Cummings . . . Catherine Gripton . . .* They sounded English, anyway. There was an open notebook and a folder containing loose sheets. Dave sneaked a look at the front of the notebook. Handwritten on the front was the name *T. Wallis*—apparently he still had the same surname. Below, in larger letters, was: *IV/A GEOGRAPHY*, and *(Tuesday 2:30 P.M.)*. Glancing at the chart of names, he pointed toward a freckled, redheaded boy near the front and to the side. "Ronald." The boy rose to his feet. "This is a test to see how well we've been doing. Please summarize to the class, very briefly, what we have covered in the last hour."

Several of the children seemed shocked. Others looked at each other wonderingly. Ronald seemed confused. "But, sir . . . you haven't asked me a question. I don't know what I am to say."

Dave thought rapidly. It sounded as if they only had experience of being drilled in rote answers. "This is a new kind of exercise," he said. "Make something up in your own words."

There were some astonished looks. After several seconds, a lean, fair-haired girl at the front on the other side of the room raised her hand.

"Yes?" Dave said.

She stood up hesitantly. "Individual viewpoints reflect incomplete information and inferior judgment, and are not to be trusted, sir. Correct speaking produces correct thought." The girl sat down.

"Thank you, but I'm not asking for a viewpoint on anything, simply a summary of what we've said," Dave replied. "This is my class, and we'll do things my way."

More gasps. Apparently such an innovation was unheard of. He nodded at the boy again. "Ronald, please?"

Ronald colored and looked around desperately, as if hoping to find guidance written on the walls. Finally he stammered, "The Federation extends from here in the west to the Japanese Republic in the east. Our major economic contributions are shipbuilding, heavy engineering, and aviation. Other important industries in the European sector are space technologies in Germany, electrical and nuclear in France, oil and chemicals in the former Moslem states, computing and electronics in Japan. China and Africa are the Federation's main trading partners in the free world."

Dave nodded. "Very good, Ronald. See, it isn't difficult. And when you say 'here,' you mean of course? . . ."

Ronald looked uncertain. "The British Republic, sir?"

"I know. But where in the British Republic? I want you to learn to be precise."

"Er . . . do you mean Liverpool, sir?"

"Much better. You used the phrase 'free world.' Can you tell me what that consists of?" Dave thought that might be a foolish question, but at once about a dozen hands shot up.

"Yes? . . . Virginia," he said, nodding at a dark-haired girl near the back. Ronald sat down gratefully.

"The free world consists of the liberated socialist republics outside the capitalist-imperialist empires of the Americas, Australia, and South Africa," Virginia recited. "It is led by the Greater Soviet Federation, which in turn is made up of the original Soviet Union, plus the protected territories of Scandinavia, Japan, Europe, and the Middle East."

"Very good." Dave stared, vaguely aware of Virginia sitting down again while he tried to figure out what it meant. It sounded as if the Euro-American crusade against the Asiatic hordes that Sarah had described might have gone the other way here. Before he could frame another question, however, a bell rang somewhere in the building. Dave waited for a few seconds. A few of the pupils began collecting books and papers together. "I guess that's it. We're done, yes?" he said.

"You haven't given a homework assignment yet, sir," the lean, fair-haired girl said.

"Oh . . . well, take a break. No homework for tonight," Dave said. Some of the looks were incredulous, but nobody was arguing. They stood and waited expectantly. When nothing happened, they each raised an arm across their chest and mumbled something that sounded like "Leader, party, and people," and the class started to disperse. Dave picked up his own items and headed for the door. The first thing was to try to find out exactly where he was before being returned to compare notes with Hugh.

A boy with tousled hair and heavy-rimmed glasses intercepted him at the door. "You didn't answer my question, sir," he said.

"Oh? Which one was that?"

"The one I asked just before you changed to that test with Harniman."

"Harniman?"

"Ronnie Harniman, sir. He just summarized the lesson."

"Oh, right. Remind me of the question."

"The party. When will it end?"

A young man who takes life seriously, Dave thought. He frowned and mustered what he hoped was a look of true socialist fervor. "End? Never. The party embodies the will of the people and is indestructible and immutable for all time. That's one that they haven't taught you yet, eh?"

"I meant the birthday party on Saturday, sir."

"What? Oh—when the last person leaves, of course. Why do you always want to know things like that? Let it end when it will. You take things too seriously, you know. Relax and enjoy life for a change." Before the boy could say anything, Dave marched out and left him looking perplexed.

Outside the door was a wide hall with students coming out of other doors, a stairway on the far side going up, corridors leading away in several directions. Dave stopped to feel in his pockets for a wallet, diary—anything that might give identity, address, phone number; but there were only some class notes and a typed timetable. He was wearing a lightweight working jacket, probably one that he changed into from his street clothes. Then he spotted a notice board on the wall at the end of the hall and hurried there to see what was on it. Among the bulletins, posters, and other things, he had just identified several items signed "Principal," or by various department heads, all bearing the heading WALLASEY ROAD SECONDARY SCHOOL. . . .

And he was back at Los Alamos. Jantowitz had come around the console and was standing facing him. Hugh was sitting on the edge of the other coupler. Dave quickly summarized his experience.

"Wallasey Road Secondary, Liverpool, England," Hugh repeated. "I guess you never made it over to the States in that world, eh? Maybe it wasn't that easy, from the sound of it."

Jantowitz finished jotting down notes of what Dave had said. "What do you have?" he asked Hugh.

"I'm on my own in a house on the coast, somewhere in Seattle. I think it's mine since the name on some mail I found is Martin Brenner. Address: 2705 Rayburn Avenue. Phone area code is 602, the number, 544-3327. It looks like I'm about to go out, but I don't know where. From what's in the briefcase on the table, I could be into some kind of engineering management."

"Well, better we get you both back quick, so Dave can call that number before your other self takes you away somewhere." Jantowitz said. "Thirty minutes this time, I give you."

Dave was sitting down in what seemed to be a staff room, with upright and easy chairs, a table by a window, shelves with books and magazines. Several people were standing around him, looking concerned. A woman in a

red woolen cardigan was handing him a cup of tea on a
saucer. "Nothing at all?" she said. "You mean you were in
class, and then all of a sudden you found yourself out in
the hall?"

"Has it happened before?" a man in a tweed jacket,
sitting nearby, asked him.

In a driveway in Seattle somewhere, Hugh stopped, put
the car keys back in his pocket, and turned to walk back
to the house.

"No, really, I'm all right," Dave assured everybody. "I
don't think I actually blacked out. It was more just getting
carried away by something and being a bit absentminded,
I think. Sorry if I got you worried. . . . Say, you know, this
tea is great."

One of the men sniffed. "Just your standard-issue rubbish.
Processed bus tickets or something. Not like they had in
the old days."

"William!" a woman's voice rebuked sternly.

Dave looked around, repeating the Seattle number to
himself in his head. There was a phone on a side table—
an old dial model with digits only in the finger holes. It
looked like the kind that would be restricted to internal
numbers. The woman in the red cardigan watched him
anxiously. She had a puddingish but genial face. The others
drifted off into conversation among themselves about what
food was on the restricted list this week. He was going to
need help from somebody. He motioned with a slight
movement of head. The woman leaned closer.

"Look," Dave murmured, "I don't want to alarm anyone,
but something funny is happening to me. I'm having trouble
remembering things. Where's the nearest outside phone?"

"Inside the front door, at the end of the main hall."

"Would you come with me—you know, in case it happens
again?"

The woman looked worried. "Trevor, what is it? We
should get you to the nurse," she whispered.

Dave nodded hastily several times and held up a hand. "Yes, yes, all right. I will. But there's a call that I have to make first. Can we just do that?"

"I suppose so . . . if it's really that important."

"Yes, it is."

Dave finished his tea and got up. The woman followed him toward the door. "Feeling better now, Trev?" the man in the tweed jacket called out.

"Fine, thanks. I think I'll get some air."

"Take it easy," someone else said.

"I'll go with him, just in case," the woman told them.

"Good idea, Beth," the man in the tweed jacket agreed. At least Dave knew her name now.

They walked through the hall that he had been in before, with staff and pupils heading this way and that. At the far end was an entrance lobby with an office and reception window, and two booths with telephone signs above. Dave let himself into one. The instrument was an old-fashioned dial pattern again, attached to the wall above a bare metal shelf that was loose at one end. He stuck his head outside again. "Is there a directory in the other booth?"

"You have to get that from the office." Beth's expression said that Dave should have known that. She went over to the window and returned a few moments later with a tattered phone book, missing its cover. "You're not all right, are you?"

"Just let me make this call."

He spent some time thumbing through the front section of unfamiliar layouts. Under "International" he finally found codes for other parts of Europe, northern and central Asia, and parts of the Middle East. But that was all. He opened the door again and showed the section to Beth. "Isn't there more than this somewhere?" he asked her.

"Where do you want to call?"

"Seattle, on the West Coast of the U.S."

Beth's eyes opened wide in astonishment. She glanced around, as if fearful of being overheard. "*America?* But you can't!"

"Why not?"

She shook her head. "Oh God, what has happened to you, Trevor? Private calls aren't authorized outside the Federation. You'd have to get approval from the External Affairs Office, and you'd need a good reason. I'm really worried now. Let's get you to the Dispensary."

During the rest of the half hour, Dave established that the United States had never become involved in the European war, and there had never been one in the Pacific. The communists had defeated Hitler and then gone on to take the rest of Europe. Japan fell to them in the fifties. Life in the Federation might be a bit drab, but it was a lot better than what the poor in the West had to put up with. That would change, of course, when the revolution had spread everywhere. Dave wasn't convinced that the people who told him this really believed it. It seemed more that voicing the approved line had simply become automatic.

On returning, he learned that Hugh had found an atlas and other books in the house, that described a world very like the one that Dave had been in. Hugh had also confirmed the existence of a Wallasey Road Secondary School in Liverpool by a call to the reference section of the Seattle central library. But when he tried placing a call, he was told that the British Department of External Affairs blocked unauthorized private calls from outside the Soviet Federation. No, the U.S. information service had no way of finding out if a Trevor Wallis was listed in the Liverpool area. It was close, but not close enough to satisfy Jantowitz that the case for an intersection was proved.

Then, after making another visit and learning a little more about life in the British Republic, Dave had an idea for trying it a different way. Maybe they didn't need to rely on telephones at all.

In a small apartment by a canal on the south side of Liverpool, Trevor Wallis sat on the couch and stared at the gas fire in its metal surround set into the wall. His wife, Mildred, tiptoed back from checking the bedroom where the two children slept. "They're out of it at last, thank heavens. I'm going to relax for an hour. The dishes can wait. Want to see what's on TV?" She made a face without waiting for him to answer. "Well, we already know what's going to be on, don't we? Dreary documentaries and crappy plays about perfect party people. But just in case there's something interesting . . ."

Trevor was looking around the room surreptitiously, as if it were all new to him. Mildred pretended not to notice. He had mentioned earlier that he'd suffered a couple of inexplicable blackouts recently. Probably all the strain at that awful school, she thought.

He glanced at his watch. "Never mind the TV. I feel like being decadent. Can we get something on Western radio—rock, anything, something with a bit of life in it?"

"That sounds like a good idea," she said. Trevor leaned across and switched on the radio by the fireplace. Then he stared at it uncertainly, as if it were unfamiliar to him. Mildred looked at him with a worried expression. "Trevor, that's no good. You have to use the VHF set to pick up the Western satellites."

"Oh . . . yes, of course." He looked around the room. "Be a love and do it this time, would you? I've had such a day."

Mildred looked at him strangely. Then, deciding this wasn't the time to make an issue of it, she uncovered a closet that was draped by a tablecloth and opened the door to reveal another unit—strictly illegal. It was a present from a friend of Trevor's who owed him a favor, who also had a cousin who smuggled contraband from South America. When Trevor saw it, he livened up at once. "Okay, let me." He moved over and began fiddling with the tuning dial. Still watching him uneasily, Mildred lit two cigarettes from the flame of the gas fire.

"Here," she said, passing him one just as he found some swinging dance music. "Oh, that's more like it. I'm so sick of all these funeral marches and singing soldiers. You're sure you feel all right now?"

He took a draw, exhaled, and nodded. "I think so."

"Maybe you need to see a doctor. I think the wait's about three weeks if it's not an emergency."

"Oh."

They listened to the end of the tune. Then the voice of the American announcer came through. "Hello once again. I'm Jack Wilder, your host for the hour, and this is WUNW on 1027 kilohertz F.M., America's music channel to the world out of Portland, Oregon, U.S. of A. For the next fifty minutes I'll be bringing you news, world reports, and, of course, the best music this side of . . ."

"Portland. That's near Seattle, isn't it?" Mildred said.

"Yes."

Mildred shook her head, baffled. "Why on earth would you want to call Seattle? Do you know anybody there?"

"No, I don't think so."

The voice of the announcer went on, "And next we have a request slot. Hugh Brenner, who just called in a few minutes ago from up the coast in Seattle, would like a number for a friend of his over in Britain. David Wallis in Liverpool, if you're listening, Hugh hopes all's well there and that he'll see you again soon."

"Wallis in Liverpool. I wonder if he's related," Mildred murmured.

But just at that moment, Trevor wasn't listening. His head was thrown back, mouthing a silent, jubilant *"Yeaaah!"* at the ceiling.

"Also, all the best from your other friends Stateside: Sarah, Theo, and Sam. Hugh says he'd call to say hi on the phone if he could, but since that's not possible here's a song instead. And the title he's asked for is 'Came a Long Way, Didn't We. . . .' "

Chapter Twenty-eight

A beep from the console announced that Sarah's transfer had timed out and the return sequence was activating. Jantowitz turned back to attend to operations on the console. Hugh, nursing a cup of coffee, was still lounging in the other coupler after returning. In the latest world to be discovered, he had found himself back in a very different but recognizable San Francisco. The aim had been to establish contact with Sarah, but he had been in a bus crossing the Golden Gate on a bridge that was nothing like the familiar design, and so hadn't been able to supply a phone number during their "flashback" to exchange information earlier.

Sarah had taken a strange liking to the city of domes, spires, and a peculiar, westernized, arabesque architecture that seemed to be where she lived. "Imagine 1930s Manhattan with ziggurats and pagodas mixed in," she had told Jantowitz. She hadn't managed to establish where it was, however.

Seemingly she was an artist again, in an apartment that doubled as a studio, and from the personal belongings scattered amid the general confusion, concluded that she was sharing the place with a husband, boyfriend, lover, or whatever, who was elsewhere at the time. The phone was not working, there was no number written on it, and nothing else that she had found told her very much. But

239

she liked the city. More than that, she liked the world that the city was part of. "How you can say that when nothing about it you can tell us, not even where it is?" Jantowitz had asked her. Sarah didn't care. She just had good feelings about it. Perhaps it was the QUADAR doing its associative thing again.

Sarah stirred and opened her eyes. "Yes, here she is," Jantowitz said. "Ah so, back from your otherwhere, you are again, yes?"

She stretched her limbs—always a subject's first reaction on coming back. "Hi. Too soon. I *knew* I needed to go back. I think I've found it. It's Sam's world."

"All very nice. You manage to do some work too in all this time, and find out where is this otherwhere, by any chance?" Jantowitz asked her.

"You'll never guess."

"Probably not. Or if I do, we take a very long time for no good purpose. Why not you tell us instead?"

Sarah smiled at the incongruity. "It's Detroit."

Hugh looked pained. "Detroit? You're kidding. You mean all those curly designs and fancy statues aren't even out of the country? I thought you meant it literally when you said it's Sam's world."

Sarah got up. "It's East and West all mixed up somehow. I don't know how it came about or how far back things diverged. I went for a walk around outside. The city's kind of old-fashioned, but it's neat and clean. People actually *live* there! There was a kind of a bar along the street, except not the heavy-duty kind of place that we think of as bars—more where people just go to meet and talk. It's okay for kids to go in with their folks, and you can bet on horse races and games, and nobody cares." Jantowitz sniffed. Evidently he needed to think about that.

"You got the phone number of this place?" Hugh checked.

"Yes."

"So who is this person that you share the place with? Do you find that out yet?" Jantowitz asked.

Sarah shook her head. "It seems he's out of town. I bumped into a girl on the street who knows us, apparently. I couldn't make out a lot of what she was talking about, but from some of it I get the feeling that he and I have got problems. His name's Barry. The studio and art stuff are his. I'm some kind of actress." She sighed. "Still the same Sarah. It seems I just can't get away from these bad personal scenes. But the world, I like. That's a good name that you used, Theo: 'Otherwhere.' I vote that's what we'll call it."

"Hm. The feeling gets me that you will be going back to this place many times," Jantowitz said.

"Well, we still haven't confirmed an intersection," Sarah pointed out.

"Forget it for now," Hugh said. "I'm still on the bus. But it sounds like it could be the same place. The suspension towers on the bridge could have been out of the Arabian Nights."

Jantowitz looked at his watch. "And I have other things I must do now today."

"That's good for me too," Sarah said. "There are some notes I'll need for tomorrow that I wanted to tidy up tonight."

"Not seeing Dave, then?" Hugh said.

"He's yours for the evening. Try not to let him drag you out to one of those bars."

Hugh shrugged in a way that said he had no control over it. "Hey, you know how it is with these English guys."

"Well, try and keep the clear head," Jantowitz told him. "Tomorrow we send you and Sarah back to this Otherwhere. And there you try again to contact each others."

"It was on the TV—all these whites in Africa," Mrs. Ryecroft said as she bustled around the table, picking up the after-dinner dishes. Only Hugh and Dave were in that evening. Jantowitz was still at the Lab. Ingram hadn't been seen since the morning before. "How they can't get jobs or any social services. They live in shacks, and some of them have to send their kids out begging on the streets. Hell, if it wasn't for us they wouldn't *have* any streets or social services. Sometimes I think we should just let loose with those space bombs and get it over with. . . . Get out from under my feet, Selby. You know we don't beg at the table, and especially not from the guests. . . . So what plans do you two have for tonight?"

"Hadn't really thought about it," Dave confessed, looking at Hugh and shrugging.

"It's about time you found him a girlfriend," Mrs. Ryecroft said, nodding at Hugh. "Then there'd be four of you to go places together. That's what people did when I was young. These days they can't even talk to each other without going through computers. What kind of life is that?"

"I've just about given up looking," Hugh said. "They're all fanatics about something. Every one of them's got a 'thing' that they either want to get me into or get me out of. Why can't they just let me be me?"

"Well, how did he do it?" Mrs. Ryecroft said, waving at Dave.

"If the ticket you don't buy, then the prize you won't get," Dave said, imitating Jantowitz.

"How about a quiet night?" Hugh suggested.

"*The Amanda Landrey Hour*'s on TV tonight," Mrs. Ryecroft told them. Hugh sneaked a look at Dave and pulled a face.

"I'll take you on in a game of chess," Dave offered. "I've got a bottle of scotch upstairs that we can open, too, while we're at it."

Hugh nodded. "You've got it."

Mrs. Ryecroft stepped back, holding a full tray. Selby backed and shifted as she moved away, maintaining an exact distance from her feet as if repelled by an invisible force field. "I can't figure what you see in it, just moving pieces of wood around," she said. "Nothing happens. I mean, it doesn't even have batteries."

"That's why I learned to play it," Dave said as he stood

up. "I grew up in a house with two brothers. Everything we owned, somebody else had always stolen the batteries out of. So chess was the only thing that worked."

"Your mind's not on it, is it, Hugh?"

Hugh returned from a million miles away. "Huh?"

Dave nodded his head at the board positioned on the low table between them. He had given Hugh the easy chair and taken one of the uprights. "Check with the knight, and discovered attack on the queen. Bad news."

Hugh snorted, grinned tiredly, and turned up a hand. "Didn't see it. You're right. I'm dead."

"Want another?"

"Oh, not really. Like you said, I'm not with it tonight."

Dave began putting the pieces back in their box. "Anything you want to talk about?"

Hugh pushed himself back in the chair and stretched for several seconds, then let go with a sigh. "Oh . . . hell, it's a mess, isn't it, Dave? The whole damn world. Everybody thinks the only way they can gain anything is if someone else loses—like kids with batteries. But it doesn't have to be like that. Life isn't zero-sum. They could be making the tide rise under everybody's boat instead."

Dave shook his head. "And I thought I was going to get a break from all this tonight. Have you been talking to Sarah?"

"But so much of what she says is so true, Dave. Governments everywhere are lying to people to make them hate others that they wouldn't have any quarrel with otherwise. You'd think they'd have learned something after two world wars, but where else can it lead than right where it's all going? Theo's right—the lunatics end up in charge of everything. Sane, normal people don't need power trips."

Dave stood up and returned the box to a drawer in the bureau. He refilled his glass from the bottle on the table and raised his eyebrows inquiringly at Hugh. "Top-up there?"

"Sure."

"All true," Dave agreed. "But was it any better in the other worlds we've seen? I mean, think about it. Sarah got trapped in an updated version of the good-old slaving days. I found a utopia where you needed permission to make a phone call. Sam was in the middle of World War III happening already—or at least, a pretty good preview. Maybe you can't get away from it. Like with dogs—farts and fleas are part of the deal."

Hugh nodded resignedly and picked up his drink. "Yes, Dave, I hear what you're saying. And yet . . ." He left the sentence unfinished, sipped, and savored the taste. "You're right. That's not bad stuff."

Dave sensed that Hugh was hovering on the edge of wanting to say something. "And yet what?" he prompted.

"Then there was that last place that Sarah and I were in—or thought we both were. You know, what she said was right: Even though she didn't even know what city she was in at first, it all had a different feel about it. I want to go back there again, just like she does."

"I thought all you saw was funny architecture and San Francisco from a bus," Dave said, sitting down along the bed and nursing his glass with his back against the headboard.

"You *knew* it was different somehow. It was the QUADAR feeding back. . . . And there was something else. I picked up a newspaper that somebody had left on the seat. And do you know the first thing that struck me as odd about it, Dave? There was hardly any mention of politics."

"Hah!" Dave threw back his head. "Take that and the advertising out and there wouldn't be much left."

"That's my point. We're so saturated with propaganda every way you look that we don't notice it. But when it isn't there, you notice. Nothing from Washington; no special interests wanting privileges; no threats, no scares; nobody telling us what we should be getting angry about."

Dave looked dubious. "So what *did* they write about?"

"Just . . . the world—people—going about its business.

It was all upbeat—as if everyone knew where they wanted to go and how to get there, and were doing it together. There was a lot on arts and sciences . . . and things about history and philosophy that you wouldn't see in our papers. *Ideas* is what I think I'm trying to say: They were written for people who liked to hear about ideas. . . . Oh, and there was something else. The German Kaiser and the Russian Czarina attended the ceremonial opening of Europe's first commercial atomic power plant. Will you just get that!"

"First commercial nuclear plant? You mean they're only just getting into it?"

"Seems like it. That was what felt good. They're not in a hysterical hurry over everything. Everyone you talk to seems easygoing, laid back."

"It sounds as if you two found an unusual neck of the woods, all right," Dave agreed.

Hugh's face remained serious. "What seemed to underlie it all was a basic difference in attitude. Life wasn't a constant war of each against all the way it is here, as if it were a . . ."

"Zero sum?" Dave put in.

"Yes, exactly. . . . For example, there was an item about a company down in San Diego that does engineering, okay? Because they'd modernized and put in better equipment, they were hiring more people, cutting hours, and upping pay scales! And a spokesman for the stockholders said they were delighted. Can you believe that? Their idea of efficiency is how many people they can afford to take on. They figure that's what a company is there for."

Dave was looking skeptical. "But how could it work? One shark could undercut everybody."

Hugh spread his hands. "I don't know. Maybe a different set of dynamics comes into play if other values become widespread enough. . . . But just for argument's sake, let's imagine for the moment that they have made it work. Just think what it means, Dave—a world without the insanity that's stampeding this one to self-destruct. People not obsessed with grabbing as much as they can get for as little as they can get away with. You say it can't work. But is what we've got working?"

Hugh's eyes searched Dave's intently. Dave sensed that he had arrived at something that he had been leading up to all evening. "Hugh, what are you driving at?" he asked suspiciously.

Hugh set down his glass to free both his hands, and licked his lips. "Think about it, Dave. When Sarah got cut off that time, nothing drastic happened. She consolidated right there, in the analog. You could make it permanent. All it would take is a bit of code to delete the recall sequences after the transfers are made. And if it deleted the director matrix as well . . . with a billion universes out there, nobody would ever set it up to find you again."

Dave stared incredulously. "Hey, wait a minute. Don't start thinking of doing anything stupid. If you're saying what I think you're saying . . ."

Hugh studied his face for a few moments longer. Then, all of a sudden, his manner relaxed and he made a dismissive gesture. "Hey, don't get all worked up about it. A thought, that's all, Dave. Just a thought."

Chapter Twenty-nine

General Ventz was suspicious both in temperament and by profession. It had long become second nature never to accept how things appeared to be or how others told him they were, but to find out from sources he trusted how they really were. The habit had served him well, and in his climb to the position that he enjoyed he had watched many others fall as casualties along the way as a consequence of their failure to develop it.

Through Colonel Elson, the spooks visiting Octagon from their base next door supplied a flow of intelligence on things going on there that the official reports made little of or omitted to mention. Two items in particular had attracted Ventz's attention. One was that the Polish professor from Berkeley, Jantowitz, should be given an out-of-the-way cubbyhole in which to pursue his researches away from inquisitive eyes, and that the very group who had been involved in his proposal for long-range experiments all spent an inordinate amount of time down there with him. The other was a copy that Ventz obtained of the day log from the TA-3 main gate, which showed the same people putting in lots of time over weekends and after hours, frequently until long into the morning. And in addition, there was the Pole's record of obstinate disinclination to be dictated to by any form of officialdom.

What it suggested to Ventz was that Sarvin's directive

was being ignored, and the long-range experiments were being allowed to continue illicitly. Such a state of affairs could hardly persist without Willard's complicity, and that was believable because Willard was subject to the influence of too many scientists. Scientists, in Ventz's experience, were too inclined to wander off in pursuit of their own fancies instead of keeping their sights on the objective. In something as crucial as the MV field could turn out to be, they had no other business than producing the results they were told to and leaving policy to others. If what he suspected was true, it would show the DRA administration to be incapable of exercising adequate supervision and provide a strong case for putting the whole MV program under direct military control.

But showing it to be true would require more than just his personal suspicions and a few circumstantial facts. In going through the original proposal that had been turned down, Ventz learned that it would have involved modifying several of the hardware modules in the coupler antenna array assembly to emulate the process that Jantowitz and Brenner had developed at Berkeley. If they had gone ahead on their own at Los Alamos in the way that Ventz suspected, then those special hardware modules would be there. But the scientists were hardly likely to leave such evidence for anyone to find when their equipment was unattended. The only chance of finding it, then, would be when they were actually there, using it. But that would entail embarrassing consequences in the event that Ventz was mistaken.

In this world, anyway. But the risk didn't have to be taken in this world. He could use Polygon to ascertain first that the evidence existed—in another world.

Polygon was right there, next door. And Polygon had been conceived to exploit precisely this kind of situation. What better opportunity for a field test could present itself than this?

He told his secretary to locate Colonel Elson at Los Alamos and get him on a secure channel to Washington.

✧   ✧   ✧

That evening, as planned, Hugh and Sarah went back to Otherwhere for another attempt at making contact with each other there. This time Hugh found himself in a restaurant. It was the first time that he had found himself instantly jealous of one of his analogs. The girl across the table from him was captivating from the moment that he returned from the initial flashback and took closer stock of his surroundings.

She had a pretty face, with high cheekbones and a pointed chin giving it a petite look, and a small mouth which just at that moment was drawn back into a soft, slightly puzzled half smile. Her hair was blond, short and wavy, sweeping down the sides of her face and curling attractively at the ears. She had bright, alive eyes, light in color—green maybe, or perhaps just picking up the hue of her dress, which was a satiny, light emerald, sleeveless, revealing tanned, slender arms, one encircled by a gold bracelet. Her nails were silvered. One hand swirled a wineglass idly while she watched him. "Well, why not? There's a good chance they would, if you can," she said.

Hugh blinked. He realized that he wasn't even aware if she had been talking to him since he "arrived."

"Is that so?" he said.

"But it would be fun, anyhow, even if they're not," she informed him.

"That's interesting," Hugh agreed. From his full feeling inside, he took it that they had already eaten. His napkin was loosely refolded on the table beside him, and most of the cutlery had gone.

The girl waited a second. "So what do you think?" she asked him.

"I, er . . . think you're astoundingly charming," Hugh blurted—then winced to himself. For all he knew she could be his sister or his boss's wife. Wife? . . . He sneaked a look. No, the hand holding the glass wasn't wearing a ring.

To his relief, she smiled. Not a vain kind of a smile switched on by flattery, or a condescension to somebody being foolish. Just a frank, simple acknowledgement of a compliment. She slid her hand across the table and slipped it over his. He was wearing a dark jacket, he saw. Her touch was delicate and smooth. "I could say the same— but you already know that." She gave him a squeeze. "This has been nice."

"Glad you think so," Hugh said. It sounded as if he'd been doing something right for a change, anyway.

She traced an outline on the back of his hand and eyed him curiously. "Do you always go off on tangents like that?"

"Oh, all the time. It's the company that does it. Sometimes I forget what we were talking about ten seconds ago."

"Okay. So what were we talking about ten seconds ago?"

Hugh shrugged and grinned at her. "I forget."

She laughed. It was a warm, easy laugh that came naturally. Nothing phony or forced. Her teeth were even and white. Something electric shivered down Hugh's spine. "I knew I shouldn't have gotten mixed up with a scientist. I was warned. You see, you can't go five minutes without your mind wandering back to atoms and whatever else you talk to all day." She sighed. "I guess it just puts me in my place. I mean, how could a girl hope to compete with *atoms*?"

So—he was a scientist again for once. He opened his hand in a gesture of mock magnanimity. "As a matter of fact—well, don't tell anyone I said so, but when it comes to company, atoms are really quite boring. They all look the same, which means they all say the same thing." He was learning how to keep his wits about him more and deal with these situations now. The thing was to just plunge in and not be overwhelmed by confusion.

"Now I feel a lot better," she said.

"I'm glad. People shouldn't work up complexes about these things."

She sipped her drink, smiling. "So, what about Saturday?"

Back to that again. There were no cues. Hugh frowned and made a show of giving the matter grave consideration.

"I'll have to think about it. Can I let you know?" he replied.

"Why is it such a big thing, all of a sudden? I just want to know if we're going."

Hugh rocked his head from side to side and showed his palms, unconsciously weighing the odds. "Sure, why not?" he said.

It was evidently the right thing. She seemed pleased. "You'll like it," she promised. "There's always a good band, the bar doesn't close, and the dancing goes on all night if people want. And we could still see the movie first."

"Sounds good to me." That was what it had all been about—they were talking about going to a dance? He squeezed her hand and released it to pick up his own glass, then sat back to see what more he could make of the situation.

From its solid wooden paneling and furnishings, white linen tablecloths, and general decor, the place could have been mid twentieth century. The jackets with ties, and stylish dresses of some of the patrons were consistent with the same notion, although there were instances of saris, kimonos, and other orientally inspired designs as well.

A waiter appeared with cups and a pot on a tray and transferred them to the table. "A brandy or liqueur to go with the coffee, perhaps?" he suggested as he began pouring. Hugh eyed his as-yet nameless date inquiringly.

"A cognac would be nice," she murmured. "Grand Marnier?"

"Two Grand Marniers," Hugh said to the waiter. The waiter repeated the order and left.

At a nearby table, a man in a high-necked, Asian-style jacket produced a red and gold pack and offered it around to the group he was with. Hugh watched some accept a cigarette, others decline. The host followed around with the table lighter, ending up by lighting his own. A wisp of smoke drifted across, and Hugh picked up the unmistakable scent of marijuana. Involuntarily, his eyebrows lifted in surprise.

"What is it?" the girl with him asked.

"Oh . . ." He gestured vaguely and left it unfinished.

She looked in the direction where he had waved. "I didn't know you liked it. Order some."

"No, it's just . . ." He groped around for something to say. "I was wondering how long it'll be before they ban it."

"Ban what?"

He realized that he was way out of line somehow, but motioned toward the other table again with his head. "Those."

"Who?"

"The government."

"The government?" She looked confused. "Why should it have anything to do with them?"

"Oh . . ." He tried to be dismissive. "I thought I read something about it somewhere." Her expression told him he wasn't making any sense. "Scientist's joke," he said. "Don't worry about it for now. I'll explain it one day." He smiled. She returned it a shade uncertainly. He leaned back, resting an elbow on the back of his chair. "How long would you say we've known each other now? . . ." His other hand made nonchalant circles in the air.

"Two months. Or is it more?"

"Did I ever tell you what kind of scientist I am?"

"I can't really remember. Was it one hundred times, or two?"

He waited, but she didn't supply anything further. "Anyhow, we're notorious for weird political jokes that nobody else understands. When was the last time we talked about politics?"

She looked at him oddly. "What is there to talk about?"

He felt himself floundering. The waiter extricated him by returning with a tray on which were two filled cognac glasses and a leather-bound folder containing the check. Hugh flipped it open while the waiter set down the drinks. One duck, one steak, wine and aperitifs—all for under twenty dollars! He swallowed hard and tried to remain expressionless. The banner at the top of the bill told him they were in The DeVere on Market Street, San Francisco. There was a phone number, which he memorized. He felt inside his jacket and found a wallet. There was enough cash to cover the amount, with an ample margin to spare. No credit cards of the kind that he was familiar with; just a plastic "Bank Validation Card" in the name of Matthew Shayne, its exact purpose obscure. He took out two tens, hesitated, not wanting to be ostentatious, and added three singles. There were a few personal calling cards and business cards, none of them his. Then he found a driver's license, giving an address in Berkeley. Also, there was a library ticket from the University of California, Berkeley, again with the name Matthew Shayne. So, ironically, after so many strange worlds, he had ended up back home.

"Looking for something, Mat?" the girl asked, watching him over the rim of her glass.

"Oh, just checking." He closed the wallet and returned it to his inside pocket. "Kind of a habit, I guess."

"See, scientists again. They always have to double-check everything."

"Maybe so, but that's what got us to the Moon."

She shook her head. "What are you talking about?" Hugh started to smile, then realized that she was being serious. "Is that another scientist's joke?" she asked.

"Right," he said, grabbing for it.

She looked apprehensive. "You must think I don't have a sense of humor at all. That's really not true. Maybe financial people just laugh at different things."

"You see, we complement each other," Hugh said. So she was a financial person. "Enough about scientists and atoms," he said. "Tell me more about financial people."

"They deal in money and investments."

"No! Really?"

"Well, it is a pretty general order. What do you want me to say?"

"Okay, your kind of financial people. What do they do, specifically?"

"It's like I showed you when you were at the office."

She shrugged. "We advise clients on stocks and portfolios, arrange deals for them, make a living off a commission. All pretty basic when you get down to it. Probably as boring as atoms once the novelty wears off." She raised her cognac and winked saucily. "Getting to know you is a lot more fun."

"Talking to atoms doesn't make you so rich, though," Hugh said. He remembered how the items in the newspaper on the bus had struck him, and wanted to see how she would react.

She made a face. "Well, if that were all that mattered . . ."

"But that's what stockholders expect, isn't it?" he persisted.

"Well, among other things. But who wants to get financially obese? . . . And in any case, why should it make any more than a good scientist?"

Hugh wasn't sure what that meant. "What would you say a good scientist makes?" he asked curiously.

"You tell me, Mat. If you're not happy with it, maybe you should get a different agent."

Scientists had agents? That was a new one. "Oh, I'm doing okay," he said. Something to think about.

She nodded. "Yes, that's what I thought. But why don't we leave all that for daytime, where it belongs?"

"Good idea."

"Why don't you ask me how Nathan got on, instead? I thought you were interested."

"All right. How did Nathan get on?" Hugh obliged.

"I wondered when you were going to ask me that. He did amazingly well, as a matter of fact. Now he's applying for a scholarship at the Technical Institute down in Pasadena. . . ."

It appeared that Nathan was a younger relative of hers— Hugh never did manage to ascertain exactly whether brother, nephew, or what—with ambitions to become an aircraft designer. He had done well in recent examinations and hoped to be moving south and learning independence. It seemed that Hugh's analog, Mat, had met him. Hugh did a great job as a listener, speaking only to fill in the occasional blank with a "yes" or a "no" on cue. All the time, he couldn't take his eyes off her.

"I hope you two get to know each other," she concluded. "Nathan believes we'll get to the Moon in his lifetime, too. He says he's going to design the rocket that will do it."

"He probably will, then."

"You see—you both think the same way. Okay, I believe it too. And we could take the train and visit him, maybe. I haven't been to L.A. for ages."

Train? Hugh raised his eyebrows. "Sounds great."

Then he looked at his watch. Time had been passing more quickly than he realized. They would be bringing him back for a check barely five minutes from now. He didn't want his analog interrupting and complicating things further, he decided; not until he—Hugh—was out of the way, anyhow. "Excuse me," he said. "I have to find the men's room. Back in a few minutes."

She smiled and settled back to enjoy her cognac. Hugh rose and made his way out to the entrance foyer. The receptionist directed him to a passageway on one side. A copy of the *San Francisco Examiner* was lying by the cash register. Hugh picked it up and opened it. The date was current, and the headline read: BAY AREA FLOOD ALERT. He replaced the paper and went through to the rest rooms.

"Okay, you are with us?" Jantowitz said. He motioned toward the other coupler, where Sarah was sitting up. "Sarah's phone is still out, but she gives us the bar on the street. . . ."

Hugh waved a hand to cut him off. "I don't have time, Theo. Take this number: area code 151, 826-1578. That's the DeVere restaurant on Market Street, San Francisco. The name is Matthew Shayne. If we fail to connect, then as a backup, the headline for today's *S.F. Examiner* is: BAY AREA FLOOD ALERT. Got all that? Good, now I need to get back, fast. Give me another hour, at least."

❖   ❖   ❖

He was in the entrance foyer, heading for the door into the restaurant. He slowed his pace and made his way back to the table. She greeted him with a smile as he sat down.

"I was thinking about that offer of yours to come over to Berkeley and see your lab sometime," she said. "Could we do it before Nathan goes to Pasadena, and bring him along too? He'd love it."

"Sure, no problem," Hugh said.

"Then you could show him that machine of yours that you were telling me about. What was it called? It sounded something like a bicycle."

Hugh frowned and racked his brains. Scientist . . . Physics? Particle physics, maybe? "Cyclotron?" he guessed.

"Yes, that was it. The one where protons go round and round and smash into atoms and break them up into all kinds of things. It sounded fascinating."

"Well, just let me know when."

"Is there any particular day that would be better for you?"

Hugh spread his hands. "Any time is fine for me." Which was true.

"And I want to meet that crazy guy that you told me about, what was his name again?"

"Er, I'm not sure. . . . Which one was that?"

"Oh, you know. The one with the trapeze. Didn't you say he has a computer that plays games? I've always wanted a chance to work a computer. A firm of brokers in town here is talking about getting one."

Hugh didn't know how to respond. He was still trying to puzzle out the situation when he was saved again, this time by the maitre d'hotel coming to the table. "Excuse me, are you Mr. Matthew Shayne?" he inquired.

"Yes."

"We have a telephone call for you, sir. Will you take it here, or would you prefer more privacy?"

"Here would be fine," Hugh said. The maitre d' beckoned to a waiter who was hovering near the wall, holding a tray with a phone trailing a cord. "Excuse me," Hugh said across the table.

His date nodded and seemed impressed. "Sure."

"Hello, Hugh . . . I mean, Mat Shayne here."

"Hi." It wasn't Sarah's voice, of course, but he knew.

"Right. It's me," he confirmed.

"It's worked, then. We have an intersection. I'm so glad it turned out to be the same place."

"I guess we chalk up another one. Where are you, Detroit?"

"Yes, in the bar here. Although judging from the phone system, I could be in the Detroit museum. How's San Francisco?"

"A lot different from what I remember, but it's nice to be back. Now, Brown's address is two-thirteen, Maple Street. You can look his number up in the book. If you do track him down and manage to get together, say hi to him from me." The last part didn't mean anything, but Sarah would understand. It gave Hugh a pretext for being called. "I'm in the middle of something right now," he said. "Was there anything else?"

"No, that's it. See you back in the lab."

"Take care." The line went dead. Hugh handed the phone back to the waiter and nodded.

"Something important?" the girl asked.

"A colleague who's at a conference out of town. He wants to look up an old mutual friend if he can."

Why was he doing this? he asked himself. These improvisations would simply pile up impossible problems for his analog to deal with later. She could well end up writing Matthew Shayne off as no less crazy than whoever owned the trapeze. Then there wouldn't be a relationship to come back to for very much longer.

He was aware how crazy it was, even as he thought it. Nevertheless, although he had no idea how he proposed handling the situation, he knew that he would be coming back. This promised to be the strangest rivalry of all time.

They left shortly afterward and had another drink at a

bar around the corner, then took a cab back to her apartment, which turned out to be on a hillside on the west of the city near Geary. She checked her mailbox on the way in, and only then did he learn that her name was Yvonne—Yvonne Petrie. Upstairs, while she was putting on coffee in the kitchen, he read the phone number.

And shortly after that, Los Alamos brought him back. He was glad that they did. He didn't know how the relationship stood. Too timorous or too presumptuous— either way it would have been too easy to spoil things.

After Hugh's return, Sarah disappeared with Dave, and Jantowitz stayed on at the lab to discuss some theoretical point with Sam. Hugh left on his own to walk the distance back to Mrs. Ryecroft's. He stopped halfway across the bridge and stood staring down into the blackness of Los Alamos Canyon below. His breath condensed into streamers that dissolved away in the chilly night air. To his left, the lights of the town stretched away along the top of the mesa, its precipitous side etched into rocky highlights by a moon skating through restless clouds. Everything about this world felt remote now, somehow, no longer significant. In a way stranger than he could explain, another world that he had glimpsed for just a few brief hours seemed more real than a lifetime's accumulated experiences. It was the QUADAR effect, he knew. That was where the feeling of affinity had come from that had been beckoning to him ever since the first time he connected to the machine on the day he started at Los Alamos. That world, from all that distance away across the Multiverse?

Or was it the person in it?

To escape permanently. The thought came back to him again. Dave had balked when Hugh mentioned it. That was understandable. It wasn't exactly the kind of thing that somebody could be expected to weigh up and respond to instantly. But Hugh had been thinking about it all day. At first he had experienced guilt at finding himself contemplating the possibility seriously—a reflex discomfort at the image of himself scurrying from the ship, pushing all else aside to pursue ends that were his alone. But then, he asked himself, what else was there? What could he do to avert the rush toward self-destruction of a world impelled by forces that were beyond his comprehension, let alone his ability to influence? Nothing.

Now all attempt at pretense was over. He had never felt so serious about anything in his life.

Chapter Thirty

Colonel Elson studied the personnel files for the scientific and engineering grades employed on Octagon, and finally selected Joyce Theale. A former electronics technician with the Air Force, she had been married to a corporate tax consultant but ditched him when his drug habits ate up their checking account, and their credit cards were frozen. She had a clean service record with good promotion prospects, but had quit to take what she saw as a better opportunity for advancement. In short, she didn't get too emotionally involved in the world, put her own best interests first, and believed in staying on the right side of authority. All of which could be used to advantage, he decided.

A Polygon spook contacted her with the message that Colonel Elson wanted to talk to her in confidence. To avoid drawing undue attention, a plain van picked her up in town during the lunch period. Elson talked to her on the bench seat at the rear while they drove over the bridge spanning Pueblo Canyon, around the North Mesa, and back again.

"What we want you to do has important bearings on national security considerations that I'm not at liberty to discuss," he told her. "But let me just mention for now that before much longer the whole MV program could be placed under military direction. In that event, your cooperation would not go unappreciated."

The implied corollary, of course, was that in the same event, her non-cooperation would be unlikely to go unappreciated either. That got her attention.

Elson continued, "Briefly, we have reason to believe that certain hardware has been modified illicitly and is being used for work not authorized under Octagon, in the area designated N2."

"N2? Isn't that the place downstairs that Jantowitz and some of the others use?" Joyce said.

"Yes, exactly. We want to send an operative from Polygon in there to check—but it needs to be when they're working there. Your part would be twofold. First, to be expecting our man over there—maybe for a technical discussion of some kind—to give him a legitimate reason for entering the Octagon building. Second, to create a diversion in N2 while our man gets a look at the couplers down there. Pretty simple, eh? Do you figure you could do that?"

Joyce frowned. What Elson hadn't said was anything about how she was supposed to explain herself afterward. "If it's that important, why can't you just go there and check?" she asked.

"It's delicate politically. If our suspicions turn out to be wrong, it could cause problems that we'd rather do without," Elson replied.

Joyce's frown deepened. It didn't make sense. "But if it turns out you're wrong anyway, what difference does it make who does the checking? The same people are still going to be upset."

Elson nodded that she was right, of course. But that was the clever part. "We let the problems happen someplace else, not here," he told her. "What we do is set up an intersection with you and our operative in a nearby universe, very close. You do your thing; he gets the information; we bring you both back. That way, nobody in our world gets to know, and the people in that world can sort things out afterward however they want." He shrugged. "Not the nicest way to treat your neighbors, I know, but hey, this is the real world. Or should I say worlds?"

✧   ✧   ✧

What the plan failed to take into account, however, was the possibility of the worlds being so close that the neighbors on the other side might have the same idea too; or that they might implement it a day earlier.

Joyce Theale was back in the lab, still mulling over Elson's lunchtime proposition, when her analog arrived, briefed and prepared. The analog took a few seconds to assess the situation and waited for the brief flashback return to her own world. There, she gave the operating staff in Polygon her whereabouts and cleared them to reestablish the transfer. Moments later, she was her other self once more, in her familiar lab in Octagon.

Phil Moody and one of the programmers were at a screen nearby, taking no notice of her. She got up from the bench and went to her desk in a partitioned area on the far side of the lab. Nobody else was there at the moment. A few seconds later, the phone rang. She picked it up. "Hello? Joyce Theale here."

"Adam calling." It was the code word for the Polygon agent from her own world. The intersection was successful. He had arrived in his analog and was across in the adjacent building right now.

"Roger, Adam. Glad you made it. I'll see you soon." She hung up, then called the security checkpoint at the side entrance from the Polygon compound. "Hello? . . . Yes, this is Joyce Theale in Signal Processing. Somebody from Polygon wants to come over to go through a few technical points. His name is Kerney. He'll be there in a few minutes. . . . Yes, I'll come down and collect him. . . . Thanks."

The plan was that they would find an out-of-the-way place to disappear in until evening. That, Colonel Elson had reasoned, was when unauthorized work down in the Bolthole would most likely be conducted.

Hugh was in a machine area inside a large building. There was an open floor, most of which was taken up by an assembly of cables, windings, and instrumentation constructed around an approximately cone-shaped framework lying sideways on a concrete foundation and accessed by steel ladders and catwalks. The assembly connected into the wall of an immense, curving structure running through the building. Although he had never worked directly in particle physics, he knew enough to guess that this was the cyclotron that his analog, Matthew Shayne, was associated with. The conical assembly looked vaguely like pictures he had seen of high-energy detectors.

He was sitting on a foam rubber mat beneath some valves and piping, looking at a lot of complicated equipment that meant nothing. Scattered around him were an assortment of tools and measuring instruments, an open binder, and several sheets of drawings. A figure that he knew instinctively was a grad student, in creased, stained pants and a blue shirt with rolled-up sleeves, was leaning under a pipe, adjusting something with a screwdriver and checking a reading on some kind of meter.

"No, we're still out by ten. Something's dragging it down. Where does the F2 line come in? . . ." The student waited a few seconds, then looked back over his shoulder. "Mat?"

"Oh . . . Yes?"

"I said, which one is F2? The blue, or does it loop back to the socket pin?"

The diagrams spread around Hugh were no help. He had more pressing things to think about, anyway. Time of day seemed to remain synchronized across the Multiverse. One of his reasons for wanting to transfer during the afternoon of a weekday had been the hope that it would coincide with his analog's being at work in Berkeley. His plan now was to find who his boss was, and if it turned out to be someone who seemed approachable, to try conveying the situation. His analog was going to be seen to be behaving strangely at times. Those around him would need to have some understanding of what was happening. The team still had qualms wondering what had been the fate of the Sarah-analog rushed off to a psychiatric clinic, whom they would never locate again.

He stood up and stepped back. "Could you take a break for a few minutes?"

"We're only just back from lunch."

"I've just remembered a call I have to make. Can you manage on your own here for a while?"

"Well, not with this. Want me to get those things that Steve talked about?"

"Sure, why not?" Hugh walked away quickly before anything more complicated could happen. He found a door leading out of the floor area and came to stairs that brought him to a corridor flanked by offices. A man in a sweater, with a black beard and spectacles was coming the other way.

"Any idea where Matthew Shayne works?" Hugh asked him.

"Good one, Mat. Having one of them days, eh?" The bearded man laughed and went on down the stairs. Dumb, Hugh told himself.

One of the rooms was empty and dark, apparently not occupied that day. He went in, closed the door behind him, and turned on the light. It looked like a secretary's office and could have belonged to academia anywhere . . . except that the furnishings were curiously ornate, with curvy legs on the chairs and carved embellishments decorating the desk. And it had a typewriter. Hugh had never seen one in a genuine working environment before. There was no com unit of the kind he was familiar with, but it did have an antiquated-looking terminal with simple keyboard and screen. The screen had moldings down the side in the form of Greek columns, and a frieze across the top. It reminded him vaguely of the proscenium arch of an old theater.

He sat down and after rummaging in the drawers found some correspondence giving the university's external number—it was still listed as University of California, Berkeley, so not everything had changed. An internal directory on the desk told him how to dial an outside line.

"Good afternoon. This is U.C. at Berkeley," an operator's voice answered.

"Oh, hi. I'd like to speak to Matthew Shayne, please."

"Can I say who's calling?"

He had expected that. "My name is Hugh Brenner."

"One moment." There was a short wait, then, "I'm sorry, but Dr. Shayne doesn't seem to be in his office at present. Would you like to leave a message, or could somebody else help?"

"Could you tell me who he reports to there?"

"Let me see . . . well, the Head of the High-Energy Experimental Physics Lab is Professor Rauth."

"Is he in today?"

"As far as I know. Shall I put you through?"

"Well, no, as a matter of fact, I think it's Professor Rauth that I'm coming there to see. I was calling Shayne to get directions. Maybe you can help. Can you tell me how to find him?"

"Professor Rauth, you mean?"

"Yes."

"He's on the top floor of the physics building, which is on the north side of the Cyclotron Complex. It's just inside the East Gate of the campus. How will you be getting here, Mr. Brenner?"

Hugh shook his head in amazement. "It's okay. I think I can find it now, thanks." This was unreal. It sounded as if the physics building was more or less on the site of Stanley Hall in his own world—next to Biophysics, where he and Jantowitz had worked. Of course, there had been no Cyclotron Complex then.

Although the name was the same, the building turned out to be a more solid and imposing affair than the regulation cuboid packed with prefabricated-partition rooms that Hugh remembered. It had character and style. The entrance was a columned arch of colored glass sitting atop marble steps; the walls of the vestibule hall beyond were lined with niches containing sculptures; and the elevator doors carried an involved design based on atomic structures and orbits, reflecting the theme of the department.

He came out on the top floor into an open area that had lots of color and indoor plants, with several people working at desks and a group talking around a table below a chalkboard. One of them waved casually, and Hugh nodded back. Some things never changed. Back in Hugh's world, an unvarying characteristic of every physics department he had ever been in was the ubiquity of chalkboards. Amputate their fingers, and physicists would be struck dumb. In many places, even the walls of the corridors had chalkboards to make conversation possible in passing encounters outside the offices.

He found a door with a sign proclaiming the domain of HERBERT P. RAUTH a short distance along a wide passage past a model of the cyclotron layout. He drew a deep breath, then rapped sharply a couple of times with a knuckle. A voice inside called out, "Yes, come in." Hugh entered.

The room had lots of books, charts on the walls, a chalkboard, naturally, an aquarium by the window, and the incongruous combination of a computer terminal wedged in one end of a huge rolltop desk. The man sitting at the desk was heavy-shouldered and solidly built, probably in his fifties, though with a full head of graying curly hair, and a ruddy face with a bulbous nose. He was wearing a red shirt with a bright green vest and polka dot bow tie.

Before Hugh could say anything, Rauth waved a piece of paper that he had been looking at. "A begging letter from ITT. They want to donate half a million to the program." He shook his head. "But I don't know, Mat. We've already expanded the budget to the limit of what's reasonable. I can't justify accepting any more. Just gonna have to say thanks, but maybe next time. . . . Anyhow, what's up?"

Hugh pushed the door shut behind him. "Professor Rauth . . ."

"What is this, a resignation speech? What's wrong with 'Herb,' for heaven's sake."

"Herb. . . . Look, some of what I'm about to say may not seem to make a lot of sense at first. Just bear with me for five minutes, okay?"

Rauth sat back and eyed him solemnly. He set down the letter, shrugged, and indicated a chair. "My ears are thine. Go on, then. Confound me."

"Quantum mechanics. What's your view of the Many Worlds version?"

Rauth's features wrinkled. "My view? Well, it's the way things are. What other view is there?"

So physical theory here was on a par with Hugh's own world. Maybe this would turn out easier than he had been prepared for. "You consider it verified experimentally, then?" he checked.

"Well, of course. Nothing else accounts for interference effects."

"So information crosses over at the quantum level," Hugh concluded, spelling out the implication.

"What is this, an undergraduate refresher?"

"So would you agree that intelligible communication between noncausally connected parts of the continuum ought to be possible?"

Rauth bunched his mouth dubiously but nodded. "In theory, maybe . . . if you knew how to build computing circuits capable of a billion calculations a second or more to unscramble it. And *if* you could assemble enough of them together in one place without melting the building."

Hugh looked at him long and penetratingly. Now, suddenly, he thought he could see where the essential difference between their two worlds lay. "But if that *were* possible, could it result in an individual consciousness experiencing the event sequence of its counterpart in a different region?"

Rauth put a hand to his chin and thought about that. Although the suggestion seemed new to him, he appeared willing to consider it honestly and candidly, with no show of the prejudice that Hugh had half expected from a scientist. "I don't know," he replied finally. "You'd have to go and talk to the mystics."

"Mystical experiences are real then?"

"Why not? Who am I to say that somebody else isn't feeling what he's telling me he's feeling?"

"Physics can't explain it," Hugh pointed out.

"Physics can't explain falling in love or a sense of humor, either."

Hugh was excited for a dozen different reasons already. He wasn't sure which of them he wanted to take up first. "Do you have any urgent commitments in the next hour, say?" he asked.

"Well, I was intending to see Gruner across on the rig sometime, but it can wait if it must," Rauth answered. "So what's this all about?"

Hugh pulled a chair closer to Rauth's desk and sat down. Although there was nothing he could do to change it, the thought of just walking out on the world he had always known still troubled him. Like a house that he had grown up in, despite its faults and times that were occasionally troubled, it had afforded shelter and nurture through the years he had needed them; he felt he was contemplating deserting, like a teenager preparing finally to move on. But now, suddenly, maybe there was something to offset that. Perhaps he had something to contribute to the world he would be joining.

"Suppose those computers were possible," he said to Rauth. "Do you think that ITT might consider that half million a worthwhile down payment for some reliable guidelines as to how to go about building them?"

Chapter Thirty-one

Sam was monitoring both couplers when Joyce Theale appeared in the outer section of the Bolthole. It was well into the evening, and people from upstairs weren't usually around. Hugh was in Otherwhere again, back in Berkeley, and achieving the first meaningful communication across the Multiverse with an astounded professor. Dave was occupying the other coupler. It had turned out that he possessed an Otherwhere analog also—back in England once more, this time as a radio astronomer near Manchester. He was supposed to attempt contacting Hugh, but it was still the early hours of the morning in England, and they were finding that the international phone system was primitive. Jantowitz was putting in an appearance upstairs and would be down later.

"Hello, Joyce," Sam greeted. "Are you turning into an insomniac too?"

Joyce stopped near the console. The couplers were positioned farther back in a recess behind a barricade of partitions and cubicles. "I see you've got Dave and Hugh on line. Anything exciting?"

"Just a routine intersection test. What gives?" Sam eyed her uncertainly as he spoke. There was something unusual about her manner—an edginess, an over-alert shifting of the eyes that was out of character. She looked around and then moved away again, stopping by one of the larger

271

cabinets standing by a main aisle traversing the building. It contained high-voltage distribution circuitry associated with the power conditioning equipment in the next bay.

"We've blown an amplifier card in one of the units upstairs, and they don't have a spare in the stores," Joyce called to him over her shoulder. "But there's a type in here that's supposed to be interchangeable. I need to get the model number." As she spoke, she loosened the front panel screws on one of the racks and slid it out on its guides. She had made a reconnaissance visit down here that morning in her own world, and had selected the rack then. All it needed now was for her to drop the piece of aluminum wire that she was carrying in her lab-coat pocket across the bare busbar connectors at the rear.

Then Sam noticed another figure in the background, by a pillar in front of a door leading from a flight of stairs. He was looking at a piece of paper that he was holding, but something in the way he was standing told Sam that he was not really studying it. His face was familiar, but not immediately recognizable as from the Octagon staff. It took Sam a moment to remember him as the spook who had asked during their familiarization tour if MV vision was tantamount to proof of the existence of God. Kerney, that was it.

There had not been enough time for the situation to register as odd, when a bright flash and a bang came from the opened rack that Joyce was stooping over. She cried out, recoiling from the cabinet, and collapsed on the floor.

Sam was across and kneeling by her in seconds. He checked her pulse and breathing. Two technicians who had been working late appeared from the chip-fabrication area nearby. "What happened?" one of them asked.

"She got a shock. One of you call Emergency, quickly." The first technician produced a hand communicator and punched in the number.

"How bad is she?" the other asked, moving closer.

"It could be worse. Her breathing hasn't stopped,

anyway." Sam checked Joyce's neck and waist, loosening any clothing that felt tight.

"What was she doing?"

"She said she was checking on a part to replace something that blew upstairs. I wasn't paying that much attention."

Two of the building's security guards appeared with blankets and a first-aid case. They checked Joyce again and had barely unrolled a blanket beneath her and covered her over, when a couple of medics hastened in with a foldable gurney. One of them pronounced that her condition did not seem serious. Only then did Sam relax and stand back.

That was when he remembered Kerney hovering nearby. He looked around, past the immediate flurry of medics maneuvering Joyce onto the gurney and the security guards assisting, while the technicians watched. Kerney was at the rear of the N2 area, peering into the equipment frames above the two couplers. He had removed the covers of the antenna arrays and was examining the chips and control electronics—precisely the special modules that Hugh and Dave had produced.

Then it hit Sam what was going on. His expression changed. "Check her again, one more time," he told the medics. "I don't think you'll find very much wrong." He walked back past the console to the couplers. Although it was inconceivable that someone with spook training would be unaware of his approaching, Kerney ignored him. "I trust you have found what you were looking for?" Sam said tightly.

Kerney glanced at him with a half amused look. There was no concern on his face, no inkling of a care. It could mean only one thing: The Kerney looking back at him was not of this world at all and didn't expect to be in it for very much longer. And if Joyce was part of the setup, then the same was true for her also. Kerney read the look on Sam's face and nodded. "Okay, so after we go back, your little group in our world is gonna have problems. But it doesn't affect you, and you can't change things for them. So why not just ease off? Let it ride."

For once Sam had trouble trying to untangle the implications. But one thing that was indisputable was the pointlessness of arguing with Kerney. He went back to the console and called Jantowitz upstairs. "Theo, can you get down here right away? We've got a strange situation. I'm not sure what to read into it."

By the time Jantowitz arrived, Joyce was sitting up on the edge of the gurney in front of the two perplexed medics, looking none the worse and being uncommunicative. Sam drew Jantowitz aside and explained the situation briefly. Jantowitz turned and confronted Kerney, who was standing by the console, evidently having lost interest in the proceedings. "Who is it who initiates this?" Jantowitz demanded. "Elson, it is, or does it come from Washington?" Kerney shrugged.

"You have no reason not to tell us," Sam urged. "You said yourself, nothing will make any difference after you go back."

Kerney, however, evidently didn't see why he should have to trouble explaining anything to anybody. Instead, his eyes opened wide, and he stared from side to side at his surroundings. "Gee, how did I get here? I was in Polygon. Have I had a blackout?" He didn't even bother trying to sound convincing. There was nothing they could do about it.

Sam turned away, exasperated. Jantowitz muttered under his breath. Then he stopped and thought; suddenly his manner changed. "Yes, the blackout, you have had," he said to Kerney. "What is it that you are doing over here? we have been asking. How do you get in?" He was going along with the charade, as if he believed it.

Kerney showed surprise for an instant, then turned up his hands in exaggerated innocence. "How would I know?"

"Then better we get you back out again." Jantowitz waved at the two security guards. "This man wishes to Polygon to return. You will escort him to the connecting door, please?"

Kerney shrugged. It was all the same to him. "Sure. Let's go." As the three began walking away, Jantowitz turned to the medics, at the same time indicating Joyce. "Never mind if normal she seems. She goes back to Medical with you, and you give her a thorough check. Taking the chances, we don't want."

"He's right." The medic in charge looked at Joyce and indicated the gurney with a gesture. "Please."

Like Kerney, Joyce had nothing to gain from arguing. She lay back and smiled at Jantowitz tauntingly. The second medic spoke into a communicator as they wheeled her away. "She's conscious and seems okay, but we're bringing her in. Heart and breathing are normal, no visible marks. . . ."

"The show now is over," Jantowitz said to the two technicians. "Thank you for your help, but if you excuse us now, we have the experiment in progress."

"Oh, yeah, sure. Any time."

"Glad it doesn't seem too bad."

They went back into the crystal etching lab.

Sam waited until sure they were alone, then turned back toward Jantowitz. Jantowitz's expression was urgent. "Okay, Theo, what gives? What are you doing?" Sam said.

"Let us now think through the situation," Jantowitz answered. "Some next-door universe sends those two to check the hardware. Why? Because someone there suspects we do our own experiments down here. What it means, very probably, is that the same peoples in this universe suspect it too. So maybe they make the same plan to find out. But when they hear what happens here, they know that their analogs in one universe screw them before they get the chance to screw some other analogs in a different universe. So far it makes sense, yes?"

Sam replayed Jantowitz's tortured English in his head and nodded. It made sense. "So it has to be Polygon people, not our people," he said. Octagon management could hardly have recruited Kerney—or would have needed to.

"Of course is Polygon. Is all lunatics, this whole Polygon

thing. So we know now that they suspect. And they will know that we know. So what then they will do? we ask."

If secrecy had been blown anyway, there would be no point now in being covert by mounting the same operation into another universe. Sam wasn't sure how the powers responsible for Polygon would react or what authority they had to invade Octagon, but there seemed a good chance of the military marching in to inspect the equipment without any further pretenses. And since a restored Kerney might, even now, be reporting to his superiors, it could happen at any moment.

"We have to bring them back." Sam returned to the console. Working swiftly, he initiated the return routines for Dave and Hugh, still in repose in the two couplers. Within seconds they were conscious again, looking around and seeming surprised.

"What's up?" Dave inquired. "I thought we weren't due to—"

Sam cut him off. "We've got an emergency. Explanations later. Get up out of there, both of you, and help reinstall the regular modules. There might not be a lot of time."

They returned the two couplers to the standard configuration and put the special modules where they were normally kept when not in use—underneath assorted other hardware in a box standing inconspicuously on one of the shelves.

But there were no immediate repercussions. Kintner called shortly afterward from his home at the east end of town. The Duty Security Officer had notified him of the incident as a matter of routine, and Kintner was simply checking.

"And she will be all right?" Kintner asked again, after Sam had summarized what had happened.

"I'm certain that she faked it," Sam said. "They only took her with them for a precautionary checkup because we insisted."

"Quite right, absolutely right." Kintner frowned, obviously preoccupied with other matters now that protocol had been observed. "What do you think they were looking for?"

"I can only guess that it had to do with something that's going on in their world." Sam wasn't feeding Kintner any leads. If Kintner knew more than he was letting on, he hid it well.

"Well, I'm glad it wasn't anything more serious. We'll talk more about it in the morning. Good night." Kintner cleared down.

The four in the lab—Hugh, Dave, Jantowitz, and Sam—debated the implications at some length. It was clear that somebody in another universe—probably somebody high up in Polygon—suspected that the DRA directive was being ignored and had decided to check. It was very possible that the same people in this universe thought the same way too. By the following morning, as much would also be clear to anyone else who learned of the circumstances. What the outcome would be was anyone's guess. There seemed little the group could do to affect it.

Jantowitz, for his part, was adamant. "Why does it matter what they think?" he said to the others. "It is the true science that we are doing. The lunatics can pester each other with their accusations and denials. Until somebody tells to my face that this work we can't do, I continue."

Kerney reverted to his normal self just after entering the main Polygon building, and Joyce Theale while she was still en route to the Medical Department. Kerney sought out Colonel Elson to report, and Theale called Elson a few minutes later. Elson raised Ventz via an encrypted channel to Washington.

"*Goddamn!* . . ." Ventz thought rapidly. The whole game was given away now. Although the incident had been the work of a different reality, the first thing others would assume would be that the same had been planned in this one. There could be no question of continuing.

"Scratch the operation and delete all records," he instructed. "We can't use Theale now. She'll be watched all the time. Maybe we'll just have to go for the direct approach and hope we're right. Arrange an inspection visit for me, Colonel. I'm coming out there."

Just before leaving the lab, Dave called Sarah at her apartment to tell her that there had been developments and he and Hugh were on their way over to update her. She heated up some chicken and put on fries. The other two picked up a pack of beer and a few groceries on their way across town.

Hugh was largely silent while Dave recounted the evening's events, going over the same arguments as they had been through with Sam and Jantowitz back in the lab, and arriving at the same conclusions. Sarah agreed that there were grounds for caution but not panic.

"Okay, so it looks as if someone in some reality suspects there are unauthorized experiments going on," she said. "And they're taking advantage of the machine to check into it in a more drastic way than they'd risk in their own world. The DRA will want to look into it, and we're going to be asked questions. But the whole of Washington isn't going to be down here by tomorrow."

Hugh looked dubious. "I'm not so sure. The result can only be a security clamp-down, and it could happen soon. The powers here can't afford any evidence showing up if there's a DRA investigation." He held Dave's eye pointedly for a second. "We can still do it, Dave. We could still get out while we've got the chance."

Sarah caught the look. "What's he talking about, Dave?"

"It's something we talked about the other night. . . ." Dave hesitated. But this was the obvious time. Sarah needed to be told. "Remember what happened with you that time you got cut off," he said. "Hugh wants to do it deliberately, for keeps—get away permanently. He wants us to move to Otherwhere."

Hugh continued, speaking urgently in a low voice. "We know that all three of us have analogs there. We could do it tomorrow. Think about it: a new beginning. A world that runs on honesty and decency. A chance to do real science, without being stifled in politics."

Sarah stared at him, astounded. "You're joking," she whispered. But it was pure reflex. She could see that he wasn't.

"Oh, he's serious," Dave confirmed.

"Isn't it just the kind of world you've been telling us you've always wanted?" Hugh said to her. "You've been there, too, Dave. . . . Well, I found out more about it today. Did you know they've never heard of Stalin or Hitler? So whose side were we on in World War II this time? There wasn't one. Nor even really a World War I. The European war ended in a negotiated peace in 1916—while respect for a defeated opponent still meant something, before everything went back to barbarism. So there were no Versailles injustices to be put right. Russia never collapsed, and Lenin was just a pest who went away. The twentieth century was peaceful and progressive, and somehow the European empires faded away without a lot of grievances and screams for revenge. The world became everybody's cultures, all mixed up. But people come first there. They've got their priorities right." He nodded again at Sarah.

"That's why it seems so quaint and old-fashioned to us in other ways. Without two world wars and a century of threats from totalitarianism, the manic drive for technology didn't happen. It's developing at its own leisurely pace. Jet air travel is a novelty there—they still have ocean liners. Railroads are the main way of travel between cities. They haven't even got to the Moon. But there's more focus on scientific basics. MV theory is taught in college—they just don't have the means to exploit it. They've got a simpler interpretation of Relativity that's news to me. . . ." Hugh spread his hands at the other two imploringly. "It's there, waiting, guys. Can you imagine what an asset the kind of knowledge we could bring would be in a place like that?"

Sarah looked at Dave dazedly. "This is crazy."

"A chance to start your life over again and get it right isn't crazy," Hugh said. He appealed to Dave. "You've heard what Sarah's said about Otherwhere, ever since the first time she went there. If you say you'll go, she'll go."

"Well, if you don't mind, I'd rather hear Sarah say that," Dave objected. "And in any case, maybe I'm not so sure yet that I do want to go."

Hugh looked exasperated. "Dave, I don't understand. What is there to not to be sure about?"

"Turning your back on a whole life and walking out isn't exactly something you do every day. There's a saying about the devil you don't know."

"And there's one about sometimes having to go for it. I say this is one of those times," Hugh said.

"*You* say," Dave retorted. "But what about the analogs? Where do they figure in all this? They've got lives of their own, and very probably they quite like their world too. We're not always comfortable about occupying them temporarily. So do we become invaders now, like some kind of alien monsters in the movies? Is that okay? And what happens when you confront their relatives and friends? What are you going to tell them?"

That was an objection that Hugh hadn't been prepared for. Dave had obviously been doing some thinking. Sarah, too, looked far from sold. "I don't have any really strong ties anywhere, I guess. . . . But it seems so, oh, I don't know . . . so callous, somehow. How do you just turn your back on everyone you've known and walk away like that—just leave them to it? It seems . . ." she shook her head, "despicable, somehow."

Suddenly Hugh felt weary. It was the same misgivings that he had felt—and Dave. The difference was that they'd had time to think about it, talk it over. Sarah hadn't.

She went on, "And Dave's right. You can't just displace the analogs permanently like that. Have you talked to Theo and Sam yet about this? If anybody's moving to Otherwhere, they should have an opportunity to be included too." Sarah was speaking mainly because she needed time, Hugh could see. But she had a point. He couldn't argue.

Dave saw it that way too. "They ought to be brought

into it," he agreed. "And when they are, there won't be any instant answers. Which is probably a good thing. This isn't something that you rush into overnight, Hugh. And it's not something we should dump on them right now. There's too much going on. I say we sit on it for now and think it through more." He looked at Sarah.

"In the meantime we can be finding out a bit more about Otherwhere," she said, keeping her eyes on Hugh. "First impressions aren't always the way to bet."

Hugh was impatient to resolve the issue but agreed to do things their way—for now, anyway.

Chapter Thirty-two

Edward Kintner sat in his office, reflecting on the events of the previous evening. He had reviewed the surveillance tapes with Willard and Calom first thing that morning, and they had talked to Sam, Jantowitz, and Joyce Theale. Theale, as they knew, knew nothing. Sam and Jantowitz had pleaded innocence, naturally, and claimed to have been catching up on routine official work. Of course, when Kintner and Calom visited the area afterward to preserve appearances—ostensibly checking over the scene as they would be expected to do—everything had been in order with the N2 couplers. They couldn't question it, naturally; to have done so would have given away their surveillance.

The obvious implication was that somebody in a nearby reality—almost certainly Ventz—suspected what had been going on and had tried a risk-free way of finding out. Very likely the Ventz in this reality had planned the same thing too—although he would deny it, and nobody would be able to argue. This much would be equally obvious to Sarvin, whom Kintner knew Willard to have taken into his confidence. Sarvin would not accede publicly to the suggestion of irregularities within his department, but with evidence of strong suspicions in the military camp, he would need to secure his position. Since he had nothing to gain from perpetuating the deception and a lot to lose if the allegation was proved, Kintner's guess was that Sarvin would order the surveillance reports expunged from the official record, and the modified hardware and illegally written code would be "discovered" just in time to preserve face.

Willard had been across to Polygon to talk to Colonel Elson and was due to hear back from Sarvin. While Kintner waited, he toyed with the challenge that had been intriguing him for weeks now: trying to create a long-range Multiverse map of his own from data extracted surreptitiously out of Jantowitz's illegal files.

He was familiar with the extended coordinate system that Jantowitz had devised—he had even added some improvements to it. He had followed the twists and convolutions of history that the group had described in their glimpses of other, distant realities, trying like Jantowitz to find the turning points that divided Sarah's Nazified world from Dave's Sovietized Britain, or the twists that corresponded to America's aligning here with one side in World War II, there with the other, and again with neither at all. As with all aspects of the Multiverse, everything was highly chaotic and unpredictable. Trends did not unfold steadily and uniformly in a given direction, but had a habit of reversing and reappearing again under the influence of subtle, unidentifiable causes buried in strange connectivities that neither he nor Jantowitz had a glimmer yet of how to unravel. Abandoning appeasement in the nineteen thirties deterred a major war only up to a point; taken too far, Anglo-French-American armed militancy became threat enough to provoke an alliance between Germany and Russia that resulted in an even worse conflagration than the second world war recorded in familiar history. The Vietnam conflict was supposed to have epitomized reckless flirting with a latter-twentieth-century third world war; yet, strangely, precisely such a war occurred in every version where Vietnam didn't. For some reason that remained unidentified, the Apollo program never succeeded in a universe where JFK lived.

The map, a composite of Jantowitz's original work and his own additions, was thin and scattered, by far the most of it still blank. The challenge that it represented gave Kintner an excitement that he hadn't known for years. It could be the beginnings of a whole new science. And now he would be expected to keep his mouth shut and act as though it had never happened. What kind of imbecility had they brought on the world that required him to pretend that the most staggering scientific feat that he had ever witnessed in his entire career didn't even exist?

And there amid all that uncharted territory of swamplands and jungles of violence and hatred whichever way one explored, like a lush valley hidden among mountain folds, was the anomaly that they had labeled "Otherwhere." Whatever improbable combination of circumstances had come together to produce it would probably never be known, but it was unique. Hugh Brenner was right, Kintner thought: young minds would never grow to their potential in the creative desert that this world had become. There would never be another place like this one they had stumbled on. "Get out, for God's sake," Kintner murmured aloud. "Go for it."

Willard finally called late in the morning. Kintner steeled himself. But instead of the terse instructions to sanitize the records and begin preparing the coverup that Kintner had been expecting, Willard greeted him with a strangely enigmatic expression on the screen. "I had a very interesting talk with Leonard Sarvin this morning. He's not the happiest of men, you know, Ed. He sees a lot of political trouble brewing ahead over the whole MV business. And his personal life's a mess. His wife took a walk last year, and the woman that he got mixed up with since has virtually cleaned him out. He's not particularly enamored at life's prospects as they stand, I'm afraid."

It was such an unusual conversation that Kintner just blinked, nonplussed. "That's . . . too bad," was the best he could manage in reply.

"What plans do you have for lunch?" Willard inquired.

"What?" Kintner shook his head. "Oh, none in particular."

"I'd like you to join me. Not the executive lounge. Let's

get out somewhere, away from this place for a change. Leonard is fascinated by this latest surveillance information from Calom. An outrageous but intriguing notion has occurred to us that I'd be curious for your reaction to. Do you think you could suspend your disbelief for an hour?"

Sam and Jantowitz had given their accounts of what had happened the previous evening. The team waited through the rest of the morning for something dire to develop. But apart from a few questions from the ever-curious among the project staff, all was routine. It seemed that Neville Ducaine might have put two and two together, for he materialized unexpectedly in the Bolthole a couple of times with unlikely excuses for poking around in the couplers; but, finding nothing amiss, he evidently forgot the matter and had immersed himself back in his own work upstairs by lunchtime. And whereas they had expected Kintner to be buzzing everywhere, it turned out that he had gone off with Willard, and they weren't even on-site.

Hugh volunteered for another visit to find out more about Otherwhere while they had the chance. Sam didn't think they should risk it until things had settled down more. Jantowitz, however, didn't agree. "Is probably the best time for it," he said. "All the crazies are too busy pointing fingers at each others today. It is this woman that he wants to see again. I say let him get on with it. Tomorrow, things may be different."

Hugh picked up the phone on the desk that he had found himself sitting at and called Professor Rauth's number. The office contained two other desks, equally untidy and overflowing with papers, both unoccupied at the moment. The wall opposite the two windows had shelves heavy with books, a couple of metal file cabinets— and two chalkboards. So this was where Matthew Shayne worked. He had discovered that the University raised its own funding from various sources and was thus free to pursue its own independent policies of teaching and research. The federal juggernaut that molded scientific reality to conform to policy was unknown. Shayne had an agent in San Francisco who negotiated his share of the discovery rights that Rauth's department commanded.

"Herbert Rauth here. How may I serve you?"

"Professor . . . Herb. It's Mat Shayne. Or rather, Hugh Brenner."

A pause. "You're back?" Rauth's voice shed its customary frivolity.

"Yes."

"Okay, Hugh. I've been doing a lot of thinking. You have me persuaded."

"I'm glad."

"Also, I have a list of questions that I'm curious about. Are you coming over?"

"Well . . . I don't want to sound high-handed or disinterested, but complications have developed back home and I could be brought back at any time. I really need to try and get over to San Francisco if I can while the chance is here."

"Oh, I see. Well, I'm sure you're the better judge of your own business. Do I take it that I'm required to cover for your sudden disappearance if anyone asks?"

"If you would, please." That was something that they had talked about when Hugh was here before. "I understand the disruptions that this must be causing in your department," Hugh added. "I appreciate it."

"I assure you I'm too intrigued to contemplate otherwise."

Hugh bit his lip. "How is it affecting Shayne?"

"He hasn't mentioned it, but I imagine having blackouts like this must be troubling. But then he's a scientist, so he'll understand when the time comes."

"You haven't mentioned anything to him, then?" That was another possibility that Hugh and Rauth had agreed might be necessary.

"Not as yet. I may have to quite soon, though—especially if he finds himself somewhere in the middle of San Francisco later today."

"I guess so. I'll accept whatever you judge to be best."

"That's something, anyway. . . . You know, this really is the most astounding business. I'm still not sure I fully believe it. I suppose you're quite used to this kind of thing."

"I don't think you could ever get used to it."

"Will I hear from you again today?"

"Probably not—unless I get into trouble and need help. But I'll be back to answer your questions as soon as I can."

"Very well. Let's hope that poor Mat doesn't get too disoriented in the meantime. I'll be keeping an eye on him. Good luck with whatever you're up to across the Bay."

"Thanks."

Hugh hung up. The office was still quiet. He picked up the phone again and called Yvonne's office number.

"Hi, this is Yvonne," she answered after Hugh was put through by an operator. It was strange how even the first sound of a voice could bring every detail of a face instantly into focus. Hugh found himself suddenly very nervous. Don't screw this up now, he pleaded silently to himself.

"Yvonne, hello. It's Mat."

She could have hung up. At least he was prepared for a certain coolness. He had no way of knowing what kind of situation he had left her to deal with when a bewildered Matthew Shayne found himself mysteriously transported to her apartment the other night. Instead she said, "My, that was quick!"

"What do you mean?"

"I only just talked to you half an hour before lunch."

"You did?" He groaned inwardly. Wrong, but he had said it before he could stop himself.

"Yes. You called and we agreed that . . ." There was a long pause. Then her voice took on an ominous note. "Has it happened again, Mat? . . . It has, hasn't it?"

Denying it would have been not only futile but counterproductive. He had made this trip specifically to straighten out the situation with Yvonne as much as circumstances would permit, before things here became too confused for any relationship to survive. And already, hearing her now, he was more determined than ever. She had only known Shayne for a couple of months. Backing off would have been all too easy—but there was genuine concern in her voice. Anyone who could handle this without freaking or sending for the white coats was one in a million.

"Yes, it has," he told her. "But whatever you and I might have said since the other night, I guarantee that what's happening isn't any of the things we probably thought."

There was another pause while she thought. That was another wonderful thing about her: She *listened*. "Are you saying you do know what it is?" she asked.

"Yes. And I have to get together with you to talk. I'm at the University now and could be across in the city in half an hour. Can I meet you somewhere?"

"But I'm already coming over there later."

"That's no good."

"Why not?"

"That's what I have to explain. Don't ask me even to attempt it over the phone."

She didn't protest that she was busy, try to badger him into giving her a clue, or otherwise give him a hard time. "Okay. I'll meet you in the Owl in . . . oh, how about forty minutes?"

"I have no idea where the Owl is."

"We must have been there at least a thousand . . . Oh, okay. Don't tell me. You'll explain later, right?" She gave him the location of the Sleepy Owl coffee shop on the Chinatown side of Broadway and directions for how to get there on the Bay Area subway system. They agreed to meet there in forty minutes.

The place served every conceivable kind of coffee, Viennese pastries, and the piped music playing when Hugh arrived was a Strauss polka. The waiter wore a tailcoat with shorts, and a bright red fez.

Yvonne looked prettily businesslike in a gray, ruffly blouse and pale blue skirt with matching lightweight jacket. They found a corner table by a window looking out over a small park. It had a lake surrounded by trees, lots of colorful people, and didn't exist in the San Francisco that Hugh remembered. She greeted him with a quick kiss and sat back to regard him, her chin resting lightly on a knuckle, looking lovely in the sunshine. "Well, can you remember why you're here, or do I have to remind you?"

Hugh had been asking himself all the way across the Bay on the subway how he was going to broach this. His experience with Rauth had given him some idea of what was likely to work and what to avoid. His face remained serious.

"I know you're a financial person," he said. "How much physics does that mean you'd have covered on your way through the system?"

She looked surprised. Evidently that wasn't what she had been expecting. "You know—the regular college basic . . ." Then she realized that maybe he didn't know. "Grad diploma level for a required area that you're not majoring in."

"So are you familiar with the Many Worlds theory?"

"Of . . . quantum mechanics or something, isn't it?"

"Yes, that's right."

"That's where the universe is supposed to be just a tiny part of this great big, branching . . ." Yvonne waved a hand in the air, searching for the word, "everythingness. I wouldn't say I understand all the ins and outs, but we touched on it. It's more or less what everyone believes now, though, right?" Hugh nodded. "And you're a physicist. . . ." She waited for him to complete the connection.

"True, but that's not really the point." He massaged his brow, grappling for the right angle. "So you're happy with the idea of all these other universes out there, all full of lots of people, many of whom are a little bit like you and me?"

"Well, I don't know if 'happy' is quite the word. I mean, it isn't exactly something I think about every day. It's a bit like the Big Bang or the Smallpox Holocaust. If that's what the people who are supposed to know say happens, I say okay and get on with life."

"Smallpox Holocaust? . . ."

"You kn— . . . Oh. That wiped out the Indians." She poured more coffee into her cup from the pot and indicated his inquiringly. He nodded without taking his gaze off her face.

"Consciousness traces a path through it all, somehow, and the sequence of events that it experiences is what we perceive as time," he said. "But all those other versions of us are experiencing their time sequences too. They're like runners on a racetrack, all staying inside their own lanes."

"Oka-ay . . ." Yvonne didn't see where this was leading yet.

"Now suppose that one of them wanders over the line into the lane next door—well, not the actual person; their consciousness does, so that it 'moves into' the person who exists in that lane. Just for a short while, say. And then it moves back again. What would it seem like to that person? . . . And more to the point, what would it seem like to the other people around, who exist in that lane normally?" He sat back, leaving it at that for now to see what she would make of it.

Yvonne stared at him with the kind of half smile that people use when unsure whether or not somebody is joking, all the time holding her coffee cup partway to her mouth as if having temporarily forgotten its existence. Finally her face lit up. "Okay, I get it. You've landed a part in a science-fiction movie and you're working on the role. Fine. But we're starting to overdo things just a little bit, aren't we? And I really don't think it justifies dragging me away from work for half an afternoon."

The last part told Hugh that she didn't really mean it. It was simply the best she could come up with without acknowledging that this was as crazy as Hugh was starting to sound. "Good try, but wrong," he complimented. "No, really, I'm serious."

"You're not trying to—"

He nodded. "That's it exactly. I am." She put the cup down slowly. This is it, Hugh thought to himself. If there was going to be an outburst or an abrupt walking out, this would be the moment. "Give me some credit," he said when the silence started to hang. "I'd hardly come all the way over here and waste your time with some kind of joke. I found myself back here, across in Berkeley, around an hour ago. I don't know how long it will last. That's why I had to call you and come over straightaway."

Yvonne was still staring, as if looking at him hard enough might cause a "true" or "false" indication to light up on his forehead. "So now you ought to remember all the things you said you couldn't remember when you faded out in the middle of dinner the other night," she said.

She caught on fast, Hugh thought. "Want me to go through it?" he offered.

She thought some more, then shook her head. "It wouldn't prove anything, would it? It could all be an act." Real fast.

"It could," Hugh agreed. "And so could it be sometime later today, when I suddenly forget all this and wonder what I'm doing here in San Francisco."

Yvonne shook her head hopelessly and sighed. "Tell me why I haven't told you you're sick or insane and left already," she invited.

"I can't. You'd have every good reason to. I was hoping that you were going to tell me. . . . Have I ever mentioned Professor Rauth to you?"

"All the time. He runs your department."

"You could call and talk to him if you wanted. He was a tough one to convince, but he's persuaded. Hardly a person who'd play games, I'd have thought—from the little I've seen of him."

Yvonne exhaled a long breath. At last she got to taste her coffee. "All right, since I still like you too much to walk out, and for some reason that I don't understand, I can't see you as crazy—when it would be perfectly obvious

to anyone with half a brain that you are—let's go along
with it, just to see where it leads. You're saying that at
the moment, you're not really Mat?"

He scratched his head and tossed up a hand. "It's kind
of complicated. All those versions of you strung out across
the racetracks connect up in a strange kind of way that's
not easy to describe—not the least reason being that I
don't really understand it myself. You could say that we're
different aspects of the same . . . person." He risked a
quick grin.

But Yvonne was keeping her emotional distance until
she had gotten this straight. "But you—the guy inside this
head that I'm talking to—you're normally a different
Matthew Shayne, who's part of a different world, not this
one."

"Right. Except it isn't Matthew Shayne there. I told
you it gets complicated."

"Who are you there, then?"

"Hugh, Hugh Brenner."

"Okay. So what does Hugh Brenner do when he's not
getting into wrong worlds and doing things like this to
innocent girls who only wanted a simple life? Is he a
physicist too?"

"As a matter of fact, yes. But that's really just
coincidental."

Yvonne bit into a strawberry flan that she had ordered.
"It isn't something to do with this bicycle machine that
Mat works with, then?"

Hugh smiled and shook his head. "No—although there
is a different kind of machine involved. It turns out that
information leaks between universes at the quantum level.
We think it accounts for all kinds of phenomena, from
what drives evolution to strange insights and mystical
experiences through the ages. The machine was built as
an attempt to investigate and amplify them. The diversion
of individual consciousnesses into different parts of their
total selves was an unexpected effect."

Yvonne scrutinized his face while she chewed, then

dabbed her mouth with a napkin. "Of course there's no question—under these circumstances we have to call off the wedding," she said suddenly.

Hugh spread his hands. "I didn't know there was one."

She studied his face intently. "There isn't. Just testing."

"That was sneaky," he accused.

"So, what kind of a girl, wife, whatever does Hugh Brenner have back in his own world?" she asked.

"He doesn't. You don't want to hear all the hard-luck stories."

Yvonne gave him a reproachful look. "Surely you're not saying that you couldn't find one woman to suit you in a whole world full of them. You had to come all this way to see if there were more?"

She was teasing, but Hugh studied her pensively for a moment. He had come here to get things straight, he told himself. If there was going to be a time, this was it. "Yes," he replied. "Exactly. And there was."

Yvonne looked at him; then she laughed. "Do you know, this could get interesting. All right, for now, let's pretend that I buy it. I didn't want to go back to the office today anyway. Let's go and sit on the grass over in the park, and you can tell me all about this world of yours."

Hugh hadn't realized how tense with anxiety he had been until he felt the relief flooding through his—or Shayne's—body. He had told her, and she was staying with him.

They got up from the table and stopped at the desk by the door to pay the tab. There was just one new aspect of it all that he wouldn't mention, Hugh decided as they walked out into the sunshine—at least not today. For the thought had occurred to him and Dave that the future they stood to face would be permanently insecure not only in this universe but in any universe that they might contemplate emigrating to. Simply put, if they could get there, now that the technology existed, so could anyone else. By the peculiar arithmetic of infinities, even though Otherwhere formed an infinitesimally small part of the

Multiverse totality, with innumerable potential source universes there was a nontrivial probability that other explorers or prospective migrants would find it too.

And there was no guarantee that their dispositions would be as benign as those of Hugh and his friends. In fact, if Earth's history was anything to go by, they were more likely to be those with the strongest urges to impose elsewhere what they couldn't get away with back home.

Chapter Thirty-three

General Ventz's adjutant came back from the cockpit. "We are cleared for immediate landing, sir. The pilot estimates we'll be on the ground in ten minutes."

"Very good, Major. And Colonel Elson does have our arrival schedule?"

"Yes, sir. A car is on its way to the strip now."

Ventz nodded. The adjutant sat down in his seat and buckled up. Ventz turned his head back to the window of the Defense Department executive jet and resumed staring down at the arid canyons and crumbling, brick-colored crags of the New Mexico desert. The signs of human habitation had become scattered from the Appalachians onward, and after the Mississippi, practically nonexistent. Yet Washington was filled with squabbling fanatics pushing blueprints for reengineering humanity, all based on the premise that the teeming, psychotic few square miles of planet contained inside the Beltway were representative of all of it. Everywhere the future of the world and the people in it was in the hands of deluded handfuls who understood neither. How things had gotten that way Ventz didn't know, but he doubted if they would change now. He had long dismissed questioning such things as futile. His job was simply to do whatever was in his power to ensure that his own brand of fanatics came out on top. Then, both he and they would survive. That was what it all reduced to. And those rules had been laid down a long time ago, by a far greater Authority than any of them.

Since the implications of yesterday's debacle would be equally apparent to everyone, it was more than probable that the evidence he had hoped to use Polygon to confirm before making open accusations—of laxness in the DRA command chain—would be swept out of sight by now. However, there was one person who would have complete information on everything that had transpired, whom Ventz's rank would empower him to prevail upon: Calom. For Calom was ex-military, and as such could be recalled to the service and required to disclose what he knew. Calom would be as aware of that as Ventz was, and Ventz was hoping that a reminder of the fact would be sufficient to induce his cooperation without need to take things to the limit. His strategy was as simple and direct as that. That was why he had come to Los Alamos.

The plane landed on the airstrip atop the mesa at the east end of the town and taxied to the apron in front of the reception building and tower, where a car with the LANL logo was waiting. A driver in Army uniform got out as the aircraft came to a halt. As Ventz came down the steps, he noticed another twin-engine jet parked a short distance away, with blue and white markings and a DRA emblem indicating that it was Washington based. On making inquiries, Ventz's adjutant informed him that Leonard Sarvin had also arrived that morning, apparently on an unscheduled visit. Evidently yesterday's incident was having repercussions in high places. A good sign, Ventz told himself. It suggested that his suspicions were well founded.

A short drive to the other end of town brought them to the LANL TA-3 site. After entering via the main gate, they proceeded across the general laboratory complex and through the inner checkpoint to the Polygon compound. Colonel Elson was waiting with his section chiefs. But it turned out that the day's agenda had already changed from the snap inspection visit—arranged for appearance but really covering for a private talk with Calom—that Ventz had planned. Elson informed him that Sarvin was with Willard across in the TA-3 Admin Building, and that they had requested a meeting with Ventz alone as soon as he could be available.

"Sounds like they're really flapping," Ventz commented to Elson. "Okay, we'd better find out what's going on. But it wouldn't do to look too eager. Fix it for an hour or so from now, say sometime around late morning."

The three met in Willard's office across in TA-3. To Ventz's mild surprise, Sarvin refused to reveal anything about whatever he and Willard had to say while they were anywhere on government-owned property, but insisted on calling for a car and being driven out from the Lab area completely. Ventz was astonished when they arrived back at the airstrip and boarded Sarvin's plane to conduct the discussion flying in a fifty-mile holding pattern at ten thousand feet. Sarvin finally came to the point with the door to the flight deck closed, when the three of them were alone with cocktails in the passenger compartment: the Deputy Director of the DRA, the Director of the National Laboratory, and a general of the Defense Intelligence Service.

"Just for once in this crazy business, let's start out by being frank with each other," Sarvin said to Ventz. "I'll tell you what we know you know, and what you know we know you know. That should save us all a lot of time and will hopefully get us down again before this thing runs out of gas." Ventz heard opening lines like that all the time, usually just before the most barefaced fabrications and falsehoods. Before he could respond, however, Sarvin went on, "Okay, I'll give it to you for free. You're right: The official policy directive on MV research in Octagon was not followed. The group who proposed a method for achieving longer-range transfers were permitted to continue with unauthorized experiments that they devised themselves." It didn't leave Ventz with a lot to say. There was the objective of his whole mission, achieved in a single sentence.

"It's amazing how much you can get through in a day when you put your mind to it, isn't it?" Willard commented.

Ventz could see now why they had chosen this setting. Everything said would be totally deniable. This could be an invitation for him to join a plot to assassinate the President, and he would be able to prove nothing. He nodded and sighed his acknowledgement of the facts.

Sarvin continued, "So where are we heading? Polygon is *the* hot item among people who know. So what's the angle? DRA management is too slack to handle it? A takeover bid from your side of the river, with all the usual knifework and shit-throwing? In fact if I'm right, that's probably what brings you here today." Ventz swirled his drink, downed a shot, and looked up in a way that admitted nothing. Sarvin nodded in a way that said he didn't have to. "Okay, so there's blood all down the walls, and heads roll. And let's say you take it. . . . Then what? The same dirt and sleaze for what— a year? Two? Three at the most? Then the whole world blows up anyway. And that's it? That's what it's all for? Are you satisfied with that return on effort expended, General?"

Ventz grimaced briefly. This was starting to sound philosophical. Not his department. "You play the hand you've got until it's time to quit the game," he said. "Do you think you can offer something better?"

Sarvin ignored the question for the moment. "Do you know what those mavericks have been doing while the rest of the world has been busy turning itself into a place where the only fit thing left for it to do now is self-destruct and be done with it? They've been finding other worlds out there that defy imagination. Universes exist in which the Second World War went the other way; or we allied with Hitler against the Soviets; and others where it never happened at all." That got the general's attention. "They've *been* in those universes! They've seen it."

"Through other versions of themselves who exist there," Willard supplied.

Ventz stared at them for several seconds, trying to fathom what their angle was. "If this is all an elaborate stunt to plead mitigating circumstances, it won't wash," he said finally. "The fact remains that an official policy directive was deliberately—"

Sarvin waved it aside impatiently. "Forget all that. Forget the whole mess that this world has gotten itself into. You asked me a minute ago if we could offer anything better. Well, the answer is *yes*. We can!"

Willard explained. "Not long after the long-range experiments began, in fact when Polygon was being installed, there was an incident. The system went down suddenly while one of the subjects—a young woman, as it happened—was connected on-line in one of the couplers. The researchers involved had always assumed that if that happened, consciousness would spontaneously revert back to the normal host. They were wrong. What happened was, she remained in the remote analog throughout the period, functioning normally, with no machine operating back here at all. She returned in the normal way later—a day later, when the system was restored—with no ill effects. As far as anyone can tell, there is no reason why the condition couldn't have been maintained indefinitely."

Ventz remained silent while he absorbed it. "In other words," Sarvin said, "for all the difference it made, her own, regular self, persona, body—whatever you want to call it—in this world might as well not have been there, in the coupler, at all." He spoke slowly and pointedly, all the time watching the general's face.

"In effect, she migrated there totally for the duration," Willard summarized.

Sarvin concluded, "And now one of the younger members of the group—Brenner again—is trying to get two of the others to do it permanently. They've discovered a remarkable world—a very different place from this one. People there don't seem to have prejudices. They just

don't care enough about other people's business to have
any strong opinions about what they're like or how they
ought to live. Brenner wants the three of them to escape
there permanently—start all over, be what they can be.
You know the line. . . . Don't you find that a fascinating
thought, General?"

This time the silence persisted a lot longer. The horizon
slid up the portholes on one side of the cabin as the plane
banked onto a new leg of its circuit. Ventz's expression
told them that he was getting a glimmer of what they were
driving at.

"It's all over here," Willard said. "Let's stop fooling
ourselves just for once. The world is stampeding toward
a cliff edge. What Leonard is saying has to be the most
bizarre thing that I've ever listened to too, but it makes
sense. It's a way out. Very likely it's the only one."

"My God!" Ventz breathed. Just at that moment he was
too stunned by the enormity of what he was hearing to
manage more.

"It doesn't have to mean leaving everything you know
behind," Sarvin urged, reading his eyes. "Nobody's talking
about tomorrow or next week. There's no reason why there
shouldn't be time to think about close relatives, friends . . .
whatever. We organize it like a lifeboat." He looked at
Willard. "In fact, I like that, Jesse. Why don't we use *Dinghy*
as a code word?" Willard nodded assent mutely.

Ventz exhaled a long, unsteady breath and ran a hand
through his hair. "What are you proposing?" he asked.
"That we go in with them or something?" He couldn't
see it. It didn't take much in the way of ruthless honesty
with oneself to recognize that he and the two men with
him, along with others they were likely to bring with them
and everything that they all stood for, were exactly what
Brenner and his friends would hope to get away from.

Sarvin shook his head. "I don't think so. My thought
was more that we form our own group as I've outlined,
and do it ourselves as a separate venture."

"Kind of ironic," Willard put in, with a wry smile.

Ventz's brow knotted. "Are you saying that we just . . ." he looked from one to another, groping for the word, "steal it?"

Sarvin raised his eyebrows as if it were the first time that he had looked at the matter quite that way, and nodded. "Yes, pretty much." It was a time for being candid, after all. "They've been under close surveillance all along. We have full access to everything they've done."

Although it wasn't really fitting in a space as confined as the cabin, Ventz got up from his seat and turned to stand with an arm braced against the side of one of the portholes, staring out at the ground far below.

The latest proposal for making Polygon more effective was to recruit defectors from rival or potentially hostile powers, or agents who had been turned—individuals who might still be in key positions today if events in the recent past had not gone as they had. The idea was that an MV transfer might put such a person in temporary control of an analog who hadn't defected or been turned. "Imagine having our own man inside the records section of the Chinese Secret Service for a day," one of the advocates had speculated in the Pentagon the day before.

The nightmare was that other powers might acquire machines of their own, with the result that anyone in the U.S.'s own military high command, intelligence agencies, or in friendly embassies anywhere could turn into another side's agent at any time. That was why the technology couldn't be allowed to get out, and what made it essential that the whole MV program be put under tight control. But it was a panic measure, a stopgap, Ventz knew. Everybody knew, if they were honest. But they weren't being honest. There simply wasn't an alternative. The Japanese were definitely working on advanced MV; the Chinese probably were. It was only a matter of time now before the whole world became one, huge asylum. And as Sarvin had said, "Then what?"

Ventz turned his head to look back over his shoulder. "How many other people are in on this?" he asked.

"So far, just Ed Kintner—obviously we need a technical expert," Sarvin said. "Jesse and I only talked about it for the first time yesterday."

"So why me? Why are you telling me all this now?"

Sarvin drained the last of the scotch from among the ice cubes in his glass. "Obviously, if it's going to be kept secret, we can't use the Octagon machine. Therefore it will have to be Polygon." He shrugged. "If you're not part of it, it doesn't fly. Simple as that. Then we found you were due here today. . . ." He left it unfinished.

Which was as Ventz had figured. "Who else knows about the experiments that this group have been doing, and Brenner's idea?" he asked.

Willard answered. "Only Calom. Some of his operatives have been involved in parts of it, of course, but only he has the complete picture."

Ventz had one more question for now. "And is it your intention to attempt recruiting Calom into this scheme also?"

Sarvin pursed his lips for a moment, then nodded. "I think we have to. For one thing, he's good, and we'll need him. And for another, we can't afford not to. You'd never keep something like *Dinghy* from him forever. Once we start asking for detailed design information out of those files, it wouldn't take him long to guess why."

Ventz nodded curtly, then returned to his seat and sat down. "I agree," he said tersely.

Sarvin glanced at Willard and then looked back at Ventz. "Does that mean that you . . . ?"

"It means that you've given me a lot to think about, gentlemen," Ventz replied. "I'm sure that you weren't expecting an immediate answer. But I will admit that what you have said does tend to reduce the conflicts that I had been anticipating between us to the dimensions of pretty foolish trivialities by comparison."

On his return to Polygon, Ventz surprised Colonel Elson by announcing that the plan to put pressure on Calom to disclose the required evidence was on hold for the time being. He gave no explanation, but in the course of further conversation inquired casually if Elson had many close family ties or if his work was pretty much his life. Elson thought it was a strange question. Ventz had never expressed any interest in anything like that before.

Chapter Thirty-four

In the Middle Ages, proponents of religious beliefs considered to be heretical were viewed not only as having forfeited their own salvation, but as threatening that of all whom they came in contact with as well. Hence, wars were fought to exterminate them. Sometimes the victims numbered entire nations. By the end of the nineteenth century, things had changed. Wars had become political, and were fought for limited political objectives when diplomacy failed. When the objective was achieved, the fighting ceased. A "civilized" notion of war resulted, with formal rules protecting noncombatants and regulating the treatment of prisoners, and terms of surrender that sought to respect the dignity and honor of the defeated side. To desire the total destruction of a nation or a people would have been unthinkable, and it became fashionable to hope that it would be only a matter of time before war was eradicated from human affairs entirely. Then came the twentieth century with its rediscovery of secular religions, and the accompanying reversion to barbarism that sanctioned universal conscription, mass internment and deportation, and the indiscriminate saturation bombing of civilian populations.

At least, that was the way it had been in Sarah's own universe. She stretched on the couch and yawned, and then returned to the books that she had brought back from the downtown public library. Piecing together the story of how things had gone differently in Otherwhere had been fascinating her for almost two hours. The only problem was her muzzy head and upset tummy. She wished that Carol, which was the name of her boyfriend-battling actress analog in Detroit, didn't party so much.

It seemed that the nations of Europe had come to their senses somewhere around the middle of 1916. The old Western system was not wrecked, but at the same time neither did it become a permanent institution for forcible suppression of the rest of the world. Instead, colonialism somehow withered away as the cultures of governors and governed became inextricably mingled across a world that was at the same time being shrunk in physical space by the sciences that the East had never developed, and expanded in spiritual space by the insights that the West had never mastered. In the process, people came to realize that most of the differences that they had squabbled about for millennia were illusory, and the few that did exist really didn't matter very much. Sam would have liked that, she thought.

The outer door of the apartment opened, and she heard someone enter. It could only be Barry, the artist. Sarah sighed to herself. She had hoped to avoid another of these encounters.

There was a shuffling of footsteps, and he appeared in the doorway—tall and bony; shoulder-length blond hair; wrinkled brown pants and a frayed sweater. "Well, don't say hello or anything. I just live here too."

"Oh . . . Hi."

"Say, what's all this?" He came into the room and picked up a couple of the books strewn around her. *"The Brink Year: 1916?* How long have you been reading this stuff? . . . *The Decline and Fall of Empire?"*

"So I like to broaden my interests. That's supposed to be a good thing. Is it okay with you?" Sarah was aware by this time that trying to talk reasonably with him didn't work.

"Oh, sure." His tone was sarcastic. "Anything that makes me look stupid, huh? I know your kind of game."

"You seem quite capable of achieving that on your own, Barry, without any help from me." *Wrong,* she told herself. It had been pure reflex. . . . Although she sometimes thought she would be doing Carol a favor if she blew things permanently with this character while she was here one day, and then disappeared back out of the picture.

Barry threw the books down on the couch and turned on her with an ugly expression. Only then did she catch the beer on his breath. But before anything further could develop, the phone rang in the next room. Barry muttered something and stamped away through the doorway to take it. Sarah waited apprehensively. This wasn't good. She knew who the caller was.

"Yeah? . . . That's right. . . . Yeah . . . *Where?* . . . Okay . . . Who the hell are you?" Sarah put her book down and got up. "Carol, it's for you." She walked through. Barry thrust the phone at her and stood watching with an accusatory air.

"Hello? Carol here."

"Hi, there. It's Dave, calling from the early hours over here." Dave had confirmed the intersection with Hugh in Otherwhere. Hugh had confirmed with Sarah. Logic demanded that Dave's being coincident with Sarah followed. Jantowitz had insisted that they verify it. Maybe Polish logic was different.

She was distantly aware of Barry trying to move his face in front of hers, at the same time muttering, "A *guy*, from *England* . . . Who do we know in *England*?" She waved him off and turned the other way.

"Look, sorry but this isn't a good time to talk."

"Just listen to this. Man, I walked in at the right time."

"Barry, shut *up*! . . ."

"Just a couple of seconds," Dave persisted. He sounded in good spirits. "I've had a horrible thought about this crazy idea of Hugh's. What if we did transfer here permanently, and it turned out that we weren't exactly

wild about the analogs here? Know what I mean? For all
you know, this guy who's a radio astronomer in Manchester
could be a hundred pounds overweight with dandruff and
bad breath. That would be a hell of a thing to find out
after you were committed, wouldn't it? And how am I
supposed to feel about a nonreturnable blind date with
this actress over there in Detroit? Hugh doesn't have a
problem. He's already fixed up."

It was so obvious that just for a moment Sarah forgot
her immediate predicament. "You're right. We need to
get together." The problem was, it would require days.

"Christ, I don't believe this!" Barry snatched at the phone.
Sarah shoved him away. He snarled and came back at her,
swinging with an open hand. She let the phone drop and
warded the blow around her, at the same time turning
inside his arm and drawing him on while her leg swept
his feet from under him to send him crashing on his back
with a bang that jarred his teeth and knocked the breath
out of him. Sarah picked up the phone again, still dangling
and squawking on its cord.

"Dave, I have to go. . . . Yes I'm okay. Talk to you later.
Have a nice trip back." She hung up and collected the
library books together off the couch.

Barry sat up, groggy and wheezing. "Shit, where did
you learn that?"

"Just something I picked up in Japan," she said coldly
and not thinking. "You'll live. I have to take these back."
She went through to the hall and opened the front door.
At least, if it happened, she wouldn't have much in the
way of ties to worry about, she reflected. And in the
meantime, maybe she had done her analog a small favor.

"When the fuck were you ever in Japan?" Barry's voice
yelled after her as she let herself out.

It was past one o'clock in the morning at the Jodrell
Bank radio observatory on the outskirts of Manchester.
Its shape traced by red warning lights, the two-hundred-
fifty-foot steel lattice dish of the main telescope stared

up into the murky blackness of a wet English night. In the control room, Dr. Nigel Cormack watched as David Vaughan replaced the phone after his long-distance call to Detroit.

Cormack was over his initial consternation now, and getting used to Vaughan forgetting who he was periodically and being taken over—so he said—by another version of himself from a different universe. At first, when it became clear that it wasn't just a silly joke, Cormack had insisted that David get himself checked, but none of the specialists had been able to find anything wrong. But when, during these seizures, Vaughan showed himself able to describe with alacrity all kinds of technological developments way ahead of anything even being speculated about currently— and the experts that Cormack checked with said that it all made perfect sense—he had started to wonder. Now, after contacting and talking to Rauth in California, who Vaughan said was in the same predicament with a colleague of Vaughan's alter ego from the same alter universe, Cormack was almost persuaded.

Nevertheless, accepting it as genuine for now, he had been horrified by some of the accounts of the kind of world that was apparently necessary to advance technology at such a rate. Worldwide wars? Slave labor camps? Cities teeming with starving children? . . . So what if they had reached the Moon as far back as the 1960s? It didn't sound as if they'd done much with it since. If those were the neuroses and pressures that it took, then Cormack was happy to let the pace that he was familiar with take its own, unhurried course.

"She's there, but it sounds as if it isn't a good time to talk," Dave announced. "No matter. It's told us what we wanted to know."

It was very different from the England that he'd known before moving to Los Alamos. There was no licensing of drinking hours, no mandatory ID documents, no passports to travel overseas, no censorship, no income tax. Health care, retirement provision, and even legal services were somehow at the same time taken care of by society in a socialist kind of way, yet not run by the government. Cormack had tried to explain, but Dave still didn't understand how it worked; it seemed to require a mind-set that he wasn't able to absorb. Sex clubs and partners advertised openly as a matter of course; drugs were available over the counter to those who wanted them—although most people seemed to look down on them as a low-class, vulgar habit; and going about armed was anyone's right, although few people chose to exercise it. Cormack had expressed astonishment that anybody should think to contest it, and remarked that doing so in Dave's world didn't seem to have done much good. And yet, there were churches, temples, and mosques everywhere; tastes in dress, manners, entertainment, and music were, if anything could be made of the strange mixtures and blendings in evidence on every side, fairly conservative; and there were more neckties than miniskirts out on the street.

It seemed to be a world where everybody—races, nations, creeds, sexes, generations—was not angry and rebelling against something. A world at peace with itself.

And on top of all that, they'd even managed to get his name right!

Cormack looked at the clock above the steering control panel. "Well, that's it, is it? How much longer are you due to be with us this time?" As an aside he muttered half to himself, "Extraordinary question to ask somebody. I'm not sure I'll ever get used to this." Cormack was every inch the English academic: tweed jacket, knitted tie; smoked a pipe; fussed around in his garden; drank pints of bitter; followed cricket.

"A little under an hour," Dave answered.

"What do you want to do, then? Fancy a quick one somewhere maybe? I made sure I wasn't expected back at any particular time tonight. You don't exactly get this kind of thing happening every day of the week."

"Sounds like a good idea to me. I can't remember how long it's been since I had a decent English pint."

"Pretty awful, this American stuff, I suppose, is it?"

"It doesn't come close to a good Sam Smith's."

"God, what a way to make a quick trip back for one. I bet the chaps who made this machine of yours never thought it would be used for something like that."

Cormack said his goodnights, and they left the night crew to their various tasks amid heavy steel cubicles and black boxes. After the environments that Dave was used to, the place put him in mind of an old movie set. "Er, I think that's yours," Cormack said, pointing to one of the coats on the rack by the door. "Don't ask me where your car's parked, though. You'd better drive with me. I'll pick Dave— the other Dave, Vaughan—up in the morning." He shook his head. "Extraordinary business. Extraordinary . . ."

They went through double doors and began descending a steel-railed staircase, the posts topped by castings that looked like minarets. "You know," Cormack went on, "with all the things you've told me, I'm amazed that the dominant cosmological theory where you come from is still General Relativity. The electromagnetic force is over a billion-cubed times stronger than gravity, and ninety-nine percent of observed matter exists as charged plasma and responds to it. Yet your people have gravity as the prime shaper of the universe. Do you really think that makes sense?" It was something that they had talked about earlier in the evening. In the models current in Cormack's world, gravity became a significant factor only after an earlier epoch in which magnetic forces produced irregularities in mass distribution sufficient for it to operate on effectively. One consequence was an age for the universe far, far greater than the generally accepted figure that Dave was familiar with.

"I suppose it wasn't relevant to making weapons," Dave replied. "It's research aimed at practical results that gets funded back there. So that's where all the talent is. There's no money or prestige in questioning basics."

"But you've got to! All the time. That's what science is all about."

"I know that, Dr. Cormack. But try telling politicians."

Cormack frowned. "Why? What's it got to do with them?"

"Well . . . they're the ones who pay the money. So they get to make the decisions."

Cormack held the door for Dave as they left the building. He looked baffled. "But surely you're not saying they run science. How can they? It's not their job. I mean, if you're sick you don't go to the post office, for heaven's sake."

"I suppose they consider it's their job to direct scientific effort onto the things that are felt to be important," Dave said.

That kept Cormack thinking all the way across the parking lot. As they climbed into his Vickers—not a make that Dave recognized; it was massively upright and had chrome scallops worked into the external trim—he said, "We'll make it an out-of-the-way place, I think. Vaughan has a number of lady friends who are likely to show up in the local pubs. None of them exactly what you'd call serious as far as I'm aware, but I wouldn't want to risk complicating the poor chap's life any more than it is already."

"Absolutely."

Cormack came back to the previous topic as he started the motor. "I'm not sure how you *can* apply scientific effort to anything important," he said.

This time it was Dave's turn to have to stop and think. "I don't understand," he said finally.

"Hm. Well, let me try and put it this way. Being scientific about something means wanting to know how it really *is*, as opposed to how you'd want it to be or how you want other people to think it is. Wouldn't you say?"

"Okay."

Cormack nodded. "In other words, being objective. But when you say something's 'important,' it means you're probably too emotionally involved with the subject to be objective. You've got too many passions and prejudices about what you want the answers to be. And once that's true, then what's going on is no longer science."

Cormack backed out of the slot and headed the car in

the direction of the gate. "It sounds as if you're saying that science is only any good for things that don't matter," Dave commented.

"Not really. What I'm saying is that you've got to make your mind up in advance that you really don't care what the answer is if you hope to understand something," Cormack answered. "For instance, Newtonian mechanics and modern astronomy only became possible once people got all the ideas out of their heads about gods and angels being involved in moving the planets around, and burning in hell if you believed the wrong thing. It sounds as if people back in this world of yours need to learn to do the same about all the things they keep fighting each other over."

It struck Dave then that that was just what had happened here. In his own world, the social zealots who sought to understand society "scientifically" were missing the whole point, imitating external appearances by swamping themselves in worthless data and playing with statistics that meant nothing. What they had failed to bring to the subject was the scientific *attitude*.

"Government here is just a kind of . . ." Dave searched for an analogy, "traffic police, isn't it?" he said. "Its function is purely passive—one of restraint. As long as people are leaving each other alone and not making an undue menace of themselves, government really doesn't have all that much to do."

Cormack glanced at him oddly from the driver's side. "Well, of course," he agreed. "What else is it for?"

It sounded like what Sam had been saying all along: the first step to seeing reality was to be free from passions and delusion. Dave could see why Sarah and Hugh had responded to this world as they had.

He was beginning to develop an attraction to it too. Although Cormack had made several references to the other Dave—the one who belonged here—Intruder Dave had not expressed much curiosity about him or how all this was affecting him. The truth was, he didn't want to get too close emotionally, to know the person as a person. For Hugh's arguments were starting to sound persuasive, and Dave was working hard on ways to rationalize the thought that if he did decide to go along, then for his analog it would perhaps be just too bad. After all, he hadn't made the rules. Sometimes life's circumstances dictated that there had to be winners and losers. . . . And then there was Otherwhere's vulnerability to think about. Now that the age had been reached in which QUADAR technology was possible, it was open to intruders from anywhere in the Multiverse. If Dave and his friends were powerless to save their own world, maybe they could contribute something to enabling this, more deserving one to do something toward protecting itself. How could David Vaughan possibly object if he knew the truth? What would be the loss of just one bundle of personal reminiscences and opinions compared to furthering a worthy cause like that?

In an operating theater in a hospital near Baltimore, a nurse gasped suddenly at the sight of the exposed chest cavity being held open by forceps in front of her. She gagged, put a hand to her throat, and hastily left the room.

Minutes later, a deck hand aboard a fishing boat leaving harbor at Yakutat, Alaska, dropped the line that he had been tying and stared around in astonishment.

Calom found himself in the plant manager's office of an oilfield in Arabia.

It was surprising how quickly Kintner had been able to duplicate the modifications and get the special couplers up and running. The first reconnaissance team from Polygon had arrived in Otherwhere to check over the territory.

Chapter Thirty-five

General Ventz's supervisory position over Polygon and his ability to operate behind a screen of military security made him key to Sarvin's scheme. Once he was persuaded, he quickly came to dominate the group and take effective charge. After sounding out their dispositions through elaborate cover stories, he began compiling a list of selected individuals from high military and civilian positions for potential inclusion, referring to them by code names and withholding their identities from each other, with the result that very soon only he possessed the complete picture. He also decided that perhaps "Dinghy" was too reserved a term to denote a project of such scale and scope, and so changed it to "Argo."

The kind of new existence that he contemplated for the Argo group was very different from that envisaged by Hugh and his friends. They were typically people whose lives were dictated by obsession with political security, which demanded influence and power. This need was made all the more acute by the uncertainties of coping in a new and unknown world. But how were influence and power to be attained when their analogs were likely to be found scattered all over the political and social spectrum?

A promising approach might be to seek the patronage of an established group that commanded both already, such as a cooperatively disposed government. After all,

317

looking from the point of their own world view, the members of the group felt that the practical experience they could bring with them of the old Machiavellian arts that seemed on the way to being forgotten in Otherwhere would give them much to offer. A whole world was just sitting there, defenseless and unheeding, waiting to be taken over by the right combination of ruthlessness, ability, and ambition.

But when one of the spooks' analogs—code name "Cossack"—walked into the Chinese consulate in New York to try an experimental sales pitch, he was merely listened to politely over a cup of tea, and then escorted back to the street by smiling officials after receiving two complimentary tickets to a new Chinese musical due to open shortly on Broadway, to show that there were no hard feelings. Clearly, this was going to require a lot more thought, research, and time.

An alternative was the age-old method of identifying some group with a grievance—real or imagined; pre-existing or stirred up for the purpose—and adopting their cause in order to be propelled to more influential heights by the militancy and support thus generated. All the members of Argo were old hands at that game; they had been chosen for that reason.

Still, problems remained that Hugh and his companions still didn't have solutions to either: how to bring analogs together over long distances when they could be controlled only for short periods; how to coordinate any long-term strategy when the analogs would revert to a condition of total amnesia whenever the connection was broken. It was true that use of Polygon meant that operating sessions could be longer than was practicable for illegal runs with Octagon, but that was only of partial help. Even spooks had to eat and sleep, and have some kind of life that needed attending to offstage some of the time. Kintner wondered if it would be possible to recruit the analogs into the scheme by initiating some kind of dialogue through written messages in the way that Jantowitz had done. Willard thought it might aid credibility to have the Argo analogs make themselves known to individuals in Otherwhere who already knew the situation and who would be able to convince others, such as Rauth in San Francisco and Cormack in Manchester. Ventz was for simply taking over the U.S. military—it was small and laughably equipped compared to what he was used to, but that could be an advantage—and going for an all-out coup.

Again, it all added up to a need for more time. And time was one thing that Ventz was not sure he could count on. It wasn't due so much to the world situation as the thought that the scientists mainly responsible for making the whole thing possible might at any time take it into their heads to go with Hugh's urgings and depart permanently.

"Where would we stand if that happened?" he asked Kintner during one of Kintner's visits to Polygon to discuss developments. "Would we feel comfortable about implementing Argo on our own, using the information we've got?"

Kintner looked dubious. "Results with Polygon have been encouraging, but I wouldn't want to try going it alone just yet," he said. "We're still merely imitating a lot of procedures that we don't fully understand." Which was about as Ventz had assessed the situation.

"Maybe it's time to rethink the policy on longer ranges, then," Ventz mused. "We can't afford to have these people irreplaceable. We need to get Octagon working on long-range methods openly. Then we'd have a solid, official, technical-support base to tap into."

"That would certainly help matters," Kintner agreed.

The other thing that Ventz was not happy about was the thought of people appearing in Otherwhere who were not part of Argo. People who were unpredictable and outside his control made him nervous. And in a situation like this, such people were more than liable to alert the wrong authorities or otherwise jeopardize the successful outcome. It was a complex enough undertaking already.

He needed some way of stopping them from migrating to Otherwhere. They could go somewhere else if they chose—it would make no difference to Ventz and his own accomplices what happened in some other universe after Argo's completion; but he didn't want any other independent group loose in the universe that he had selected now as "his." Simply having them arrested wouldn't work, because Kintner would need their cooperation in setting up an official long-range program for Octagon. And until that was off the ground, Ventz was reluctant to reveal that they had been under surveillance and that their own plan was known, for fear that they might refuse all cooperation and so scuttle both plans permanently.

How to reconcile the requirements of stopping them from going without giving the game away was far from immediately obvious.

Sarvin issued a revised DRA directive authorizing a preliminary investigation into the possibility of adapting the QUADAR to longer-range capability along the lines proposed earlier. Commencement of work on the requisite hardware modifications and supporting software was approved accordingly. Willard called a meeting of Kintner, Ducaine, Mulgrave, and their various section heads to announce the news, which caused considerable excitement. Hugh and Jantowitz were present to explain their work at Berkeley, which provided the conceptual basis for the new undertaking. The ensuing flurry of technical discussions and planning activity provided a convenient smoke-screen for continuing, whenever they got the chance, their own private explorations of Otherwhere.

So did others who were only newly introduced to it.

Calom—his Otherwhere name was Jack Frazer—stood outside a hut wedged between towers of pipes and machinery, looking out across the Arabian wastes. At a trestle bench in front of the metalworking shop nearby, one of the engineers was standing with a group of young teenagers—boys, girls, brown and white—watching while one of them tried his hand with a welding torch. In bygone days, children had learned the ways and skills of adulthood in the home or out on the farm; in Otherwhere it was not uncommon to take them to one's place of work.

"Has it ever occurred to you, Jack, that this planet comes like a packet soup?" the man standing next to him said. His name was Singrit—Indian or Pakistani, Calom was not sure which. He had a Herculean build and was wearing greasy orange coveralls with a white pith helmet.

It never had. "How do you mean?" Calom asked.

Singrit extended an arm. "Most of the world is like this. It's all there—good for just about anything you want. You just have to add water. Instant planet."

Calom wasn't used to hearing thoughts like that. People in his experience talked mostly about how to kick ass or to protect their own. "That's one way of looking at it," he agreed.

"Well, the water is all here too, but they're not mixed," Singrit said. "It's all ocean in one place and sand in another. We only live along the fringes of where the two happen to come together—coasts and river valleys. Most of the surface isn't used yet. You could support, oh . . . fifty billion people easily. Plenty of time to learn how to get off the planet."

Always, there was plenty of time for everything. Another thing that Calom had difficulty getting used to. "How are you going to mix them?" he said dubiously. "It sounds like it would need a pretty big spoon."

"Energy," Singrit said. "But not with oil. The new atomic reactors could do it, though. They've got the concentration to desalinate economically, and the yield to pump anywhere you want. All that out there will be green one day."

In Calom's world it was radioactive. The latest news was that one of the bases in Arabia had been taken out by a tactical nuke. Nobody was admitting responsibility, but it was believed to be in retaliation for more planes being shot down by U.S. carrier forces off Oman. Ventz was trying to bring forward the timetable for Argo. It seemed it might be more urgent than they had thought.

Tom Felada was Sarvin's brother-in-law. He was also state governor of Texas and an oil billionaire whose holdings and political connections reflected years of international dealing that had secured U.S. options on major reserves in territories that were judged to be reliable. Tom knew the locations, extent, and quality of deposits from Alaska to the Caribbean to the other end of Siberia; he was conversant with deep-water drilling technologies developed only in the last twenty years—the kind of knowledge and experience that it was thought would stand to get the right people's attention in Otherwhere.

He opened his eyes in one of the couplers in Polygon and looked around to regain his bearings. Members of the elite chosen as possible Argo candidates were being brought incognito to Los Alamos, ostensibly to be introduced to the existence of an MV program. Ventz was watching with Kintner. A Polygon scientist was operating the console. Ventz didn't care too much now if the Polygon's existence became known to too many people, since he didn't plan on being around to be affected by the consequences. And if Argo didn't happen, it wouldn't matter much anyway.

"My God, it was incredible!" Felada exclaimed. "I was back in my office in Austin with a guy whose name I won't mention, but who's been a pain in the ass about something for months." Felada was stolid and phlegmatic by nature, and the excitement that he was radiating was uncharacteristic. "I almost didn't make it here today because we had trouble with the plane, and at one point I was about to put off the trip. . . ." He waved a hand about. "But in that world I was in just a few minutes ago, it *happened!*"

Kintner smiled thinly and nodded. "That's the kind of thing you get. It's one thing to hear other people describing it. But nothing compares with the actual experience."

"But there's more. See, as things are, I'm due to see this guy tomorrow—in this world. Yet I learned a few things today that would have caused me to play very differently if I'd known about them to begin with." Felada grinned crookedly. "But you see, back here now, I *do* know about them to begin with. So boy am I gonna have a ball with this asshole tomorrow." He looked at Ventz. "This is worth more than all the explanations. Now I can see what Polygon is. No wonder they're keeping it under such tight wraps."

Except that the real reason for bringing Felada here was not to clue him in on the capabilities of Polygon at all.

"Well, since you're so impressed, let's send you off again in a slightly different direction," Ventz said.

"Okay." Felada settled himself back. Ventz looked at Kintner. Kintner sent a slight nod in the direction of the scientist operating the console. The scientist quietly activated the coordinates obtained via the tap into Jantowitz's files in Octagon, that would direct the transfer to Otherwhere. Ventz and Kintner watched Felada's face curiously.

After several seconds he refocused within the room and frowned at them, puzzled. "What's wrong? It doesn't feel like anything's happening this time."

Kintner's brow creased. "You're sure?"

"Sure I'm sure."

"Negative connection function," the scientist at the console confirmed. It meant that Felada didn't have a connected analog in Otherwhere.

"It's all still very new," Kintner said. "Sometimes we do get these minor hitches."

Ventz sighed silently to himself. Scratch another one off the list. It also meant he would have to pass the word to Sarvin that sorry, brother Tommy wouldn't be going.

It only occurred to Ventz later that it was the obvious way to make sure that Brenner and his companions would never be able to migrate to Otherwhere, or make any kind of trouble there, either: Eliminate their analogs.

"Talk to Calom and get as much as you can on Matthew Shayne in Berkeley, David Vaughan in England, and Carol Yeats in Detroit," Ventz instructed Elson. "I want details of where they live and work, regular habits and movement patterns—you know the kind of thing. Observe maximum discretion. If Calom asks, it's just routine to complete our records."

"I understand," Elson answered.

"Also, I want a listing of all Polygon operatives who possess an Otherwhere analog, and in each case, where the analog is normally located. Also, occupation, situation regarding freedom of movement, and any infirmities or physical disabilities."

Chapter Thirty-six

It was the first time that Hugh had seen Matthew Shayne's apartment in Oakland. It was a cheerful and sunny place, near the water, facing westward across the Bay, with a fine view of an elaborately ornamented Bay Bridge. The bridge carried a road and rail connection through a pagoda-like tower on Treasure Island that contained a casino, hotel, and entertainment complex.

He found himself stretched out along a couch with a Civil War spy novel propped against his knee—the last century hadn't produced much in the way of military excitement, and writers were forced to cast back farther for material in that vein. There had been some squabbling over territory when the former colonial empires broke up, but they had been mainly localized affairs that didn't really get adrenaline flowing like the good-old flag-waving, drum-beating issues of days gone by. Like most people, Shayne felt a peculiar fascination toward such times and wondered what it would have been like to have lived in them. The records of the brutality and suffering were repugnant; but the depictions of gallantry, bravery, and comradeship that came with them evoked a certain admiration and curiosity that couldn't be denied.

He set the book aside and got up to wander around the rest of the apartment. A kitchen with a small dining table opened off from the living room. Beyond was a bedroom, spare room, bathroom, and a couple of closets. He came back to the living room with its French window and veranda with garden furniture, facing out across the bay, and stood looking around, puzzled. There was an eerie feeling of familiarity about it all, somehow. A door on the far side was open and led through to a study containing bookshelves and a desk. He went across to the door and looked in. A white, business-size envelope was wedged under the paper–bail of the typewriter, with something written on it in black ink, positioned to be readily visible. He moved closer and peered at it. The words read: <u>HUGH BRENNER</u>, and were underscored.

He had just taken the envelope out and was about to open it, when the phone rang. He sat down to take the call from the extension on the desk. Even before she spoke, he knew it would be Yvonne.

"Hello, Mat. It's me."

"Hi."

"It was interesting. There was a lot there that I think you'd have liked. Anyhow, I've had my fill of cultural inspiration for today. Is there anything you want me to pick up?"

"No, I don't think so."

"So what have you been doing? Did Jerry call yet about next week?"

"Not yet. Oh . . . I've just been relaxing with a book. Figured I'd earned it."

"Good. That's what I've been telling you. So, I'm on my way."

"See you in about ten minutes, then."

"If not sooner." Yvonne blew a kiss down the phone and hung up.

Hugh stared at the receiver in his hand and replaced it slowly. He let his gaze wander again over the room that he had never seen before, yet in some strange way felt at home in; then he opened the envelope that he was still holding in his hand.

It contained a three-page letter from Matthew Shayne.

Hugh ran his eye over the sheets absently. Mat had talked to Yvonne and Rauth, and now had a better idea of what was behind the sudden blackouts that had been affecting him lately. At least it was nice to know that he wasn't physically ill or coming apart at the mental seams. All the same it was weird, to put things mildly, and not a little scary. On the other hand he was a scientist, frankly curious, and if he was honest, admitted to a certain degree of excitement despite his apprehension. Either way, since it appeared that Shayne didn't have a lot of control over the situation, he guessed he was pretty stuck with it. Finally, he couldn't get over how fortunate it was to have somebody as intelligent and thoughtful as Yvonne, who actually wanted to stick around and be involved instead of throwing her hands in the air and running away screaming. He hoped Hugh wasn't about to do anything to mess that up. Hugh scanned over it to the end of the last sheet, but he didn't really read it. He didn't have to. Because he more or less knew already what it said.

And yet even now, while he reflected on how that could possibly be, he was aware of a part of himself asking why that should be so surprising.

There had been something odd about everything, right from the beginning of this transfer. He went over it and tried to reexamine everything that had gone through his mind since he first found himself on the couch, reading the book.

How had he *known* this was Oakland, and what was outside the window before he had really looked? And how come he knew what was inside the tower with a tunnel running through it, halfway across the Bay Bridge? He had known what the book that Shayne was reading was about, even though he had barely glanced at one or two sentences, and he knew Shayne's reactions to it. He had been expecting Yvonne to call. Something was happening that he hadn't experienced before. He was still puzzling over it when footsteps clattered on stairs outside, and the doorbell rang.

She greeted him with a bright smile and a kiss, smelling perfumy and wonderful. Hugh made no attempt to dissuade her, although he was unable to prevent his mild but pleasant surprise from showing. She noticed at once, took a step back, and looked at him searchingly. "You're Hugh, back again, right?"

"Yes."

She studied his face for a moment longer, then frowned. "Something's worrying you, though. What's up?"

"I'm not sure. Come in." She did. He closed the door behind her. "You don't miss much."

"I suppose it's something I've gotten into the habit of watching for. But why the strange look all of a sudden?"

They went through to the kitchen. He took her coat and hung it on one of the pegs near the door. There was no need to ask her if she wanted coffee. He went over to the counter by the sink, opened one of the unit doors above, and took out the tin. Then he turned and showed it to her. "See. I knew where it was. Funny things like this have been happening ever since I found myself lying on the couch in the next room reading a book, just a few minutes before you called."

Yvonne took down two mugs from a rack by the toaster, looked in the refrigerator, and produced a carton of milk. Hugh told her about the book, the apartment, the tower across the Bay, and the letter left in the typewriter. She listened without speaking while she filled the mugs from the pot. "So you were here already—you'd arrived here, I mean—when I talked to you on the phone," she observed.

"Right."

She nodded as if confirming at last. "You knew I was at the art gallery. You said you'd see me in ten minutes."

"Did I?" Hugh had missed that himself. He hadn't consciously registered anything about an art gallery. This girl was quick. And her composure in handling something as outlandish as this whole situation was uncanny—or was that something that came with growing up in Otherwhere? "A lot of him is still here," he said.

"Who?"

"Matthew—he isn't totally suppressed this time."

But it went farther than that. Although Hugh had referred to Shayne as "him," an internal feeling of somebody "separate" from himself—properly described in the third person—refused to form. It was not like having another voice talking to him inside his head, something apart. Rather, he felt it as part of an expanded awareness that embraced more than the person he was used to being. Although the Hugh Brenner part with impressions of life up to Los Alamos was dominant, it existed as just one side of a composite consciousness that extended into this reality too. Of course there had been no need to read the letter that he had found waiting for him. It wasn't simply that he "knew" what the content would be. He *felt* all the things that had induced Shayne to write it.

They took their coffees outside and sat at the table on the veranda. The docks both on the near side of the Bay and across in San Francisco were larger and more extensive than those in Hugh's world. The tide was high, and several large passenger liners were moving through the Golden Gate. Ocean travel still predominated here. Jet air travel had arrived, Hugh had learned from Rauth, but it was still a novelty.

He had meant to ask Yvonne more about the workings of business here, which had still been puzzling him. But now that he was here, he found that there was really no longer any need.

Along with the Shayne part of his awareness came a glimpse of the insight possessed by those who belonged here, which had so far eluded him. By the unquestioned tenets of his own world, the purpose of business was to make money; the particular form of activity engaged in was merely a regrettable prerequisite to that end. Human talent, in other words, was developed and utilized as the means to create profit. Here, simply, it was the other way around: Business was merely a means to develop talent.

Yvonne wanted to know more about the world that

Hugh was from, especially its mass politics and global-scale militarization, which were unheard of in Otherwhere. Hugh tried to portray it, but she was as incapable of conceptualizing the mind-set that had produced Dresden, Pol-Pot, Apartheid, and the Gulag system as he would have been of understanding corporate elections without the new perspective that he had started to acquire. Yet at the same time, he found himself, also, more deeply disturbed than he remembered ever being before. Phrases of Sarah's came to mind, familiar but with a difference: no longer did he merely hear the words; he *felt* them. It was, he realized, the Shayne part of him, reacting in the only way that sensibilities tuned to Otherwhere could.

They stood by the veranda rail, watching the sun dip behind the Golden Gate and transform the Bay into a lake of luminescent copper. Yvonne drew nearer. She was more sure of herself now. There was no stranger here, but, as he had claimed from the beginning, just a deeper, mysteriously more alive version of the person she had known all along. She didn't want the moment to come when part of him would leave again, and he would revert back to what he had been. She didn't say so. It wouldn't have been fair to the Mat who would remain. He sensed her movement and turned toward her.

"How long is there?" she murmured.

He hesitated, trying to read her eyes and her face. But there was a part of him still present now that knew her—knew her better than the confused awareness from another world that had only glimpsed her fleetingly. She sensed it too, and was responding to it. He drew her to him. Their mouths sought and found each other's as their bodies pressed together.

"A while yet." Hugh took her hand and led her back inside.

It was the first time for him that it had happened this way: with everything right, the way it should be. It made him feel doubly like a god. How could he shrink back to being just plain Hugh Brenner now?

✧　　✧　　✧

And, indeed, when he returned he did feel just a pale counterfeit of the extended self that he had experienced for those few hours. He felt like a fledgling that had opened its wings and felt the wind, only to be drawn back into the egg.

"It must be something to do with repeated stimulation of the same analog," he told Dave and Sarah as soon as they were alone together in a corner of the lab, and he was able to describe his latest experience. "Until recently, the transfers were to different analogs all over the place— never to the same one twice. It's a new phenomenon that we haven't seen before. You can't really put it into words. You're an expanded version of yourself—a merging together of complementary sides of the two personalities. Coming back again is like losing half your vision."

"Do you think it could be another way of achieving the deeper awareness that Sam talks about?" Sarah said. "They're really the same thing: expanding consciousness farther into the MV?"

"I don't know. Maybe," Hugh answered. "But whatever it means, I've made my mind up. I'm checking out. The only question now is, are you two coming or not?"

There was a silence. Dave looked questioningly at Sarah. He was beginning to like the new version of a free-and-easy England, not degenerated into a police state, that he was getting to know. And from what Hugh was saying now, maybe the other David—David Vaughan—wouldn't have to be eliminated from the equation after all. "I could go for it," he said cautiously. When Sarah didn't respond immediately, he went on, "There still might be some way for us to help them protect themselves—even if it's no more than educating them about what to look out for. We can't do anything for anyone back here."

Sarah looked at him searchingly, and for a moment the other two thought she was about to come around. But then she shook her head. "Not until we've talked to Theo and Sam. They have to have their chance to be included too."

"They'll want to see it for themselves first," Dave said.

"Then the sooner we tell them about it, the better," Sarah answered.

Hugh nodded. "Okay, then let's do it," he agreed.

In Otherwhere, Matthew Shayne lay back against pillows and stared out through the window at the lights across the Bay. Yvonne snuggled contentedly in his arm, her head against his chest.

"Did I ever tell you that I used to be the same thing in that other universe too—a research scientist at Berkeley?" he asked.

"No."

"Except it was a very different Berkeley. There were mobs, violence, police on the streets. Everything was run-down and decaying. Even this place—here where we are now—was a wharf with derelict warehouses. And the bridge out there was ugly—just bare steel girders. . . . It probably still is, in that world."

Yvonne frowned at the sudden strangeness of what he was saying. He had said "I" and not "he." She moved her head and looked up at him. "What are you trying to tell me?"

"This time wasn't the same. It wasn't a complete blackout. I can remember you arriving here, me opening the door, the things we talked about. And those things about Berkeley . . ." there was wonder in his voice, "I can still *see* them! You see what it means? Even though the connection is broken, a part of the Brenner side of me is still functioning. I don't think I'll ever be the same person again now."

"You *are* the same person," Yvonne said. "You're just discovering more of yourself, that's all. And it makes you a lot more interesting." She rubbed her cheek on his shoulder and kissed it lightly. "So don't worry about it."

Chapter Thirty-seven

Inside the main Polygon building, the operative code named "Picador" settled back in a coupler that had been arranged to keep an occupant comfortable for twenty-four hours or more if necessary. A scientist activated the transfer routine, and moments later Picador found himself to be once again Arnold Miller, an American gymnast with a team currently touring in the Otherwhere version of France. In fact, that was why he had been picked for the assignment. It was early morning. The transfer had been timed so that he would still be in his hotel room.

He selected one of Miller's smaller bags and filled it with toilet articles and clean clothes for several days, and went down to the desk, where he supplemented the amount of cash in his possession with as large a check as the hotel would cover, drawn on Miller's account. Then, after inquiring about local travel services, he had the hotel call him a cab and drove to the railroad station in the center of town in time to catch the 9:00 A.M. fast train to Paris. The city's Metro took him out to the principal international airport at Orly, and he left in the afternoon aboard a British Northern flight direct to Manchester. He bought a large-scale map of the Manchester area at a newsagent's in the airport, rented a car, and drove into the city.

An ad in the evening paper took him to a camera, instrument, and gun store on the west side, where he had no difficulty purchasing a .38 caliber "BSA Gentleman's," made by the Birmingham Small Arms Company, and some ammunition. After that, he found a pharmacy and bought a bottle of fast-acting sleeping pills. Then he had dinner at a Moroccan restaurant in the city center. The restaurant's cashier gave him directions to the radio observatory at Jodrell Bank and recommended several hotels that were conveniently close.

Picador checked into a traditional style guest house called the Derwent and retired to his room shortly after 11:00 P.M. The sleeping pills made sure that Arnold Miller was unconscious by midnight when Picador was recalled to report, and he was able to feed and exercise his own body, shower and shave, without risk of a suddenly restored analog panicking at the other end. Miller, as such, wouldn't be functioning again until the mission was completed. Picador would endeavor to get him safely back to France before relinquishing control, however. Analogs in Otherwhere accessible to Polygon were difficult to come by, and then not always usefully placed. It wouldn't do to just leave one to be caught and locked up on a murder charge. There was no telling when he might be needed again.

Carol Yeats sat with her suitcase and a smaller travel bag in a bus shelter in a suburb of Detroit. She was confused at the changes taking place in her head, yet at the same time seized by a strangely exciting conviction that something very exceptional was happening to her. She wasn't sick or going out of her mind; she no longer worried about that. Her most recent "blackout" had been different from the earlier ones. Instead of coming out of it with her mind a complete blank, this time she had been left with feelings of inspiration and a new sense of inner confidence, welling up from a source that she didn't understand. And even now, when it was past, she had not reverted fully to her former self. A residue of whatever had been taking possession of her remained.

It was like being able to see the world with suddenly

broadened vision, as if an additional part of her mind had become active that she had never used before. Somehow it brought with it feelings and reveries that seemed to belong to another world. They were not all especially pleasant or comfortable, but in adding to the frames of reference by which she judged the world, they altered and expanded her perspectives of just about everything she had experienced in life. In a way, she felt as if she had begun metamorphosing into a different person.

"Carol, could we talk, please?" Barry's voice jerked her out of her thoughts. He had appeared at the end of the shelter, leaning against one of the posts supporting the roof. Just when she'd thought that she was getting herself together, confusion erupted inside her all over again. When she left the apartment she had meant to just slip away—Joan would send her other things when she had an address in New York. Then, after she arrived at the bus shelter and thought things over, it had seemed a cowardly way out—like the other times. If she was going to start over and get it right, it should be a clean, honest break, she had told herself. Now she wasn't sure either way.

Barry went on, "Look, I know I've been pretty shitty to you at times. And I'm not gonna start trying to snow you with excuses now, because you're right. But it doesn't have to be that way. We had a good thing going at the beginning, didn't we? I don't want us to throw that away. It could work again."

It was true that he had changed some and was easing back on the drink—ever since she shocked the life out of him by almost breaking his back. That was one of the times that had been a complete blackout. She was glad that they were having this final face-to-face clearing of the air after all. But bigger things were happening in her life now. She needed space.

"It's not just that," she told him. "There's a more complicated side to it that I can't really talk about. I'm not sure that I understand it myself."

"You haven't been well lately, Carol. This isn't the time to be taking off. You need someone to take care of you."

"I . . . just think it's best."

"But where do you even have to go?"

"Home—New York. I'll find somewhere there okay."

"But not like this. Come back and give it a week—at least until you've got something fixed." She shook her head, but inside she could feel her resolution crumbling, the way it always did. Barry sensed it, the way he always could. He moved closer. "Take a break for a week and rest up. You owe that much to yourself. If you still feel the same by that time, then okay. But give it a try. We can work something out."

The part of her that had always responded to him was ready to give in. But the new element present within her resisted. She agonized, unable to resolve the tussle either way. Barry took the moment to decide for her and stooped to pick up her suitcase.

And then she felt her personality transform. The remnant of new awareness that had persisted as a minor adjunct to her normal psyche expanded suddenly to dominate her consciousness. It was happening to her again, only instead of blacking out into oblivion, she was continuing to function as part of the process.

Straightaway, Sarah could feel there was something different about this transfer. There was no moment of disorientation while she took in where she was and what was happening. She *knew*. Or rather, the Carol Yeats part of her that was not completely suppressed knew, and she was sharing the knowledge. The same thing was happening to her as Hugh had tried to describe.

Then she was back in the lab again. "Do we go or abort?" Jantowitz asked from the console.

"Go!"

She was at the bus shelter. Carol was about to leave for all the right reasons, as she should have long before. Barry was putting on the I-can-change routine that the Carol part of her knew was an act but was powerless to fight— as had always been the case before. But the Sarah side was dominant now.

She took his hand and removed it firmly from the handle of the suitcase. "No, Barry. It isn't going to be that way this time."

"But . . . hey, no. You can't be serious. We need to talk."

She'd torn up the script. None of his prepared lines fitted.

"I'm being serious for the first time. Look, there isn't any need for hard feelings, and I'd rather there weren't any."

"Carol, that's all I'm trying to say, for Christ's sake."

"You don't understand. A lot of complicated things are going on that change everything." To Sarah's relief, she saw the bus turning into the far end of the street. She stood up.

"What complications? Don't you figure I'm due some kind of explanation?"

"I can't explain. Just take it from me that there couldn't be any going back to the way it was. That's over."

Barry's feeling of futility turned to anger, and the mask fell away. "Suit yourself, then," he sneered. "So who is it? The jerk who phones, or some other dick that you've been keeping on the side?" The Carol part wanted to retaliate, but the Sarah side that was in control ignored him and moved to the edge of the sidewalk as the bus pulled up. Barry's voice rose to a whine. "I always thought you were pretty worthless anyway, know that? Don't think I'm gonna shed any tears. And don't waste your breath coming back when he wises up too. Do you hear me? Are you listening to me?"

The driver climbed down to take the bags. Sarah mounted the steps without looking back. She was conscious of the Carol component absorbing and sharing new feelings, wondering why she had never seen something so obvious before.

✧   ✧   ✧

In the Seashell Bar a block from the apartment, Barry
ordered a beer and vented his feelings on Leo, the
bartender. "She walked, man—took off on me. Can you
believe that? I always figured she was no good. They're
none of 'em any good. All the same."

"That's too bad. Any idea where she's heading?" Leo
said.

"Back to New York, she said. Farther the better as far
as I'm concerned." Barry took another swig of his beer.
"Shit, know what I'm gonna do? I'm gonna go on a tour
of the neighborhood and get good and drunk. So I'll
probably see you again later, Leo." With that he downed
the rest in a long gulp and left the bar.

Leo waited a few minutes and then called the number
of the hotel a couple of streets away where the stranger
with money, who had been asking questions earlier, said
he was staying. The stranger was in. The desk put the
call through to the room.

Leo glanced around and kept his voice low. "Hello? . . .
Yeah, this is Leo at the Seashell. You were in earlier asking
about Carol Yeats who comes in here. . . . Right. I've got
something for you. She's blowing town and heading for
New York. Just took the station bus. . . . The City, I guess.
That's where she says she's from. . . . No, I dunno. . . .
Aw, I'd say less than an hour ago. . . ."

Dave sat up in one of the Bolthole's two couplers and
blinked his eyes. He looked excited. Sarah was waiting
anxiously with Hugh to hear what he would say. Jantowitz
was at the console. Sam was settling down in the other
coupler, which Sarah had only just vacated. They had at
last told Jantowitz and Sam about Hugh's idea of migrating
to Otherwhere permanently. Jantowitz and Sam had raised
the same reservations about suppressing analog personalities
permanently, but were reserving judgment in view of the
new phenomenon that was affecting Hugh and Sarah. In
the meantime, they wanted to see something of this other

world themselves. This was to be Sam's introductory visit.

"Well?" Sarah prompted, looking at Dave.

"The same thing," Dave said. "The Vaughan personality was still functioning this time—reduced to a minor component, but definitely there." It was what they had hoped. The same effect was manifesting itself with him. As Hugh had suspected, it seemed to be a result of repeated stimulation of the same analog. If the analogs were retaining an awareness of what was going on, it put a different picture on the prospects of bringing them together to meet.

"But a sense of this other David, this David Vaughan, you don't bring back with you?" Jantowitz checked.

Dave shook his head. "No. Back here, I'm purely me."

Which again was what Hugh and Sarah had found. It made sense. The transfers had all been from the regular world to Otherwhere, not the other way around. There was no reason why any aspects of personalities that existed in Otherwhere should be brought back.

"What's the news with Carol?" Dave inquired while Jantowitz attended to initializing the coupler that Sam was occupying.

"She's split with Barry, finally," Sarah said.

"Good."

"Moving back to New York City. I'm not sure exactly which part—I'll have to wait till next time to find out. She almost didn't make it, though. Barry was there when I showed up, and had almost talked her out of it—I remember feeling that it was the usual pattern. But I got her on the bus and left some new thoughts in her head. With luck she'll be okay now."

Dave started to say something but stopped when he saw that Hugh was no longer paying attention but watching Jantowitz. Jantowitz was frowning at the screens on the console. Then Dave saw that Sam was still alert in the coupler and looking toward Jantowitz with a strangely expectant look on his face.

"What is it, Theo?" Hugh asked, but a catch in his voice betrayed that he already knew.

Jantowitz tapped at keys, watched the screens for a few seconds longer, and shook his head. "There is no connection. The T-matrix has zeroed, and the forcing function check confirms. Sam's world, it is not." He looked across at Sam. "You have no analog in Otherwhere, my friend."

Dave was speechless. Sarah shook her head in protest. "No analog? But that can't be true. . . . There has to be. Check it again, Theo."

"There is nothing to check. Is no connection possible, I am telling you." Jantowitz looked around the circle of faces, all of them stunned except Sam's, which was calm and accepting as always. Jantowitz responded as he always did when people started acting as if their feelings might alter facts—by getting irritable.

"Why you three dummies standing there like is raining day at funeral?" he demanded. "This is not big surprise that nobody expects. We know this can happen. Sam is man of real world."

"Theo is right, and you all know it," Sam told them. "Statistically, three in five was over the odds—so maybe it was an unrealistic hope to begin with." He thought for a moment, then smiled distantly. "You know, the Buddha's final act of compassion was to renounce his own liberation in order to show others the path. Maybe this is God's way of saying that now it's my turn."

"God?" Jantowitz repeated.

Sam shrugged. "God. The strange workings of the Multiverse. It's the same thing. Either way, let's not waste any more time on it." He motioned Jantowitz toward the other coupler. "Let's get you checked out."

Jantowitz stared at him for several seconds longer. Then he shook his head. "Bah! No. If you have to stay, I stay too. You need somebody to keep company with here and make sure you stay out of trouble."

Hugh threw out his hands. "You mean you're not even going to check it out?" he protested. "Theo, you can't! You have to give it a try."

Sarah looked imploringly from Hugh to Dave. "We can't

just leave them," she insisted. "Forget Otherwhere. . . . We'll find somewhere else, another world."

Jantowitz shook his head stubbornly. "Sam just told you, you could look against odds for the rest of time. And then there may not be some other place like this one you describe. In any case, is probably for best. What business does a professor at my age have gallivanting around other universes, anyway? You three, you go. Is young people's world that you tell about. We already say, maybe you can be something useful there—show them how they watch for other peoples coming from other universes. Here, you can do nothing."

Sam nodded in answer to their inquiring looks. "Theo's right," he told them. "There's something going on with all this military involvement that gives me bad feelings. Go while you've still got the chance."

Dave looked bemused. "Like when? When are we talking about?"

"We do it for you right now, why not?" Jantowitz answered.

Hugh drew a long breath, then nodded. "A bit more sudden than I'd have liked, but I could go for it," he declared.

It was too much for Sarah. "But the analogs? What about them?" she said.

"Go first. Sort out with analogs later," Jantowitz answered. "In any case, maybe is not so much a problem. You already tell us you are becoming same peoples."

But Dave was balking too. "They haven't even met. . . . Vaughan and Carol, I mean. It's different for Hugh. We can get them together in Otherwhere now. It would only take a day or two. Let's give ourselves that long to be sure, at least."

Jantowitz snorted, looked at them balefully for a few seconds, and then glanced at Sam. Sam nodded silent agreement.

"Then this is what you do," Jantowitz pronounced. "This Carol, already she is going back to New York, yes? So that is where you meet. The other two analogs—the physicist who is in Berkeley again, and the other David in England—you make them forget about their other plans for now, and you bring them also to New York. Then the six of you work it out together." He looked at Sam and threw up a hand hopelessly. "Six of them! And you and me as well, they wanted to go. Here with the simple life, we are better off staying. Is so, my friend, yes?"

Chapter Thirty-eight

In his hotel room in Manchester, Picador was awakened by an early-morning call. He spent fifteen minutes doing calisthenics to give Miller's gymnast's body the exercise that it felt as if it needed, and then took a long shower, letting it run cold to dispel the effects of the sleeping pills. After that he called for a pot of coffee to be brought to the room, dressed while he waited, and began his work for the day.

Vaughan's home phone number and the number of the observatory where he worked had been given in the mission briefing. How Colonel Elson had obtained them or why a radio astronomer living in a different reality should be a target were questions that Picador had been trained to exclude from his considerations. Matching the home number against the Vaughans listed in the directory gave him the address, which from the map that Picador had bought at the airport, was located in what looked like a residential area about three miles away.

A little before 7:00 A.M., he turned into the street on a reconnoitering tour and drove slowly by the house. It was a small, Spanish-style residence with arched porticoes and a miniature campanile, situated in an estate of mixed architectures scattered among trees. A blue Peugeot was parked in the driveway; the morning paper was wedged in the letter box in the front door; and he could see a figure moving behind net curtains in a lighted window that looked as if it belonged to the kitchen. Nobody else was about. It would have been straightforward to go in and complete the job right then, but the rules wouldn't allow it. Positive identification of the target had not been obtained. Picador noted the registration of the Peugeot and found a cafe in a mall of shops not far away where he could get breakfast. It was still well before 7:30. While his order was being prepared, he called the observatory's listed number from a pay phone. A man's voice answered.

"Jodrell Bank observatory."

"Hello. Who's this, please?"

"The office opens at nine. This is the front gate."

"Oh, hi. My name is Anderson. I'm visiting the country, and I want to look up somebody I met a while ago, who works there somewhere. His name is Vaughan, David Vaughan. I know that astronomers work all hours of the day and night. Could you tell me when might be the best time to get ahold of him?"

"Vaughan, you said—with a V as in Victor?"

"Yes."

"Let's see . . . Ah yes, David Vaughan—Dr. Cormack's group. He's down here as regular day shift at present. You'll normally get him in the Main Telescope Control Room or the Interferometry Lab. Staff tend to show up at any time between nine and ten, depending on how many pints they had last night. I can only suggest that you try calling back then."

"Okay, I'll do that."

"Any message I can pass on?"

"No, that's fine. Thank you."

Estimating that Vaughan wouldn't leave home until 8:30 at the earliest, Picador ate a leisurely breakfast and took the opportunity to familiarize himself more with the map while he was drinking his coffee. When he returned to the street where the house was, the blue Peugeot was still in the driveway, the paper had gone from the letter box, and there were no lights showing. It looked as if

Vaughan might be ready to leave at any moment. Picador waited and watched from the end of the street, but by 9:30 there had been no sign of movement. An instinct told him something was wrong.

He found a public phone box on the next street and tried calling the house. There was no answer. He called the observatory again. David Vaughan hadn't been seen that morning in either of the locations that the gate supervisor had mentioned. A technician in the Interferometry Lab thought that he was going away somewhere and wouldn't be back for some time. He had Picador transferred to the departmental secretary.

"Hello. Mrs. Greaves here. Can I help at all? I believe you're looking for Dave Vaughan."

"That's right. We met at a seminar some time ago, and I promised I'd give him a call when I was in this part of the country. Do you know where he might be today?"

"Oh dear! You've just missed him, I'm afraid. He left for the United States this morning."

"The States?" Picador thought frantically. Clearly the mission here was over. The target would have to be picked up again on the other side. "Can you tell me where he's heading for, exactly?"

"I honestly don't know. It's to do with something personal. Dr. Cormack knows more about it, but he won't be in until later. He's taking David to the airport."

Picador went back to the house to see if he could find out more from neighbors or local shops, but all he learned was that the paper had been stopped for a week. There was nothing further he could do until noon, when there would be a brief recall to Polygon for him to report. He drove out of the city and parked in an out-of-the-way spot by a field and a canal lock to wait. Arnold Miller would be able to do little there that could cause problems in the ten minutes or so that it would take. So he could occupy himself with admiring the view and trying to figure out where the hell he was.

✧   ✧   ✧

San Francisco International Airport was built closer to
the city than the one that Hugh knew. It consisted partly
of an artificial extension out over the Bay, and had service
piers for flying boats as well as regular runways. Hugh
was surprised when he arrived with Yvonne on the subway
link from the city to find a complete absence of airport
security. Yvonne couldn't understand why there should
be a need for any. He tried to explain about terrorists
and hijackings, but she couldn't comprehend why anyone
would want to hijack an aircraft.

"What would they do with it?" she asked. "Where would
they find pilots and a maintenance crew, and where would
they get spare parts?"

"No, you're missing the point. The idea isn't to acquire
the plane. It's to get visibility for political causes."

"Oh." Yvonne didn't press the matter. It was clear that
she really didn't have a concept of what he meant.

The plane was a Lockheed turboprop. Hugh had never
flown in a turboprop before. It had four engines and twin
tail fins, and apart from the unfamiliar airline name—
"American Pacific," which sounded more like a railroad—
looked the way airliners should. Hugh suspected that
aircraft in any universe would be pretty similar—for the
same reasons that caused sharks, porpoises, and submarines
to end up pretty much the same shape. Their flight time
to New York would actually be longer than Dave's from
London, which would be with one of the new European
jets. An aviation journalist had commented that trans-
Atlantic jets might be carrying as many as two hundred
fifty passengers before very much longer. Wow, Hugh
remembered thinking to himself.

He had told Rauth some things about twenty-first-
century air travel, warfare, and aerospace technology back
in his own world. Rauth had passed a few details on to
friends of his in the business, who had laughed it off as a
joke until they checked the claims with some of
Otherwhere's designers and engineers. Then, all of a
sudden, Rauth was inundated with calls that they wanted

to hear more. Hugh had spent some hours in the LANL library, cramming his brain with facts and figures on things like aerodynamic performances, radar navigation systems, laser ring gyros, and high-efficiency turbofans before his next transfer, and now a lot of people wanted to talk to him.

It seemed that a market for information trading across the Multiverse was there, in very much the way that he had speculated with Dave and Sarah back in the early days. But they would have no access to it if they burned their bridges and migrated permanently. That fact had caused Hugh to do some hard thinking and reevaluating.

And then Rauth had come up with a thought whereby even that might turn out to be a temporary problem. As a physicist, he couldn't help but be intrigued by the QUADAR, and in one of his more fanciful moments he had wondered about the possibility of building a simpler version of it in Otherwhere. On closer examination the thought had turned out to be not so fantastic. Most of the required knowledge of MV physics was already in Hugh's head, and Rauth knew most of Otherwhere's leading quantum theorists personally. The reduction of MV data required enormous processing power, and it was true there was nothing in existence that came close to being able to provide it. But hardware design was Dave's field, and with the world's principal industrial and academic research centers available to draw on, it was conceivable that a crash program could produce something workable in as little as five years. A world war followed by a cold war, predatory international commercial rivalries, a lunar landing program, and all the other factors that had spurred things along in the old world didn't have to be necessary preliminaries.

And the most amazing thing to Hugh was the openness of it all. There was no cult of secrecy in Otherwhere. Rauth was perfectly frank about the source of his information when he talked to others, and as many of them had smiled or sneered as had taken him seriously. What others chose to believe seemed to be generally acknowledged as being their business. Already, there had been several calls to U.C. Berkeley from reporters wanting to talk to the scientist who said he'd been taken over by an intelligence from another dimension. Hugh had the feeling that if a QUADAR-like device were ever to be built here, it would be a very different affair from the sinister business going on in his own world—probably with a public opening ceremony attended by movie stars and hosting regular tours of schoolchildren.

The other area where the openness of Otherwhere had astounded Hugh was in the reaction to the threat of other intruders from other parts of the Multiverse showing up with other motives. Hugh had finally broached the subject with Rauth, and Rauth had conveyed it elsewhere to invite opinions. The general feeling was that the way to deal with it would be to inform the population at large of the possibility and what to look out for, and to set up some kind of coordinating network to report suspected instances to. Vastly outnumbered, any invaders ought to be easily isolated and contained. No coverups, cover stories, official denials, covert surveillance programs. He could quickly get used to this place, Hugh thought.

He squeezed Yvonne's hand as it lay lightly in his. She turned her head from watching wisps of cloud slide across the craggy faces of Yosemite below, and smiled. "It's wonderful," she said. "A lot better than the train down to LA."

"Wait till you try a jet."

"We'll see what David from England thinks about it. This is going to be so strange, meeting these friends of yours. I can't imagine what it will be like with three of you around."

"They're great people. You'll like them."

"I think I might have to. Now I've gotten more used to you, it makes everybody I've known before seem dull." She eyed him impishly for a second. "You might be stuck with me for a long time, you know, Mat."

Mat. That was something he was just going to have to get used to, he guessed.

Although, that wasn't really true because by this time "he" was as much Matthew Shayne as he was Hugh Brenner. There was no longer a subordination of one by the other but a composite awareness that combined both equally. The pictures in his mind of Brenner's strife-torn, rubble-strewn Berkeley ranked alongside those of the home in Sonoma where Shayne's father owned a share in a winery. The irrigating of the Sinai deserts in one world was as familiar as the tank battles fought there in the other; the annual Berlin Music Festival, as the onetime Berlin Wall; Chinese garden cities, as Chinese orbiting bombs. Nothing of him remained suppressed now. He was simply more alive and alert, more conscious, more perceiving—an expanded version of what either of them had ever been.

And the indications were that the condition would persist if the connection to Los Alamos were abruptly broken. Hugh had thought about going it alone and writing himself a one-way ticket. In fact, one night when he had worked late alone in the lab, he had written and installed the code to do it, intending to make his decision irrevocably the next day.

Then, for some reason that he didn't quite understand, a feeling of guilt at the thought of abandoning his own world had afflicted him again and caused him to pause. The struggle and conflict of that world had produced the relentless striving that had brought him here. It was the people of that world who had expended the lives, endured the suffering, uncovered the knowledge. He owed them, all of them. If there was just some way he could reciprocate—even if only to lessen their pain.

On a train pulling out of Binghampton, New York State, Sarah studied the other people sharing the compartment. She had been watching people all the way from Detroit, and in the process had finally put her finger on what had enabled Otherwhereians to create the kind of world that they had. They minded their own business. It was amazing how agreeable people could be when others let them be and think what they wanted, even when they disagreed with their choices. The Carol part of her was amazed that the Sarah part should find it amazing.

The same blending of personalities was taking place with her as Hugh had described—though not yet to the same degree. When the QUADAR link was established—as at present—she was more Sarah than Carol; when it was broken, she was more Carol. The combining of their differing perspectives into one viewpoint was a new, vividly revelational experience for both. Now she understood what Dave and Hugh had meant when they talked about seeing everything in ways they had never grasped before, which they found impossible to describe.

It reminded her of Sam's repeated assertion of the connectedness of all people, all life, and ultimately all things; that the perceptions of separateness and alienation that form the roots of strife are illusions. She still didn't understand it—not in any way she could have put into words; but, to some degree at any rate, she could *feel* it. Sam believed that what mystics tried to describe was the freeing of consciousness—deliberately or otherwise—from the restraints that normally define identity, into the quantum-connected paths of the Multiverse. Now, she thought she was experiencing the same thing on a smaller scale across the bridge of connectivity that united her and Carol.

Although she had not faced the issue squarely in her mind as yet, there was already a part of her that knew there could be no going back now to what she had been. Making it permanent was the only other option. That made both sides of her, each for its own reasons, all the more anxious over the forthcoming meeting with the radio astronomer from Manchester, who at that moment should be somewhere over the mid-Atlantic. This had to be the strangest blind date of all time—in either universe.

Elson had been pressing for all the information that Calom could provide on Otherwhere—and in particular on the analogs of Brenner and the other two that he was trying to talk into escaping there with him. However, the surveillance tapes were yielding less information than usual. Brenner and the others were not talking about their plans and movements so much now after they returned. Calom got the feeling that their Otherwhere analogs were communicating even when they weren't connected, although he had no idea of how that could be. He put the question to Kintner, but Kintner didn't know either. It made it all the more important that the Bolthole people were not allowed to suddenly disappear. Kintner was for detaining them as a precaution until he had unraveled what was going on. Surprisingly, it was Ventz who demurred. He said that everything was "under control." But he ordered surveillance to be stepped up to include continual direct monitoring of the Bolthole area in addition to the later analysis of tapes.

Calom sat in his office in the Administration Building, brooding over Argo, the plan that Willard and Sarvin had revealed to him for moving a selected elite to Otherwhere. At first he had been surprised that they should want to include him—he hardly thought of himself as belonging to the social elite. Then he realized that it was for their own protection. They couldn't risk having somebody in his position who was not one of them, and so had been forced to take the risk.

And in many ways, such a prospect should have appealed. After making several more "visits"—more from curiosity than any real demand of his job or of the project—he had decided that there was a lot to be said for being a plant manager at an oil installation in Arabia. Jack Frazer had a fine wife there, as well as a teenage son and daughter, both at college and doing fine. Good pay, first-class working crew. A world that was sane and had a future.

That was the problem. In some strange way that he had never known before, Frazer was becoming a part of him. Up until now Calom's life had consisted of a series of encounters with individuals who were threats, rivals, aids to attaining ends, or simply objects to be processed as the job demanded . . . but never *people*. So why this vague but persistent concern for somebody he hardly knew, in a world he'd never heard of?

It wasn't just Frazer, his family, or the team of black and white, Arab, Indian, Chinese, but the whole coterie of humanity all mixed up together that they were part of, the whole world of Otherwhere that seemed present in each one of them as much as they were contained in it. He had heard Argo's plans for seeking out approachable governments and exploiting vulnerable minorities to gain influence after the first phase was completed. And those who made the plans would depend on professionals like himself to do the work, as they always had. Nothing was going to change. They were the same powers that he had always served unquestioningly because he stood to gain when they did, and in any case he had never really cared. So what was it about this other reality of strangers that made it different now? Because that was the difference. For some reason he *cared*.

He was still brooding when his secretary announced an incoming call. It was Mike Schlager of the state's Anti-Terrorist Force.

"Bruce, I've got something on the item you were asking about," he said without preliminaries.

"I'm still interested." There hadn't been anything else since they talked about Howard Turner.

"I'll be driving north from Santa Fe later today. There's a truck stop at the intersection of 502 and eighty-five. Could you meet me there?"

"When?"

"Say about an hour. Make it four?"

"I'll be there." Calom cleared down and called his deputy, Nick Guerntz, in the basement monitoring room. "Nick, I'll be going out for a while shortly. Keep an eye on things till I get back."

"Sure."

"How's it going down there?"

"Oh, pretty quiet. Nothing exciting right now."

It was the machine affecting him, he told himself as he drove out of the main gate and across the bridge to the main road. He had heard the scientists talking about it, how for some of them reality never seemed quite the same again. Turner had been one, before his abrupt departure. It impaired professionalism, and that was why Calom had refused to have anything to do with it. Then things that Sarah said had made him curious and caused him to change his mind.

And now something was happening to him too. Something that he didn't understand.

In the larger of the two Polygon buildings, Picador was recalled on schedule and reported that Vaughan had left Manchester to fly to the U.S. via London. "Sandman," the spook analog who just missed Carol Yeats in Detroit, had already given the bartender's information that she had left for New York City. That made it as good as certain that Vaughan was heading there too. There was already one spook analog in New York: "Cossack," who had made the abortive visit to the Chinese consulate there. Elson told Sandman to reconnect and take the first available flight out of Detroit to at least get his analog into the right area as well while they worked on finding out where in New York Yeats and Vaughan were going. The other item to be taken care of was Matthew Shayne in San Francisco.

The spook analog located nearest to San Francisco was a woman by the name of Dorris Desota, Polygon code name "Amethyst," who managed a furniture restoring business near Dallas, Texas. Elson instructed her to find out Shayne's whereabouts and movements from there by phone first, before launching another chase halfway across the country. The result was as Elson had anticipated.

"Shayne left town early this morning," Amethyst reported on recall. "Rauth wasn't in, and that was all anybody else at the university knew. I called the office in the city where his girlfriend works, Weller Financial, to see if she knew anything, and it turns out she went with him. But we've got a break. She left a number where she could be reached. It's the Kennedy Hotel in Manhattan, on Fifth Avenue. I called there to check. Shayne, Yeats, and Vaughan all have confirmed reservations for tonight."

Elson contacted Ventz in Washington and relayed the information. "Then we can move," Ventz said. "Cossack is there already, and Sandman's on his way. Two of them ought to be able to handle it. But as backup try and get Amethyst on a P.M. flight out of Dallas as well. By tonight I want that escape hatch closed—for keeps."

Chapter Thirty-nine

Lincoln International Airport was on the east side of the Bronx, extending out into Long Island Sound on the peninsula that in Hugh's world was the urban battleground known as Pelham Bay Park. There was no airport on the shore of Long Island south of Queens, and Yvonne had never heard of JFK. The Kennedy hotel chain was owned by a Massachusetts-based family that she thought might be of Irish descent. She couldn't imagine them going into anything as mundane as politics. Hugh asked her who the current President was. She said she thought his name was Howell—but she had to check with another passenger to be sure.

There was a subway terminal inside the airport, but they decided to take a cab—staid, black, and gleaming, with a radiator grill that looked like a church organ, and high-backed seats of red leather. The cabbie wore a red beret, bow tie with vest, and a Scottish kilt. A sign outside the terminal said NO PARKING **PLEASE**. Hugh blinked. This was New York?

It was—but nothing like the New York that he knew of or remembered from the few visits he'd made when he had to. The streets had a lot less of the waffle-iron regularity, and the buildings were not all monotonous concrete-and-glass variations on stacked cubes. They were high, all right, but showing mixtures of colors and styles that formed scenes of a different quality in every direction. It was like the cheerful chaos that he had encountered in San Francisco but on ten times the scale. And whereas San Francisco had exhibited a distinctly Asiatic influence, here it was more European. Intermingled with the rectangular, functional forms—and in many cases, fused with them—were neo-Gothic pinnacles and soaring windows, French chateau rondels, Byzantine domes, Romanesque towers, Russian spires, and Islamic minarets. Ground level was reserved for automobiles. Pedestrian life went on above, along terraces and plazas extending along multiple, neon-lit levels connected by a canopy of bridges. Yvonne had only been there once before, when she was young, and remembered little about it. She asked about the New York in Hugh's world. He tried to describe it, but although she could picture destruction and decay, she had no comprehension of the forces that drove societies to it. The suggestion of race conflict in a modern age mystified her. It was something that should simply have gone away a long time ago—like animal sacrifices, or blood feuds between families.

The cabdriver held the door open for Yvonne, carried the bags up the hotel steps, and refused when Hugh tried to give him a tip. He was paid okay for the job and didn't need any more. "But thanks for the thought, all the same." Yes—this was New York.

The lobby atrium was an airy extravaganza of marble pillars and arches, profusions of greenery, and alcoves with seats and tables surrounding a central fountain and ornamental pool. Hugh stared at several girls, heavily made up and expensively dressed, who were sitting in one of the alcove areas chatting and flipping through magazines while they smiled at all the men who passed by. They had to be hookers. Nobody seemed to mind. "The one in red, with the long black hair is pretty," Yvonne remarked. "I love her dress."

The desk clerk was as surprised as the taxi driver when Hugh produced cash to cover the room. Apparently, expecting guests to pay in advance would have been considered an affront. He gave them two sturdy brass keys to room 612.

In the elevator, Yvonne leaned against Hugh and rested her head on his shoulder. He slipped an arm around her waist and pulled her close through her coat. There was a tension in both of them that demanded release, not just because of the long day behind them, but also from rising anxiety about the encounter that lay ahead with the two people that neither of them had seen before. They both felt it and acknowledged it. There was no need to speak.

To Hugh, the room was quaintly vintage: a king-size bed with heavy oak headboard; matchingly imperial chairs, window table, vanity, and writing desk. But it was clean and bright, with fresh flowers in a vase. The bathroom had marble fittings with framed mirrors, and porcelain-capped faucets; there were robes and slippers in the closet, and toothpaste and brushes, a razor and blades in the bathroom cabinet besides the regular soap and shampoo. No chain or security lock on the door.

There was over an hour yet before Dave's plane was due to land; then it would be thirty minutes at least on top of that for him to get into the city. Carol's train would get her to Grand Central—there was a Grand Central— at about the same time. Hugh was due to be recalled before then, it was true—but they still had long enough.

They showered in turn, saying little, then slid naked among the silky sheets. The bed was the softest, most enveloping luxury that Hugh had known. Yvonne was the tenderest, warmest, most giving. This whole setting, the situation, the experience, were unlike anything he had ever known.

After they had finished making love, he lay staring up at the ceiling with its decorative moldings, waiting, feeling Yvonne's breathing light on his shoulder. He could feel simultaneously the Matthew side of him's elation, the Hugh's certainty of purpose, now. Never had "he" felt such inner calm, such contentment. Already, Los Alamos and

the world that it was part of seemed like a fading dream.
Now, he told himself. Do it now—when he was called
back. There would never be another moment like this.

There were two couplers in the Bolthole. Dave and Sarah
would want to be using them when David Vaughan and
Carol finally met. But if Hugh made this recall his last,
he could be back here again by then and present too, fully
committed. Then, the Hugh Brenner body back in the
other world would never need a coupler again—or anything
else, come to that. People back there could hook it up to
life-support gear and drip nutrients into it if they chose.
He would have no further use for it.

He turned his head and looked at Yvonne. Should he
tell her before the recall happened, share it with her, let
her be a part of it too? . . .

No, there was no need. He knew how she felt. It should
be his decision and his alone. It needed to be. To seek
assent or approval now would be somehow to doubt her.
There was no doubt. He wanted it to be something over
and complete when he told her—a clean break with the
past, and only the future left for them to think about.

But *this* was the time to do it. There was no question.

Below, in the lobby, the analog of the spook code named
Cossack returned to the desk. He had a Tyrolean-style
hat and sported a thick black mustache. In his own life
his name was Vingini. He was of Italian descent and worked
as a steel erector.

The clerk took a message slip from a pigeon hole and
came over. "Shayne checked in about an hour ago with a
woman," he said in a low voice. "They're in 612. Stick
around, and I'll give you a nod when they come back down."
He pushed the slip across. "And a guy left this for you
about fifteen minutes ago. Said he was going to get a
sandwich."

The message was from Sandman, saying he had arrived
from Detroit and giving his room number. He would meet
Cossack on the seat between the two plants, over by the

fountain. Cossack slipped the clerk a ten, which was apparently big money here, and picked up a copy of the *Tribune* off the desk. Then he strolled over to the nook among the plants, surveyed the seats there, and settled down in one from where he could admire the hookers.

Calom was waiting at a corner of the truck parking area away from the pumps, when Schlager turned off Highway 85 North in an unmarked Chevrolet. He saw Calom's car and drew up alongside, pointing the other way so that the two driver's windows were facing. Calom rolled his down and looked out.

Schlager shook his head. For a moment Calom thought it meant that the answer was negative. Then he realized it was because Schlager didn't know what to make of it.

"Man, that was a mean business," Schlager said. "Your guy was taken out. It was an undercover Army hit team flown in specially from Alabama, operating across the border. The wife survived the assault. They had to mop her up afterward."

"I see," Calom said woodenly.

Schlager shook his head again. "I don't know what goes on. I thought we were all supposed to be on the same side in all this. Aren't there enough problems?" He looked across from his window. "What did you say this guy wanted to do—take care of kids someplace? It doesn't sound as if staying popular was his thing."

"It's a long story."

Schlager spread his hands on the wheel briefly. "Well, there it is. I can fill in more details if you need 'em. Anything else on it I can get?"

"No. Thanks, Mike, that's fine. I owe you one."

"Okay, well, you can stand me a trick at Madeline's one night."

"You've got it."

On the drive back up the Hill, Calom was again conscious of changes that had taken place in him, although he was still unsure what they meant. When he asked Schlager to check on Turner, he had been skeptical of Sarah's insinuations, but curious. No more. Why did he feel not a shred of surprise now? Nor surprise that there was more going on behind Argo than he had been told about. It was as if he had known all along what Ventz had meant by everything being "under control" and why Elson had wanted so much information on those three analogs, but he had repressed the awareness even from himself. That was the key word in what felt so different now. "Awareness." So much that the world was tearing itself apart over didn't matter. Just delusions. Sam had once described the machine as typically the white race's way of repeating at enormous cost what had been achieved three thousand years before. Calom took in the living colors of the desert, the sky, the sides of the valley leading back up to the mesa. And he felt that he had emerged into daylight for the first time in his life.

Chapter Forty

There were things in his room at Mrs. Ryecroft's that Hugh had brought with him from San Francisco because of special attachments that they held, because of the memories they brought back. He sat with some of them spread out on top of the bed, lost in the thoughts and images that they evoked.

There were photographs, of course. His parents and an assortment of relatives that really, he hadn't kept in touch with that much—but they were what he had. His mother had died young after surgery when he was in his teens; his father was at sea somewhere on a Navy supply ship. The gang from college days; boyhood camps and vacations; swimming near Monterey; helping an uncle build a boat; the pretenses at romances that never came to anything. There was a collection of attempts from the time when he had tried his hand at being a cartoonist; a signed menu from his dinner with a world-famous quantum physicist visiting from Brazil. His familiar books . . . Even never wearing again some of the clothes that he had grown used to would be like losing old friends.

And then there were the things that would never be done now: unfinished notes and papers from the lab; books marked and magazine articles copied to be read; items to pick up at the store. Yesterday they had all seemed so important, just like most of the things that people distracted themselves with through their entire lives instead of discovering the few things that mattered. Another of Sam's delusions. He found a couple of unpaid bills, wrote checks and attached them, and left them prominently on the desk.

And that was it. He took a final look around what would be his last abode in what had been the only world and life he had known. He moved the drapes and looked out at the familiar view of the yards behind the houses on the next street. The children were playing; their dog was yapping. Hugh dropped his keys onto the night table by the bed, walked back across the room, closed the door.

Mrs. Ryecroft came out of the kitchen with Selby scampering around her feet as Hugh arrived at the bottom of the stairway in the hall. "It's Hughey. What are you doing here at this time?" she trumpeted. "Did they throw you out?"

"What? Oh." He mustered a smile. "No such luck. I just had to pick up a couple of things."

"There's this great thing on TV—about psychics and how they can do all kinds of things just by holding pendulums. Wanna come and see?"

"Thanks. . . . But there's something else I have to do."

"Suit yourself. Will you be back for dinner later?"

"I don't think so." Hugh looked at her silently until her expression became puzzled. Then, on impulse, he kissed her on the cheek. Then, leaving her gaping with astonishment, he hurried from the house.

He walked briskly back toward TA-3 but stopped halfway across the bridge that he crossed every day, to take in his last impressions. He tried to picture what the scene would be like today if there had been no Manhattan Project or World War II—without the labs and the town that had grown with them. He would come here again with Yvonne, he decided. They would look out across the mesas, and he would recall all of this in his mind and tell of the things that had happened in this place in another world, in another time.

He showed his pass and entered through the familiar

main gate, crossed the site to the P2 building, and went inside past the security checkpoint. And even then, as he approached the bay where the Bolthole was situated, his feet swerved in another direction, suddenly, and carried him into the men's washroom by the plating shop. Neville Ducaine was in there, rinsing his hands.

"Ah, Hugh. You've been causing a panic. Theo's been looking all over the place for you."

"I . . . had to go over to Admin about something. Do you know where he is?"

"Isn't he around the corner in his hole?"

"I didn't look. I've only just got back."

"Well if he's not, try Sam's office upstairs. We're having a lot of fun with the long-range stuff, by the way. Peter Mulgrave is totally hooked on it. He found himself in a world where he's a stand-up comic. *Him!* Can you imagine it?"

"That's a joke in itself."

"Exactly. Anyhow, if I see Theo I'll tell him you're back. Catch you later."

"Right."

Ducaine left. Hugh stood before the mirror above the sinks and stared at the person that he had watched changing day by day as it had stared back at him for twenty-eight years. He looked pale, he could see. He felt nauseous—then realized that he was shaking uncontrollably. A slow paralysis was starting to creep into him. If he didn't force the effort now, he never would. He sucked in several long, unsteady breaths, expelling them sharply. Then he turned and went back out the door.

Dave was in one of the couplers; the other was unoccupied. Sarah was making adjustments at one of the consoles. Saying nothing, Hugh went to the other and activated the primary screen.

"Hi," Sarah greeted. "You're back. Theo has been ranting all over."

"Neville told me."

"Where were you?"

"There was something I had to do over in Admin." The code was initialized, unlocked, ready to go. The sequence would self-activate ten seconds after he hit the command.

Sarah went on without looking at him. "Dave has landed and is on his way to the hotel. I left Carol on her own for a while to stretch my legs when she made Grand Central. I'll go back in a few minutes. It feels like my first high-school date all over again. We've had some crazy situations since this business started, but never anything like this. It's a pity we couldn't have had three couplers and all be there."

Hugh stared at the empty coupler. All he needed to do was stroll across and lie down in it—make it slow and casual. It would be over before Sarah knew what was happening. He could explain it all later, when he saw them in New York.

But it wasn't just Sarah and Dave. He couldn't do it this way. "Where is Theo?" he asked. The words came out as a croak. Sarah turned her head.

"Up with Sam, I think. . . . Hugh, are you all right? You look terrible."

"It's nothing. I'll be right back."

He went out of the Bolthole and took the building's central stairwell to the computing area. From there he followed the corridor that led to the Theoretical Group's offices, and stopped at Sam's door, which was open. Theo was inside. They were both holding pieces of chalk and gesticulating at something between them on the wallboard.

"Excuse me." They both looked around. "Sarah said you were looking for me."

"So, is back from the vanishing trick you are," Jantowitz said.

"I had to go out on something. Was it important?"

"I need the file that we talk about last night at the house, but then I find I have it already, so is okay. Is all going okay with other two when you are down there?"

Hugh glanced around behind him to make sure there was nobody within earshot. "Dave's landed and due at the hotel any time. Sarah's off the train and back, taking a break."

Jantowitz looked at his watch. "My God! Time it is for their New York meeting, almost." To Sam, waving with the chalk: "We talk more about this later." To Hugh, "You want to come too? Interesting, this will be, I think."

"I was going back down anyway," Hugh said.

Jantowitz dropped the chalk into a pocket of his lab coat and moved to the door. Hugh turned after him and then stopped when he realized that Sam wasn't following. "You're not coming too?" Hugh said.

"I've got a meeting with Peter and Dennis in five minutes. Besides, we've always agreed to try and avoid having all of us down there together. I'll look in later. I'm sure they'll fall in love at first sight all over again." Sam's face became serious as he saw that Hugh wasn't really listening. "What is it?" he asked.

Hugh came up to him and put a hand on his shoulder. He looked at him, opened his mouth and tried, but could find no words. He shook his head helplessly.

Sam stared into Hugh's face with his dark, depthless, searingly intelligent eyes and scanned silently. Hugh had the feeling that they could read every thought that had ever gone through his mind. Sam nodded. There was nothing to ask. "Good luck," he said quietly. "Be kind to each other. Remember: Hatred, Greed, and Delusion. Their world is learning to forget such things. Leave yours here." Hugh clutched Sam's shoulder hard with his fingers for a moment. Then he left the office and hurried to catch up with Jantowitz.

Jantowitz was at the consoles, watching over Sarah's shoulder, when Hugh appeared and stopped a short distance to one side of them. "All going okay," Sarah said, acknowledging his presence. "Dave was almost there when I flashed him back."

There was no way to do this as Hugh would have liked. He moved to the other console, reactivated the code that he had prepared, and entered the command. He had ten seconds.

"What is this?" Jantowitz said, looking across.

Hugh put an arm around his shoulders and hugged. "Theo, this will make a lot more sense a few minutes from now. . . . But thanks for everything. You were right." And with that he released his hold, moved quickly away, and sat down in the coupler.

Sarah looked up in surprise from what she was doing. "Hugh, what are you playing at? You can't use that. I need it to get back to Carol."

"This won't take long," Hugh called at her.

Jantowitz came over and stood in front of him. "What in hell you do, you think? You know in minutes she must go."

"No time, Theo! No time!" Hugh extended a hand. Bewildered, Jantowitz clasped it. . . .

And it became Yvonne's. They were dressed again, in fresh clothes, about to leave the room. At once, Hugh felt his consciousness expand again to become Hugh-Matthew. He stopped as he was about to open the door, and stared around—as if needing to make sure that it was real. Yvonne looked as if she had been about to say something. She checked herself and studied his face keenly for a second.

"That was a lot longer than you said," she told him.

"I . . . had a lot to do," he said.

She gave him a mock-hurt look. "Well tell me next time. You had me getting worried. I was starting to think you'd had a hitch or something, and maybe you weren't coming back."

Hugh turned his back to the door and pulled her close. She was firm and voluptuous in a revealing dress. Her hair tumbled softly against his face. She had put on a new perfume and smelt wonderful. This dream was real.

"You don't have to worry anymore," he said. "There isn't going to be a next time."

Chapter Forty-one

"What's gotten into him, Theo? Dave is practically at the hotel. I need that coupler *now!*" Sarah released a vexed sigh and switched to the other console. "Well, if he can't have the decency to explain what he's doing, I don't see why we should have to put up with it. I'm bringing him back." She scanned over the screen that Hugh had used, looking for the recall identifier. Her face became puzzled. "Theo, could you have a look at this? I don't understand what he's done."

Jantowitz shuffled back from the coupler that Hugh was reclined in and peered past her. "Eh? I don't know. What is this he does? . . ." He frowned, grunted, and entered a test string, muttering in Polish. Then, suddenly, he fell quiet and went very still.

Sarah saw the look on his face and became fearful. "Theo, what is it?" she whispered.

Jantowitz remained silent for a long time before answering. He understood now what Hugh had meant. "He is gone, Sarah," he said expressionlessly. "The connection is broken and the recall function erased. He has done it. We won't be bringing him back ever again."

In the monitoring room below the Administration Building, the duty operator turned and called across to Guerntz. "Hey, Nick, something just happened here that you oughta see. Wanna come take a look?"

Guerntz got up from his desk at the back of the room and rolled an empty chair up to the panel. "What?"

The operator backed up the last thirty seconds and redirected the replay to an auxiliary screen, keeping the current realtime view on the main screen with the audio turned down. Guerntz followed the exchange between Jantowitz and Sarah. "Looks like Brenner just turned in his chips," the operator said.

This was serious, Guerntz decided. He thought for a moment, then used another of the screens on the panel to call Calom's secretary upstairs. "Is the chief back yet?" he asked when she answered.

"Not yet. He called in about five minutes ago and said he's on his way back up the Hill. That's all I can tell you."

"Okay." Guerntz cleared down. He thought about calling Calom direct on his personal communicator and decided against it. It was customary to use direct personal channels sparingly. Unnecessary intrusions were considered tackiness at its worst. Besides, Calom had specifically told him that he was in charge until Calom got back. That was what delegation was all about. All the same, in Guerntz's judgment the development was too significant for him to just sit there and not do anything. He got on the direct line into Polygon and asked for Colonel Elson.

Sam stood over his desk, sorting out the papers that he needed for the meeting with Mulgrave and Ursell and slowly absorbing the meaning of what Hugh had done. Sarah and Dave would follow soon now, he had no doubt. He would miss the youthful optimism that their presence had brought to these somber surroundings, but it would be best for them. The world they were going to would let them grow.

On his way to the door, he stopped by the window and gazed out. It overlooked the compound between P2 and the two connected, portable Polygon buildings, with the wire fence and its guarded connecting gate leading out to the general TA-3 area. He could have done with a more uplifting view, he reflected.

He would have liked to have seen Otherwhere, even if just once. . . . But then there was the possibility that he might have taken to it too and decided to stay also. And that would not have been right because there was so much to be done here. And the need was going to get worse. Otherwhere was capable of taking care of itself.

And then figures appeared from the side door of the nearest Polygon building. Elson was in the lead, followed by a couple of other officers and a squad of guards carrying weapons unslung. Sam's brow knitted. The group marched swiftly across in the direction of the Octagon building. Sam frowned to himself. Hugh would have departed only minutes previously. This couldn't be a coincidence.

And then it hit Sam that they must have been under surveillance all along. He dropped the papers and rushed out of the office. "Oh, Sam, I was thinking that . . ." Peter Mulgrave's voice floated from somewhere, but Sam didn't even hear it.

His footsteps clattered down the central stairwell, and he burst through the door to the lower level, knocking a bottle of cleaning fluid from the hands of a technician who had been about to enter. He heard it shatter on the floor behind him as he turned the corner into the corridor. He knew already that he could never get to the Bolthole in time to make any difference. But not to try was out of the question.

Hugh and Dave were in the couplers. Jantowitz was by the consoles, wearing a wooden expression. Sarah was standing over Hugh, looking shocked. There wasn't a second to be wasted. Sam rushed past her and began heaving Hugh's inert form out of the coupler. She started to protest. Sam silenced her with a sharp shake of his head. "Get in," he ordered curtly. While he laid Hugh out alongside the coupler, and Sarah obeyed mutely and totally bewildered, he shot a look across at Jantowitz. "Dave is there already, right?"

Jantowitz nodded, equally mystified. "He is. But Dave is not the problem. Hugh has—"

"I know. Now we have to do the same for these other two too, and just pray that it's the right thing."

In the coupler, Sarah's eyes widened. "Wait a minute, I—"

"There's no time. You have to trust me. Do it, Theo."

Jantowitz was already hammering commands into the console. He knew Sam well enough not to question. Moments later, Sarah sank back into the recliner, and her features relaxed.

Sam ran to the other console. "Now the recall sequences. We have to . . ." But already he could hear the crashing sound of booted feet approaching at a run.

"Freeze!" Elson appeared around the dividing partition, holding a pistol. The guards with him fanned out to cover the area. "All right, everybody freeze right where you are." Sam didn't move, but his eyes strayed down to the keyboard. "Don't even think about it," Elson told him. "Right, now hands on your heads, both of you. I want them where I can see them, well away from any of those panels." He nodded to a uniformed doctor who was with the group and indicated Hugh. "See what you can do."

A Polygon scientist who had also accompanied them came forward and inspected the displays. "It's okay," he announced. "They're on regular transfers. The recall functions are here."

"You can bring them back?" Elson checked.

The scientist nodded toward Hugh, on the floor, where the doctor was unfastening his shirt. "Not that one, I guess. But the other two, sure. I'll do it right now."

Hugh and Yvonne came out of the elevator, into the main lobby of the hotel. She was clinging tightly to his arm, still in a rapture at what he had told her just before they left the room. Hugh felt light and elated, as if a huge load had been removed. It was done. All the agonizing was over. Dave and Sarah would follow now. And then there would be just the four of them, a new world, and the future.

There were more people about than earlier. On one side, what looked like a school group of about a dozen children were assembling to go out somewhere. In the alcove opposite, the hookers were having drinks with prospective clients, and the atmosphere seemed quite partylike. Hugh and Yvonne went over to the desk to inquire if there was any sign yet of Vaughan or Yeats.

A tall, dark-haired young man was just turning away after checking in. He was broad shouldered, clean shaven with firm, not-bad-looking features, wearing a black blazer, and carrying a tan raincoat over one arm. He gave a suitcase and a shoulder bag to one of the bellhops to take upstairs while he stayed in the lobby. A tag on the suitcase read: BRITISH IMPERIAL AIR. He seemed to be looking for somebody. A hunch told Hugh that it had to be. He stepped forward, waited to catch the man's eye, then grinned tentatively. "Dr. Vaughan, I presume?"

The man turned to face him fully, looked at him curiously for a few seconds, and then grinned. "Hugh? Or is it Mat?"

"It depends which Dave is asking."

"I'm not sure I know the difference myself anymore. You see—only one name to worry about. You've got it easy."

The Brenner and Wallis parts of them wanted to throw their arms around each other; they were restrained by the Shayne and Vaughan parts, who were inclined merely to shake hands. Instead of doing either, they stood looking each other up and down. It was all too strange. None of the personalities grappling within could find words that seemed to fit. "How was the flight?" they both said together, finally. Then Hugh remembered that Yvonne was there too.

"Dave," Hugh said, bringing her forward. "You're right— I do have it easy. . . . Dave, this is Yvonne. Yvonne, Dave. I don't have to say a lot. You've both heard all about each other."

Dave and Yvonne looked at each other, hesitated, and shook hands formally; then they decided that they knew each other better than that, smiled, and changed it to a hug.

"I can see now why you wanted to come all this way. . . ." Dave began, then stopped and looked uncertain. "What do we call you?"

"It's always been Mat to me," Yvonne said. "That isn't going to change now."

"I guess I'm gonna have to get used to it," Hugh conceded. He exhaled a sharp sigh. "Well, you two seem to get along." He gestured toward Dave and looked at Yvonne. "What will Sarah—Carol, whoever—think, do you think?"

Yvonne nodded at Dave reassuringly. "I don't think there'll be any problem," she said.

A girl had come into the lobby, seen them talking, and moved closer to listen. She was smaller than Yvonne, slim, and had long black hair, and alert, inquisitive eyes, set in a face that was immediately striking, though not what would be called beautiful in the fashion-model sense. Right now her face had something of a strained look, although that could have been from the effects of a long day. With her, she had a suitcase and a smaller travel bag. She was standing staring at Dave, ignoring the other two. Then he noticed.

He turned slowly, letting their eyes do the talking. Hugh and Yvonne waited. Dave moved a step forward . . . but somehow this wasn't the moment that it should have been. He stopped, puzzled, sensing something amiss. "It *is* Sarah?" he said. "Or Carol, whatever? We've been having the same problem." He realized that it could be a huge mistake.

But she nodded. "Sort of."

Dave didn't understand. "So what's wrong?" He looked down at himself. "Am I that bad?"

The dark-haired girl shook her head. "You're very handsome, and you sound charming. But it's only the Carol part of me, mainly, that's giving the opinion. Sorry to spoil it. Sarah was supposed to be here by now, I know, but she . . ." And then, even while she was speaking, her expression changed. Hugh and Dave knew the signs and tensed expectantly. Yvonne looked from one to the other of them questioningly. "I think I spoke too soon," Carol said.

Dave took a pace nearer. "Sarah?"

"Hello, Dave. Yes, it's me." He started to put a hand on her arm, but she seemed tense and agitated, and looked right past him. "Are you Hugh?" she asked Shayne.

"Yes. Look, I haven't had a chance to tell Dave yet—"

But Sarah cut him off. "Something else happened after you bailed out. Sam showed up in a panic and—"

"Told me what?" Dave interrupted. "What do you mean, bailed out? What's been going . . ." He stopped speaking abruptly and seemed surprised.

Hugh looked worried. "Dave?"

Dave ran a hand through his hair and shook his head. "He's gone. There wasn't supposed to be a recall, was there?"

They both looked at Carol. But before she could say any more, the change that had taken place in her a few moments before seemed to reverse visibly, and she was once again the confused girl from Detroit who had watched them from the side of the lobby. "Sarah's gone again as well. It's just happened to me too," she said.

"Hugh?" Yvonne's voice was apprehensive. "What's happened? Something's gone wrong, hasn't it?"

He shook his head. "No. It's just a glitch. Everything will be fine. Let's give it a few minutes."

Inside, he was a lot less sure. Something had gone wrong. Very wrong.

On the far side of the lobby the man with a Tyrolean hat and a black mustache, who had been joined by a red-haired man and had been watching them, was called to the desk to take a phone call. Amethyst had arrived from Dallas and was on her way from the airport now.

Dave was back in the coupler in the Bolthole. He started to sit up, then stopped and stared around him, stunned.

A man that he didn't know was at the console, and the place was full of military with guns. Elson seemed to be in charge and was shouting orders. Jantowitz and Sam were standing by a wall with their hands up on their heads. Hugh was unconscious on the floor, with a medic and an assistant bending over him.

"Okay, on your feet. Over against the wall by those other two," Elson called out. His mind in a daze, Dave got up slowly from the coupler.

Then Sarah stirred in the other coupler close by. She saw Dave and started to sit up, then froze as she realized the situation. "Oh my God," she gasped.

Chapter Forty-two

They sat apprehensively around a table in the lobby bar of the New York Kennedy. It was a semicircular open-plan area of tables and booths, divided from the lobby floor by a balustrade partition with trellises of climbing plants. An appetizer bar with trays of chicken wings, meatballs, seafood, chips, and various dips and sauces was laid out by the entrance.

This wasn't the way that any of them had imagined it would be. "It couldn't happen to me anyway," Hugh told Dave. "I can't go back. I've done it—wiped the recall code. Sarah had just found out. Yvonne already knew. That was the big news. That was what I was about to tell you."

The Vaughan part of Dave that was left uppermost knew nothing, while the residual Wallis component had been in Otherwhere for hours now and was unable to be of much help either. "We didn't have any recalls scheduled?" was all he could say yet again.

"No," Hugh answered yet again. "Just the opposite. Sarah was due to come back on a long connection until midnight to join you. I only needed a few seconds. That was why I slipped in ahead. That way, I figured I could be here as well and give you guys the big news." The idea had been for the four of them to celebrate over dinner later, but by unspoken agreement any further thought of that was postponed for the time being.

"Sam was certainly in a panic over something," Carol said. "Sarah had never seen him like it before. And Theo didn't know what was going on." As with Dave, her Otherwhere part had retaken control. Using the first person to refer to recollections that were purely Sarah's didn't feel natural.

"Which has to mean it was somebody else who took them back, and it wasn't good news," Hugh completed. He threw up his hands helplessly. "I don't know what to say. . . . Jeez, what have I gotten you three people into?"

Yvonne searched for a philosophic angle. "Well, I did say that life before seemed dull by comparison," was the best that she could manage, sighing.

The others reflected on it in philosophic silence. Finally Carol said, "I haven't even checked into my room yet. Why don't I take care of that while we're waiting for something to happen?"

Yvonne finished her drink and put down her glass. "I'll come with you and give you a hand," she offered. "It'll leave the guys some time to talk guy talk."

"Great. Thanks," Carol replied.

They got up. Yvonne took one of her bags. "Where are we going?"

"Room twelve-twenty."

They left. Some things, it seemed, were the same in any world.

"Secure this whole area, Lieutenant. Nobody is to approach any of this equipment without express authorization or until you hear personally from me. Is that understood?"

"Yes sir."

"The rest of you men will escort the prisoners back to the Polygon building with me. Okay, let's move it." They had taken Hugh away on a gurney. Elson waved for Dave and Sarah to close up behind Jantowitz and Sam. The guard detail formed up on either side, and the procession began moving in the direction of the side entrance. Curious groups of technicians and researchers from the surrounding areas assembled to watch them pass. Dave turned his head toward Sarah. "So what did you mean—"

"No talking!" Colonel Elson barked.

They came out of P2, crossed the compound, and entered the larger of the two Polygon buildings. It was the first time that any of the four of them had been in there. The surroundings were quieter and more orderly than in Octagon, more doors and partitions, less open floor area. Figures moved about their business silently, many of them in uniforms. The air hummed with unseen machinery and the flow of power. It was a bigger-scale operation than Dave had realized.

He thought he knew now what the sight of Hugh apparently lifeless meant. ". . . bailed out," Sarah had said. Hugh had done it. He had tired of the excuses and the shilly-shallying around, and done what he'd said he would do. Probably he had reasoned that it would be enough to make Dave and Sarah forget their reservations and follow after him as Jantowitz had urged. Now it wasn't going to happen. If only they had listened while they had the chance. Sarah would have agreed. He felt sick at what he saw as his own indecisiveness.

The four captives were taken to a small, windowless room at the rear of the building, with several easy chairs, couches by two of the walls, and a low table. It looked like a coffee lounge or relaxation area—maybe for resting between machine sessions. Elson posted two guards outside the door, then went to call General Ventz to report and request instructions.

A red-haired man stepped in after them just as the elevator door was about to close. "Twelve?" Yvonne checked.

"Right," Carol said.

Yvonne looked at the man inquiringly. "The same," he grunted. She pressed the button. The car lurched and began rumbling upward.

"So . . . what do you think of him?" Yvonne asked after the short, customary period of elevator silence.

"Dave? *I* think he's terrific. Sarah didn't really . . ." Carol became conscious of the bystander and let it ride. "I guess with you and Mat it was all okay anyway," she said instead.

"That hardly makes it any easier to get used to. I'm the only one who doesn't have a piece of both sides."

"Oh, right—I was forgetting that. It may even mean you have the toughest part . . . after this present thing gets straightened out."

Yvonne nodded. "Exactly."

Carol looked at her and smiled. "Somehow I don't think you'll have much of a problem handling it, though."

"Thanks. I only wish I had your confidence."

They got out at the twelfth floor, taking one of Carol's bags each. Carol scanned the sign on the wall opposite the elevator doors. "Twelve-twenty. That way." They began walking. The redheaded man turned in the same direction. "What do you do?" Carol asked.

"Financial consulting and investment. A lot of it's to help corporations avoid embarrassing profits with people like Hugh cutting the costs of everything all the time. How about you?"

They came to the door. Carol set her case down and inserted the key. "Oh, the last thing was an actress of sorts. "But I always seem—*What!*—"

The redheaded man had stopped just behind them as if searching for something in his coat pocket. As soon as Carol had opened the door, picked up the case, and gone in ahead, he pushed Yvonne hard in after her, causing them both to collide and fall down over the bags. Before they could recover, he stepped into the room behind them, kicked the door shut behind, and produced a gun.

"*Up! Quick! Hands in the air!* . . . That's it. . . . Now move back across the room, re-eal slow."

Carol was almost gibbering in her confusion. "Look, mister, we don't know what this is all about. You've got the wrong people. We only just—"

"That's enough! Now over by the window. Both of you,

sit down with your backs to the wall." They glanced at each other. The man waved the gun menacingly. He was serious, all right. Yvonne gave a faint nod. They complied shakily.

Sandman was not sure what to do. If it had been only the target from Detroit, he could have gotten it over right then and been clear. But his orders said nothing about the blonde. He didn't even know who she was. He'd have to get directions from Cossack.

Keeping the gun trained on the two women, he sat down on the edge of the bed and pulled the phone across. "Hello, desk? I want to leave a message. If someone asks there for Mr. Sandman, could they call me? I'm in room twelve two-oh. . . . Right."

He replaced the phone, stretched his legs out along the bed, and leaned back against the headboard. Cradling the gun in his lap, he reached into the side pocket of his jacket, drew out a pack of cigarettes, and lit one with a match from the book on the bedside unit. Then, as an afterthought, he tossed them across so that they landed between Yvonne and Carol. "One at a time, ladies," he invited. "Help yourselves if you use them. It looks like we might have a little wait."

Downstairs in the lobby bar, a man in a bright blue blazer presented himself at the table where Hugh and Dave were sitting. He had a heavy black mustache, muscular build, and Mediterranean complexion. "Mr. Shayne, room six-twelve?" he inquired.

"Yes, that's me," Hugh acknowledged, looking up.

"Hotel security. Look, I'm sorry to bother you. But the guest who had your room last night was moved to another room, and she's missing something valuable. Housekeeping have no record of anything, but she insists that it's in there. We want to search the room, and we'd prefer it if you were present. Would you mind? The hotel would be happy to stand you a complimentary round of drinks for the inconvenience."

Hugh looked at Dave. Dave spread his hands. "Oh, by all means. Let's help keep the peace."

"I'll be right back," Hugh said, standing up.

"Want me to get you another while you're gone?" Dave asked.

"Sure. . . ." Hugh paused and stared at him. "It's uncanny. You two are so much alike."

"I thought we were supposed to be the same person," Dave replied.

"Thank you so much," the man in the bright blue blazer said as they moved away.

They stood aside for the people getting out of the elevator, and then stepped in behind a couple with a small boy. "What did she lose?" Hugh asked casually as the doors closed.

"Oh, a ring that she says is an heirloom going way back in the family. I'd have left it until tomorrow, but she's in the manager's office right now, going ballistic. You know what some people can be like."

They were silent the rest of the way to the sixth floor. Hugh sneaked a closer look at the man as they got out. The tie went okay, but the shirt wasn't right for a bright blue blazer. And the shoes were street shoes.

The corridor was empty, with a laundry cart parked on the corner of the branch corridor leading to the room. Hugh quickened his pace and drew ahead, at the same time feeling in his coat pocket as if for his key. Then, when he was abreast of the end of the cart, he turned without warning and shoved it as hard as he could into the other man's path. It caught the man by surprise, hitting him in the midriff and doubling him over the end. Hugh accelerated the cart, running the man backward with it across the hall and slamming him against the far wall. He went down, wheezing and clutching at the cart. Hugh upended it on top of him and raced for the door to the stairs.

It was saying that the woman was "going ballistic" that had given it away. Hugh had no idea who the man was, but he sure as hell wasn't with hotel security. The phrase derived from missile parlance. It described the transition of an ICBM warhead from the boost phase after launch to its freefall trajectory outside the atmosphere.

ICBMs were unknown in Otherwhere.

Chapter Forty-three

Jantowitz sat staring morosely at the floor in the small lounge in the rear part of the Polygon building. It had all been too easy. The readiness with which he had been given a convenient, secluded part of the building to work in; their accessing of resources not connected with their official work, never being questioned; the long hours and heavy computing usage that they had, never questioned. He, the iconoclast whose idea it had been, and who had exhorted them to go it alone. The fearless defender of principle and honesty, who would outwit the straitjacketed mediocrities; Perseus slaying the bureaucratic Medusa; an intellectual Hercules cleaning the stables of political strangulation; a Horatius holding the bridge of unfettered science. . . . And the authorities had been following every move, all the way from the beginning. If he had bothered to stop and look and think, it had been staring him in the face. Perhaps if he had come from a different environment, he would have read the signs. . . . But no, he was old enough to know the way the world worked. Didn't he spend enough time telling others? There could be no excuse.

Sam was watching him, and as always seemed to read the thoughts. "It wasn't only you, Theo," he said. "We were all blind. Over-enthusiasm can be intoxicating. It sweeps away reason and caution. I was as much a victim too—me who always warned everybody else about being carried away by their delusions."

Jantowitz dismissed it with a wave and a weary shake of his head. "What they do with me now is no matter. But these two here . . ." he gestured at Dave and Sarah, "these young peoples, that is the tragedy. They should be gone while they have the chance. I tell them the words, yes, but is not the same thing as making them. Now is no chance."

"Theo, quit blaming yourself," Dave told him. "We all had the same chance. We were there too. We saw what Hugh saw. You told us the same as you told Hugh. He listened, and we argued. That's the only difference. It's thanks to you that he got out. And he'll do just fine there. Think more about that."

Jantowitz stared at him, wanting to believe it. "You think he will be okay? He will make out, yes?"

Dave nodded emphatically. "Professionally, he's practically an international sensation there already—I know, because I talked to Cormack, who's in touch with Rauth. He's got Nobel laureates filing applications to meet him. And as for personally, he couldn't do better than Yvonne. I only met her for those few minutes after I got to the hotel. But what a lady! You don't have to worry about him. He'll do just fine."

"I only got a glimpse of her," Sarah put in. "And yet I got the feeling straightaway that she and I could have been really good friends. Isn't it strange how you can pick up such strong impressions in a few seconds."

Sam stared thoughtfully into the distance. "He knew from the beginning—ever since the first time he ever used the machine. I wonder what it was that was drawing him— her, that whole world, or the set of possible futures that it led to. Perhaps you responded to something similar."

Sarah's eyes came back to rest on him. "You've always said it was due to communication across the Multiverse, haven't you, Sam?" she said. "Inspiration, intuition—the strange hunches that people get."

"Exactly." Sam smiled and nodded.

She thought back. "Do you remember that city that I told you I used to dream about—the one that I was convinced really existed somewhere? I knew, somehow, that all the different places I saw were part of the same place."

"Yes."

"That was it. I knew it the moment I walked out of Grand Central. And Carol grew up in New York. The connection was there all the time. The QUADAR just amplifies the effect."

"That was what it was originally meant to do," Sam reminded her.

Voices sounded outside. They stopped talking. A few moments later, one of the guards opened the door and stepped in. Calom was outside with a drawn automatic. "These people are wanted for interrogation," Calom said to the guards. "Would you bring them, please?"

"You heard," the guard said to the four occupants. "Everybody on your feet. Up."

They rose and moved to the door. The other guard stood aside to let them pass, while Calom moved ahead to lead the way. He met Sarah's eyes for an instant and looked away expressionlessly. She chided herself for imagining at one time that she had made some kind of contact with him; that the beginnings of some feeling approaching human had flickered behind that impervious exterior. Delusion, she told herself. All delusion.

They walked past olive-green partition walls and featureless doors with numbers stenciled on them in black. Calom opened a larger door that formed the end of the corridor. "Wait here," he told the two guards.

Chapter Forty-four

Dave thought that the Wallis part of himself would have possessed enough information to make more sense of the situation than this. Throughout the flight from London, he had absorbed the exhilaration of the newly resident side to his personality at the freedom of the world in which he found himself, his fascination with the different values and attitudes that prevailed here, the delight he experienced on coming into New York City. At the same time, he had been conscious of a worldlier, somehow more mature awareness that was seeing all these things. As he adjusted to the strangeness, the composite personality that was forming warmed to the idea of making the condition permanent.

Then had come the meeting in the lobby, here at the Kennedy, with Matthew and Yvonne. And then, at last, he'd come face-to-face with the other self of the mysterious Sarah, only to discover that Sarah herself hadn't managed to make it on time—on this of all occasions. And when she did finally show up, she had promptly vanished again, as had Wallis. The good news was that in the meantime he was quite taken with the Carol who had been left in the same predicament as he, and the feeling seemed to be pretty mutual. Mat, on the other hand, was apparently equally stuck but the other way around—he couldn't go back at all, ever. The scary part was that even the residue of Wallis that remained didn't know what was going on. The apprehension emanating from that source, as he sat at the table in the lobby bar waiting for the others to return, was seeping through the rest of him.

"Excuse me." A woman's voice came from behind him. He turned his head. She was on her own on a bench seat by the wall—quite close, but he had been too absorbed in his thoughts to notice her. She was in her mid thirties, maybe, with curly auburn hair and a snub-nosed, not unattractive face, and wearing a short gray coat with black slacks. There was a black leather purse on the ledge by her. "I couldn't help overhearing when your friends were here earlier. You're English, aren't you?"

Dave returned from a million miles away. "Er, that's right. Yes."

"I have some friends from over there. It sounds such a nice place. I keep meaning to visit one day and promising them I will, but I always end up putting it off."

"Oh, well, let's hope that next time you manage to get it right." Dave smiled just enough to be polite. The strained look that he imparted with it tried to convey that this really wasn't the best time.

But she either didn't notice or wasn't going to let it put her off. "What's that you're drinking?" she asked.

"Oh . . . ah, Guinness. Long flight. . . . Gives one a thirst." Wrong, he thought as he said it. He felt a sinking feeling as he saw her eyes brighten with interest, and she leaned closer.

"Did you only just get in today?"

"Yes."

"Oh my, what a long trip that must have been! Can I buy you another?"

"Well, it's very nice of you to offer, but I am—"

"No, really, I insist. Kind of a welcome to the United States."

"Very well. But my friends will be back shortly. We won't have much time for socializing, I'm afraid. There are some personal matters that we need to discuss."

Seeming unperturbed, the woman picked up her purse and slid onto the chair that Carol had vacated. "A little bit of socializing of our own won't do any harm while you're waiting, will it?" She caught the eye of a passing cocktail waitress and signaled for two more. "I'm Jenny-Lee, by the way."

"Oh, er, David."

"Yes, you look more of a David than a Dave. I think it's the dark hair and the blazer—very British. Is it your first time here?"

"I was over a few years ago. That was to Boston—MIT."

"I love Boston! . . . MIT? What do you do?"

"I'm a radio astronomer, actually."

"Oh, how fascinating!" She eyed him silently for a few seconds, teasing her teeth mischievously with the tip of her tongue. Her voice fell. "I do have a room here. What do you say we slip away for an hour? You could always say that you got called away by a phone call from England— somebody just discovered a new galaxy or something."

Dave massaged his brow and smiled, at the same time looking embarrassed. "No, really . . . I'm sorry, but I don't think you understand the situation. My time is committed, I'm with company, anyway, and—nothing personal, but— not in a mood to be interested."

Very well. Amethyst had given the easy way a chance. She moved the purse below the edge of the table and let him see the gun before transferring it to the pocket of her coat. The mask dropped, and her tone became sharp. "No, I don't think *you* understand the situation, Mr. Vaughan. We get up, and we walk quietly to the elevators. Or you can have a messy scene here right now, if you want. It won't make any difference to me. Midnight, and I'm out of here."

She said it in a strange way that made Dave stare perplexedly despite the chill that had seized him. Then he realized what she meant. "You're one of them too . . . from that other place. Look, I'm not even Wallis. He went back. Would you believe it if I told you I have absolutely no idea what this is about?"

"Would you believe it if I told you that I don't either? I just have my orders. Let's go."

"But this—"

"I *said* let's go."

Dave looked at her face. She wasn't fooling. He rose shakily to his feet and moved toward the trellised archway leading out to the lobby. The woman followed, keeping close but out of arm's reach. As they reached the entrance, Hugh-Shayne appeared from the other direction, breathless and at a run.

Perhaps because he was on an adrenaline high, the pieces registered and came together instantly—the woman's unnatural closeness behind Dave; her involuntary tensing at the sight of him; her hand starting to move from her pocket. He reacted faster than she did, sweeping a tray of shrimp and dip from the appetizer bar and hurling it at her without even stopping in his tracks. She reeled backward, upsetting a table of drinks while startled guests shouted and jumped aside to the clanging crash of metal and the shattering of glass. She pulled herself back up, but her foot skidded on the spilled sauce, and she careened into another woman who was trying to get out of the way. Several people had started coming toward her, but they froze or backed away when they saw she had a gun.

In the confusion, Hugh caught Dave by the sleeve and dragged him out into the lobby. Dave was too bewildered and panicky to be capable of framing any words coherently. "I don't know what the hell's going on either," Hugh yelled, before he could even try. "We need to get back to Yvonne and Carol. They went up to twelve."

With Hugh propelling Dave in a semi-daze, they ran toward the elevators, knocking over a porter who was carrying a vase of flowers, and leaving indignant guests shouting in their wake. As they approached the elevators, one of the doors opened to reveal a man with a black mustache, wearing a bright blue, hotel-security blazer.

"No! He's one of them too!" Hugh shouted, steering Dave away.

At the same moment, Amethyst appeared in the trellis arch from the bar on the far side of the lobby. She raised her pistol and aimed after them, and somebody behind her in the bar behind her shouted a warning. Guests screamed and scattered across the lobby. Others ran out the main doors to the street. The reception clerk grabbed a phone and dived down behind the desk with it. Seeing Cossack in the line of fire, Amethyst lowered her gun and gave chase. Hugh and Dave disappeared into a stairwell. Amethyst confronted Cossack at the elevators.

"They're heading for twelve," Cossack snapped. "Yeats is in twelve-twenty. You take the elevator. I'll go after them." Amethyst ran past him into the open elevator door. Cossack drew his own gun and sprinted for the stairs.

Hugh and Dave tumbled out of a service elevator into a corridor on the twelfth floor. Hugh checked the direction of the room numbering and beckoned frantically. "Come on, this way."

1228 . . . 1226 . . .

An elevator door opened at the far end of the corridor behind them. "Mat," Dave's voice warned ominously. Hugh looked back. The woman from the bar had emerged and was coming after them.

1224 . . . 1222 . . . "Keep going," Dave gasped. "There isn't time."

1220.

And then the man in the blazer came around the corner of the corridor ahead. They looked back; the woman was advancing, gun drawn. There was no other way to go. Dave rapped sharply on the door of 1220 with his knuckles. *"Carol!"* The two assassins closed relentlessly.

Hugh hammered with his fist. *"It's us. Open up, for God's sake!"* They heard the lock turn. The door opened. It was Carol.

But Hugh could tell from her face that something was wrong even as he was pushing Dave through past her.

"Who's out there?" a man's voice called from inside.

"It's us," the man with the black mustache answered from along the corridor.

Yvonne was sitting on the floor, her back against the wall. A red-haired man was standing by the head of the bed, covering everybody with a gun. "Just leave the door as it as," he told Hugh. "Now, all of you, over there with her, by the window."

Kintner was in the main Polygon building when the panic erupted. He was not informed or consulted, but from what he was able to make of things after Elson went dashing off with a detachment of guards and a couple of the Polygon scientists, Hugh Brenner had done it. Inwardly, Kintner felt a twinge of satisfaction. He had advised Ventz to forget about trying to conceal the surveillance any longer, and to detain the whole bunch of them. Then, once Argo was on a solid technical foundation, they could be removed from the project and forgotten as a potential source of mischief permanently.

He sat before screens in one of the control rooms, consolidating the files on the candidates for Argo that had been processed that day. There were two—one of Ventz's military buddies, and a senator's wife that Kintner didn't think could be trusted not to talk too much. Not his department, he reminded himself.

And then he came across something that puzzled him. Some of the data tables showed status summaries of couplers that were active in Polygon at the moment. There were a number of spooks on practice missions, hidden away in various rooms and recesses, a couple of scientists engaged in research, an engineer testing a circuit modification, a repair being checked out. What had caught Kintner's attention were the target coordinates logged for three couplers in the building that Kintner was in, at the rear in a secluded section that he normally didn't go into. He had been told that the area was reserved for spook training. The numbers wouldn't have meant anything had it not been for his familiarity with Jantowitz's maps. They were the coordinates that specified Otherwhere. That didn't sound very much like training.

His curiosity got the better of him. If he was going to do a little investigating, this would be the time—while half the guards who normally stayed at the back of the building were in Octagon. He got up and wandered casually into a maintenance gallery that led toward the back of the building behind the bays of cubicles.

There were banks of racking, aisles of cabinets, partition walls carrying bundles of cable. Everything was more closely packed together than in Octagon—close to what Kintner imagined the inside of a submarine would be like. It was dark and shadowy farther back. There was nobody about.

He found them all together—two men and a woman—in an area screened off by walls on three sides. A gap between the equipment led to another area beyond where there were three more couplers, at present empty. The trio were about in their mid twenties, the typical age for spooks—somehow still looking keen and zealous, even in unconscious repose. The mystery was, what were three individuals that he didn't know about, hidden away at the back of the building, doing in Otherwhere right now?

Before he could consider the matter further, he heard footsteps and voices behind a door on the far side of the adjoining, unoccupied coupler bay. Moving reflexively, he slipped into the shadows among the cubicles separating the two areas.

He was surprised to see Jantowitz and Sam enter, followed by Dave and Sarah; then came Calom, holding a pistol. Calom said something to somebody outside, presumably guards, and closed the door. Sarah and Dave looked around them in bewilderment. Jantowitz seemed confused. "What kind of a place for interrogation is this?" Sam demanded. At the same instant, Kintner registered the look of horror on Sarah's face as she stared at the gun in Calom's hand, and the protest written across Dave's. He was on the point of intervening, when Calom waved at the empty couplers. "Get in," he told Sarah and Dave.

They gaped at him, not comprehending. "Get in the couplers," Calom said curtly. "We may only have a few minutes."

He turned to Jantowitz and Sam. "Are those consoles like the ones you're used to? Can you work them?"

Jantowitz activated a panel, tried a few entries, checked the responses. "Is same," he told Calom. "They use our procedures."

"Get their profiles loaded over the link from Octagon," Calom said, indicating Sarah and Dave. Dave was sitting down in one of the couplers. Sarah was still on her feet, gaping at Calom.

"You mean you—"

"Go now! Move!"

Still as if in a trance, Sarah sank down into one of the other two couplers. Sam moved across without saying anything and activated the second panel. Calom stood by the door, his pistol at the ready, prepared to buy them a few more moments if necessary.

"We have profiles through now," Jantowitz confirmed. "Coordinate priming is set. . . . Transfer function is active."

"Check here," Sam murmured after a few seconds.

Sarah looked from one of them to the other. "There's such a lot I want to say. I wish it didn't have to be like this."

"I tell you all along, is best way without all the talk," Jantowitz answered gruffly.

Dave let his head sink back under the antenna array assembly. "We're going to miss you guys," he said.

Sam smiled and raised a hand in a silent salutation. . . .

And they were gone.

Working swiftly, Jantowitz and Sam erased the recall routines to make the transfers irreversible.

"Now, there's just one more thing," Calom said. "I'm pretty sure Ventz means to send a hit squad after the analogs at the other end. The coordinate system is on a Grapevine code. We have to take it out everywhere."

"Grapevine" was a high-security provision for protecting

sensitive information by making sure that no stray copies survived in the event of a decision to delete—a kind of computerized shredder. All copies of information protected by Grapevine, existing in Octagon or Polygon, were linked such that a "General System Purge" command would erase all of them. Purging the Otherwhere coordinate directory would ensure that nobody would ever be transferred there again. With effectively billions of worlds out there across the Multiverse, the chances of anyone's hitting it at random again were as good as zero.

But Jantowitz shook his head. "Code is Grapevine, yes. But is Executive-level privilege. Access authorization, I do not have."

Calom stared at him, appalled. He shifted his eyes to Sam. Sam could only show empty palms and shake his head too. It had all been for nothing. For once, Calom had overlooked something.

Then the figure that had been watching moved out from the shadows.

"I do," Kintner said quietly.

Chapter Forty-five

Sarah wished that it didn't have to be this way. Her last impressions of the world she had known all her life were a confused mixture of Sam's and Jantowitz's features etched out in the shadows by the glowing screens; Calom indistinct to one side by the door; the dark outlines of steel cabinets and cables in the cramped room; winking lights, flickering displays, the subdued pulsing of unseen machinery. Her final conscious thought was that it was Sam's victory, not hers.

There was a sharp rapping on the door. *"Carol!"* It was Vaughan's voice. The red-haired man got up off the bed quickly and moved to where he could cover the whole room. He waved at Carol with the gun.

"You, up!"

She climbed to her feet weakly.

The knocking changed to a frantic hammering. *"It's us. Open up, for God's sake!"* Shayne this time.

"Do what he says, then stand back out of the way," the red-haired man ordered.

Carol opened the door, and Vaughan almost fell through with Shayne on his heels. "Who's out there?" the red-haired man called.

"It's us," a voice from the corridor answered.

The red-haired man waved the gun at Vaughan and

Shayne. "Just leave the door as it is," he told them. "Now, all of you, over there with her, by the window."

At that moment Sarah rejoined Carol, and immediately felt the fear, sickness, and despair that had brought Carol close to collapse. It was no longer like the earlier transfers. Her consciousness merged with the one that had remained—she was aware of the things that had been happening.

Seconds later, the same thing happened to Vaughan. The Wallis persona came back, assimilated the circumstances that it had come back to, and immediately wished that it hadn't.

"Jenny-Lee" appeared in the doorway. Behind her was the man in the blue blazer who had come out of the elevator downstairs. They both had guns. The man in the blue blazer pushed the door shut behind him, moved into the center of the room.

"Wonderful," he pronounced. "We've got all three of them together."

The red-haired man indicated Yvonne, who had risen to her feet and was clutching Shayne's arm. "I wasn't sure what the score was with her," he said.

"She's Shayne's girlfriend from San Francisco," Amethyst supplied.

"Look, whatever this is about, she's got nothing to do with it," Shayne protested.

Cossack looked at her. He didn't have any orders about girlfriends from San Francisco either. What did it matter? he thought. A couple more hours and they'd all be out of this place for keeps. Best to make it safe.

"Her too," he replied nonchalantly.

"Ventz is more than just meaning to send a hit team," Kintner told Calom. "The team's there already." He jerked his head to indicate the direction past his shoulder. "Their couplers are back there, in the next area behind." Calom strode across to look, then turned on Kintner accusingly. Kintner shook his head and moved past Calom to the console serving the adjoining area. "I didn't know until a few minutes ago. Why do you think I'm doing this? Disarm them and immobilize them. I'm recalling them now."

Calom took a moment to absorb the situation. Then he nodded to Sam and Jantowitz to help, removed the sidearms from the three agents, and handed them a weapon each. "Cover them," he instructed, then looked around. The cables trailing from some of the cabinets had been tied into bundles in places with wide, adhesive tape. Calom unwound several of the pieces. "Throw me some of those," he said to Jantowitz, indicating an assortment of power cords and connecting wires hanging on a rack.

Tony Vingini had been relaxing at home in the tub. The next thing he knew, he was standing in a room with six people he didn't know, pointing a gun at a young man standing near the window with a good-looking, very terrified blonde clinging to his arm. Vingini stared, dumbstruck, looked at the gun, and let his arm drop limply. "What is this shit?" he managed finally. "Who the hell are all you people? Where is this, and what the hell am I doing here?" He looked down and pinched out his lapel to inspect the blue blazer that he was wearing.

A man with red hair, also holding a gun, looked at him oddly. "What's the matter? Don't tell me you lost your nerve. . . ." His face clouded with suspicion suddenly. "Cossack? It *is* still you?"

"What are you talking about?" Vingini demanded.

There was a curly-haired woman in pants and a gray coat covered in what looked like shrimp dip, again with a gun. "I think he's been recalled," she said.

Yvonne felt Mat's arm tighten around her. She wasn't sure what this meant, but the new hope that he felt all of a sudden communicated itself.

"*Who are you?*" The red-haired man suddenly looked at the woman in bewilderment, then around at everyone else in the room. His last recollection was of painting a door. Now, all of a sudden, he wasn't even sure if he was in Detroit.

Dave and Carol were staring at each other incredulously. "They've found them!" Dave whispered. "Calom and the others have found them, back there. They're taking them back."

The only thought that crossed Amethyst's mind was that she had possibly seconds left to carry out the mission. She aimed determinedly at Shayne . . .

"Holy Christ," Vingini breathed.

. . . but the red-haired man pushed her arm up. "No!" he yelled. "I wanna know what's happening here."

And suddenly the woman screamed at the sight of the gun in her hand, and let go of it. *"Take your hands off me!"* she shouted at the red-haired man. "Who are you?"

Guests from nearby rooms were crowding around the doorway, aroused by the commotion.

"Somebody should call the desk," one of them said.

"We already did," another answered.

"Heavens, they've got guns in there! I think I'll go back to the room."

The sound of police sirens approaching and dying as cars drew up came from outside the building.

Cossack's first thought on finding himself back in the coupler inside Polygon was that this shouldn't be happening. When he tried to move, he discovered that he was gagged and bound. Figures were moving nearby to one side. Raising his head, he saw the Polish professor and the Buddhist, both holding guns. Moments later, Sandman's voice from one of the other couplers started to echo his thoughts: "What the hell is—" Then it cut off into a stifled mumbling.

"Don't move. You are covered." Cossack recognized Calom's voice but couldn't see him. He tried straining against the wires that were holding him. No chance.

CONFIRM GENERAL SYSTEM PURGE

ENTER AUTHORIZATION CODE

At the console, Kintner responded and supplied a completion sequence. . . . And Otherwhere disappeared back into the strange convolutions of the Multiverse as all pointers to it vanished from the system. Nobody would be going there to import alien notions of conquest or power, to assassinate analogs, or for any other reason, ever again.

Calom gagged the woman before she was recalled, and finished securing the second of the two men. Then he tied her, ignoring her muted protests. When he looked toward the console, Kintner had disappeared. He had never been there. Calom understood.

He waved to Jantowitz and Sam to leave. They followed him through the adjoining coupler area, pausing for a last look at the inert forms of Dave and Sarah. Then they tossed the guns down in the third, empty coupler and turned toward the door.

"The others will remain here," Calom told the two guards outside. "I'm taking these two with me. Stay there until you are relieved."

And the Buddhist, the scientist, and the security officer walked quickly away along the corridor.

Curious people watched from all sides as the party came out of the elevators into the hotel lobby, escorted by New York City police, the manager, and the security manager. Yvonne hugged close inside Hugh's arm. "So Dave and Sarah are back now?" she said.

"Yes, they're back."

"For good?"

"I hope so."

Vingini, a watchful policeman on either side of him, looked at Hugh searchingly. "You mean somebody knows what's going on around here? Would you mind sharing it with me? I've got the feeling I could be in some real trouble."

"Don't worry too much about it," Hugh told him. "We'll all be on your side. You haven't really been yourself today. Take it from me. You'll have some good witnesses." He turned to the plainclothes officer who seemed to be in charge. "Those three people might need to be kept under observation for a while," he said. "I've got a hunch that they won't be bothering anyone again, but let's wait until we're a bit more sure."

"Mind telling me what it's all about?" the detective officer said.

Hugh sighed. "It's going to be a long story," he warned. "And it'll take some believing. Before we get into it, there's a professor in California that you might want to talk with first."

Hugh looked at Dave. "Is it for keeps now—you and Sarah?"

"I think so," Dave said.

Sarah, pressing close against his shoulder, nodded. "It has to be. There was no other way to read what Calom had in mind. That was why he needed Sam and Theo there."

"What does Calom have to do with it?" Hugh asked.

Dave expelled a long breath. "That's a long story too." He looked at the others. "You know, after traveling all day, I've suddenly got my appetite back. Maybe we could have that dinner after all, and we'll tell you about it then."

Hugh thought about it, then nodded. "Suits me," he agreed. Yvonne liked the idea too. So did Carol.

"Dinner tonight is compliments of the Kennedy," the manager informed them.

Hugh, Matthew—whoever he was—slipped an arm around Yvonne's waist. "So . . . do you have any more surprises like that lined up?" she asked him as they began walking.

"No, I think that's it."

"For a while, I thought you'd decided that this dull world of ours needed a little livening up."

"No, not at all," Hugh told her. "I'll settle for it absolutely, just the way it is."

Epilogue

Calom eased his car to a halt at the TA-3 site main gate. The sentry checked his pass, peered in to identify him visually, recognized his two companions, and waved them through. Calom accelerated out and across the bridge and made a right to take them past the town. The thing was to get down off the mesa and well away on the Interstate by the time the alarm went out. Twenty miles north there was a gas station owned by a man that Calom knew, who would switch the car without asking questions.

As he drove, he pictured again in his mind the glimpses that he had seen of Otherwhere. There had been a moment in those final minutes back inside Polygon when he had been tempted by the thought of going too. With the Grapevine code obliterated, he would have been free from pursuit and interference there. But some kind of power coming either from outside or deep within himself had overrode him, and he had let it pass. And now, from his position of greater detachment, he saw that this had been the wiser guide. That world belonged rightfully to the three young people who had gone. Unlike him, in harmony with it, they would grow. Yet he was conscious of an unaccustomed sense of fulfillment; of bringing things to be as they were meant to be. For the first time in his life, he was content.

"What are your plans now?" Sam inquired from the seat behind.

Calom came out of his mood of reverie. "First we have to get you two out of sight," he answered over his shoulder. "The heat's going to be on everywhere. Next, you and Theo need to do your own disappearing act. Make a new start somewhere else. Fortunately, I just happen to know the right people to show you how."

"And then, what about you?" Jantowitz asked in the passenger seat next to Calom. "Where do you go? Or is that the secret that you keep?"

Calom bunched his mouth and made an openhanded gesture on the wheel. "Not really. . . . I might end up overseas. There's a certain children's orphanage in Paraguay I heard about, that could use some help. It's not something I've tried my hand at before, but then, maybe there are times when everyone needs a change."

In the seat behind them, Sam also knew contentment. He had become a Buddha. His enemy was now his friend.

And then, slowly, awe overcame him as enlightenment dawned on the meaning of what had happened. He suddenly understood the wondrous power of the Multiverse to heal itself.

First it had happened to Kintner; then Calom. The very act of expanding consciousness outward into the greater self extending across the Multiverse caused new, widened insights to replace the petty delusions and obsessions appropriate to the shriveled reality of minds only partially functioning. Like a body sealing off a wound, the Multiverse contained poison in cells of its own making to prevent the infection from spreading. When the cell was ready, the same process that enabled it to extend itself would make it whole. The harder it tried, the faster it would be transformed. In the long term, Argo could never have been a danger to Otherwhere any more than life emerging from the ocean could hope to turn the continents into abyss. It, not the continents, would change.

The irony was the guilt that Hugh and his companions had felt over what they'd thought was abandoning their own world, when what they had accomplished had given it the one means of eventually putting right its ills. Sam only wished he'd understood it sooner and could have let them know. But he had a feeling that they would come to see it for themselves, in time. Everything in its own way, in its own time.

The road ahead wound down between the sandy hills and the crags, into the gathering night. Above and behind, the lights of Los Alamos grew smaller against the outline of distant mountains, looming in the last glow of the dying sun.